THE·ESCAPE·OF·SOCRATES

THE ESCAPE OF
SOCRATES

ROBERT PICK

NEW YORK · ALFRED A KNOPF 1954

L. C. catalog card number: 53-9480

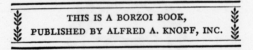

THIS IS A BORZOI BOOK,
PUBLISHED BY ALFRED A. KNOPF, INC.

FIRST EDITION

IN MEMORIAM
H · B

AUTHOR'S NOTE

THIS IS A NOVEL. *As is obvious, it is based on classical sources, including Plato, but I have not hesitated to invent scenes and characters to serve its purpose as fiction. As for the Athens of 399 B.C., I have invented nothing.*

THE·ESCAPE·OF·SOCRATES

PROLOGUE

Whoever has lived through violent political changes and watched their aftermath at close range must have found himself, on occasions, amazed by the tenacity of ancient custom amid such upheavals.

There was Athens a few short years after her final defeat at the hands of the Spartans. . . . Now consider the wounds inflicted on all and sundry by usurpers and tyrants whose misdeeds had capped twenty-seven years of warfare; think of that citizenry in their precarious enjoyment of civic rights restored to them after a fratricidal struggle—men grown all but insensitive, through sufferings past and anxieties present, to the Periclean splendor still about them; imagine their empire lost, their countryside bearing the sores of war's fury, their exchequer depleted, their harbor forts garrisoned by the uncouth victors, their city rent by mutual mistrust, with everyone blaming the common disaster on everyone else. . . . And then stop to recall the fact that these same men conformed with a custom dating back to the days of King Theseus—the annual dispatch of the Sacred Ship to the temple island of Delos—and you will agree with the playwright, dead for some years at that time, that "wonders are many, but none is more wondrous than man."

You might say that the living-together of men is one thing, and their observances another. Granted, for argument's sake, it is—still the unchanged adoration offered the Delian god must remain a matter of marvel. The god, Apollo, had done precious little to deserve such great devotion. In the latter stage of the war his oracles had grown unreliable to the point of leading the armies of Athens straight into defeat and dragging her navy down to the ocean's bottom.

Not that the other deities had done better by her. Athena herself, the virgin goddess, had failed to stay the ills besetting her town, or counteract the blows that crushed the men in the field. She had watched the plague ravage her Athens for more than a year, deaf to the supplications poured forth at her shrines, blind to the hecatombs sacrificed at her great altar. Indeed, even before the city's downfall it was whispered about that the gods had grown jealous of the Athenians and had forsaken the town—or else no longer commanded the power assumed in them for so long.

Yet such doubts interfered as little with the solemn punctilio employed at the Sacred Vessel's departure, or the cheers of the crowds come to the Piræus to watch it, as did the sight of the run-down roadsteads, or, for that matter, the thought of the poor state of affairs in their homes.

To be sure, conditions had improved considerably since the war was over, domestic peace restored, and popular government in power again. Men could till their patches of land again without the numbing thought of likely destruction. A great many olive trees had been replanted. Grain ships from foreign parts put in regularly again at the Piræus. Work in the silver mines had been resumed.

As for the future of the commonweal, the way one looked at it was, of course, primarily a matter of temperament. It also depended—such is man—upon one's own fortunes. Some men had fared better than others in the ups and downs of the long tribulations, and there were those who had not done badly since.

To that favored group belonged the man in command of the Sacred Vessel in the first year of the Ninety-fifth Olympiad (to be computed, much later, as 399 B.C.). His name was Cleomedes.

The voyage to Delos, a state pilgrimage to the island's festival, complete with a trained choir, was an expensive affair. In the old days its costs had been defrayed out of a special fund. With that fund squandered during the war, it had become customary to have some wealthy citizen pay for the repair of the overaged bireme, rig and equip her, hire the crew, and buy the provisions and the offerings for Apollo. The man undertaking all that—or rather, the man talked into it—would then be declared the Sacred Vessel's commander.

However, not many citizens were any longer in a position to disburse such large sums; and fewer still were those the purity of whose political record and whose comportment matched their fortunate circumstances. But the men in power now—the men of popular rule—while fond of displaying a homespun plainness, yet were eager to give its due to the dignity of time-honored public functions.

Cleomedes, a citizen of inherited means; a man with a smattering of Homeric education; a lover of the city who had gone into exile directly the Council of the Thirty came into being under the eyes of the Spartan victors and made its will the sole law in Athens; a soldier said to have been second to none in the battles through which the small band of exiles had defeated tyranny—Cleomedes, then, filled the requirements to perfection.

He also was a remarkably modest man. On the first

day of the voyage he said to his pilot: "Do not expect me to give orders in matters nautical, Xenias. I lay no claim to seamanship."

Xenias, a man no longer young, was seated on his narrow bench at the tiller. He said: "Every Athenian is also a seaman."

"Hearing you say so reminds me of the mockery of certain people in saying: 'Every Athenian is fit for any office.' "

"No mockery is in my mind."

"At any rate, Xenias, this one Athenian will abide by your experience till we put in at Delos."

The steersman tightened his grip on the tiller with one hand; then, shading his eyes with the other, he looked at the large orange-colored square sail.

The slightest of breezes ruffled the deep-blue water of the Saronic bay. So softly did its waves lap against the ribs of the vessel that the rhythmical wash was intermittently deadened by the grating of the oars in their locks or the boatswain's pipe, which gave the time to the rowers below.

Xenias said: "I felt gratified this morning when you paid no heed to the clamor of the choristers. It was uncalled for, to say the least. Who ever heard of sailing out of sight of the coast before Cape Sunium is rounded? Those choristers are a high-strung lot."

"They are young."

"Impatient to get to Delos ahead of the pilgrims from other cities! Crazy I call it. There is no distinction attached to being there first. But as long as you, Cleomedes, keep in mind that speed is of no importance, within reason . . ." He left his sentence unfinished, or perhaps the wind, livelier of a sudden, carried away his words. He stared out on the water, sidewise.

Cleomedes, who was leaning against the wickerwork bulwark, took his eyes off the helmsman. He glanced, past the sail, up to the high brazen prow decked with garlands of laurel. A rim of radiance quivered about the festive wreaths. Cleomedes found himself somewhat troubled. He had rebuffed the choir's demand out of a sense of solidarity with his pilot. Or so he had thought. For in truth he *had* been told, shortly before going on board, that time did not count for much on this voyage. Two men—trustworthy citizens, as trustworthiness went nowadays—had taken him out of the crowd, one after the other, and from behind a crooked hand at the side of the mouth had warned him against "racing the unwieldy old craft." Particularly on her return trip, so one of them had whispered, the commander should exercise prudence. Unless Cleomedes wished to presume that this counsel had been offered to taunt him, the words of those two men sounded much like some cabal, a scheme perhaps to discredit the magistrates responsible for his appointment. Again it occurred to Cleomedes, as it so often had in the four and a half years past, how greatly his exile, brief as it was, had estranged him from his fellow Athenians' delight in intrigue and their petty malice.

"Of course," said Xenias after a while, "I would not think of slowing up our voyage deliberately."

"Did anyone urge you to slow it up?"

The helmsman gazed down at the long silver-scrolled wake. "Urged me? Who save those foolish choristers would give me unbidden advice? This is my eleventh voyage to Delos. But perhaps I should not mention those ten voyages," Xenias went on testily, "or rather, one particular voyage. I take it you heard many people say I ought to have been replaced long ago."

"Not many. Some."

"I assume they justified their opinion."

"They did, according to their lights."

Xenias shook his head several times to rid his beard of the spray which had collected on it; and that motion seemed to support his tone of defiance when he continued: "It is true. It is true that I sailed with the brother of Critias on that one particular voyage."

No one in Athens ever referred to Critias, the late headman of the Council of the Thirty, without calling him "infamous" in the same breath. Cleomedes was a little astonished that Xenias pronounced the name with no such explicit derogation. Still he said: "How could you help it? You are paid a salary by the city."

"Even so, I might have gone to Critias and told him: 'I shall not steer the Sacred Vessel this year. I loathe you. I will not have any truck with your brother. Since you made him the ship's commander this year, you must pick some other man to sail her to Delos.' Thus I might have spoken. It would have meant death for me, and for my family, destitution," Xenias said, adding: "I realize that sort of thing is hard to grasp for a man who was not in the city in those evil days."

Cleomedes said nothing. He knew that citizens such as Xenias, men who had lived through the terror of the Thirty, looked at those who had not as utterly inexperienced. The memory of the sufferings within the town had paled the exiles' glory. Times had changed since the day when the populace, running wild with joy, led the returned exiles, the liberators, up the hill to the great shrine of Athena in triumphal procession! It was that melancholy thought which caused Cleomedes to say that it was not among the returned exiles that Xenias must look for his detractors.

"You speak wisely," the helmsman affirmed. "The worst are those who ought to know better themselves. It is they who willfully ignore my predicament under Critias. How else could they call me—what? A henchman of the Thirty? A friend of Critias? It is such names they call me, is it not?"

"Why listen to slander?" Cleomedes said. He wondered why he kept humoring the touchy man.

"How can I refute it?" Xenias said listlessly. "By declaring truthfully that I was in favor of popular rule all my life? 'You were, whenever being in favor of it served your own ends,' they would tell me. Referring to my persuasions would be of no proof of my having acted in accordance with them. Those whose own persuasions were spared a test ask for more than persuasions. They ask for recorded actions. The only proof that they might accept of my hatred of Critias would be my having allowed him to put me to death. And who," the pilot proceeded, ignoring the step that Cleomedes made away from him, "who ever chose death only to make his actions fit his feelings, and thus prove their sincerity to the men who will live when he no longer does?"

"Such a choice would indeed be absurd," said Cleomedes. The stiffening wind and the clatter of the sail filled him with a sensation of well-being. "Everybody knows the words of the poet: 'Rather than rule over all the dead I would be a poor man's slave.'"

"I *am* a slave," Xenias said with a low voice, "I am the slave of fear, Cleomedes."

"That is an awkward remark to come from a seaman."

"Storms and wild currents and sunken reefs and even the pirates who would think nothing these days of attacking even this ship—all those perils put together do not

frighten me half as much as does the thought of my
enemies. At this very moment some of them may be trying
to have me disfranchised."

"Trying they may be. But how could they succeed?
Even if steering this ship under the brother of the infamous Critias ever could be considered a crime—which it
never could—is there not the Great Amnesty, my good
Xenias?"

"I have three sons," said the helmsman. "What is to become of them should their father be disfranchised, disgraced?"

"You exaggerate."

"Do I? Look at what is happening to Socrates."

Cleomedes, who had taken another step to midships,
spun round. "What about him?" he asked.

"Will he not be accused of having been the teacher of
Critias?"

"There is not one word about Critias in the indictment,"
said Cleomedes, drawing closer again. "I saw the parchment hung up outside the Royal Hall with my own eyes.
Not one single word."

"Of course not. That would be against the amnesty. But
there are other means of dragging in the name of Critias.
It need not necessarily be the accusers who drag it in."

"Who then would?"

"There will be many men in the Great Court tomorrow."

"If it is the five hundred and one jurors you are talking
about, Xenias, jurors do not accuse."

The pilot put his shoulder to the tiller. "Accuse! Think
of this: what will Socrates do if a hundred men, or only
twenty, shout that it was his teachings which made Critias
the monster he was? How can he prove—prove to shouting men—that his intentions in teaching the young Critias

were honorable and pious? He can prove that as little as I can convince anyone of my having hated Critias."

"These are conjectures," Cleomedes said on a note of dismissal, "in Socrates' case as well as yours. You imagine things. You listen altogether too much to gossip."

"What Athenian wouldn't?" mumbled Xenias. He threw back his head, glancing up the whole length of the sail, which the breeze blew out with soft round contour.

Upon a command from the boatswain's pipe the oarsmen on the upper benches had stopped rowing. The wind came steadily now from the north; and in the intervals between the strokes of the lower-bench rowers one could hear the long-drawn-out groanings of the mast. The shore, blurred by a slight haze, was sliding by in the distance.

"Sun and wind augur well for the voyage," Cleomedes remarked before he stepped away.

"They do," Xenias confirmed, his eyes still on the billowing sail. He did not seem disconcerted by the curt manner in which the commander had broken off their talk.

In fact, the forthcoming trial of Socrates was about the last thing that Cleomedes wished to discuss with the moody pilot, or with anyone, for that matter. Few men inspired him with greater admiration than Anytus—one of the three citizens who had convinced the magistrates that Socrates offended against the law.

Had Anytus asked Cleomedes beforehand, the latter might have told him he failed to discern the good that could possibly come from the trial. He might have suggested that charges brought against one of those "lovers of wisdom" would serve only to enhance the reputation of them all. Now some people were certain that Socrates differed from the rest of those self-styled "lovers of wisdom." Others contended he was nowise better than the Sophists, those itinerant foreigners who had overrun the town in the prosperous years. Cleomedes had even heard some men say that Socrates was no more honest than the ventriloquists at the Piræus, who baffled the mob by declaring that an oracle was talking out of their innards. Cleomedes himself had no opinion in the matter. He was glad he had none. Whether the jurors would uphold or throw out the accusation which Anytus had submitted— together with Lyco the orator and the poet Meletus—that was not at all likely to change Cleomedes' feelings for his old friend.

They hailed from the same class of the citizenry. The father of Cleomedes had been a shield-maker risen to wealth in the early years of the war. Anytus' father had been a tanner, and he himself had expanded his business in a fashion novel to the city: a string of slaves was producing leather goods in his workshop. For such ingenuity Cleomedes felt great respect. He also admired the skill with which Anytus had retrieved his possessions after his return from exile.

Many Athenians admired Anytus the tanner. Cleomedes had been devoted to him ever since their days of exile in Thebes. They had fought side by side in the civil war. Side by side they endured the rigors of siege in the snowed-in mountain fastness of Phyle, and side by side sallied forth onto the plain to give battle to the infamous Critias. When Anytus rose high in the exiles' army, Cleomedes, far from envying him the career, took great pleasure in it. Also, Anytus gave Cleomedes greater honor than due his rank. When the last battle was won, and Critias slain, Anytus kept Cleomedes by his side while negotiating with the defeated for the removal of the men killed in the fighting—a hallowed obligation unshaken even by the frenzy of the struggle thus ended.

Cleomedes thought it no more than just that Anytus had assumed a place of prominence in the pacified city. The qualities that had turned the "simple tanner" (as Anytus was fond of calling himself) into a warrior of distinction also made him a man to reckon with in the Assembly. He had become one of the prime movers of the measures by which the men of popular rule were striving to restore the ancient spirit of Athens. If Anytus, then, in keeping with these efforts, wanted to put Socrates in his place—who was he, Cleomedes, to question the wisdom of that decision?

All that came back to Cleomedes, in the way matters decided upon once and for all run in one's mind, while he walked toward the mast, his eyes half closed against the salty spray. Xenias had begun to round the ship up into the wind. The upper-bench oarsmen had come on deck and were shouting good-natured taunts up to a couple of sailors who had begun to climb the mast. In the fair wind, the ship was gathering speed.

On the forecastle deck some of the choristers stood about. This was their first pilgrimage to Delos, as could be concluded from the band of wrought silver they still wore on their heads, for more experienced choristers always laid aside that "Delian crown" once the ship was at sea and did not don it again before disembarking. Coming closer to the young men, Cleomedes noticed that they were surrounding a boy somewhat older than the others who sat on a coil of cordage. Their contracted lips and their frowns revealed the attention with which they listened to him. None of them seemed to have noted the commander's approach. The youth on the cordage—his graceful body was stripped to the waist—went on talking, his countenance shining with the awareness of some superior knowledge. But the air, resonant now with the sounds of the whipped-up waves and the hull's creaking, blurred his words to Cleomedes' ears.

Suddenly one of the choristers stirred and, turning round, exclaimed: "The commander! He will tell us the truth."

"The truth about what?" Cleomedes asked sternly, while the young men opened a lane and the boy on the cordage fell silent. Cleomedes cast a glance over his shoulder as though attracted by the yells of the sailors aloft who had begun to shorten the sail. He was determined to thwart any further discussion about the ship's course.

But what the young choristers were discussing was merely the history of the Sacred Vessel. Prince Theseus himself was said to have sailed her to Crete. Now, did he really voyage, as it was said, on this ship when he took it into his head to slay the monster feeding on human flesh on that island?

"So Theseus did," replied Cleomedes, relieved. However, as some more queries were hurled at him, he became uncomfortably conscious of the problem presented to him. It was by no means novel.

The Sacred Ship, so the question proposed, had been repaired innumerable times since the misty days of King Theseus. Every last part of the craft could be assumed to have been replaced any number of times. "Now *is* our ship Theseus' ship still?" the boy on the cordage concluded. "Is she the same, the self-same vessel?" A hush had fallen on the group. Their spokesman—he was very handsome indeed—got to his feet.

Even while he talked, an incident not thought of for four years or so had drifted back to the mind of Cleomedes. On one of the long winter nights in the fortress of

Phyle, when the exiles sat round their fires and talked about the city, wondering whether they'd ever see her again—on one of those nights, one of them, a taciturn man by nature, had advanced a peculiar observation. Athens, so he said, was not different from the Sacred Vessel: as each of *her* parts had been exchanged many times over for a new one fitting into the place of the old, so the law-givers of the earliest Athens had been replaced by a long succession of men, each of them in his turn taking the place someone else had held before him. One could see with one's eyes the men alive at one's time; one was told, or could read, about their precursors. But what made each of them take the right place in the city's structure—what made him function as a part of her order as though he had been part of the original structure himself—that could never be seen, never be perceived with the senses. Yet that unseen and unseeable thing was what distinguished Athens from the townships of foreign people, no matter how rich or victorious in battle.

Recalling those remarks, Cleomedes was not altogether certain that to draw a comparison between the city and a seagoing craft, however highly esteemed, was the thing to do in conversing with men so young: did not such comparisons suggest the kind of playfulness which some of those "lovers of wisdom," those windbags, had made the fashion in discourse? But that doubt did not take shape in Cleomedes until, challenged by the boys' prolonged silence, he started repeating to them what he himself had listened to on that long-bygone night in Phyle. So he went on to tell the story. But as, through some prank of his memory, the present predicament of old Socrates came back to his thoughts and more and more drew them away from the tale, his words did not come out well, and soon trailed off in a murmur. "My dear boy," he said in a lively tone, "you are sailing with the Sacred Ship! Is that not enough to make you proud and proud of your city?"

The young man said it was, and gave a short friendly laugh, and so did the others, and some of them turned around to wave a hand at the sailors on the mainyard.

These youngsters were not malicious, Cleomedes said to himself. Nor corrupted. Their thoughts, if alighting easily on some subject, could also be deflected with ease. It was good to know that a new breed was coming of age —young men with un-Sophisticated minds and indifferent to speculation. Anytus would like these choristers . . . and their behavior also might show him that Socrates and his like no longer constituted too grave a menace for the youth of Athens.

A great opalescent cloud had come up, and the water beneath it darkened. Cleomedes felt a chill. He wrapped his cloak more tightly about him and wiped the wet from his face. Then he abruptly turned his back without so much as a nod toward the boys, so strongly did a new, poignant thought assail him.

He knew suddenly why the two men on the wharf had urged him not to hasten his homeward voyage: as long as his craft had not put in at the Piræus, Socrates would be safe even should the worst come to the worst at his trial. For since time immemorial it had been accounted unholy to put a man to death in the city as long as the Sacred Ship was not in, back from Delos.

According to the indictment, Socrates had offended against the law by denying the gods whom the city revered—replacing their worship with new practices—and by corrupting the young. Socrates' three accusers, as was their right, indeed their duty, had suggested the penalty which in their opinion befitted those crimes: they had asked for Socrates' death.

Like most Athenians, Cleomedes realized that the king
archon's taking charge of the case had turned it into a
grave one: in a hazy manner, Athenians looked upon this
high magistrate as though he really were the successor of
the priest-kings of yore. Still, a sentence of death had
seemed improbable to Cleomedes before the thought of
the two meddlesome men on the pier leaped to his mind
again. Now the motive of their officious advice was clear:
friends of Socrates, or men who had listened to him with
approval at some time or another, they were trying to
have the period of grace extended should the improbable
come to pass and the court condemn him to die.

Cleomedes reproached himself with having been slow-
witted. He reproached himself with not having paid the
proper attention to what people were saying about the
impending trial. But was there not always some law case
being guessed and gossiped about in Athens, this most
litigious town in the world?

Cleomedes was to worry about this one law case
throughout the outbound voyage. He was, throughout it,
to worry a great deal about the two men on the pier.
Sometimes he saw them in his dreams and was wakened
by his impatience with their increasingly secretive whispers. Then he would wonder in whose behalf, if in anyone's, they had talked to him on the wharf, and whether
there existed any sizable clique fearful of the decision of
Socrates' judges. Cleomedes, though a rebel in his time,
had no intention of antagonizing powerful cliques, one
way or the other.

Once, dreaming again, he saw Anytus standing between
the two men on the jetty. The two had stopped talking,
nor were their hands any longer cupped over their mouths.
Anytus talked. In fact, he shouted, across the becalmed
harbor, out to Cleomedes, who stood—so he felt in his

dream—in the bow of the homecoming vessel. But no matter how much he strained his ears, he did not grasp Anytus' words. When Cleomedes awoke, not even their tone was left to his recollection. Once, on some other night, Socrates came into Cleomedes' dream. Untidy as ever, his overlong woolen tunic carelessly girded and hanging without folds down over his paunch, his feet bare, the squat man stood close before him, unmoving, hands clasped low on his back. But of Socrates' face Cleomedes could see only the untrimmed gray beard—and above it, the ugly mask of Dionysius' companion, Silenus, whose little effigies, as the dreaming Cleomedes knew, the artisans made to open in the middle and reveal the god's own image inside. "Where did I hear that story about Socrates and Silenus?" Cleomedes wondered in the morning.

Such goings-on in his dreams of course alarmed him; and whenever that uneasy mood took possession of him, he was to grow resentful of the role into which the Fates had cast him when they permitted the magistrates to appoint him this year, of all years, as the Sacred Vessel's commander. Looking for diversion, then, he would stand for hours by the side of the pilot, now contemplating his weather-beaten face, now bending over the bulwark to watch the foaming wake and hearken to its murmurs. He would on occasions not mind listening to Xenias' talk about his fears and about the self-righteousness of so many fellow Athenians in times when, as he loved to put it, "any man may find himself tossed about one day in a rudderless boat, a prey to inscrutable powers, and with nothing to steady his heart save the memory of those rare mortals said to have been rescued by the gods from tempest and darkness."

PART I

I

At the Piræus, the throngs come to watch the rites had
begun to thin away as soon as the Sacred Ship had maneuvered out of the inner harbor and they could see, beyond the arc of the twin breakwaters, her sail—the much-
talked-about new sail—being hoisted. And soon after,
most of the men were on their way back to the town—back
to Athens. Ever since the Spartans had made the Athenians throw down the strong walls that used to protect the
five-mile highway, people had preferred to walk on it in
groups, for gangs of waterfront riffraff were said to roam
the vicinity of the road.

Among those who nevertheless decided to stay at the
Piræus some hours more was Meletus the poet. He wanted
the company of a Corinthian woman known as Glycera,
who had moved to the port from Athens some months
previously. Moreover, Meletus foresaw that, should he return to the city, he would hardly remain in his house on
this balmy day, and he had no wish to run into Anytus
again. He was weary of the tanner's contention that the
king archon had deliberately set the trial of Socrates for
the tenth day of the month of Thargelion while every
schoolboy knew the Sacred Vessel must sail on the ninth,
leaving the city powerless to carry out a sentence of death
until she returned.

While the priests were decking the brazen prow of the

ship with garlands of laurel, and the choir aboard was singing out one farewell chant after another, Meletus had managed to banish from his mind those conjectures about the
"trickery" of the king archon. Yet no confident mood took
hold of his heart. The cheers that went up on the wharf
upon the boatswain's first signal and the first concerted
strokes of the rowers sounded like mockery to his ears.
When the ship began to drift out of his sight, he had also
seen drift away the hope that Socrates, found guilty, would
without delay be compelled to board a vessel himself—the
Stygian ferry to the land of the Shades. . . .

Of the crowds, only some small groups of men had
stayed behind on the pier. They were loitering about
the warehouses or staring at the canvas and cordage, the
anchors and oars, the carved figureheads and the oaken
rudders, piles of which could be seen through the open
doors of the Great Arsenal, still so called. Some other men
walked to and fro on the embankment, and some others
still sat on the edge of the quay wall, their feet dangling
over the water that sluggishly beat against the stone.
Meletus stood close to one of the bollards, arms crossed
over his narrow chest, and gazed out on the glassy surface
of the water; and while he watched the broad fishing-
boats come in, their dirty sails swinging lazily in the still
air, and the mounds of their night's catch glittering in
the light of the cloudless hour, he could not help listening to a man who talked about the old days and how the
two capstans on the breakwaters' battlements would drag
a huge chain across the mouth of the harbor directly a
large craft had departed. Meletus did not turn his head
to look at the man or at his hearers, who kept interrupting
the wistful tale with curses meant for the Spartans who
had dismantled that marvel of Athenian ingenuity. For
some moments the poet felt like stepping up to those day-

dreamers and telling them that it was useless to glory in grandeur gone, that they had better think about dangers present. . . . But the conspicuous lack of recognition with which he had met throughout the ceremony warned him against rebuking strangers. On his way down from the city, in the limpid coolness of the early morning—and when, later, he had crossed the whole length of the harbor town—Meletus had been certain that he would be the object of great curiosity on the pier; he had all but seen the men there nudging one another at his approach, had all but heard them whisper his name with awed anticipation. As it was, no one had so much as stepped aside to make room when he tried to elbow forward in the throng to get a good view of the Sacred Vessel.

Farther off to the eastward, the slim rowing-craft of the port's commander, which had lain alongside the jetty during the ceremony, was now being steered toward one of the roofed ship houses, which, built at right angles to the edge of the water and tilted up toward the land, still lay in the shadow. Meletus, turning slowly, cast one single glance up to the rock of Munychia and its citadel, whose forbidding dark stonework stood out, serenely, against the azure. With a short sigh, the poet walked away from the embankment.

He strode across the wide quay, picked his way through the commotion about the arsenal, and turned into the thoroughfare that led away from the waterfront. There was surprisingly little traffic in the lower part of this straight wide street lined with houses greater and in better repair than most secular buildings in Athens proper. However, after passing the temple of Aphrodite, Meletus heard the hum of voices grow louder, and after another two hundred steps or so he found himself amid the flow of men on the road leading to the highway. Knots of them, and some women and children too, stood in front of the workshops on both sides of the cobbled street, in some places packing its whole width. Meletus, not interested in the wares on display—or, for that matter, in the artisans sitting at work behind them or haggling with some prospective buyer—advanced, almost gingerly, through the multitude. Their ceaseless gay babble failed to lift his low spirits. At one turn he was jostled a little by some young fellows, and he was on the point of upbraiding them for their mischief, though his small stature surely was no match for their big muscular bodies. As he retreated to a near-by corner to rearrange his cloak, two streetwalkers, poorly clad though pretty young things, caught his attention, but he did not respond to their calls, and even took his eyes off them, disgusted by the vulgarity with which they thrust out breasts and buttocks. Surely such a sight could not but fill with contempt a man about to join a Glycera!

He walked on briskly, keeping close to the high rear wall of what looked like a rich merchant's house, and in fact succeeded in keeping out of the bustle. Also, there were no shops on this upper part of the thoroughfare, and the men returning to Athens, no longer engaged in banter and loud-mouthed jesting, were moving faster.

An offensive odor of refuse hung over the entrance to the narrow street on which Glycera's house stood. Meletus, bringing index finger and thumb up to his nostrils, turned the corner, only to find himself blocked by two half-naked slaves trying vainly to make a pannier-laden donkey move from the spot. The poet did not hesitate to abuse the two men soundly, raising his voice over the animal's braying until they succeeded in flogging it into the alley. Although anxious to get away from the foul smell, Meletus followed them and their jackass at a distance, aware of his dignity.

The noise of the thoroughfare soon was out of hearing, and it grew increasingly quiet about him. At one time he heard the clatter of a loom, and at another the song of two women at some splashing fountain near by. At last he saw the hetæra's house among the foliage of a cluster of bay trees, and after a few steps he halted in front of the outer wall.

He called, and repeated his call, and then there was a rattle of bolts and iron bars behind the heavy door; and as the dark-skinned keeper opened the door a crack, the twang of a cithara rose from somewhere in the rear of the building.

"Go and tell your mistress that Meletus the poet is calling on her," he said, and when he elicited no more than a surly grunt from the man, he added, patronizingly: "I haven't seen you here before, my good fellow, or have I?"

The doorkeeper half turned to calm a fiercely barking dog; and Meletus, annoyed by what he surmised was deliberate vacillation, was about to shove the ill-mannered slave to the side when he heard a female voice—not Glycera's—inquire who the visitor was.

"Meletus the poet," Meletus announced through the widened crack of the door to the girl, who was crossing the courtyard.

With a gesture oddly poised for one so young, she asked the doorkeeper to admit the caller. Then, having halted near the small statue of a nymph that stood in the center of the courtyard, she bent down to stroke the dog, which had come over to her. "What do you think, my pet?" she said. "Should we tell this impatient man how early it is? And that Glycera is still having her hair curled?"

"Her beautiful golden hair!" exclaimed Meletus while the door was shut behind him. "Ah, how greatly the sight of that gold is missed in Athens!"

"It must be," the girl said, her eyes following the dog on its slow retreat toward the rear.

Meletus stepped into the courtyard, and as he nimbly slipped off his sandals, he let his eyes roam about with the expression of a man pleased to find a familiar place unchanged. The eastern wing of the building still cast a long shadow upon the flagstoned quadrangle. "The music—" he said. "Is it the blind old woman who is playing for our Glycera?"

"Glycera might be willing to send her out here to divert you."

"I would not dream of so imposing on her goodness," objected Meletus, at once realizing he would be kept waiting for some time. Glycera was not likely to go out of her way to accommodate a caller with so slender a purse as his; gone were the days when women of her calling might give their favors to a poet for nothing.

"Well, then, Meletus, son of Meletus . . ." the girl said with a mellow voice and lifted a hand.

Her knowing him gratified Meletus, though he did not like the way in which she addressed him. He wanted to ask her how she came to know him so well, but when he had formed his question she already had disappeared under the covered walk in the rear, probably behind the vermilion curtain of the central hall of the house.

Although of good health and still fairly young, Meletus never had been a happy man. Not the least of the troubles eating away at his heart was the fact that his father, Meletus the elder, had named him Meletus, and that the ridicule attached to the work of his father as a playwright seemed to have blighted his own career. On the other hand, Meletus the younger could not help comparing his father's vast output to the trickle of his own genius. It was very well for him to know that his good taste was

bound to spare him such scandalous failures as tainted
the name of his father; surely he, Meletus the younger,
never would come forth with a drama about Œdipus,
the Theban king, as Meletus the elder had done, challenging the great Sophocles himself! But reminding himself
of what he had not done and of what he never would do
afforded but small satisfaction to Meletus the younger.

Of late, to be sure, that sickly preoccupation with his
calling had given way to some doubts about the place of
poetry as such within the order of things—

Walking to and fro in one of the twin colonnades that
lined the longer sides of the courtyard, Meletus several
times had glanced at the low couch he had kept passing.
Now he stopped in front of it and tested its cushions. He
took off his cloak—the customary large oblong piece of
bleached woolen cloth—and spread it over the couch. The
poet had a sensitive skin (which was also the reason why
his tunic, the girdled garment reaching down over the
knees a couple of inches, was made of linen).

He lay down and clasped his hands behind his neck.
He began to wonder whether the news of his recent distinction had preceded him to this house. Glycera was
likely to have heard of his prominence in the case against
Socrates. But had she also heard that it was he, he alone,
who had worded the writ of accusation?

No such writ could be submitted to the king archon
directly. First, the lower magistrates had to be convinced
of the gravity of the charge. The accusers had no means of
employing persuasion; they simply would, at that hearing,
take an oath attesting that their case was a just one, to the
best of their knowledge. Thus it was, above all, their writ,
the "complaint" of popular parlance, that had to plead
their cause at this stage—or, rather, the city's cause, which
they had taken upon themselves to defend against infringe-

ments. The wording of the "complaint," then, was of the most decisive importance. Also, a special statute imposed a heavy fine on anyone whose "complaint" the lower magistrates dismissed as unfounded. That danger, in the present instance, was past. Not so the greater one: the heaviest of fines, topped by the permanent loss of the right to institute any proceedings, and even disfranchisement, threatened those whose accusation failed to obtain a fifth of the jurors' ballots in court.

Now if things should come to that pass in the present instance, the wealthy Anytus of course would also have to pay the fine of the impecunious Meletus. Therefore the poet had not protested against Anytus' wish to consult a legal expert—the orator Lyco. But the orator, instead of simply stating his fee, declared he wished to be a party to the "complaint." Socrates had been an eyesore to him for countless years: had he not nettled men of his profession always, and scoffed at those who were "selling words for money"? He, Lyco, was willing to prove his selflessness to that street-corner rhetor—prepared to stake his entire future upon Socrates' prosecution!

That fervor had sounded sincere: Lyco's livelihood depended on his composing the speech for an accused today, for an accuser tomorrow; should an accusation co-signed by him be found groundless, who would be eager to secure his services any longer? Claiming that he, then, of the three "complainers," was running the greatest risk, Lyco set out to draft the writ of accusation. "To accuse a citizen of impiety," so his draft began, "is by many considered hard and even vexatious, for everybody is tempted to think that a law appealed to only seldom may be infringed with impunity—"

Meletus would have none of it. The law was clear. The introduction of new cult practices—of deities, really—was criminal, if ever anything was. To discuss the law against impiety, or stress its not being obsolete—that would be nothing short of disastrous, for didn't Socrates just love that sort of discussion?

In the ensuing struggle between the two associates of Anytus—and when Meletus, having prevailed, began to compose his own draft—he had experienced a sensation so keen that he at once perceived its import for his whole outlook on life. Arranging words with a view to their effect on the very existence of a human being exerted on him an attraction far stronger than the lure of whatever it was that used to fire his poetic genius. What proof had he ever had of the power of his verses? What proof had any poet ever had of the might of his verses, except for the public's talk—words resulting from words? Indeed, the howl of an animal preparing to kill commanded a power greater than even the war songs of a Tyrtæus!

Egged on by that startling discovery, Meletus yet had used his habitual circumspection in approaching his work. Time and time again he had erased still another draft of the "complaint" from his wax-covered writing-tablet until he was satisfied and had satisfied Anytus and felt assured that the grudge of Lyco was soothed.

As to further procedure, Lyco spoke the truth when he said that public opinion no longer favored professional rhetors in law courts. Though it was legal for any of them, as it was for any Athenian, to stand up as an accuser and deliver his speech in the court, as any accuser had to—why not, in this case of a joint accusation, have Meletus, who after all had drafted the writ, also take over the role of the "main accuser"? Anytus could have intervened, claiming that role for himself. But he had evidently put more trust in Meletus' talent than in his own.

Thus the poet's victory had been complete. In his elation he had dismissed any thought of Socrates' fabled deft-ness with words, bound to make his own task by no means a light one. He had thought only of his success.

But was it still success, what with the alleged trickery of the king archon and its unknown motives? Had the strict language of the writ given pause to the king archon? Why, *if* it had, had he handed down an indictment? For days Meletus had pondered those questions. However, having tasted defeat so often and fearing the image of an-other defeat, he had in reality avoided searching his soul. Waking early this morning after a troubled night, he had found his doubts anything but dispelled.

Still lying on his back, Meletus bent his knees, put one leg across the other, and for a while watched the wiggling toes of his foot. Then he directed his eyes up to the quadrangle of sky, one of whose corners the colonnade's roof obliquely cut off from his vision. Absorbed by the thoughts of his hopes and his misgivings, he failed to hear the curtain being drawn aside from the aperture in the opposite colonnade; and as Glycera wore the thinnest of sandals and moved with feline slowness, he did not notice her until she stood over him, smiling. The music indoors stopped.

" 'To lowly folk the good unbidden come,' " she said.

"If Homer there must be," the poet rejoined, sitting up, "why not quote the better verse, my Glycera: 'To the good the good unbidden come'? I would have sent you word beforehand under different circumstances. As they are—"

"I was told how busy you were," she interrupted him, softly. Her lips remained parted, and her protracted smile, together with the humorous daintiness guiding her hand up to her hair, seemed to stress her quizzical tone when she continued: "Your visit therefore flatters me doubly. I take it you were at the harbor." From under her painted eyelashes, her glance went out to the spindly legs of Meletus and the traces on them of the dust of highway and wharf.

Sitting on the edge of the couch, he made a disparaging gesture. Glycera's station excluded her from attending certain rites, and he felt he was acting in very good taste by belittling his own attendance at the Sacred Vessel's departure.

The slave girl came out, and put an earthen cup half filled with wine at the foot of the couch.

"You must excuse me for not joining you," said Glycera. "I was drowned in wine last night. They drink hard at the Piræus, and I still haven't grown accustomed to it."

The poet's eyes rested on the girl who stood close to him, holding a figure-painted lipped vessel in a pose of abashed indecision. When she had leaned over the cup to pour water into the wine, the shoulder clasp of her knee-length white gown had loosened and it had slid down past the nipple of one of her breasts. Meletus took the jug from her hand. "I shall mix the drink myself, child," he said. "Or perhaps I shall leave the wine untouched. Your mistress doesn't seem to approve of drinking at this hour." As the girl thanked him and walked off, it occurred to him that it was a pity to keep banned from the city a woman who was training her slaves so well.

Glycera leaned against one of the slender columns of the covered walk. She wore a long purple-hemmed linen robe whose modest half-sleeves would have been fitting for a matron. Whenever she moved her head, her silver earrings tinkled a little. She observed her visitor water the wine. "They say you will speak in the court yourself to-morrow," she said.

Across the rim of the cup, which Meletus had put to his mouth, he looked at the hetæra.

"But then," she went on with a sigh, "whatever I am told is no more than hearsay. How could it be otherwise? The foreign sea captains and the merchants who come to this house—what would *they* know? Most of them, for all *I* know, are still ignorant of your new friendship with Anytus the tanner."

"We did not become friends to be talked about."

"Assuredly not," Glycera said. She relaxed her posture abruptly, came to the couch, and sat down by his side. "So why talk about it at all, my Meletus? There are so many things I am eager to talk about with a friend from the city. Oh, Meletus . . ."

"I know you are not happy here."

"Oh, Meletus, there must be *someone* in Athens to take up my case again. *You* know I was wronged. It was a ludicrous accusation. They never could have found me guilty without that wretch of a Syrian slave. They put him under torture—"

"Such is the law," Meletus interrupted in a mild tone. Her physical nearness pleased him. Although it also made him notice the lines at the corners of her mouth and a premature fold on the nape of her neck, he would have taken her into his arms forthwith on the slightest encouragement. He said: "You have lived among us for a long time, Glycera. You should know that no one can bring his slave to court as a witness unless he consents to having his man stretched on the rack if it so pleases the court. And a wise law it is, for who would endanger the health of his slave without the assurance that his own cause will benefit from the truth, which torture of course brings out?"

"The truth! Will not a slave always say what benefits his master?"

"Now the foreigner speaks out of you. *Our* slaves—"

"That law is stupid."

Meletus raised a finger. "With us, Glycera, laws are made and enforced by men who themselves submit to those laws. Furthermore," he said, slightly vexed by a shrug she made, "if memory serves me right, the necklace was found in your house. They could have put you to death for thievery, as you know."

"The necklace was given me as a present."

"The slave declared that his master had bought it for his wife."

"How would a Syrian slave know his master's thoughts so well?" Glycera asked with a sigh of resignation, and placed a hand on his knee. "The affair was simple enough if looked at as I think it must be. A Glycera robbing, though not through thievery, mind you, a citizen's wife of a costly token of his affection—a sentiment rare among you Athenians—what is there to suit a law court better these days? Law courts abide by the spirit of the new Athens."

"That is an odd way to look at our law courts."

"Are your law courts above the sympathies of those they consist of?"

"The law is," Meletus said not without dignity. He thought to himself that brevity made for his most felicitous utterances. Brevity had made his "complaint" effective. He wondered how brief the main accuser's speech could possibly be in a court presided over by the king archon.

Glycera said: "Tell me, Meletus, how did you come to hate him?"

"I do not hate him," he said, not in the least surprised by the frivolous lightness with which she changed the subject.

"You are asking for his death."

"The three of us are. And how many besides us! He must die so that the law may live."

"That is a lofty way of looking at a man's life," Glycera remarked, adopting Meletus' own tone of some moments earlier. Then she asked: "Have you talked to him often?"

"Who ever tried to talk to Socrates without finding himself talked to, instead?"

"Has he, then, talked to you often?"

"Would he talk to a poet? He has no liking for poetry. He once suggested that poets' work was the result of inspiration, not of thought. And of course inspiration is something far lower than thought! However . . ."

"However—?"

Only when he had satisfied himself that the hetæra was in earnest did Meletus say: "I heard him talk on poetry in a different vein on one occasion. But being very young at that time myself . . ."

"What did he say about poetry on that one occasion?"

"He compared it to love," Meletus replied after a pause, "in a way. . . . Come to think of it, he may have been joking, as he so often is, that lover of wisdom. Still, he talked a great deal about love on that night. In fact, all of those present did. Those were carefree days, and it was a carefree man's house where all of them talked and drank till dawn came."

"Tell me more about that night."

"I told you I was a mere boy then."

"How did you happen to be in that house?"

"The gentleman had *not* called me in—if that is what your question aims at. I was not a handsome youth."

"So you were eavesdropping?"

"I heard Socrates mention poetry."

"You were not a poet yourself in those days, were you?"

"My father was," he said gloomily, his desire to embrace the woman dwindling.

"I regret that you no longer seem to recall what Socrates said about love on that night. Or what the others were saying."

"Aristophanes, the comedy writer, was among the guests," the poet said. "He suffered from a hiccup."

"Did *he* talk about love?"

"Who would remember what Aristophanes says?"

"You do not wish to talk to me about love," she said when Meletus failed to proceed.

Having caught a glimpse of her pursed lips, he said to himself that this sulkily pouting woman could not really annoy a Meletus these days! Why not tell her that the love she wanted to be talked to about was not exactly the one uppermost in the gentlemen's minds on that long-ago night? Such an intimation might stop her precious prattle: women of her kind had no sympathy for men's love of fair boys. But would she not turn the tables on him, saying that Socrates, for one, was known for being like a father or older brother to his youthful companions? And then, only a boor would allude with derision to the love of young men; and though Meletus was not altogether certain that he might not do so in the court tomorrow, should he be offered an opportunity by some heckler, he did not wish to harm in this house his reputation as a man of refinement.

Glycera had taken her hand away from his knee. She leaned backward, propped her elbows on the pillow, and lifted her feet from the ground, hunching up her knees a little.

Meletus contemplated her delicate ankles, and then, over his shoulder, her face with its small straight nose and her eyes shut in a pretense of lassitude. He found himself willing to forget the sharpness of some of what she had said. "I was a mere boy then," he began again, "an eaves-dropping boy. Granted. Still, some of what those gentle-men said has stuck in my mind. The thing I recall most clearly is the trick Socrates performed at that party. He pretended that he was giving an account of what a certain wise woman, a seeress, had told him many years before, and into her mouth he put his most presumptuous words. No one could call him impious. It was all very reverent toward the gods. Only many a year later did I realize that he would take a word and turn and twist and squeeze it till it assumed an entirely new meaning while he kept paying lip service to the old." The poet, looking into space, made a mental note not to let Socrates play a similar trick upon him tomorrow.

"What was the new meaning he gave to the word 'love'?" the hetæra asked.

"I no longer remember. And in fact, I do not care. The memory of that feast disgusts me, with drunken Alci-biades flaunting his frivolity and in the next breath hold-ing forth in praise of the matchless Socrates!"

"Alcibiades . . ."

"No other," he confirmed, lifting his voice to rebuke her for the wistful tone with which she had pronounced the late archtraitor's name. Was the legend of Alcibiades' beauty and daring to survive the record of his unspeak-able crimes? "Why do you wonder?" he said and rose. "You must have heard that Alcibiades was Socrates' fa-vorite pupil. Yes, my good woman, the man who more than any other is to blame for Athens' defeat was Soc-rates' pupil. And so was Critias, her scourge. On these two counts alone Socrates would have deserved death long ago."

"Does Athens punish teachers for the misbehavior of

their pupils? Long as I have lived among you, I still am not conversant with the finer points of Athenian law."

"You resent Athenian law for personal reasons," he said, while he drew away from the couch, "and I do not say I condemn you for it. But as for Socrates, you must know why we ask for his death. Any number of men must have talked over with you my complaint."

"Any number of men? With how many men do you think a Glycera discusses such matters? With how many men do you presume she lies every day—even a Glycera reduced by your laws to living at the Piræus?"

"I did not intend to hurt your feelings. 'Any number of men' was only a figure of speech. And well you know it!" he burst out, whirling round. "You enjoy making a fool of me."

"It is not I who am making a fool of you, Meletus."

"And to think," he said, plucking his meager beard, "that I came here to forget awhile the great responsibility descended upon me!"

"Do you wish my slave girl to keep you company?"

"I didn't say one word about that slave of yours."

"I am neither blind nor dumb."

"Perhaps you are not quite as clever as you think you are."

"I am clever enough to see who really is making a fool of you—or, to put it correctly, who is using you for his own ends."

"Who is?"

She sat up and let her gaze travel from the poet's dust-covered feet up to his sallow face and its long nose, which at this moment was twitching a little. "Anytus," she said.

Meletus threw up his arms. "I was wrong, my beautiful Glycera! I was wrong in employing that figure of speech, 'any number of men'! Few indeed must have been those who visited here of late, and fewer still those who knew what they were talking about when they gossiped about Meletus the poet. Who, I wonder, can be so ill-informed as not to know that Anytus is as clay in my hands? I do not mean to belittle him," he said, his self-possession faltering under her upraised glance, "and perhaps the simile I just used was not chosen aptly. Yet Anytus would be the first to concede that he has no talent for drafting so important a document as a writ of accusation. He was wise enough not to entrust it to a professional orator, either. He left the whole matter to me once he realized I was the best man for it. Anytus, the son of Anthemion, is a great man, though he keeps calling himself a simple tanner—"

"That is the point."

"Modesty in a man of his wealth should delude no one—"

"He is a tanner and maker of leather goods."

"So I said."

She drew a deep breath. "Tell me, Meletus, where does a tanner get the hides he needs for his trade?"

"From sheep, from cattle."

"From live cattle?"

"Certainly not."

"From slaughtered cattle, then."

"Naturally."

"And who, tell me, is slaughtering cattle these days? Actually not many are. Few people can afford to buy a steer and have it slaughtered for their family. Most people have to make goat do. However, it is oxhides a tanner needs."

"Correct. He buys them from the acolytes at the temples."

"In other words, the acolytes sell to the tanners the hides left from sacrificial offerings."

"Precisely."

"Therefore, those who make sacrifices are about the only people who buy oxen, and by so doing provide Anytus with oxhides."

"Certainly they do not sacrifice in order to provide him with oxhides."

"Certainly not."

"Moreover, you are innocent of present-day conditions on farms. There's precious little livestock left."

"Would you say that farmers own more than they did four years ago, or less?"

"More, of course."

"Can it therefore be assumed they will own still more oxen four years hence?"

"That may be assumed."

"They must worry who will buy them in the future. To think that the only regular buyers are men anxious to offer to the gods!"

"Not the only ones, surely."

Glycera nodded indulgently. "To sum up, then. Those who are offering to the gods are a most welcome sight to cattle-breeders as well as tanners."

"They are a most welcome sight to any right-thinking Athenian."

"Granted. Now, Meletus, tell me, is it not common knowledge that those who offer to the gods regularly have become quite rare?"

"So have those who can afford it."

"Would not their forebears, under similar conditions, have sacrificed to the gods first and thought of their own needs afterward?"

"So they would have."

"Might it not, then, be salutary to remind their present-day descendants of their first and foremost duty?"

"It might be."

"And can you think of a better reminder to that effect than punishing a man said to fulfill his duties toward the gods only slackly? Especially if such a man is said to invite others to share his alleged indifference toward the gods? And more especially if those rumored to be influenced by that man happen to be well-to-do citizens on the whole, or their sons, and thus, as we agreed, the only people in a position to purchase oxen regularly?"

"What rubbish!" Meletus said with the nearest approximation to haughty disinterest his growing confusion permitted him to assume.

"Suppose—" she began again, affecting the tone grownups adopt in explaining an everyday occurrence to children who refuse to apply their minds to it properly, "suppose your tanner goes to see one of his cattle-breeding friends. 'It is not easy to come by oxhides regularly,' he says; 'do you people skin your oxen before driving them to market, and throw the hides on the dungheap?' You see, Meletus, I imagine your Anytus to be in a waggish mood, what with his farmer friend treating him to some well-seasoned cheese and fresh quinces and plenty of wine—"

"Go on."

"I will, my Meletus. You have grasped the jocular query of Anytus, haven't you? To it, his friend replies: 'Why should we drive oxen to the market? There are no buyers for them.' Asks Anytus: 'Why is that so?' 'Come, come, my excellent Anytus,' the man says, 'you must be aware that people do not purchase steers unless they plan to make an offering. And you must be equally well aware of the growing reluctance of people to make such offerings.' Thereupon Anytus declares: 'They must be led to make regular offerings again.' His farmer friend agrees heartily. 'Rely on me,' Anytus says, drains his cup, and takes his leave."

"You are a good teller of tales," Meletus managed to say. The cithara-playing inside the house had been resumed. "Right so! A fantastic tale should be accompanied by some music." Inclining his head on his raised shoulder, he gave the appearance of letting the tune engross him.

"This, Meletus, is how Anytus thought of having Socrates called to task for not worshipping the gods the city worships," Glycera proceeded, and her suddenly dreamy-sounding voice did not detract from the obvious merci-lessness of her intent. "But forming a decision and carry-ing it out are two entirely different things. Returning to his house, then, your Anytus engages in some serious thinking. Will not the citizenry question the purity of his motives in accusing Socrates of impiety? Not all citizens breed cattle. Far from it. How about the vast majority of Athenians whose only possession is their citizenship and who could not afford to buy leftover meat from the tem-ples even if the supply were greater than it is because of the lack of piety on the part of the rich? Well, your tanner friend is not really worried. An army leader of a sort, and a successful one, too! And just as hapless army leaders—this is another of your wise laws—are dragged into court for their failure, a lucky one can rely for some time on the gratitude of his fellow Athenians. Still, still . . ."

From the corner of his eye Meletus watched the hetæra support the image of Anytus' troubled irresolution with a slow fluttering motion of her spread fingers.

"Someone else must take the initiative in accusing Soc-rates—that is the solution your tanner arrives at. And who would be the best person for that, the man least likely to sting people into searching for selfish motives in the complaint? Well, who but a poet? Of course, a poet! A man acting only upon inspiration!"

Had a stranger entered the small courtyard at this moment and come upon the Corinthian hetæra and her visitor, who was gaping at her—red-faced, his teeth set, his thin lips a-quiver—that stranger might have presumed it was the man, and not the woman, who had done all the talking, so strained and hoarse was Meletus' voice when he finally said: "Yours is the most venomous mind it ever has been my misfortune to encounter. Greed is the only motive of human action that vicious mind of yours can conceive of. Ah, your judges showed a keen understanding when they passed the sentence of banishment on you for your greed—"

"Did they not do so for thievery?"

"Stop it!" Meletus cried out, and, conscious though he was of the poor figure he cut, began to hop from one foot to the other and to throw his arms about him as if fending off a persistent gadfly. "Stop pulling apart my every word!"

"I merely corrected a minor error of yours," Glycera said with an expression of naïveté so nearly perfect that it choked the poet into speechlessness. "I was not banished because of my greed—if greed, then, should be in my nature. I was punished for the alleged theft of a necklace studded with precious stones. I admit that the crime of theft in most cases is motivated by greed; and probably those of my judges who let themselves be persuaded that I had stolen the necklace did not doubt that greed *was* in my nature. Yet surely they wouldn't have voted for my banishment if they had not believed that I had stolen the necklace. Or would they? Perhaps one can arraign people in Athens and punish them for something objectionable in their nature, something that might lead them one day into transgressions and crime. I do not know, Meletus. Maybe you do. Or perhaps Anytus the tanner does."

Meletus no longer followed her arguments. A short while earlier he had been torn between his intention to tell Glycera that he had *not* taken the initiative in accusing Socrates and his wish not to destroy the legend which apparently maintained that he had. But the slander leveled at Anytus and their common cause had all but numbed him. Its very enormity deprived it of a rational effect on his mind.

"Does the music annoy you?" Glycera asked, looking with mock sympathy at his twisted features.

Unable to face her accusation squarely, the poet had begun reading her mind. He sensed the extent of her concern with the fate of Socrates. He was astounded: he always had held that people who thought themselves wronged were the last to be interested in the welfare of others.

"I hope my little story did not overtax your patience," Glycera said. "You also must excuse its artlessness."

"I certainly do not take exception to the artlessness of your treacherous tale," the poet said through clenched teeth, at the same time trying to smile superciliously. In actual fact, he felt an unwilling admiration for the semblance of consistency that she had given her story, making its conclusion fit the preconceived scandal. While, to hold off even the dawn of a doubt, he muttered such words as "absurdity," "evil fantasy," "women's prattle" or "laughable nonsense," he said to himself that here was another piece of evidence in proof of the havoc wrought on Athens by those "lovers of wisdom." Their warped manner of putting facts together at will and embroidering on them with speculation had entered even the habits of a woman whose business it was to keep company with men of breeding, listen to their talk, and entertain them through her wit and subtle caresses. Instead, this Glycera, to suit her fancy, had attempted to discomfit him with as vile a piece of Sophistry as ever had come his way! That thought steadied Meletus' bearing at last. "The absurd," he pronounced, opening his arms wide as if to limn in air the immensity of the realm of the absurd, "the absurd never bothers a man of my kind. But neither does it amuse him." And with that, he lifted the cup from the flagstones and, before raising it to his lips, poured some drops of the wine on the ground; earlier his great thirst, or perhaps his impatience to lie with the woman, had made him forgetful of his duty to the gods.

When he had drained the vessel and put it down, Glycera got up from the couch and clapped her hands. The music stopped instantly. With an obliging gesture she answered the puzzled look of the poet, who picked up his mantle.

Grasping it adroitly, he threw it over his left shoulder and then, holding one end in his armpit, drew the cloth across his back and under his right arm, and finally tossed the other end of the cloth over his left shoulder again— all that with the care fitting of a man of distinction.

"Do not leave," Glycera said, "she is waiting for you." A solid beam of sun had made its way to where she stood, and she shut her eyes to its glare.

And as she also averted her face from Meletus, holding her body motionless, he said no further word. He hesitated for another moment. Then he turned to advance toward the rear of the courtyard.

There, in the right-hand corner of the short covered walk, lay the dog. He must have been lying there all the time. Barely pricking his ears at the man's approach, he seemed to have been expecting him all the while to direct his steps toward the narrow door.

It stood ajar, and Meletus saw the slave girl standing in the bluish light of the small room. She extended her arms in a motion of welcome, both studied and lewd. She was naked, except for a saffron-colored Egyptian veil which fluttered lightly in the breeze that had sprung up.

11

Anytus left his house this morning at his habitual hour and then attended to some of his habitual business—as though to prove to himself that this day's events did not interfere with routine. At daybreak the Eleven—the committee of penal overseers—had dispatched two of the city's Scythian police slaves to Socrates' home, and by now Socrates had been for hours in the prison house halfway up the hill.

Shortly before midday Anytus went to his barber's shop; and from there he walked down to the marketplace, though he was not one of its regulars and as a rule left the buying of the day's provisions to one of his slaves.

A well-built man, if somewhat broad of hip, the tanner looked, when seated or standing up, every inch the citizen of consequence that he was. His graying beard, which encroached high on his cheeks, and a constantly furrowed forehead, together with a perpendicular crease over his small hooked nose, gave him the appearance of a man asking much of himself and much of others. It was his uneven jerky gait that impaired this impression of self-assured sternness. It made him look hurried even when he was not. There was a joke about that: Anytus, people said, tried to outrun the tannery stench sticking to his clothes.

On this midday, too, emerging from the dingy lane of

the barbers, he arrived on the square as though pushed
into its swarms by some unseen power behind him. But
as the slave he had with him had fallen behind in the
crowded alley, Anytus stopped and, for a moment, let
his eyes wander sidewise toward the Royal Portico, at
whose western end he had halted. He was uncertain
whether he would later enter the long covered walk—
which, supported by fluted columns on the side of the
square, bounded it on its southern edge—and mingle
there with the idlers.

Before him, a sea of white tunics and cloaks—here and
there dotted by the gayer colors of some foreigner's garb
or that of some fop—flooded the western part of the spacious plaza, up to the row of public buildings, from whose
walls and columns and statuary the forenoon's shadows
had retreated. The great marble sanctuaries uphill shone
in a stream of sunlight. Close though they were (as the
crow flies) to the teeming humanity here below, they
seemed aloof from its noisy bustle.

Anytus, the slave by his side again, started threading
his way through the confusion of wickerwork stalls and
plank booths and roughly arranged sunshades, waving a
lofty hand at some of the sellers or buyers who, interrupting their chatter, called out a loud "*Chaire*, Anytus!"
But he rarely greeted anyone himself and barely looked
at the men.

Having turned east, he advanced along the line of
quadrangular stone posts that bisected the width of the
plaza, each surmounted with a crude head of the god
Hermes. He paid no attention to the yells of the vendors
of unguents and cure-alls whose tables he then passed by
—or to the clanking of coins with which the money-
changers were trying to attract the eyes of people—and
made straight for the booths of the flour merchants. De-

ciding quickly, he bought, after the usual haggling, a good measure of flour, and the slave poured it into the large basket he carried.

In the fishmongers' corner, then, Anytus took his time choosing a well-sized tunny. Somewhat farther off, a donkey had upset a row of earthenware piled on the ground; and while the slave was stowing the fish into his pannier, Anytus was listening to the foul-mouthed altercation between the hapless potter and the animal's owner which was wafted over to him. But unlike the men standing near by, he was not amused by the incident. His face remained immobile.

Then he turned to proceed along the northern edge of the market, past the City Hall's brazen portal, toward the Round House.

A thin train of smoke from the Sacred Hearth, which was kept burning day and night beneath the peaked roof of this ancient structure, met the tanner as he hastened past its weather-worn pillars. But not before another ten steps or so did he become aware of the abrupt manner in which a small group of men about to leave the building— members of the City Council—had halted as he had come near, and had fallen silent one after another.

At the same time, Anytus felt that he was being followed. He slowed his pace, as if to contemplate the flower-vendors' garlands of oak leaves and myrtle, but did not look behind him.

Suddenly he said to his servant: "Come to think of it, I needn't buy any wine. There's plenty of it in the house. And oil, too." And having said this, he changed his direction to recross the plaza.

At one of the hermæ he made a brief halt to buy some garlic and also some dried figs from the old man who squatted at the base of the post. He even leaned down to read a small parchment fastened to it, which offered for sale a three-year "noble steed, perfectly trained." And all the while he knew for a certainty that he was being watched.

Striding on again in his usual jerky fashion, he soon had reached the Royal Portico. "You may go home," he told the slave and then said that he wished to eat a couple of figs; and as he stood between two of the colonnade's columns, his head bent over the pannier and looking about him from under his knitted brows, he at last saw the man who was following him. It was Simmias the Theban.

Had Simmias been just another of Socrates' hangers-on, the tanner and maker of leather goods might have chosen to overlook the salute with which the young man tried from some distance to catch his attention. But the father of Simmias had been Anytus' host in the days of his exile in Thebes; and there was no denying that, but for him, Anytus would have fallen into the hands of Critias. It was Simmias' father who had prevailed upon his fellow Thebans to reject the Spartans' demand for extraditing the refugee Athenian rebels—whom they, in turn, planned to hand over, with glee, to the infamous Critias. Simmias' father, then, had saved Anytus and his companions from certain destruction. Yet after his glorious homecoming, Anytus' thoughts had only seldom returned to the good man in Thebes, and less frequently still to his son, a mere lad in the days of the tanner's exile. In fact, his memory had needed some prodding when, on a wintry day about two years before this morning, Simmias had come up to him in the square. Anytus had inquired after the arrival's business in the city. Simmias said that he had come to study. "So, so . . . to study?" Yes, with Socrates. "With Socrates?" Yes, with no other; and was not to partake of his wisdom worth leaving one's home? The tanner said that there was a lot of talk about that wisdom, not all of it favorable. When Simmias showed no response, Anytus asked him how his excellent father had fared in the intervening years, and how conditions in general were in Thebes now that Sparta was the supreme power in all Greek lands. That had been all of the welcome Simmias received from Anytus in Athens.

It had not been difficult to keep the young Theban at a distance in the subsequent two years. He himself seemed to be eager to avoid his father's onetime houseguest—who soon forgot Simmias again. When, later, the design of complaining against Socrates matured in Anytus, no thought of Simmias and his devotion to the accused, and no thought of the consideration the father of Simmias might deserve, troubled Anytus' resolve. One day—the king archon's indictment was on everybody's lips by then—Anytus, to divert himself, went to look at some cocks to be trained for a fight at one of the wrestling-grounds, and there he ran into Simmias. "Oh, Anytus," said the young man with true or pretended surprise, "I received a letter from my father this morning." Anytus asked after the health of the man in Thebes. "The years sit lightly on him," Simmias answered, "and he is gladdened by the news I gave him of your enduring good fortune. These are his words: 'No doubt, the gods deal justly with a just man.'" And having said that, Simmias stepped away from Anytus to join a man carrying a small cock under each arm. If Anytus suspected the Theban, then and there, of adopting his teacher's much-talked-of ironic manner, and of trying to censure Socrates' pursuer by reminding him of the man in Thebes who had once rescued *him* from *his* pursuers—if that suspicion *should* have come to Anytus, then and there, it certainly had failed to stick in his mind. Not until he now looked across the shortening distance at the young man did it occur to Anytus that he might be bent upon calling in the debt of gratitude owed his father.

And with that thought the tanner entered the portico and turned sidewise to contemplate one of the frescoes adorning its wall, as though he had not seen all of them innumerable times and did not recall them even with their colors unfaded.

"I see that not only foreigners missed the ceremony at the Piræus," said Simmias, standing close behind Anytus —who, even before facing the young man, noted the strain in his voice.

He nodded, took a bite at his fig, and said, munching: "I shall be at the Piræus when the Sacred Vessel puts in, Simmias. The rites will be far less elaborate then. Still it will be a feast day for me."

"That remains to be seen."

"So it does," said Anytus. He put the other fig to his mouth, and began to walk without encouraging Simmias, through a word or a gesture, to join him.

But Simmias stayed by his side.

Anytus said to himself that, for all the young man's present rudeness, he had no genuine dislike for Simmias. He used to be fond of him in Thebes. Once, so he recalled, he had told Simmias the elder that having the lad about reminded him of his own son, a boy of the age of Simmias, and in a way hard to explain strengthened his hope for his son's survival in an Athens ruled over by his own archfoe. "Survive he did," Anytus thought with great bitterness while he glanced at the handsomely regular face of Simmias, "survive that boy of mine did—to become a drunkard!"

"Anytus . . ." Simmias began, "I came here to ask you a question."

"You used to ask many of them in Thebes five years ago," the tanner said amiably. "I wish you had asked some since your arrival in Athens. I might have warned you. I might— What is it you are anxious to know?" he interrupted himself, having caught a glimpse of the smile flitting over the young foreigner's face.

"It is about the amnesty. How do you reconcile the trial with it?"

Anytus wiped his mouth on the back of his hand. "The king archon appears to do so," he said.

"It is your opinion I am curious about."

"Is not my opinion evident?"

"How did you arrive at that opinion? You must have been more mindful than most men of the Great Amnesty, my Anytus," Simmias said, and in the following moment had to fall behind in the bustle. The portico was swarming with men, some strolling in one direction, some in the other.

"You are well informed," Anytus said as soon as Simmias caught up with him again. "Having been one of the movers of the great pardon in the Assembly, I have been mindful of it indeed ever since it became the law. You are well informed—but not well enough, I dare say. The amnesty was born from our longing to have concord restored among us. But great though that longing was, it never could have made us sacrifice our gods."

"That is a curious expression."

"I was never taught the art of picking words, and in my untutored way I don't think that expression out of place. Would not standing by and watching a felon insult our gods be tantamount to denying them ourselves?"

Simmias made no immediate reply, and it crossed Anytus' mind that this unbeliever of a Theban might be busy gauging the strength of his own beliefs. Finally the young man asked: "In other words, the amnesty cannot be applied where your law against impiety is involved?"

"If it could, the amnesty, far from restoring order—"

"Was it not meant to restore concord? Now you say it was order."

"Do not split hairs, Simmias. As I was saying, the amnesty, by forgiving such crimes, would open the gates to disorder and anarchy," Anytus declared. He was struck by the lofty ring of his own words: they had come to his mind from Lyco's discarded draft of the "complaint." The din of the marketplace was farther off now. There was less commotion in the eastern section of the square at this hour.

"Does the amnesty cover only offenses committed while Critias was in power," Simmias went on to ask, "or also those a man is accused of having committed before that time?"

Two substantial-looking citizens overtook Anytus and Simmias. They turned their heads to greet the tanner, who waited until they were out of earshot before saying: "Did not your teacher, Simmias, infringe on the law after the amnesty was proclaimed, as well as long before that? Is not your own way of asking questions and talking lightly about impiety—the speech of a man, mind you, who came to Socrates only yesterday, so to speak—is it not living proof of the recentness of his transgressions? Socrates offended against the law yesterday, and thirty years ago, and while the infamous Critias was in power."

Simmias remained silent. They passed the great mural that depicted the capture of Troy; and now it was Simmias who seemed to be absorbed by a painting, so often did he turn his head as they walked by the fresco, to admire the still-blazing tints of Priam's castle afire. "Talking about Critias," he at last said, "only the other day I was told a story about Socrates and the Tyrant."

"Oh?"

"One day," Simmias continued, looking straight ahead, "Critias summoned Socrates and told him: 'I forbid you to hold discourse with the young.' 'The young?' Socrates asked. 'Such as are under thirty years of age,' said Critias. Whereupon Socrates: 'Suppose I wish to buy something, and a man under thirty years of age has it for sale; am I forbidden to ask him at what price he sells it?' And so—"

"And so your Socrates went on needling the other and making him sound foolish."

"The other, Anytus, was the infamous Critias!"

"What of it? Does not your Socrates needle his friends also? Moreover, I have known that trite anecdote for a long time. I fail to see what you wish to prove by it. That Socrates had no love for Critias? Perhaps he had none—though he remained in the city when the Thirty took over. Still, I do not deny he may have disliked Critias. It's immaterial. . . ." His tone grew fretful. Some moments earlier he had been certain of the ease with which he'd draw out Simmias and learn something about Socrates' plans for his defense. But surely he did not plan to insert that hoary tale into tomorrow's proceedings! "I do not see," Anytus repeated ill-humoredly, "what you are trying to prove by that dated story."

"This, Anytus. Critias forbade Socrates to hold discourse with the young. You say he corrupts them by holding discourse, and for corrupting them you ask for his death. The Tyrant molested Socrates; you men of popular rule set out to destroy him."

"Not we men of popular rule! We—Meletus the poet, Lyco the orator, and I. In our city, my good Simmias, political parties do not accuse a man and bring him to trial. Nor do political parties interfere with law courts. Oh, no! I said that you were well informed on matters

Athenian. You are not. First you involve me in an entirely immaterial discussion about the Great Amnesty—"

"How great is its greatness, Anytus?"

After a moment of puzzlement the tanner said, with a snort: "I think it useless to discuss its spirit with you." The Great Amnesty had not only granted immunity for criminal offenses committed before the return of popular rule. There also were property matters involved in the pardon—the thorny problem of the restitution of land and moneys seized by the Tyrant and given away to his hench-men or sold for the benefit of the exchequer. And Anytus, vexed by Simmias' effrontery, wondered at this moment how well informed the Theban was on that aspect of the amnesty and on his own past troubles in retrieving his possessions. . . . The tanner looked out at the two stat-ues in the open space of the square, erected to honor the two illustrious Athenians who, more than three genera-tions before, had killed the tyrant Hipparchus; and though Anytus had never gone so far as to liken his own to their great deed, he now felt tempted to tell the young foreigner at his elbow that an Athenian who had fought despotism as bravely as he must not be annoyed with senseless and disrespectful questions! But while Anytus' sidelong gaze still rested on the defiantly thrust-out swords of the two statues, he also recalled the privilege that the descendants of those two heroes enjoyed; and this was a melancholy re-flection. For even if Athens were still as grateful to her benefactors as she had been in the days of *those* tyrant-slayers, Anytus' drunkard son, unlike theirs, would not be given a lifetime seat at the City Hall's public table—

At last Simmias remarked rather sheepishly: "Socrates showed great courage when Critias ruled in your city."

"Once the infamous Critias was done away with," Anytus retorted, and with a start took his eyes off the two marble effigies, "the town resounded with tales about such courage." And while Simmias again kept silent, the tanner reflected: "He's probing one point after another. He was ordered to find out what we accusers will dwell on in the court. Most probably he volunteered for this venture, boasting of our old acquaintance, or even of the service his father rendered to me." Why had he permitted the Theban to drag him into this profitless talk? Not really out of courtesy for his father, and a regret at not having shown such courtesy earlier!

Suddenly Simmias asked: "Are you happy, Anytus?"

"Giving the gods their due makes a man happy," Anytus answered, using a stock phrase; and then, following a whim, he said: "The trial is not over yet. I may have to pay dearly for my attempt to give their due to the gods. But even in that unlikely case I still would feel happy, knowing I made that attempt. When I decided to complain against Socrates, I was not unaware of the risks I was running. Is there a love without risks? Why should the love of the gods be without them? When I made up my mind to have your teacher brought to trial, I recalled one instance in which the city paid a high price indeed for upholding the gods' honor. I recalled the mutilations of the busts of Hermes, and how Alcibiades came under suspicion and was indicted for that outrage. He happened to be in command of our expeditionary force in Sicily. Yet he was ordered to return to Athens and stand trial. He had to hand over his generalship to a man everyone knew was inferior to him in daring. Athens knew that she imperiled her victory. Looking back on that decision in the light of what resulted from it, you might say that Athens traded victory for giving the immortals their due."

"Alcibiades, if I am well informed, was indicted for sacrilege. Surely you do not call Socrates sacrilegious."

The tanner puffed up his cheeks and blew out air, much like a man suffering from great heat.

"Alcibiades—"

"Enough about him," Anytus broke in gruffly. He had inserted the story on the spur of the moment, but actually was less in favor than ever these days of having Alcibiades' name brought up too often. It was well to remind people that Socrates had been the teacher of Critias: the recency of the Tyrant's misdeeds still kept afire the hatred of *him*. It was something else again to conjure up Alcibiades' shade. No longer did all Athenians curse him and his treacheries with the proper fervor; and were there not some to whom his name suggested the splendor of the bygone adventurous days? Anytus was as proud as any Athenian of the dazzling past of the city, and only a little less willing than most to forget for a short while her downfall. But far more important to him than glory past was the city's present order; and the memory of the extraordinary—even where it had not led to crime, as it had in Alcibiades' case—never was conducive to order!

"You failed to tell me," said Simmias, "whether you equate impiety with sacrilege."

"You have a legalistic turn of mind," Anytus remarked. "I am astonished you didn't pick one of the Sophists as a teacher. Well, then, did not Socrates himself inform you about the law that brings him to trial?"

"It seems a nebulous law, ill-defined."

"So it might seem to a man not born and bred in the city. It doesn't to us. We know precisely when to apply it." And having repeated these words with the tone of the deepest conviction, he started to talk about the "intrinsic clarity" of the law, which, so he said, was lodged in the "unerring feeling" of people who had no master over them save the law. He enlarged on the "typically Athenian instinct for justice" with waxing eloquence; and though the law against impiety had been made less than a generation before, he referred to it as though it were as ancient as the city herself.

When Anytus concluded his speech, Simmias, turning his head to the side, lifted both hands. "I beg of you," he said, "think it possible you might be mistaken . . ." and there was no effrontery in his voice this time, and his words came out with the childish-sounding blurs of the Bœotian accent that Anytus remembered as having so often amused him.

Against his will he tried to retrieve from Simmias' features the face of the boy he had been. "Mistaken, my Simmias?" he at last echoed. "Mistaken—in explaining the law?"

"In applying it to Socrates."

The tanner shook his head. To himself he said it was time to bid a good-day to the young man. He could have left him at this moment without being discourteous, for they had arrived at the portico's end.

It abutted on a small square enclosed on three sides by the Old Halls of the Magistracy, so called, and on the fourth—to the left of where Anytus and Simmias stood—by the iron bars setting the Great Court apart. There was no one in the square at this hour. But Anytus, stepping out into the open, saw in his mind's eye the assemblage which would be pushing against that barrier tomorrow—whispering, laughing, nudging, munching garlic, pressing against the bars, and twitting the harassed police slaves whose duty it was to keep back the spectators.

The long wooden benches of the Great Court stood deserted. In the wide passageway that intersected their rows, a sleek-skinned dog ran hither and thither. The noonday breeze stirred the plane trees lining the large rectangle's farther long end.

Slowly, as if hesitantly, Anytus shifted his eyes toward the dais and the high marble seat overtowering its oaken boards in the rear. Set off against the ocher-colored rear wall of the Royal Hall and the graven inscriptions in its stonework—the laws of Solon and Draco—the marble seat looked to Anytus more austere in its emptiness than it ever had with the king archon in it. The stark midday light lent a purple hue to the barren boulder-strewn slopes that stretched away, at both sides of the Royal Hall, up to the Place of Assembly and farther up, to the Gate House of the temple compound on the plateau of the hill.

Of a sudden Simmias had gone. He had not followed Anytus into the open, and had gone without bidding him good-by. Anytus saw him cross the corner of the marketplace and walk away, along the four-foot-high brick wall that separated the eastern end of the marketplace from the court. Some men stood near the farther end of the low wall; and as Simmias approached that group, he walked faster. Anytus did not strain his sight to identify the men; he could have recited their names: custom forbade Socrates' friends to keep him company in the prison house on the eve of the trial. But nothing forbade them to peer, as they seemed to be doing, across the low brick wall at the place they would stand in tomorrow—the small semicircle formed by the gradual recess of the wall to the left of the dais.

"Give it to him tomorrow, Anytus," said a fat man who, apparently having strolled down the portico, halted level with him. "And be on your guard. He is a slippery eel, if ever there was one."

"I shall keep that in mind, Cinesias," said the tanner, still gazing toward the farther end of the wall.

"Good."

Anytus turned his head to Cinesias. He had no illusions about the man. Enthusiastic as was his support in the Assembly these days of whatever the men of popular rule would propose, his earlier record was muddy; by some he was talked of as a turncoat. Yet Anytus said: "I shall also warn Meletus the poet."

"Meletus, Meletus . . . It was you who saw this complaint through. It is you who started this affair. Affair! It's an issue. That's what it is, an issue. But who am I to tell you that? You know yourself that hundreds—what do I say—that thousands of good Athenians are waiting to see the old corrupter cut down to size. And once and for all, too. Why, more than one of my friends would gladly chop off a hand if by so doing they could get those jurors to return the right verdict tomorrow." And pointing his thrust-out chin at the empty benches, he let the edge of his flattened right hand come down, like a knife, on the wrist of his left.

"I know that a great many citizens approve of our action," Anytus said.

"'*Our* action, *our* action!'" Cinesias said, and began to blow his nose, turning refinedly to the side. "Is it your son or Meletus the poet's whom Socrates corrupted? In fact, that poet has no son, and is still unmarried. It is your son whom Socrates corrupted, my excellent Anytus. Give it to him, and good!"

"You are being stupid, Cinesias," Anytus said severely. "It so happens, you know-it-all, that my son did not turn out well. Alas! I had to leave him behind when I went to Thebes. I left him in the care of an educated slave, who I suppose did his best. But his best wasn't good enough. With my workshop closed, my house sequestered, my moneys seized—what could the boy imagine his future would be? So he began to listen to this man and that. If you people—" he continued with rising choler, "if the whole lot of you who stayed in the city had been less callous than you were toward the sons of the men who meanwhile were fighting your battles, the boy might have turned out well! It is true that he also talked to Socrates. Probably he told Socrates that he wished to take up higher studies—which made some sense at that time, considering the hopeless state of my affairs. But upon my return that unfortunate son of mine, though he'd say he had no liking for my trade, did not utter one word about Socrates' teachings. He had by then already taken to drinking. Oh, I do not mind the truth," he exclaimed upon a mimicked protest from Cinesias, "I am not squeamish. I am the last to deny that the interest in learning my son paraded was merely designed to conceal his wish to loaf and drink un-watered wine. But one thing is sure: Socrates had nothing whatever to do with what became of my son. And you had better keep that in mind, Cinesias. Who are these two men?" he asked brusquely, somewhat out of breath, scowling at a couple of strangers who had posted them-selves behind Cinesias. "Acquaintances of yours?"

"In a way. They are islanders. Detesting Spartan rule, they recently moved to the city."

"What do they want?"

"Go away," said Cinesias to the two men; and even be-fore they had turned he said to Anytus: "You are a high-minded man. The way you pardon Socrates—"

"Who are those two friends of yours?"

"Oh, they? They are very poor."

"So they look," said the tanner, eying the shabby pair as they withdrew.

"They were rather well off some years ago. As long as their island was allied with Athens—that is, under Athenian jurisdiction—they were rather well off. Justly so."

"Informers, eh?"

"Yes, my Anytus."

"I knew their ilk. Of course they were well off, those island informers. Exacting money from one rich man today by threats, and accusing another tomorrow and having him summoned to Athens on their trumped-up charge; and while he'd wait for his trial in the city, they would grab his property at home." Anytus did not sound indignant; he sounded almost amused. "And now? What are those two birds doing in Athens?"

"They have fallen on evil days. But they are adaptable. In case you should need some information . . . Their fees are laughably small, Anytus—"

"Leave me alone," the tanner interrupted the officious man, whose vulgarity began to infect his own speech. From the group that Simmias the Theban had joined, a tall shape now had detached itself—and Anytus recognized the white beard.

So did Cinesias. "Crito!" he said, his voice overcast with amazement, and brought the palm of his left hand up to his mouth.

"You must go now," Anytus said, but he added: "My good fellow."

III

Nothing about the old nobleman, as he approached Anytus, showed that he might be aware of the delicacy of the enterprise into which he seemed determined to plunge. He walked erect, measuredly, putting his tall staff before him at every step, barely leaning on it. As he came closer he raised the staff a little and called across the intervening space: "*Chaire,* Anytus!"

"*Chaire,* Crito," Anytus responded and went to meet him halfway. His keen wish to read embarrassment and apprehension in Crito's face was disarmed by a beautiful smile.

A life well spent had lent an incomparable ease to the nobleman's bearing. His big eyes did not flinch from the piercing stare of the tanner. The smile was still on his face, and made it, seamed though it was, belie the silvery beard. "There are men," he said, "who would censure us both for talking to each other today."

"Small men I'd call them," Anytus said with marked civility.

"But is not exposing oneself to misunderstandings the coin a man has to pay for bold action?"

"Very true," Anytus said, and when Crito nodded and for a while did not stop nodding, he wondered whether the old man was not feigning an infirmity from which in reality he was free.

"A bold man must not be afraid of slander," Crito went on. "What indeed would an Athenian do were he afraid of scandal? Of all the ills besetting the city, slander certainly is the most persistent."

"Slander is like a bad odor. Though the merest whiff of it pollutes the air half a mile round, it does so only for the shortest of times. Athenians itch for a new scandal every day. How, then, could any malicious rumor last?"

Crito had entered the little square and gone to the iron barrier; and leaning his back against it, he propped his elbows against the top of the bars while with his staff he began drawing small circles on the soft ground. "I disagree with you," he said to the tanner, who stood in front of him, arms akimbo. "It is true that our fellow citizens are quick to spread an evil rumor—the more far-fetched it is, the quicker they are to spread it—but do they forget it as quickly? Is not what we tell one another about Athenians gone filled with rumors of bygone days? But I know," he went on, inclining his head and closing his eyes for a moment, as though listening to the hum of the more distant part of the marketplace, "Anytus is aware of all rumors, far-fetched or not."

"He is."

"Some of them are nasty."

"So they are," murmured Anytus, and quite suddenly asked: "Does a Crito perchance so lower himself as to allude to those oxhides I need, according to the most far-fetched of all present rumors? What dismal nonsense!"

"Rank nonsense."

"Everybody knows I do not depend on day-to-day business."

"Everybody does. Everybody does today. It may be different at some future time. Some day that story may seem more than a barbed joke to certain Athenians. Some day, looking back upon your complaint against Socrates, some men may say: 'Anytus was a businessman. Businessmen never forget what is good for the growth of their fortune. They have a second love of money, as it were. They don't love it for its possible use. Their affection for money resembles an architect's love for a house he has built, and that kind of love is prone to enslave a person. Even when a businessman no longer depends on day-to-day business, he remains the slave of his affection for money, and whatever he undertakes he does at its command.'"

"Any businessman?"

"That is what some men may well say, some day."

"Is it—even if the businessman they are talking about also happens to have done well by the city?" Anytus asked, his voice hoarsened. In view of Crito's own lifelong detachment from money-making pursuits and his family's ancient wealth, his remarks were in the poorest taste! And things had come to a pretty pass again when such a gentleman dared to mock a man of popular rule right in his face! Why not tell him that *his* class had committed crimes worse than being fond of amassing money? Why not remind him of the monsters *his* class had given birth to, an Alcibiades, a Critias?

"You have taken the words out of my mouth," Crito replied belatedly. "There always will be men in Athens to correct a view in need of correction. In your case, I would tell those people myself that a prosperous entrepreneur who, going into exile, deserted his property, knowing the Thirty would descend on it like a pack of wolves—that such a citizen must not be called selfish. I assume I would also know how to silence an argument running about as follows: 'True, Anytus jeopardized his property when he went to Thebes. But he merely acted shrewdly. He foresaw that Critias would plunder rich men, whether they had stayed at home or gone into exile, and, into the bargain, would put to death some of those within his reach.' "

"He did not plunder all of them!"

"That precisely would be my answer. 'Look at me,' I would say, 'Critias didn't plunder me.' "

" 'You happened to be a kinsman of his,' those men would counter your protest."

" 'True,' I would reply. 'But just as I could not rely on my kinship to Critias—did he not in fact rob and kill some of his kinsmen later?—so Anytus could not foresee what you men say he foresaw.' "

"To that," Anytus said with acerbity, "one of those men would probably object: 'Do not read a nobleman's thoughts into the head of a tradesman, my lord Crito. Anytus, as a sworn partisan of popular rule, and a well-to-do man to boot, surely was in greater danger than your like. He realized that his possessions were as good as forfeit the day Critias came into power. Fearing worse, he ran for his life.' "

"Did he?" asked Crito with a changed voice.

"No, Crito, he did not. What he thought of in going to Thebes was Athens' life, not his. On my return, I was praised for that thought. However, that praise did not delude me. I knew that what good an Athenian does is soon forgotten."

"His errors are not."

"Errors in law cases are punished on the spot," Anytus said on a note of provocation. "Should the complaint against your friend Socrates be judged an error tomorrow, I shall pay the fine."

"A thousand drachmæ, is it not?"

"It is."

"Ten minæ of silver, that is."

"Ten minæ of silver."

"A respectable sum even for a man of means."

"So it is."

"To see you convinced of how greatly you have erred, Anytus," Crito said under his breath, "I would not mind parting with twice that sum."

"Do not forget you are free from that enslaving 'second' love of money," Anytus said after a startled silence. "My excellent Crito. You first say: 'Beware of what might happen to your good name should your accusation be found just.' Then you say: 'Beware of what might happen to your purse should your accusation be found false.' May I dismiss that second warning of yours and return to the first? We agreed that men are prone to forget the good an Athenian does. Well, since nothing but good will result from the trial, men will forget it soon, together with the part the gods gave me in bringing it about."

"Are you thinking of the trial's results, Anytus? I am thinking of its outcome."

Anytus told himself that it must be an aged man's fatigue that reddened the eyes of Crito. How had he ever come to attach himself to Socrates? What had caused him to remain loyal to him for forty years—or was it fifty? "Result or outcome!" he said with a growl. "Do not involve me in squabbles about the meaning of words."

"I did not come here to squabble," Crito said, slowly shaking his head, and again that motion did not stop for a while. "I came here to say this. Men *will* ask, some day: 'What prompted Anytus to have Socrates haled into court?'"

"Will not one of them say: 'It was his love of the city'?"

"Every Athenian takes that love for granted in himself. In his neighbor's actions, every Athenian searches for motives other than that love."

"Does he search for motives he would not want others to find in him?"

"Preferably so."

"Are you back at those oxhides, Crito?"

"No, my Anytus."

"Are you, by any chance, referring to my son?" the tanner asked after a pause. "*You* know that Socrates hardly ever talked to him."

"But did he not talk to you about him? Did he not warn you against the severity with which you treated the boy?"

"He did. Once. What of it?"

"You hate him for it."

"If every man Socrates foisted his uninvited advice on should hate him—hate him to the point of forgetting justice—Socrates would have been murdered long ago, Crito."

"You never wished him any good."

"Wishing no good to a man and thirsting for vengeance are sentiments a world apart. I am not a vindictive man. Is not the amnesty proof that I am not? Did I not do more than any other man to make it the law?"

"You did."

"Well, then!" Anytus exclaimed. His was a minor triumph at this moment: Crito had thrown back his head, exposing it to the full impact of the sun, and Anytus noticed, under the finely textured skin of the old man's neck, the rapid pulsation of the jugular vein. His serenity was no more than a mask!

"Yes, my Anytus," Crito began again, "men will discuss the Great Amnesty for many years to come. That is one thing bound to keep your name on their lips. Can you not imagine some of them wondering: 'What manner of man was this Anytus, really? Was he really eager to see justice done? Was equity always in his mind? Was there not, shortly after the civil war, some puzzle about the restitution of his property? What with the amnesty, and many sequestered properties having changed hands several times under the Tyrant, many men had to fight in the courts for what was theirs. Not Anytus. It was then bruited about—was it not?—that, aware of the plans for the pardon, he got ahead of it in his own case.'"

"Will anyone ever so distort the facts? My property had come into the hands of an alien resident close to Critias—"

"And that alien fled the city even before Critias was slain, and—"

"And so I retrieved what was mine—"

"Even before the exchequer could claim it, as was done generally in cases of property seized and later abandoned by those who'd received it as a present. There was nothing unlawful in what you did. Anyone who says that you bribed the magistrates is lying. In fact, there were no magistrates to bribe, in the confusion of those days. No one knew who was in charge of the exchequer."

"Do you imply I would have bribed the magistrates had there been no such confusion?"

"I, Anytus? Are we not imagining, in common, what some men might be saying some day?"

"Is that the kind of reasoning Socrates has taught you? Let us stop that game, my Crito. What do you want?"

"What is it you want yourself?"

"I want justice done," the tanner replied. "I want the old respect for our gods to return. I want Athenian piety, Athenian ways to return."

"These are grand words."

"I do not propose to examine them. Everyday Athenian parlance must do. Grand words? That they are. What makes them grand, Crito, is the assurance that they will mean tomorrow what they stand for today. Discourse about words must stop. It falsifies words. It falsifies the citizens' knowledge of things as they are. I beg your indulgence for talking about knowledge, simple business-man that I am. Your Socrates calls himself a lover of knowledge—"

"Of wisdom."

"Of wisdom, then. I, Crito, am merely a lover of the city." Anytus clenched his fists. "What did you hope to accomplish by sending that Theban boy after me in the square? What was in your mind when you came here yourself after I turned my back on him? What is it you want, Crito?"

Crito, no longer leaning against the barrier, opened his mouth twice before he said, in a pleading tone: "Do not push matters to the extreme tomorrow, Anytus."

"Why—" the tanner asked in an irritated whisper, "why didn't your friend take himself away to some other city when he was indicted? Why did not *you* urge him to go away?"

"I did," said Crito, passing a hand over the wreath of his white hair, "I did, my Anytus."

A long silence ensued, with Crito's eyes glued to the tanner's dark face, and Anytus staring into nothingness. But when he saw Critobolus, Crito's son, walking along the low wall in their direction, he said dryly: "I shall see you tomorrow, then, you and all the others of Socrates' friends," and with a movement so abrupt it nearly threw him off balance he left Crito and went back into the portico.

Soon Critobolus' voice fell on his ear, but Anytus strode

on; he was not in the least curious to hear what son and
father were talking about. He noticed the two informers,
Cinesias' friends, squatting, in islanders' fashion, at the
base of one of the wall's pilasters; and one of them scrambled to his feet when Anytus came near. Ignoring the
tattered fellows, he called a huckster who had come into
sight in the square, bought a small pot of spiced honey
from him, and hastily started to ladle it out with his
fingers, for his throat was as parched as though he had
been talking for hours. When he looked behind him,
Crito and his son were nowhere to be seen.

Anytus put the half-emptied honey pot down at the
column at which he had halted, and while licking his
right hand's fingers clean one after another, he drew himself up. Then he left the covered walk again, and far more
slowly than was his wont crossed the corner of the marketplace, as good as deserted now.

At the low brick wall he stopped, jerking his shoulders,
propped his elbows up against the top of the wall, and
lowered his bearded chin on his joined fists, his unseeing
eyes on the empty benches of the Great Court.

The final question that he had asked Crito had not come
to Anytus offhand. Ever since the indictment had been
hung up in front of the Royal Hall, he had expected Socrates to leave Athens. To go abroad would have been the
most sensible step for him to take under the circumstances.
A sizable number of men had followed that course under
circumstances far less pressing.

Anytus had grasped at once Crito's unspoken contention
that Socrates' reasons for refusing that course were too
lofty to fathom. He did not dispute that lofty considerations might move a man to follow a course all his own;
had he not himself translated into action a lofty resolve
by going into exile? But what loftiness could there pos-

sibly be in a man's decision to stand his trial when in a
position to avoid it? There was none, Anytus concluded—
and no purpose either, except for Socrates' wish to set his
conduct apart from a pattern accepted as such by his
fellow Athenians!

Throughout his life he had tried to talk them into seeing
things upside down. Had he, the teacher of countless
young men, not been heard to say that he had no intention
to teach them and only aimed at "learning in common"
with them? Did he not drive that studied modesty to the
point of declaring he had culled what wisdom was his
from ordinary men's opinions on the most trivial issues?
Had he not, in fact, made it his habit to stop hoi polloi
for a chat in the street—while what he in truth craved
was the company of well-bred, well-groomed, quick-
witted young men about town? Had he really fooled
those ordinary people with his pretense of curiosity—his
asking questions about matters no one gave thought to
himself, while he of course had the answers ready? Was
he conceited enough to think that those people loved him?
He could not be! Why, then, had he stayed on in Athens?

Most probably he regarded his trial as merely another
opportunity to parade his eccentric disrespect for the established and the wholesome. The humiliation of an appearance in court surely seemed to a Socrates not too high
a price to pay for that chance. True, he must know that
this price might go up. But even if he should not count
on an acquittal, the actual dangers, as he seemed to see
them, were not immense: a fine most likely was what he
envisaged, should the jury return a verdict of guilty.
Every accused had the right to propose a penalty himself
in that case, irrespective of the punishment which his accusers demanded. The exchequer's sorry state had made
law courts agreeable to accepting fines. Socrates, then,

apparently counted on getting off scot-free, with the fine being paid by his wealthy cronies!

That, to Anytus' mind, was the picture which Socrates was painting to himself of the trial's outcome; and in the beginning Anytus had come close to making that picture his own. The first sign that things might take a different turn had come to him when the king archon set the trial for the tenth day of the month of Thargelion—which indicated some doubt on his part as to the willingness of the court to accept any penalty other than death should Socrates be judged guilty. But the king archon's action revealed also—this had come as a shock to Anytus—his concern for the fate of the accused.

Anytus had talked about his worry to Meletus. The poet replied that the king archon had no means of influencing the judgment: was not the decision to accept or reject the counter-proposal of the accused, was not pronouncing judgment, incumbent upon the jury alone? Were not the jurors, in Athens, both jury and judges? They were, so Anytus had conceded, welcoming Meletus' steadfast assurance as a man swallows a tonic knowing its effect will not last.

Apparently the poet had not grasped what actually was troubling his associate! "Suppose," Anytus had asked himself time and again, "the king archon wishes to protect Socrates—why did he not dismiss the accusation, in the first place?"

By now the tanner had solved that riddle.

Although more than half of the one-year tenure of the present king archon had elapsed, the complaint against Socrates happened to be the first case of its kind presented to him. The approaching end of his archonship made him increasingly mindful of his audit—that investigation of actions and omissions which any magistrate had to undergo upon relinquishing office. While the populace, at this juncture, did not seem to be taking sides on the question of Socrates' guilt, there was no telling how the trial itself would affect their feelings, and which way those feelings would veer. And who didn't know that Athenians loved nothing more than reproving a retiring magistrate at his audit, and that a king archon, in spite of the formal veneration paid him while in office, was, once out of it, the supreme quarry of those dreaded investigations? The present king archon was cautious; he was playing both sides. To those who should, at his future audit, reproach him with having taken lightly the gods' worship, he would say: "I indicted their worst offender, did I not?" Should, on the other hand, with a sentence of death passed upon Socrates and carried out, some men scold the ex-king archon for it, well though they knew it couldn't be blamed on him—but what nonsense was not introduced at those audits!—he would say: "At least I managed to have the execution postponed, hoping for some event that might stay it!" As an experienced politician, Anytus understood and even sympathized with the king archon.

Not being in the magistracy, Anytus did not have to fear an investigation of that kind. Yet harm might come to any man found to have acted wrongly in public life—as a later day might conceive of wrong and right. And Anytus realized that Crito's platitudes about his own future good name had been, in effect, a warning of far more tangible harm. Anytus had acted sternly on occasions in the Assembly, and once or twice had ridden roughshod over dissenting opinions. Still he had never cowed men into yea's, to the best of his knowledge. There had been no need for that: the reasonableness of his views, as well as his fame as the Tyrant's virtual slayer, must have won him the hearts of men!

But did not fame and opprobrium feed on the same meat? Was there not legend in opprobrium, as well as in fame? And did not opprobrium's legend encourage attacks on the same man whose legend-fed fame had formerly muted opposition? Was not, to pursue that train of thought to its chilling conclusion, anything threatening to invite censure some day also likely to revive opprobrium's legend — gossip, malicious rumor, calumnies, scandal?

Crito had not beaten about the bush. He had spared Anytus none of the vilifications that had tainted his name at one time or another. None—none but one! And thinking of that one, Anytus let his head sink deeper down on his hands, and he started combing his beard with slow-moving crooked fingers.

He would not have been mortified had Crito said to him, earlier: "Your present enterprise must remind you of the day when you stood accused yourself in a law court. Eleven years ago, was it not? The charge against you was harsh. You had been inexperienced in the field, and it had been folly to put you in command of that bastion. Nevertheless you were responsible for its loss to the Spartans. Trials of that sort always end badly for the accused, do they not? Yet you were acquitted. You happened to be a well-to-do man, and the suspicion of bribery presented itself to some citizens, so I seem to recall. That old tale will come back now that you proclaim so loudly your love of righteousness and of justice." Anytus simply would have shrugged off the story, and told Crito that the long-disproved lie was most unlikely to bias anyone judging the rightfulness of his own present action. "You cannot be in earnest, Crito," he would have said, and Crito might have admitted that he was not.

But Anytus no longer carried on that imaginary conversation with Crito at this moment. His own memory brooked no evasion. Money *had* changed hands at that trial, landing in the palms of some greedy jurors. . . . "And what of it? Do none but the blameless have the right to denounce an offender? And who *is* blameless?" And then: what he had done at that time, though not good in itself, had been all to the good! If that jury had sent him to his death, would not his courage have been sorely missed in the fight against the infamous Tyrant? Would popular rule not be all the poorer for it? Had not his acquittal saved a man destined to save the city? Unwittingly, those veniremen had acted wisely. Seen from the vantage of what benefited Athens—and did any other exist?—they also had acted justly. Little did it matter that the Fates, to make those jurors act both wisely and justly, had had them bribed!

Snapping out of his posture, Anytus lifted his head high. Gropingly, he drew up his cloak, which had slid from his shoulder. Whatever his detractors might say, tomorrow or later, his deep love of the city made him a righteous man. For what, in a citizen, *was* righteousness if not his determination to keep evil away from the city?

I V

Later in the day Anytus decided to look up Lyco the orator. But Lyco was not in his house—as at least one other person was to find out, the wife of Socrates, Xanthippe.

Defying custom, as well as some curious milling about the house, she had left it all by herself when the shadows grew longer.

When Lyco's doorkeeper, not concealing his surprise at facing an unaccompanied matron, informed her that his master had "betaken himself on a stroll," and, if gently, tried to shut the door in her face, Xanthippe flared up. "Now, really!" she exclaimed with her naturally strong nasal voice, folding her arms across her generous bosom. She took it for granted that everybody knew her by sight; and though she had never made up her mind whether to enjoy her popularity or to dislike it, she now found herself as much annoyed by the lack of recognition on the part of the slave as by the failure of her undertaking. For failure it was: she could not possibly wait in the street for Lyco's return.

The slave, opening the door wider again, said: "You might find my master in the Great Court tomorrow. There you might venture to approach him. Whether he will be inclined to lend you his ear, that I do not make bold to foretell."

Under different circumstances the pompous speech of the man might have amused Xanthippe; as circumstances were, it vexed her, and glowering at the fellow for a long moment, she vented her annoyance in a loud snort. Then she spun around and walked off.

Sharp-tongued observers had often commented on Xanthippe's "waddling." In fact, her slightly lurching gait and the continuous forward-and-backward motion of her large head, which followed the rhythm set by her feet, supported that impression. Yet she was not devoid of some grace—an aspect of youth, at variance by now with her ample figure. As for her face, the gods must have ordered her forty years to be good to it. No wrinkles marred the full smooth-skinned cheeks, no folds slanted the lips at their corners. Not one shimmer of whiteness could be detected in her rich brown hair; she still had her front teeth; and now and then her dark eyes still sparkled —not always in mirth, to be sure. Had Athenians been in the habit of discussing the looks of respectable women, even her husband's friends, who had no liking for Xanthippe, would not have denied that she was handsome. Nor had Socrates' poverty or his indifference toward his own outer appearance turned his wife into a sloven. Even amid this day's excitements, the pleats of her long gown were in their proper places and the woolen mantle, neatly clasped on the left shoulder, was spotless, though one could see that she had worn it for years. In short, there was an aura of good breeding about Xanthippe; her ancestry, of the equestrian class, showed.

Xanthippe had married beneath her family's station. And, odd to say, her misalliance had been in her thoughts quite a bit this day—as though the kind of calamity which had befallen her husband hadn't also, at one time or another, descended upon citizens of the most exalted lineage.

Truth to tell, Xanthippe's thoughts, in the course of this day, had not always moved in the cool channels of reason, though they *had* risen above her emotions at certain moments.

"My father—" she had reflected, "my father used to say that good breeding never proved itself as clearly as amid adversities. He was right. No man of distinguished descent would let his anger carry him away to the point of spiting custom with loud-mouthed scorn. I am a good wife. But I cannot say a man behaves as he ought to simply because he happens to be my husband. When the two Scythians came at daybreak, I thought again about what I had reminded Socrates of for days—my appearance in court. I asked him at what time he wanted me to come there with the two little ones. Having knelt down to roll his cloak, he glanced at me over his shoulder; but he did not open his mouth. I asked him where he wanted me to stand in the court before, in his speech, he'd begin to talk about his family, entreating the jurors to have mercy on them. He said: " 'I will have none of those antics.' 'Antics, my husband? Is it thus you feel about ancient custom?' 'If it is an ancient custom,' said he, 'it's high time it fell into disuse.' I was speechless—and those gossip-mongers who say that Socrates has no chance to put in a word edgewise in his own house should have seen me gaping at him without so much as a murmur. And when Socrates got to his feet and shouldered his cloak, he chuckled at the sight of my speechlessness. That is another thing a man of fine breeding would not do in front of police slaves.

"But why did my father, if he thought fine ancestry so important, give me away to Socrates, an obscure stonemason's son who no longer was young? My father had no dowry for me, that is why. He could not afford to turn down a suitor. I was eighteen years old, and men are re-

luctant to marry a girl past the age when she can be taught
without much effort. There is some reason in that—to
teach *me* must not always have been easy. Still, I learned
what my husband taught me. I have cared for his wants
as well as I could. Few women followed their husbands'
orders as well as I did during the plague; no one suc-
cumbed to the dread disease in our house.

"It is true that my firm voice at times may have lent a
ring of contradiction to the questions I'd ask of my husband. But I never contradicted him, really. I never reproached him with his neglect of his family's needs—

"How *do* I manage to get him his meals, on top of
scraping up the little ones' food, out of what he brings
home every other day from the square? I am a resourceful
housewife! He must have known that.

"He also must have known that I wished him nothing
but good, though I never assured him that this was so, and
once or twice even said I wished he'd run into some un-
pleasantness likely to convince him how greatly mistaken
he was in his ways. Gods, he must have known I did not
mean what I said then. Any untoward event coming down
on his head was bound to strike me and the children, too
—and so he must have told himself that I did not really
wish for any such blow. I have been a good wife.

"No less a person than the noble Crito once said so to
me. He came after me into the back yard that night when
Alcibiades made fun of me inside the house. Or, rather, it
was Socrates who was making fun of me when Alcibiades
mentioned my habit of asking questions. 'I am used to the
noise she makes,' Socrates said, 'as you are to the cackling
of the geese on your country place.' And when Alcibiades
rejoined that his geese at least gave him goslings, my husband said: 'Doesn't Xanthippe give me offspring?' Now,
really! I stood behind the curtain, eavesdropping, and if my

disposition were actually as bilious as certain gossips say it is, I would have thrust the curtain aside at that moment and flown at my husband, in the face of custom. But I merely stepped out into the dark back yard, so that the impudent boys Alcibiades had brought with him and who were all over the place would not see me in tears. Crito must have seen me, though. 'Never mind the jesting, Xanthippe,' he said as he joined me, 'you are a good wife, and Socrates knows it. He pretends to be amused by Alcibiades, who is drunk, and he wants to amuse him.' As Crito left me standing there, it was for the first time borne in on me that we women are nothing. Exposing me to ridicule, together with his firstborn son, did not seem too high a price to Socrates to pay for making Alcibiades smile—

"The coxcomb! The traitor! Ah, Socrates must have loved him a great deal. Once Alcibiades had disgraced himself, there was no one with whom he would joke in that fashion. Something seemed to have gone out of him on the very day it became known that Alcibiades had fled to the Spartan king instead of coming back to Athens as ordered and standing his trial. Never once since that day has my husband so much as pronounced Alcibiades' name. Not in all these years—

"Yet he has not really changed in all these years. . . . Many a woman have I heard bemoan the changes time wrought on her husband. They'd dreamily talk of the flower-crowned bridegroom who led them out of their father's gaily lit home to the chariot among the songs and railleries of the neighbors. *I* have no recollection of such merrymaking. The feast my father prepared was meager. My mother had told me that Socrates was not as pleasing to look at as were the figures of bridegrooms which artisans paint on walls or earthen vessels. Therefore I did not look up at him through my veil. His voice sounded very even as he kept talking to me. But not until we stood in the chariot, with Crito between us, did I grasp what Socrates was saying. He said that he didn't mind our simple wedding. Crito laughed and said: 'You will get used to your husband's manner of speaking, my little Xanthippe, and to his unending questions, too. Remember always to answer: "I agree," "Such is the fact," or "Quite so." You will not be the loser for it. You will extract much wisdom from him.' Perhaps I did not always remind myself of Crito's advice, later. Wiser I did become, just the same. I also came to like Crito a great deal, later. He was to be the only friend I ever found among the companions of my husband. But when we were riding that night to Socrates' home I nearly detested Crito, though my father had impressed on me the honor of having him as our groomsman. But did I not, on that ride, hold fast to my detestation of Crito in order to stifle the terror which gripped me more tightly with every turn of the wheels?

"O gods, why do you draw my thoughts back to that night, today of all days? Do I not today fear for my husband's life? Why, then, do you make my mind wander back to the hour in which I feared *him*—him and the power you gods lent men?

"You did well by our husbands, gods—that much I will say even in this hour. I say it without bitterness. My bridal terror turned long ago into mere wonderment at your doings, gods. My scorn at what men win now from the power you gave them—that scorn long ago lost its sting.

"I still recall how as a small child I stood in awe before the statues of the immortals. A notion had formed in my head that it was the male parts on the gods' bodies which distinguished them from humans. I forgot that foolish be-

lief soon enough. But was not a faint echo of that childhood fantasy in my fright when Socrates led me into the
chamber prepared for me in his house?

"We women are nothing. We are given to our husbands
as a piece of land is. It is true the goddess makes us give
life to seed. But do we not accept our husbands' seed life-
less ourselves, as it were? Unchanged, we are the receptacle
of our husbands' seed at any hour they choose, or which
the gods choose for them, changing their very bodies and
making their own power come over them as in a storm.

"Not all women bemoan that order of things. Some
claim that their husband's power transports them and
makes them share in the divine gift that is man's. 'His
manhood subdues me,' they'd say, if only in whispers, 'but
being subdued affords me bliss. Rob me of my will though
his power may, it yet does not tame me.' Or: 'I do not
know to whose delight I succumb, mine or his. My yearning's fulfillment is within me, but it is his raptures that
bring it about.' To my mind, those ladies are shameless
liars. Fulfillment, my eye! There is none. Perhaps those
ladies also lie to themselves. Of course they can't help
overhearing some of their husbands' prattle about the god
Eros and his doings, and the gentlemen's talk goes to the
women's heads. Thus they might put themselves, in their
thoughts, in the place of those foreign women trained for
the plays of love. Only recently did a story reach me about
a young lady who tried to imagine she was a lovely boy, to
please her husband. Now, really!

"This is one thing I must admit: my husband always
has kept his dignity in my chamber. Considering how
little he cares about dignified deportment otherwise, that
is strange. It struck me as curious on my wedding night,
for my mother had warned me a husband was not quite
himself when he came to the couch of his wife.

"But, then, Socrates' face never seems to express his emotions. The wilderness of his beard, the short nose that looks as though he were wrinkling it all the time, the small watery eyes with the crisscrossed bags beneath them —there just is no room in that face for the ordinary signs of emotions. . . . On my wedding night, when I finally raised my eyes to Socrates and in the light of the festive lamps beheld his face, it seemed to me different from any human countenance I ever had seen. Or does my memory mix that first impression with the feeling of utter strangeness that all but paralyzed me later in the night when he lay with me and his head was over mine and so close to my eyes that I could no longer make out his features?

"Nine months from that night Lamprocles was born, my son, his gosling.

"His gosling . . . There were times when I wanted to pity Socrates for not seeing what was beautiful and good and true in life: his family, and what he owned, and what he might add to it, and our venerable customs, and how they safeguard a householder's station. But Socrates would not be pitied. He could not be pitied. Not even the best of wives can pity a man who refuses to discern the good in life and instead speculates about things no one but he discerns, or pretends he discerns—I still don't know which.

"Of all the tales Socrates' friends tell about him, the one I dislike most is the story of his thinking bout in the camp before Potidæa—how he stood on one spot staring into space, 'thinking through a problem,' taking no food or drink for all the heat of the summer day—and how some of the soldiers, when the shadows grew, came out to watch him, and how he could not be talked to, and how throughout the night he remained standing there without stirring a limb, till the new day broke. Now if someone had approached him with bad tidings from his family, would he have snapped out of his stupor? Once I asked him that question. He said: 'I think that the voice—the voice I hear on occasions—would have come to me then and urged me to break off my thinking.'

"Why, that 'voice,' those 'signs,' that 'thing coming from the gods,' nearly drove me crazy at times. Not that I disapprove of oracles. Auguries may move the gods to indicate what is to our advantage, and if Socrates, to observe portents, had preferred the shrine in his house to those at the temples—of that too I would have approved, for many men are known to do so. What so unnerved me was his listening to a voice that came to him without preceding supplication, irregularly, so to speak, and not seldom in the midst of ordinary business.

"For all I cared, that voice could have talked to him while he was gabbling with his hangers-on outside the house, or watching the boys on the wrestling-grounds, or having a good time at some well-laden table. But to have that 'voice' around when we were with each other only, husband and wife, to have such a thing in my very chamber, ready at any moment to interfere with what Socrates was saying or doing, whereas I could not hear one sound of those supposed injunctions—now is there one decent woman in Athens who would have put up with that? Impropriety I call it, among other names.

"To talk to him about that 'voice' was impossible. He would have discussed a toothache with me, or an upset stomach. But never once could he be drawn out about that 'voice.' Yet is not finding oneself compelled to listen to a voice that no one else hears a disease, too?

"Once I lost my temper over it. A woman at the fountain had told me that Socrates talked about that matter in public. Now, in general I was not concerned with his marketplace conversations and his question-and-answer games. To be sure, in the early years I hoped that despite his undignified methods he'd make a name for himself as a teacher, and our household would profit from it. After I saw that my hopes were vain, I ceased to be curious about his doings in the square. Nor was I on that occasion curious about them. But is not that voice 'of his' a personal matter? Is it not my business at least as much as that of strangers picked up in the street? So I asked him: 'Why don't you ever tell me what sort of voice that "voice" of yours is?' And I repeated my question. I repeated it several times. It got me nowhere. I said: 'Talk to me. Talk, Socrates. You never are at a loss for words outside the house. You are reported to have torrents of them for anyone coming your way. And some of those torrents give people some pleasure, so I was told—though it cannot be the right sort of pleasure, or else they would offer you a recompense, which they evidently do not.' Then, finally, he said: 'What I told my friends about the divine voice did not amuse them. It gave them pause.' 'What gave them pause?' I asked; 'what *did* you tell them?' Not one further word could I drag out of him. He did not even look up from his mud-caked feet, which he was nursing. 'The truth is,' I said, 'you tell them nothing. You merely juggle with words. My family have always said that's all you do. And what would come in more handy in such word-juggling, which has no bearing whatever on reality, than a voice whose existence cannot be proved? And do you know,' I continued in my anger, 'what your glittering skill with words in the square suggests when I compare it with your tight-lippedness at home, my husband? A butterfly that would turn into a caterpillar at every sundown!' And as I repeated, rather beside myself by then: 'Caterpillar, caterpillar!' Socrates burst out in laughter so uncontrolled, I could not but flee his presence. But suddenly he was on his feet, ran after me, and exclaimed: 'I may be a caterpillar at home, my clever Xanthippe, an eyeless slow-moving caterpillar. But in the marketplace I am not a butterfly—I am a gadfly, Xanthippe! A gadfly—that is what I am to my fellow citizens!' And with those senseless words, he started to dance round and round and toss his arms about as in a revel. Never shall I forget his conduct on that occasion. Never was I to ask him again about that mysterious voice.

"I only hope he will not bring up the matter in court tomorrow. His accusers would just love it. I can imagine them saying: 'A voice! He says it comes from the gods. From which, from what gods? Surely not from those the city reveres, or else some of us would have heard that voice, too.' And I would not altogether blame his accusers for giving him a piece of their minds on *that* score!

"I planned to warn him this morning not to mention that voice in the court. But the two Scythians came before I rose, and I could not of course talk to him about such a delicate affair in their presence.

"But could I ever talk to him in the days before that? Could I ever talk to him about his defense? He did not listen to me whenever I so much as alluded to his speech in court. I know that he shrugged off Crito's suggestion to engage a legal adviser, whom Crito himself would have paid, too. It was as though this one accused, Socrates, the son of Sophroniscus, were not expected to deliver a speech of defense in the Great Court.

"I never have made out the man I am married to. I have heard it said that there was something un-Athenian about him, and even something definitely un-Greek. Sometimes I wondered how much studiedness was behind his ways. On the other hand, I was told that what people enjoyed most about Socrates was his lack of studiedness. Come to think of it, that may have caused those gentlemen in the old days to take him on as a pet, as it were. His blunt manners amused them. But would they have taken his bluntness equally kindly if he had charged them a fat fee? Or only the usual one? Why did he give them for nothing what they were said to value so highly? Did he not do so to be free to talk to them in his blunt manner? So my good husband indulged his fancy, eh? He argued himself out of the obligation to take proper care of his family, he denied his children good clothing and sometimes their very food—and all that to indulge his fancy! I do not think I ever put it to him in these words. I should have. . . . I have a good mind to go to the prison and tell him what I have been thinking all along about his being 'not wise enough to take money' from his listeners. I too could accuse Socrates—

"Now, Xanthippe—you do not really want to enter the prison house and ask your husband questions, with the jailer within earshot? You do not really wish to add ridicule to his plight, do you? Of course not. . . . Also, such reproaches might sound as though I were berating him for not having brought me presents ever, bracelets and such like. Actually, I never cared for trinkets. I never wanted anything for myself.

"Only some time after the birth of Lamprocles did the callousness of my husband begin to fill me with consternation. I must have shown it. I must have asked him certain pertinent questions. Yet I do not think it was because of those questions which I'd ask that he avoided my chamber for years. He kept away from it because he realized that I had no desire to lie with him. There was understanding in his restraint.

"But is it true that throughout those years I had no desire to lie with my husband? Is it? . . . When he came back to my couch on that one night, I believed I had been yearning for nothing with greater abandon in all those years. He did not come that night to subdue me, blinded by the urge of his manhood. And as he never got drunk, however hard his drinking, I knew he didn't come to me bereft of his reasoning power by wine. He came to me, in that night, driven by fear!

"He had reason to be alarmed. A mob had followed him to the house all the way down from the Assembly, shouting abuse, and some of the men had threatened to put the house to the torch. He was scared. He was—while my own fright was more and more drowned by the startling knowledge that a Socrates could be frightened! Or was it something else that drowned my panic in that hour? Did I in that night—for an hour's time or a mere fraction of it—feel what those boastful ladies called women's bliss?"

There had been no other hour like this one in Xanthippe's life; and had it not been for the older of her two little ones—who owed his existence to that night—she might have dismissed it as a dream, and thought of her experience very much as people recall with a smile their having sailed through the air in a dream. As it was, the memory of that night had clung to Xanthippe with so strong a sense of reality that even the events which drew Socrates, in his fear, into her arms had remained vivid in her recollection.

Off the Arginusæan islands, Athenian ships had defeated a Spartan flotilla. The men in command of the city's vessels, then, had been victorious and were deserving of gratitude. Yet most of the citizens in the Assembly clamored for having action brought against them for their crime, in a body: they had failed to rescue some shipwrecked men, and to salvage from the sea the bodies of those killed, as was a general's most sacred duty! The six generals claimed they were innocent: night had fallen when the battle was over. One of them was the son of the late Pericles. But that august name, far from soothing the temper of the Assembly, only fired its wrath. Pericles' son was a citizen by courtesy only. His mother was Aspasia of Miletus—a woman no better than a hetæra, for all her erudition—and the law deprived of citizenship the off-spring any Athenian had by a foreign woman. Yet Pericles, before marrying his beloved Aspasia, had wangled from his fellow Athenians the promise that sons of that union would be considered Athenians. Was not, so some hotheads now asked, what had happened off those islets an evil bound to come down on a city that took its laws lightly?

Having been picked by lot, Socrates was in the president's seat. He said no one suggested that laws should be taken lightly. Quite the contrary: the Assembly must keep in mind that to accuse several men in a body was unlawful.

At that moment a wounded man was brought into the Assembly, a blood-soaked bandage across his forehead. The only one lucky enough to reach the shore after the battle, he told the Assembly that his shipwrecked com-rades-in-arms, fighting the surf and with their powers sinking, had urged him to denounce the abominable neglect whose victims they were. And then the mothers and widows of those victims, clad in mourning, marched in, in a lugubrious procession—called by no one, so they contended—and began to weep and wail and to shout that the Shades of their beloved ones, with their dead bodies not taken care of, never would be able to cross the Stygian river! A shudder swept the Assembly, and for a while all the men sat as if frozen. The women's appearance in the Assembly was illegal. But no one stopped to consider that trespass; everyone was appalled by the crime he was convinced he discerned. "A motion was made!" cried the most violent of the men. "Put the motion to the vote, Socrates." "To the vote!" shouted the entire Assembly.

Socrates did not attempt to call the men to reason. Dusk was approaching by then. He said: "Night comes, men. No one could possibly count the raised hands in this uncertain light. I rule adjournment."

That was the account which Socrates gave to his wife later that night. He lay by her side, supporting her head with one arm, the other on her chest, his mouth close to her ear. And that time there was no nay-saying meddlesome voice in Xanthippe's chamber, coming to her husband from the gods or from nowhere, and it seemed to her as though something of his nature were flowing to hers as water runs from a fuller vessel into an emptier one. "I saved the city," he said over and over again, "for I saved the law."

He had not saved it. The following day he was overruled in the Assembly, and the six generals were made to stand trial in a body. One of them proved that he had been shipwrecked himself and driven off by the current; yet this did not save him. The Assembly, which tried them, found the six men guilty, and, sentenced to death, they were made to swallow the hemlock potion within the hour.

"But so, afterward," recalled Xanthippe, "were the evil men who managed to sway the Assembly on the first day. For repentance came soon to the Athenians, and they brought their seducers to trial for disregarding the law. They were judged guilty and put to death.

"From that moment on, Socrates appeared to have forgotten his great fear on that night, and how he'd talked to me to silence his fright. He merely rejoiced in the trial of the seducers. Its outcome vindicated his conduct.

"It must have been my disappointment, in the subsequent months, at my husband's failure to allude to that night which gave rise in me to a peculiar suspicion. 'Might it not be,' I was asking myself, 'that the death of those six generals seems to Socrates not too high a price to be paid for having his conduct regarded as wise and just after all?' True, I was pregnant when that suspicion took root in me, and the judgment of pregnant women must not be trusted. But even today I feel it is permissible to say that what delights my husband most of all things is being found to have been in the right. I know: most mortals enjoy being told that they were right—told so by those who first disagreed. But the pleasure of Socrates is of a different kind: his advice rejected, he seems only to wait for an event likely to vindicate his opinion. Does he not, in reality, *prefer* to have his advice rejected so as to gratify later that supreme passion of his?

"O gods, what price will he pay tomorrow for being called just and wise later on by the wrestling-ground boys and marketplace gossips? What price will he make his family pay for that future pleasure of his? Will he stop to think of the two little ones before courting the jury's disfavor by words, on top of flaunting his contempt of the court by not bringing his family to the trial? . . ."

These, then, were the thoughts that a capricious deity infused into Xanthippe's anguish on this day. Some of them were in accord with the fears natural in the wife, docile or not, of an accused. Some others astounded, and some others still shocked Xanthippe. Yet the commotion in her head did not prevent her from grasping at once the plan that emerged from her confusion when the shadows grew longer.

Xanthippe did not hate the prospect of the jurors' telling her husband that Athens did not approve of his ways. No one could approve of them less than she did. However, the prospect of seeing her husband punished was a different matter. This was why the image of herself beseeching the jurors after a verdict of guilty—of herself begging for their mercy, not for Socrates' own sake, but for the sake of his family—had taken possession of her mind so strongly; and this was why his refusal to let her abide by that custom had upset her so greatly.

Reared in the countryside, Xanthippe had never quite freed herself of its more primitive notions. Thus it seemed to her now as though some magical power, while already sharpening the jury's will to find Socrates guilty, was at the same time relying on her to save him. "But how can I save him if I am not to appear in the court?" she had asked herself. And in her predicament she had come close to wishing a "voice" would come to her and advise her.

Perhaps it did. In the late afternoon she suddenly formed the resolve to go and see one of the accusers. Common sense told her it would be unwise to go to the house of Anytus, which was likely to bulge with kinsmen, well-wishers, retainers, and slaves. As for Meletus, she had never talked to a poet; and though the small esteem in which that profession stood with her husband made it rather attractive to her, she felt that she would hardly be at her ease in the company of a poet. Lyco, then!

"Lyco," she had planned to say, "I want you to know that there will be a breach of custom tomorrow. I shall not come to the Great Court. Nor will the small sons of Socrates be brought there. As for Lamprocles, our first-born, he has been staying with my brothers on their farm for some time now. Lyco, do not hold it against my husband that his family, then, will not be in the court. *I* refused to do as usage demands. I cannot bring myself to shriek and wail in public. I cannot bring myself to coax my little ones into weeping and whimpering. I don't wish to appeal in that manner to the men, husbands and fathers all, whose duty it is to administer justice. I recall the mothers and wives of the men killed off the Arginusæan islets, and how those misguided women lured the Assembly away from justice, and thus had their share in bringing about a decision that was to pain Athens a great deal afterward. True, those women acted contrary to custom, while I only would abide by it in coming to court. Still, would I not be acting as they were? Would I not be trying to influence the emotions of men sworn to uphold the law? It is not for women to criticize ancient custom. But I cannot, Lyco, conform with this one. Pray urge Meletus to refrain from blaming Socrates for that irregularity. Should some of the veniremen take exception to it, pray repeat to them what I have told you."

When Lyco's absence from his house thwarted Xanthippe's plan, she at first felt relieved. She had been conscious of her intent to overstep her womanly station. Further, she had realized that her artifice might give birth to an ugly suspicion: mightn't Lyco assume that her stressing the breach of custom was designed to incense her husband's judges still more? Xanthippe had no illusions about her repute as a tender spouse; over the years many people must have heard her asking her husband questions in her strong voice. . . . But then she told herself that any other woman as cruelly wronged as she was by tittle-tattle *would* be careful to avoid any such suspicion, even though avoiding it might be harmful to her husband; and a very peculiar pride invaded Xanthippe's heart: the pride of being different from her sisters.

That, actually, was why she had with so much sincere

indignation said: "Now, really!" when the slave told her that Lyco was out on a stroll. But as she walked away from the orator's house, in her oddly rhythmical and somewhat waddling gait, she only felt that the Fates once again had foiled the goodness which she knew was in her.

V

"By Hercules, what brings him here?" Meletus said to himself as soon as he caught sight of Lyco. The poet approached the Piræic Gate walking level with three elderly men. They had fallen in with him on the highway, and all the time had discussed, across his head, the choice this year of the Sacred Vessel's commander. Although in talking about Cleomedes they had also mentioned Anytus, they seemed oblivious of the forthcoming great event. Nor did they seem to know who *he* was.

Lyco sat atop the ruin of one of the highway's twin walls (which the Spartans had left standing at this spot as a token of their contempt for the Athenians' sense of beauty). Clasping his hunched-up knees, his head deep between his shoulders, the orator squinted toward the sun, which stood low in the sky.

As Meletus stepped away from the three men, Lyco, without changing his pose, turned his eyes to the other side, as if attracted by the talk of the guards at the gate. But when the poet was within hearing, he said: "I take it you feel like talking to me, Meletus." And as Meletus halted his steps, Lyco took his legs down from between the grass overgrowing the top of the truncated wall and let them dangle over its edge. Although the men at the gate, who had begun to throw dice, had no eye for him, he kept his voice low when he asked: "Should not the accusers exchange their final views on the eve of the trial?"

Meletus, standing in front of Lyco, glanced up at the orator's nearly fleshless face. It had always reminded the poet of the head of some bird, so leathery was the skin of that face, so thin its aquiline nose, and so cavernous the eyes' sockets. "If he knows of the oxhides-and-leather scandal," it crossed his head, "now is the moment for him to bring it up."

With a sigh, Lyco let himself slide down from his precarious seat. He stretched his long legs and then stamped his feet several times to overcome their numbness. His studiedly apologetic smile bared the one front tooth the gods had left him. "Will you walk with me toward my house, Meletus?" he asked, raising his voice over the rattle of an ox-drawn cart that was approaching the gate.

"As it happens," Meletus said, "your way is mine up to the temple of Hera."

Lyco had already started to walk away. But as the cart stopped in the gateway and the guards began to exchange some banter with its driver, the orator halted in front of the large stone post surmounted with an ancient bust of Hermes, which stood to the right of the gate close to the high wall; and while Lyco let his fingers run over the laurel garlands that the priests, early this morning, had hung on the iron pegs protruding from both sides of the square pillar, he kept looking back at Meletus with marked impatience.

At last the poet followed Lyco, stepping forward briskly. He had made up his mind to dissimulate his fatigue. It had been a long day for him. He had got more than he had bargained for at the Piræus. . . .

Only some time after the two men had passed between

the thick columns of the gate did the orator speak again. He said: "You were late in setting out on your road back. You were wise to wait for company, though."

"Those three simpletons joined me by mere chance," Meletus remarked. "I was not afraid of the dangers of the highway. I am not easily scared." In fact, those dangers had been absent from Meletus' thoughts on his five-mile march. He had not been able to break away from the memory of the hours spent in Glycera's house. They had left him with the most ambiguous of feelings.

As he had lain with the slave girl, lording it over her body, a sensation of limitless power had taken possession of him, seeming at the same time to assure him of tomorrow's success. But even while that feeling swept his whole being, and lent to the delight the girl's docility gave him a refinement never extracted from his manhood before, it had come to Meletus that in lying with her he himself was obedient—obedient to her mistress, that teller of slanderous tales! Later, on the road, he had admonished himself to think of Glycera's story as "whorehouse prattle"; but his scorn could not allay the smarting awareness that he had gone to the slave girl's couch on Glycera's command—that he had been Glycera's plaything.

And as Lyco now said that "the thoughts of two clever men combined" must give twofold strength to a plan, Meletus resolved nowise to be the plaything of Lyco. "He has come here to humiliate me," he said to himself. "He still resents the minor role he has been reduced to."

In actual fact, Lyco had not gone to the Piræicgate shortly after midday, and waited there for hours, in order to humiliate Meletus. Alarm had driven him there.

A composer of speeches to be delivered by others, he was accustomed to having others put their fate into his hands —well-experienced and nimble hands, as he was entitled

to call them. What had made him put his own fate into
the hands of Meletus? Anytus had said: "We agree that
your presenting yourself as the main accuser in court
might provoke criticism. I might shoulder the task myself.
But should not Socrates, indicted for corrupting the young,
be confronted with a more youthful accuser?" Why had
he, Lyco, replied to that subterfuge: "This is a sensible
consideration," instead of saying, for instance, that no
one ever brought a horse into a law court to have a horse-
thief convicted? Had he grown so subservient to Anytus
as to refrain from examining the tanner's motives? Why
should he have been subservient to him, to begin with?
Surely not on account of the small pecuniary present received!

Ever since Lyco had joined the accusation, something
inscrutable seemed to have guided his conduct. Hating
enigmas, he had devoted not a few thoughts to that first
step. He had told himself that what made him co-sign the
"complaint" must have been his wish to counteract the
decay of his prestige, a hope to boost his business by becoming a much-talked-about public figure again. In an
aging professional man, that was a likely consideration—
and therefore Lyco had pursued his self-search no farther.

At any rate, his ruminations during this day had confronted him with a matter more pressing than past action,
however fateful. Whereas, according to earlier gossip
among legal men, Crito had engaged one of the most successful of Lyco's competitors to draft a speech for Socrates, Lyco this morning had learned that Socrates would
do without the services of that rhetor. As Lyco had not
until recently disclaimed the rumor that he was to plead
the accusation before the jury himself, he now grew convinced that Socrates, mistrusting his eloquence as long as
he assumed he'd have to meet a Lyco on the dais, had

stopped worrying about his defense once he knew Meletus would be the one he'd face there. Socrates' carelessness should have pleased Lyco; instead, the low opinion of Meletus which it implied aggravated his misgivings. To be sure, he would be in a position to remedy the imperfection that he foresaw in the poet's speech: in cases of joint "complaints" the law gave each accuser a chance to have his say at the trial. However, the brief speaking-time allotted to any but the "main accuser" dulled the effect of all the speeches save his.

In this roundabout way, then, Lyco came to gauge the whole magnitude of the peril into which his resentment of Meletus had cast him, and to admit to himself that ordinary pique had kept him from counteracting that menace as best he could by forcing his expert advice on the poet. He had come to the Piræic gate to undo that mistake.

The streets were all but empty of men at this late hour. Only now and then, some younger men on their way to a friend's house, or a slave girl hurrying toward a street-corner fountain, a pitcher on her head, crossed the progress of the two men.

Meletus had remained silent for a good while, casting covert glances at Lyco. At last he decided to talk, and talk bluntly. He said: "If that ludicrous piece of gossip should trouble you, my good Lyco, you may save your breath."

"What piece of gossip? Which piece of gossip?"

"About Anytus' trade," Meletus said prudently, with an edge of contemptuous dismissal.

"I don't know what you're talking about. Let us waste no time. Precious little of it is left."

"I am listening," Meletus said in a new tone. His fear, so he persuaded himself at once, was groundless: if

Glycera's base scandal had not reached Lyco, a man no doubt particularly alert to every hearsay for reasons of his profession, then it was clear that the story, originating in "that whorehouse," had not got beyond it.

"Well, Meletus," Lyco began, "the one thing a man pleading before five hundred and one jurors must never think of is the fact that two hundred and fifty-one of them, should *they* find the accused guilty, would serve his purpose. Not for a moment must the accuser flinch from his determination to win all the five hundred and one over to his view."

"To win them over to justice!"

"Quite so."

"The one thing I shall think of, Lyco, is that we rose to avenge the offended gods. Justice is of divine origin."

"So it is," Lyco said, his animation flagging. Either this poet was trying to make game of him, or the assignment had gone to his head! Or was he planning to engage Socrates in a discourse about the nature of justice? Lyco himself always had stayed aloof from the modern discussion as to what justice was. To inquire after its nature, or its relation to the statutes—that, for a man of his métier, would have been about the same as an artisan's stopping to examine the "nature" of his hands!

"And that divine origin of justice," Meletus was going on, "will also inspire those called upon to judge of Socrates' crimes."

"Will it? So why deliver speeches before them? They saw the complaint written out—so let them proceed to cast their ballots!"

"You are angry."

"I am. Do you know what your talk about 'inspiration' reminds me of? Of that ungodly 'voice' of Socrates."

"You wrong me," Meletus said.

"Meletus, I offer you what knowledge I have of the means that lead to success at a trial. I have spent a lifetime in law courts."

"I respect your experience."

"So let me go on," Lyco was quick to say, "to tell you what, next to the accuser's iron resolve to win over the whole jury, is most important at a trial. Under no circumstances must he bore the jury. This may sound coarse to a poet's ears—"

"Whatever gave you the impression that I might bore my listeners? Five hundred and one of them—or, for that matter, the thousands in the Theater? I presume you are not familiar with my poetic work, and happen to have listened to some envier of mine."

The orator, bending down, put his arm round the shoulders of the poet. "I am not unfamiliar with your work. I think highly of it. However, I know little about meter and cadence, and you would gain nothing did I comment on the merits of your work or the finer points of your art. Moreover, time presses. So let me repeat: an accuser can do far worse than amuse the jury."

"Amuse them? I am not a comedian."

"You have an excellent instrument handy to make the jurymen laugh tomorrow."

"I am not partial to telling jokes. I am not a comedy writer."

"Aristophanes is."

"He does not make *me* laugh," said Meletus, aware instantly of what Lyco was driving at.

"You are too young to recall the sensation Aristophanes caused with his *Clouds* twenty-odd years ago."

"I know the comedy. I also know it was not a success."

"It was a daring stroke to bring Socrates onto the stage."

"The 'Socrates' Aristophanes brought onto the stage was a puzzling figure, to say the least."

"The play was ahead of its time. Is that not often the case with the very best of our writing?"

"The comedy was anything but ahead of its time," Meletus said, deaf to Lyco's obvious flattery. "That play was outdated even in its own day. The 'Socrates' your Aristophanes put on the stage was a man searching into matters under the earth and above in heaven. That sort of investigation was out of fashion even twenty-five years ago."

"Not so, however, ten years before that! About ten years before Aristophanes' comedy was produced, the man who excelled most in those under-the-earth-and-above-in-heaven speculations—Anaxagoras—was indicted for impiety. He fled—"

"I know everything about Anaxagoras."

"I know you do," Lyco said patiently. "My point is that the memory of *that* indictment will interest *our* jury, especially if brought back to them in the entertaining manner I recommend. That memory will make them conscious of precedent—"

"And remind them of how Anaxagoras absconded, instead of standing trial! Oh, my Lyco, bringing up that precedent would only serve to remind the jurors that Socrates, unlike Anaxagoras, decided to stand his trial. To us, as to a great many Athenians, that decision reeks of spite, of an arrogant self-assurance, of levity. But might not some other men be tempted to talk of courage, or even to say that nothing short of the conviction of his innocence could have prompted Socrates to stay in the city? At any rate, I can see no point in dragging in that obsolete play. Everybody knows that Socrates does not engage in speculations about the cosmos, as Anaxagoras did, or, for that matter, the character given the name of Socrates in *The Clouds*."

"That character was not meant to lampoon Anaxagoras. Not only Anaxagoras, that is. Aristophanes, as you must recall, made that character also engage in speculations of a very different kind, and—"

"And what are those other speculations? Pedantic, hair-splitting discussions of problems of grammar, plus some Sophistry reminiscent of—of Socrates? No. Rather, of men like—"

"Men, you wish to say, with whom Socrates took issue himself on occasions. Granted. But was that not, in a manner of speaking, a family quarrel? To my mind, and not only to mine, Socrates has a lot in common with those greedy foreigners, the Sophists. And though we've gotten rid of the worst of them by now, the hatred of them is not the least effective sentiment to count on under the circumstances."

"That greed, that's another thing," the poet rejoined. "The money-mindedness of the stage-Socrates in *The Clouds* is another trait the real Socrates does not share with that bizarre figure. It is common knowledge that Socrates is not money-minded—which, as I need not tell *you,* is part of his arrogance. But be that as it may, the jurors wouldn't identify the accused with that compound figment of Aristophanes' imagination. I admit there are some innuendoes in that comedy which, on men of our cast of mind, might make the impression you think of. But let us not overrate the subtlety of plain citizens, Lyco."

"It certainly is not their subtlety I advise you to count on, Meletus. Just listen to these lines from *The Clouds:* 'How could I deal with matters of the heaven,/ Did I not bring the subtle essence of my mind/ Up here, to let it mingle with its kin,/ The air? . . .' Not bad, eh?"

"Bad verses."

"Never mind that."

"Believe me, Lyco, not fifty jurors out of the five hundred and one would understand what I was aiming at by quoting those lines. Perhaps a hundred of them (for older men may have seen the comedy) might understand what the 'up here' in those lines refers to. But the rest of the jury—"

"You must explain, wittingly, that in that scene Socrates is shown reclining in a wicker pannier suspended high up—"

"*I* know it."

"You must point out the insolent disposition of the stage-Socrates and his wish to set himself apart, even bodily, from the run of Athenians. Would not the picture of that lover of wisdom in his basket high up, if you recite his highfalutin' nonsense with the appropriate gusto— would not that picture be of great help in molding the jurors' opinion of the real Socrates and *his* disposition?"

"They would laugh in my face."

"They would laugh and feel good," the orator said with emphasis. They were walking uphill, along the narrow street of the stonemasons. One of them still was at work: one could hear the noises of his hammer and chisel. Lyco drew a deep breath before, in a summing-up tone, he declared: "Those investigations of the cosmos which Aristophanes exposed as a fraud in his comedy are far less widespread today than they were twenty or thirty years ago. True. But plain men often feel the blow of a new doctrine only long after it has been brought forth. You may rely on those Anaxagorean doctrines to anger plain citizens greatly even today whenever they are reminded of them."

"As I said before, Lyco, some of the jurymen certainly

know the play. Would they not take exception to my singling out from it only verses meant to ridicule speculations about the cosmos? If, on the other hand, I also refer to those other speculations of the stage-Socrates, those bodyless musings—"

"Pursuits even more Athenians detest, and even much more so, and which *are* in certain respects suggestive of that 'examining of man' in which Socrates glories."

"But that double role of the stage figure—"

"—is all to the good! Do you really fail to see, Meletus, that what Aristophanes had in mind was to expose those two different trends of higher learning at one and the same time? Dissimilar as they may be, they are both equally odious to right-thinking men."

"To those same men who booed down *The Clouds?*"

"To those same. And to their sons. For their sons have learned—learned the hard way—what harm those two trends did to Athens. May I come to my conclusion? By quoting from *The Clouds* and commenting on your quotes, you will in an entertaining way confront the court with those two obnoxious trends of higher learning. I repeat, with both those trends. Those who twenty-odd years ago booed down the play will be ashamed of their former lack of judgment. Those who applauded *The Clouds* will become aware of how right they have been all along. In fact, all of them of a sudden will be convinced that they know the play and have always liked it. All of the five hundred and one! They all will feel at their ease. Do not say," Lyco continued, catching his breath, "that such tactics are beneath the righteousness and the nobility of our cause—"

"Aristophanes' verses are!"

"May I go on? Every art has its technicalities. Just as I wouldn't dream of asking you why, once an exalted feel-

ing has matured in you, you should start racking your
brain about the appropriate meter, so I beg of you not to
press me for an elaborate explanation of my counsel. The
accuser's primary task is to touch a kindred chord in the
veniremen before him. You will do so by warning the jury
against those two great dangers inherent in modern teaching. You must lead the jurors to see those dangers in all
their immensity. Should they come to feel that you are
not in favor of any kind of higher teaching—I for one am
sure such a boorish aversion is alien to you—no harm will
be done either. The untutored among the jurors will be
proud of being untutored. But, untutored or not, jurors
ask for guidance. The stuff the threads are made of by
which you guide them is a matter of secondary importance. Should you also entertain them while steering them
in the right direction, you would lighten their task and
yours."

When Lyco, spreading his arms wide and dropping
them in an impressive gesture, fell silent, Meletus said:
"Whatever you may read into *The Clouds*—and I must
say you read a great deal into the play—it is still a very
poor comedy. Aristophanes has been an uninspiring playwright all his life, besides being a man devoid of good
taste, and in his bawdiness relying upon the basest in-
stincts of the audience."

Lyco stood aghast. He had expected Meletus to find
fault with the tenor of his advice, and would have known
how to cope with an outburst of indignation. Nor had he
been unprepared for being rebuked for the low esteem in
which he held juries. It was the mode of the day to talk
about them with exaggerated respect. The lists of citizens
eligible for jury duty included men of varied means, to be
sure; but these days it was chiefly the impecunious among
them who on the day of a trial would appear at the law

courts before sunrise in the hope of being picked by the lot and earning the juror's fee, three obols, a pittance; and as if to gloss over that state of affairs, people referred to juries in a vein that might have suited the old days, when no such thing as a juror's fee existed. Lyco had not been unaware of his boldness in departing from that convention. He had intended to shock Meletus—shock him into examining his plans for the trial once more. Meletus' immaterial and trivial response left him speechless.

Lyco was known for the pride he took in his memory. But it had failed him this time: the humiliation that Aristophanes some years earlier had inflicted upon Meletus the elder had slipped the orator's mind. Meletus—Meletus the younger—had been thinking of it all the time Lyco was talking about *The Clouds*. The poet did not think it possible that any man could have forgotten that other play in which the comedy writer had shown a character named "Meletus" descending to Hades and begging the illustrious dramatists' Shades to lend him a plot for a drama! Meletus was not blind to the imitative leanings of his father, and no longer pitied him for the derision he had, after all, brought on himself. But he feared lest people say: "Like father, like son." Had not Lyco been saying just now, in effect: "Don't be squeamish about borrowing another man's verses and thoughts—cribbing runs in your family, let's face it, my boy"? Yet despite his annoyance, Meletus finally said coolly: "I shall think over your suggestions, Lyco."

"Think them over! When do you propose to think them over? In your sleep? I marvel at your equanimity."

The poet was about to make a heated reply when he suddenly had to jump out of the way of a slave boy darting from a door to empty a bucket of dirty water into the street. "Curse you!" Meletus shouted, shaking a fist at the door, which had been shut almost at once. He stopped and lifted one leg and then the other to get the wet off his sandals. Lyco, on the other side of the alley, walked on.

Behind them, the sun set. Lyco lifted his eyes to the purple sky, overcast in the east by the hues of the evening. There the Virgin's Great Temple still shone in the light; and in a mood whose loftiness touched the orator's heart, he recalled his recent visit to that fane, with Anytus by his side, and how they both had stood for a long while in front of the goddess' ivory statue, mourning in pious silence the inlay of gold of which the much-sung image had been bereft long before. There also, but later, in the twilit hall of this sanctuary, Anytus had first spoken of his wish to have Meletus appear as the main accuser in court. . . . "O you gods," Lyco now thought to himself, "I could then and there have threatened to withdraw from the complaint, and Anytus, afraid of scandal, would have thought twice before leaving the whole matter in the hands of this nincompoop. Why did I not do it? Now I am reduced to currying favor with this dwarf!"

Meletus was at Lyco's elbow again, still grumbling.

Lyco said in a very soft voice: "We are agreed, my Meletus, that the one thing which counts is that justice be done."

"That is the one thing which counts."

"Your high-mindedness augurs well for tomorow. High-mindedness is a trait not common to all young men nowadays, alas! Nor can one say that they are all public-spirited. Come to think of it, that is curious. Do not the young stand to lose most when justice is not done in Athens? They will live in this city when we older men have departed. Must not they, above all men, be eager to make Athens a good place to live in?"

"They certainly must."

"And must not therefore the young be most eager to have order reign in Athens?"

"Justice and order are twins."

"The right order," Lyco added in a murmur, and then, talking distinctly again: "Young though you are, you are old enough to recall the horrors that issued from the collapse of the right order, from the downfall of popular rule. I cannot imagine you but burning with zeal to protect it. So, in fact, I told myself when I yielded to the recommendation of Anytus to let you draft our common complaint." Lyco looked with intense eyes at Meletus, and noticed a frown of attentiveness on his face. He began to feel that his words, for all their lack of outspokenness, had not been ineffective. He had not wanted them to sound outspoken. This was hazardous ground: Anytus had been refraining consistently from touching on politics in their talks, and surely he hadn't acted differently in talking to Meletus alone, for if he had, the poet would have been flaunting his knowledge.

"You puzzle me, my Lyco," he said. "The benefits of our popular rule are self-evident to me. Aristophanes, however—whose praises you sing—is anything but a devoted friend of popular government. True?"

"True. But in politics, as in war, you must use the weapons that happen to be at hand."

"Politics, Lyco?" Meletus asked. Politics never had tempted him as a field for gaining distinction. Now he suddenly wondered whether it had not failed to attract him simply because it had never offered him an opening wedge. Or had he, dreading failure, turned a deaf ear to some earlier clarion of statecraft?

Lyco was turning into the street that led past the pilastered side wall of the Temple of the Enthroned Hera; to his satisfaction, the poet did not seem to consider taking his leave. "Popular rule," he said, his arm about the poet's shoulders again, "would not have been destroyed five years ago if traitors had not weakened the city long before that."

"Alcibiades!"

The orator nodded.

"A pupil of Socrates. A man on intimate terms with Socrates."

"On terms of intimacy," Lyco said with a crackling laugh.

"Quite so. What more do we need in order to expose the wrong political persuasions of Socrates?" asked Meletus.

"Remember, we did not denounce him for them. The problem is this," Lyco went on, and put a rigid finger to the tip of his nose, crooking it a little. "The problem is how to make the most of Socrates' wrong ways in public affairs—"

"Most men take his ways' wrongness for granted. Why dwell upon something few jurors will question?"

"Because, my Meletus, our veniremen love to be told in court what they were thinking themselves even before being picked to serve on the jury. Let me go on. You cannot possibly say: 'Socrates does not favor popular rule—'"

"You are being repetitious, Lyco."

"Nor can you accuse him of deriding our way of government," the orator continued firmly, "for everybody is free to talk about it as he wishes in this fortunate city of ours. What you can and should say, however, is that Socrates has been deriding our institutions in conversing with the young. He is under indictment, in Count Three of the writ, for corrupting the young."

"So he is."

"Now, is there any more sinister way of corrupting them

than scorning, in their presence, the institutions of restored popular rule and our laws?"

"There is none."

Lyco nodded contentedly. He was congratulating himself on his dexterity: he had mentioned the laws and present-day popular rule in one and the same breath, and for all practical purposes equated the one with the other. He proceeded to say: "Many years ago I heard a story about Socrates from Protagoras the Sophist. You must know that I attended some of his lectures, though his fees were unreasonable and I was not the son of a rich man. And, by the way, that was long before Protagoras was indicted for impiety—"

"And expelled."

"And expelled, yes. . . . What I wanted to point out was that I deserted Protagoras not merely on account of his outrageous fees. I sensed the impiety of the great man, as misguided people used to call him. This is by the way. Here is my story, or, rather, the story as told by Protagoras of Abdera. One day Socrates and Protagoras and some young men were talking again about one of those imagined problems thrown up by speculations as bubbles are on the surface of boiling water. This is what Socrates had the temerity to say (I no longer remember how it bore on their problem): 'Whenever we Athenians meet in the Assembly and discuss, say, the construction of a new public edifice, we summon skilled builders and listen carefully to their views; when the matter in hand relates to naval craft, shipwrights are called in; and so forth. Anyone volunteering advice and who has no training in the art in question is laughed down and jeered at. And if he persists in offering his counsel, the police are ordered to push him out of the Assembly. But when the matter under consideration happens to be an affair of state, then everybody is free to open his mouth. Carpenter, tinker, coppersmith, sandal-maker, rich or poor—anyone who feels like it stands up in his seat and holds forth to his heart's desire, and no one so much as reminds him he had no training in statecraft.' Thus spoke Socrates in the presence of several young men."

"Strong language."

"To say the least," Lyco affirmed. He had not been free of apprehensions in retelling the anecdote: what if someone had told it to Meletus earlier—his father, maybe, a man notorious for retaining the tales of others? It also came to Lyco, through the haze of the intervening years, that he had not recounted the whole story, and that its context lessened the harshness of Socrates' criticism of the Assembly. But he also became aware, more strongly than ever before, of how utterly loathsome that context—that "imagined problem"—had been to him, even then. In actual fact, it was Protagoras' lectures which had imbued Lyco with his passionate dislike of speculations on things the senses could not perceive. He had come to hate the famed Sophist for his fascination with them—and he hated Socrates for it!

And while Meletus, after having asked whether Lyco, considering the amnesty, would deem it wise to repeat the old story in court, and while Meletus, after having gotten no answer, went on to inquire how many of the jurymen might be devoted to Anytus and grateful to him for what he had done for the city, it occurred to Lyco that he in reality hated Socrates more than he hated his crimes. The effortless grasp that he seemed to have of those dreamed-up notions—a gift the gods had not given Lyco—was more loathful to him than the dangers that those speculations seemed to hold for the commonweal. That was not a noble feeling to become conscious of—and Lyco did not flatter himself that it was. But at last he knew why he had become a party to the "complaint": his detestation of Socrates, waxing over the years, had grown so strong that nothing short of taking a hand himself to crush the criminal could ever have stilled the urge of his hatred. It had refused itself to argument. It was like the wrath of the gods . . . and did not that wrath smite mortals irrespective of their "innocence" or their "guilt"? And suddenly the wish that Socrates would feel he was innocent flashed through the orator's mind, and he thought: "I almost hope he *is* innocent. I indeed hope he is, for how much more then will his punishment smart him!"

Dusk was slow in coming. Pearl-colored cloud strips hung in the sapphire sky.

Meletus had fallen silent. Occupied only with himself, he did not realize how far the thoughts of his interlocutor had swung away from his own momentary concern with forensic tactics.

"The amnesty . . ." Lyco began again—this one word lodged in his ear, out of the many Meletus had spoken— "try not to be a stickler for legalistic matters. For one thing, you have no experience in that tangled field. And then, it is not always what you say that sways the emotions of the jurors. Rather, it is the spirit of it—your own emotion! The jurors must come to feel that before them stands the truest lover of our institutions. They must be shamed into feeling that they themselves do not love them enough. They must feel that they stand accused themselves, in a manner of speaking."

"That is a good point," said Meletus absently. In the fading light, a new discouragement gripped him. How did the orator's crafty recommendations fit the cause of the insulted gods? Was it not for their sake that Socrates must be punished? But then, it was the goal that counted,

not the road. The road on which the insulter of the gods
was to be made to suffer the penalty commensurate with
his transgressions—the road surely did not matter!

They had left the Hera temple behind them, and slowing their steps, strolled past a two-story building that Lyco
pointed out as belonging formerly to a "scandalously prosperous" alien; and after passing the empty lot which separated that structure from Lyco's own house, they soon
halted before it.

The orator, feeling suddenly weary, leaned against the
high stone relief of the three-bodied Hecate inserted in
the wall of the building next to its door. Inside, close to
the entrance, a lamp, or two of them, had been lit in expectation of the return of the master, and the yellowish
light trickled out into the gloom.

Glancing up to the foliage of the trees whose outlines
rose over the stone wall from the garden within, Meletus
cleared his throat and said: "My excellent Lyco, be assured I shall put your various hints to good use. The fruits
of your vast experience will not have been wasted on me."

Even though Lyco had not called, a dog began to bark
behind the wall, and presently the approach of rapid footfalls was heard. When the huge bolts inside were pushed
back and the chains removed, Lyco stepped up to the
door. But there, instead of lending his ear to the slave who
started talking to him in pompous whispers, Lyco spun
round.

Meletus had drawn back a pace or two, but still stood
within the rectangle of brightness which issued from the
thrown-open door and whose flickering emphasized the
changing expressions that traveled over his face.

"He will change his mind a score of times before sunrise," Lyco said to himself, astounded at once by the dis-
passionate tenor of his observation. It was as though the

god-like hatred of Socrates which he had discovered in himself were numbing his thoughts.

Night had fallen.

"Well, then, my Lyco—"

"I shall lend you a boy with a torch."

The slave in the doorway shouted out the order, across his shoulder, while Meletus said:

"You are very kind, Lyco," and then, "Do not worry in the least," and then, "The gods will not desert their defender."

The boy came out, carrying the lighted torch close to his body. Upon the doorkeeper's gestured command, he rushed past his master up to Meletus, protecting the gleam of the torch with hand and forearm, in his wake the smoke of the sputtering flame and its resinous scent.

Before turning, Meletus called out a word of farewell to Lyco; and at the same moment the flame of the torch went up with a hiss.

Lifting it high, the boy followed Meletus, and his light, blazing now, flung the shadowed walk of the poet ahead of him on to the ground. Entering the narrower stretch of the street, he began to walk more slowly—and with the boy slave now at his elbow, and the torch level with his head, the black shadow of the long-nosed face folded at the foot of the two-story building and rose on its wall; and for a moment Lyco, watching his associate out of sight, had the impression that this grotesquely elongated shadow, dancing upward, was to blanket the very roof of the house and the roofs of the houses beyond, to mingle with the great darkness which, at this hour, was Athens.

PART II

V I

A cock was crowing. The chill of the waning night came up to Socrates, who was lying on the trestle bed, his knees hunched up under the coarse garment that served him as a cover. Before falling asleep he had spread his cloak over it, but the mantle must have slid down later. It was still pitch-dark in the spacious prison room—

Why had the dream had to vanish? Why had it vanished even before he awoke? Had the beauty of the apparition been too great to keep company with him even in his sleep? Or was it his knowledge that had banished the image?

At first there had been no sign about it to reveal the name it could have asserted its right to, save the image's incomparable beauty—or, rather, the awareness it gave to the dreaming Socrates of his being in the presence of perfection; and no sooner did its identity accrue to the fair specter than it had vanished. It was as though the spark of recognition, penetrating the dream, had driven off the beloved—back, across the river of forgetfulness, to the mansions below—leaving his laughter, at once prideful and teasing, lodged in the ear of the lover.

But was it not natural for the dear Shade to tease him? Had not the living Alcibiades always been teasing him? Had he not held out to him countless times the picture of excellence, only to make him realize its elusiveness within the hour? And had he not seemed to take a mischievous pleasure in proving that human excellence was no more than a mirage? And when all was lost—

A moan escaped from Socrates' lips. He was wide awake now. A smoky grayness had begun to drift into the deep gloom. The jailer's donkey was stamping the ground in its stall.

Never until the past day had Socrates, in all of his seventy years, set foot inside the prison compound. The low walled-in building, situated about midway between the Royal Hall and the Place of Assembly, had never aroused his interest.

In certain cases, tax defaulters were kept there until they paid their debts. But on the whole, Socrates' Athens did not believe in incarceration as a penalty. And because only citizens arraigned for a capital crime were (on the eve of their trial) taken into custody—and because the law, wary of venal veniremen, restricted any trial's proceedings to one single day—the prison house was more often than not empty of prisoners.

In fact, there had been complete silence about Socrates throughout the past day. Only a seemingly distant buzz had reached his ears, sounding at times like the excited chorus of men loitering somewhere on the slope or on the stone steps that led up to the prison. But as this monotone failed to fade when the shadows grew longer, Socrates recalled the beehives he had seen in the back yard and he understood that it was the bees' hum that had been coming to him all the time.

"My having been taken to this place did not upset my fellow Athenians any more than did the unjust complaint against me," he had said to himself before falling asleep . . . and had gone on to reflect that to be upset by a man's alleged impiety men would have to be pious themselves; and to be pious they would have to know first what piety was. And then he started to inquire of himself whether his fellow citizens, in offering large sacrifices, did really assume the gods were agreeable to such deals, and how those men could fail to realize that gods susceptible to bribes no longer would be gods—

His eyes fixed on the aperture in the wall—still only a rectangle of blackness of another hue—Socrates recalled the train of these thoughts quite clearly; but he also remembered that his attempts to expound them to himself had been overtaken by sleep.

If sleep had not come, and he had been allowed to meditate on the way the city was worshipping her gods, would not his speech of defense have taken shape in his mind? Would he not now be rid of the echo of Xanthippe's nagging contention that ordinary spite had kept him from preparing a speech for the court?

He had prepared it! He had prepared it all his life— as he had been telling Crito the day after he had followed the king archon's summons and gone to take the oath at the Royal Hall, attesting that he was innocent, to the best of his knowledge.

"But how could you prepare a speech all your life," Crito had objected, "not knowing you'd be indicted?"

"I've always known that some Athenians reproached me with being the man I am," he had replied. "Now they have indicted me for being the man I am, for that in reality is the charge against me. Well, then, I am above all a man who has speculated all his life about what is just and unjust, and has tried to avoid acting unjustly. Is not that my defense?"

But when Crito said that to rely on the righteousness of one's cause did not suffice in a law court, and mentioned those many trials in which juries had been swayed by the accuser's eloquence or moved by the speech of the accused, Socrates no longer felt like withholding the truth from his old friend, and said:

"I tried to compose a speech, Crito. I buckled down to it several times, but my attempts were interfered with every time. I was forbidden to prepare my defense."

"Forbidden?"

"The voice made itself heard, my Crito, and forbade me to go ahead."

How well Socrates knew the kind of silence which Crito had opposed to that information. It always had been his friends' reaction to his merest hint of his intercourse with divine powers. Yet that intercourse could not, as such, really perplex them, for despite everything that had happened to the city, few men would regard oracles as mere contrivances of priestcraft. In fact, most citizens would at one time or some other, driven to the gods' shrines by man's fear of the unknowable future, implore the immortals to let them peep into it. What bewildered Socrates' friends, then, was his truthful statement that he for one knew of no way of asking the gods questions, and that he for one was made to listen to their agent at their own good pleasure.

No one in Athens ever had grasped the matter-of-course existence of the divine voice within his being, the utter naturalness with which it manifested itself, and the all but sensuous spontaneity with which it spoke up and mastered his senses. Many a time had he pondered its injunctions and realized their rightness in the channels of reason; and aware that it was part of a man's excellence to share with the whole city whatever inkling of the right way was his, Socrates had often been saddened by his apparent inability to convince his friends of the realness of the voice that made itself heard at the gods' own good pleasure.

But then he would hear it again warning him against downheartedness—and he would conclude that his endeavors alone were pleasing to the gods.

Thus his had been only part of a part of excellence all his life. But once—once in all of his seventy years—he had felt as though he might be able to bring forth excellence in another mortal, so that men would say about him in days to come: "Socrates? He was the one who made Alcibiades what he was: the delight of all who at last saw a man's inner being perform *all* the services it is capable of—intelligence and wisdom, fortitude and moderation, truthfulness and justice." But the gods, as the saying went, had been jealous. . . .

The whole city had been enamored of Alcibiades from the beginning. Men of all classes would stand on the wrestling-ground watching the youth, enthralled by his wit and his charm as well as by his incomparable beauty and skill. He had a lisp in his speech which lent a persuasive turn to his words; but the precocity of his mind disarmed even men armored against persuasion. Adored even by those who as a rule censured the young for the smallest of trespasses, Alcibiades soon took it for granted that the entire town would condone his own, no matter how great. Soon pranks such as many wealthy youths of the equestrian class engaged in, in those exuberant days of the imperial Athens, no longer satisfied his high spirits. He was bristling with an altogether frenzied ambition. To contend, to overcome, to be the first, the only one in a chosen field, to be gaped at by all and sundry—such were his goals, and never once did he pause to consider a purpose past them. He adopted affectations a Socrates would merely smile at—sporting outlandish clothes and effeminate finery, or adorning his horses' harness with silver—yet in Socrates' smile there was love as well as simple forgiveness. When Alcibiades returned from those never-to-be-forgotten games at Olympia at which he won three chariot races—a feat never attained by any athlete before —Socrates stood in the cheering crowd and waved both hands high over his head, eager to catch the eye of the laurel-crowned champion as he rode by holding the reins of his steeds ever so lightly.

At that time Socrates had not yet spoken to Alcibiades. He had merely been "stalking the priceless game," as certain men would put it when drinking hard. Not till the day before Alcibiades was to make his first appearance in the Assembly did Socrates talk to him and for the first time perceive, behind the fair veil of flesh, the potential excellence of the youth—

The prisoner on his cot did not move. He had not taken his eyes off the opening in the wall. A strip of sky had become visible there, with slow-traveling mother-of-pearl tints paling its deep blueness. The air smelled of the sea and of ripening barley and of acacias in bloom—

Had it been curiosity that had turned Alcibiades to him? It had been . . . but even on this day, almost thirty years after, Socrates could not bring himself to doubt that it had been a curiosity of the highest order. He had not then, either, given credence to the youth's assurance that he wished to hold discourse with him merely to become an effective speaker in the Assembly and outshine all men in public affairs.

Yet Socrates had done as bidden. He told Alcibiades that a man bent on influencing the affairs of state must know what is best in each case under discussion. He must know what is good. *Therefore,* he went on with a twinkle, such a man must know how to distinguish between right and wrong, between the just and the unjust. The just and the unjust? Alcibiades retorted with a sneer unbecoming to his smooth face; was it not widely known that what was just need not necessarily be profitable also? Not profitable to whom? Socrates proceeded to ask; to the one citizen who happened to be talking in the Assembly? Or to his friends? Or to the rich? Or to the poor? Or to the strong? Or to the weak? Might not to act justly be profitable to justice—which alone made Athens different from other cities and a good place to live in, and thereby guaranteed its citizens the only genuine happiness man could gain, his and his sons' only lasting profit? "I must take refuge, as Ulysses did from the Sirens!" Alcibiades cried out in exaggerated despair; but when, after many more days, Socrates convinced him of his fallacy in judging of right and wrong according to his and his friends' momentary profit, tears rolled down Alcibiades' face and he admitted that in his ignorance his life had been wretched as a slave's.

Such moods passed, though; and Socrates knew that, out of his sight, Alcibiades would succumb again to the blandishments he was exposed to. He returned, a new swagger in his gait, inflated and arrogant, to tell Socrates that all that right-and-wrong discussion was so much balderdash, and he for one had learned what was right precisely the way he'd picked up his speech. Socrates said that everybody agreed on what a stone was, or a piece of wood, and that no one therefore had any doubts in such matters. But in matters of justice and righteousness opinions differed, as could be seen from men's differing actions in identical situations. "You learned how to talk from scores of men and even from women, Alcibiades; but inasmuch as opinions on right and wrong differ, as we just agreed they do, how could you possibly have learned from scores of men how to act justly?"

In that manner they wrestled for months, for three

years, in fact—now bantering, now striving in great earnestness to agree. And if Socrates, in the early days of their association, wondered sometimes whether Alcibiades' beauty did not delude him into taking it for the true mirror of excellence, the youth's waxing determination to think with his own head more and more dispelled that tormenting doubt.

At last, Alcibiades' pride in his body's perfection seemed to be tamed, and his ambition spurred beyond getting the better of men by bewitching their eyes and their ears. And at last he admitted to the dissatisfaction which had grown in him, in step with the flatteries offered his self-love, and he declared that Socrates was the only man alive who might quench that discontent. He went on taxing the citizenry's patience with many an insolent frolic; yet he would listen, patient himself, to his older companion. So high did Socrates' hope soar in those days that all the youth's madcap behavior tarnished his picture, to the mind of the older companion, no more than the dust of the road whirled up by a breeze in springtime would stain the fringes of a meadow in bloom—

"If I had no more than twenty-odd days to live," Socrates said to himself at this point in his reminiscing—conscious at once of the inappropriately cautious wording of that premise—"if I had only twenty-odd days to live and were permitted to relive an equal number of days out of my past life in this last span, these are the days I would choose—the days when I built the loftiest hope of all upon the youth I could not help loving!"

He still lay unmoving. His cheek still reposed on his joined hands. Not until he felt his beard rub against them lightly did he realize that he was smiling. Could he still smile at the memory that now had risen to his mind?

He had smiled *then* at what he thought was Alcibiades'

eagerness to show himself to his older companion as a household's master, and had joined the youth at his meal. And then he joined him several times. But every time he left immediately after their dinner.

One night, however, Alcibiades drew him into a long discourse, and when he finally wanted to leave, the youth prevailed upon him to stay in his house overnight. So Socrates lay down again, and when the lamps had been snuffed out and the servants had withdrawn, Alcibiades, who also had lain down, asked: "Are you asleep, my Socrates?" And when Socrates said he was not, Alcibiades said: "Do you know what I have been thinking for some time? I have been thinking that you are the only man in love with me who is worthy of my beauty, but that you are reluctant to talk about your passion. Therefore, *I* must talk about it, and I say that I'd be a fool to refuse myself to your desire, my Socrates. No one ever helped me as well as you have to fulfill my one and only ambition—to come as close as possible to true excellence— and therefore all wise men would chide me for a refusal to give in to your craving, while only the ignorant multitude might find fault with my yielding to it." Socrates said: "My dear boy . . . My dear boy, I am glad to hear you talk so firmly about your sole ambition; and that I seem to succeed in helping you in its fulfillment, that too makes me glad." But then, to suppress the joy mingling with unease which swept him, Socrates changed his tone and said with a chuckle: "Still, there's a bit of trickery in your offer, my boy. You seem to discern in me a beauty higher in kind than your own, and by offering me yours you try to get a share of what you assume is beautiful in me. In short, Alcibiades, you're trying to trade brass for gold—the spurious image of perfection for what may well be true human beauty. Be that as it may, you ought to make sure you haven't judged rashly of my worth. Think it over, then, as I shall, and let us talk at some other time about your proposal." But Alcibiades got up from his couch and came over to Socrates and threw his mantle about him, for it was wintertime, and crept under Socrates' cloak and clasped his arms around him—

Almost thirty years had passed since that night. Yet not one sound of Alcibiades' solicitations had been lost to Socrates' memory. Once again, in this hour before dawn, did he hear the lisping voice implore him to comply with its entreaties; once again did he feel that night's seduction—his desire to keep listening to the pleas of the beautiful youth in whose arms he was lying, pleas that seemed to turn him, Athens' ugliest man, from a lover into the beloved. And once again, in this hour thirty years after, Socrates tried to sever the memory of that night from the knowledge that was to shatter its bliss.

Having lived with divine agencies since childhood, Socrates was also aware that their manifestations sometimes escaped his consciousness afterward; once he had heeded their warnings and abstained from doing what they had spoken against, he sometimes assumed that he had acted merely out of experience. Thus, he had never been certain that it was the gods' injunction which made him spurn Alcibiades' beauty during that most perturbing night of his life. Had he himself not perceived Alcibiades' wish to have a certain notion of his confirmed—the disdainful suspicion that his older companion's love was not in truth different from the desire of the coarsest and the most forward of his suitors? And had there not been an overweening presumption in his proposal, issuing from his inability to bear the thought of not being yearned for? In a sardonic mood, Alcibiades had switched roles, as it were: he, the most adorable youth ever to tread the soil of the city, was wooing her least sightly man—

A good many years later, at a gay party, Alcibiades told that night's story himself—and how he rose from Socrates' couch in the morning as though he'd slept by the side of his father or older brother. He declared Socrates to bear a strong resemblance to those figures artisans made of Dionysus' ugly and dissolute companion Silenus, which, hollow inside, when opened in the middle disclosed the god's own noble image. And the admiration that Alcibiades kept voicing on that occasion for the "monstrous self-control of this wonderful man" seemed to prove that he had long before overcome the humiliation suffered while he held Socrates in his arms, realizing that he was being rebuffed.

Their friendship had survived the great shock. Perhaps it had survived because Alcibiades did not look through Socrates as Socrates had looked through him. . . .

Socrates' love of him had not been fired only by the hope of raising to excellence the youth's inner being. This love had also fructified his own thought and uplifted his own existence. As the bacchantes possessed by the god were said to draw honey and milk from springs yielding mere water to others, so had he, exalted by the sight of perfection, reached in his thinking peaks of clarity such as he never before could scale. And however disenchanting the knowledge that one night had forced upon him, however cruel the misunderstanding between the beloved and himself, he could not for many years after do without the nearness of Alcibiades' matchless beauty.

When they finally parted company, some said that Socrates of course had stopped being attracted by an Alcibiades grown to full manhood. In actual fact, it was

Alcibiades who cut the ties of their friendship; and the praise he lavished on Socrates at that gay party—the speech of a man drunk with more than wine—had been his farewell to the old companion.

He had no use for Socrates on his new road! His power over men had begun to intoxicate him, and he in turn had begun to infect his fellow Athenians with his own lust for conquest. Was he not, soon afterward, to drag them into the most foolhardy of all their undertakings?

In the years gone by since the great armada, to the city's undoing, set sail for the rich Sicilian shores, Socrates had pondered countless times the sacrilege committed on the eve of the fleet's departure; countless times had he asked himself whether Alcibiades, as accused, really was that crime's author—whether it really was the once-beloved who had defiled the statues of Hermes, hundreds of them, all over the city.

Level-headed men, though incensed to the utmost, spoke of a senseless outrage perpetrated in the wantonness of a drunken debauch. Senseless? Wanton? . . . None of those men had heard Socrates tell his young companion many years earlier, in answer to a question, that the great respect paid those statues was justified simply by its being in accord with the law. Might not Alcibiades, by doing them shame, have intended to say to his discarded companion: "You urged me to think with my own head, Socrates, and my own head told me I was a law unto myself, and therefore whatever I do is in accord with the law"?

Socrates sat up with a start and lowered his legs from the bed. He was staring at the opposite wall and the iron chain coiled up against it, which caught the first glint of the oncoming dawn. "So you were thinking with your own head, my Alcibiades, were you? About what, if I may ask? About success and power and the dazzle of glory (and money, too, for you had run through your own and also the dowry extracted from your father-in-law) and about how you might get all those things by freeing your gifts from all shackles! Did you ever stop to think about those great gifts of yours, and about their employment on what we agreed was the right way? Did you ever pause to examine your own life? Yet I proved to you, several times, that an unexamined life was not worth living—and did you not admit that my proof was sound and conclusive? . . . They call you the archtraitor, my Alcibiades—because you went to Sparta instead of standing trial in Athens after they recalled you from Sicily, and because you betrayed your city to the Spartan king, and because you betrayed *him* with his adulterous wife, and because you betrayed his generals to the Persians, and because you betrayed one of the satraps there to another, and because you betrayed all of them to Athens again, and then again Athens to the Great King . . . betraying all and sundry, down to your unglorious death in the tent of a Phrygian woman! I am not chiding you for betraying my love, boy. Nor for betraying my hopes by becoming a traitor to what we agreed on. You committed a worse kind of treason, the only one for which there is no pardon. You were a traitor to yourself, Alcibiades—"

The bolts of the door had been pushed back. "Rehearsing your defense?" asked the jailer even before entering. "I was not eavesdropping, Socrates," he remarked apologetically when the prisoner turned his head, slowly, rigid, eyes wide open.

"So I was talking aloud to him—"

"To them, Socrates, to the five hundred and one of them," the short ruddy-faced man said, and advanced with gingerly steps from the shadowy recess of the door, careful not to spill the bowl of porridge he was carrying in his hands. "And a good way of rehearsing it is—talking aloud, I mean," he went on while he put the bowl down at Socrates' feet. "Now you must eat. A man about to go before his judges must eat. Frankly, long though I've lived in the city, I never came to share the Athenians' dislike for a morning collation. Here, take my ladle. You must eat," he repeated and stepped back, contemplating Socrates with round-eyed curiosity.

Socrates, his head lowered again, lifted the bowl and took a spoonful of the cornmeal, and then sat immobile. From under his brow he was squinting sidewise up to the aperture and the soft light that streamed through it into the room. And suddenly he saw the dream image again, and he saw it more clearly than he had in his dream. . . . The young Alcibiades stood with his back to the translucent haze of the early hour, and a quivering brilliance was about the honey-colored hair stirred by a breeze that Socrates did not feel. Alcibiades' face was in shadow, but now and then a flicker of brightness illumined his features, and the charming apparition seemed to smile enigmatically and to nod toward the old companion and to raise the chin in the hint of a reassuring, promising, beckoning gesture—

"Socrates, day has come," the jailer was saying.

Socrates made no answer. Now at last he knew that Alcibiades—the Alcibiades of those earliest months of their association—had not by chance come into the dream of this past night. He had come as a messenger of the beautiful—of beauty pure and clear, not clogged with the vanities of human life and not polluted by its errors. The image had been an illusion then, as it was now. But an inextinguishable radiance emanated from it—

"Eat, Socrates. The voice of a man who's eaten properly is all the firmer for it. Think of this. Those jurors who wish most to hear you defend yourself well may be seated far in the rear of the court, and wouldn't it be a pity if your voice did not reach them?"

"You are experienced in these matters, my good friend," Socrates said, and after taking another spoonful of the meal, put the bowl down on the floor.

"I am not," said the turnkey. "I am not experienced in matters of law courts. I hardly ever attend a trial. I'd love to attend yours, though. People say you are a witty man, and if I may say so, I am fond of witty repartees. Now, you may well ask—" he went on, only to stop and say in a changed, very low tone: "Socrates, the Scythians have come. The Eleven have sent four of them."

Socrates got to his feet. He picked his tunic up from the cot and slipped it on, fumbling with the girdle of the overlong garment, and meantime the jailer reminded him that there was a trough near the outer wall, with clear water flowing into it from the rocks.

"As I was saying," he remarked when Socrates, having closed the pin on the slit of his tunic, seemed to glance past him again, "I'd love to be at your trial. Nor am I the only one eager to hear you speak today. An acquaintance of mine, coming from down there just a short while ago, told me that never did he see a greater number of venire-men assembled at the barrier of the Great Court, and I am sure not all of them went there today to earn their three obols. Well, they must be picked by now, your judges—"

"I am ready, my friend," Socrates broke in.

"So you will not eat," said the jailer with a chagrined expression, but in the next moment exclaimed: "Your cloak! Do not forget to take it with you, Socrates. It is your only one, isn't it? I'd hate to have you come here tomorrow and tell me you were cold at night in your house and why hadn't I reminded you of your cloak?"

But Socrates was walking toward the door.

"Maybe the nights aren't that cool, after all," the man added. "Thargelion is a pleasant month."

"That it is, with scents and sounds of still warmer days to come," Socrates affirmed, waiting for the jailer to follow him into the dark hallway. But as the man kept busying himself in the room, Socrates went out by himself.

When he stepped out of the door of the low building, the sun was rising as in a burst above the cragged ridge of the hill, and for a moment he shut his eyes. The bees were buzzing again, and he tried to listen to them—and perhaps his blank mien at this moment gave the impression of a blind man's face, for one of the Scythians came up to him and put his hand on the prisoner's arm.

"I am ready," Socrates said, looking up at the four tall men. Then, asking for their permission, he went to the trough and wet his face and forearms and wiped them on his garment, and then took a sip of the water, drinking from the hollow of his hand. Without lingering any longer, he marched through the open picket gate of the high outer wall, setting his bare feet firmly down on the rough ground, and the police slaves followed behind him.

Except for some pollards close to the wall, there was nothing but naked rock between the prison compound and the stone steps, about twenty of them, which led from the small plateau down to the path on the slope.

Limpid coolness was still in the air. Red spring anemones and the ghostly pallor of asphodel specked the stiff grass at both sides of the pathway. Some clumps of small oak trees rose from amid the scrub. The Scythians had walked ahead of their charge down the steps; now, on the road obstructed by prickly leafage, they fell back. None of them said a word.

Of course Socrates was familiar with the descent from the hill, and knew which of its turns would offer him the first sight of the Royal Hall's ocher-colored façade. Yet the sudden vista from on high took him by surprise. The sun had swept the last remnants of the dawn's obscurity clean off the russet roof of the building, and in the stark light of the young day its dimensions seemed curiously dwarfed. Even the men milling in front of its closed portal seemed unexpectedly small and unmoving to Socrates' eyes.

To the right a clear brook now had begun to accompany the downhill walk of the five men. Soon the Cave of the Nymphs, still so called, came into sight on the farther bank of the silvery water, while to the left the bay trees surrounding the temple of Haphæstus gradually cut off the Royal Hall from their vision. Shortly after, however, the hum of men's voices, which had been with them all along, grew suddenly louder and more distinct; and after some more steps on the now broadening path Socrates saw the first of the men who had come to watch his trial.

They were sprawling up here in the sparse shade of some brier, or standing atop some boulder, with their palms protecting their eyes as they gazed downward. And when the prisoner and his escort were about level with them, some called out *"Chaire!"* or "What's the news, Socrates?" Only one man darted onto the road with fists raised and shouted: "Hey, Socrates, is it true our gods ain't good enough for you and your boys?"

Socrates walked on. A cluster of weather-beaten wayside shrines narrowed the road again. Some men were squat-

ting with their backs against the stonework, and the
Scythians had to shoo them away to make room. Amid
this little commotion, it occurred to Socrates that it was
not against usage for the friends of an accused to join him
on the last leg of his way to the court, and looking about
him, he thought he heard Simmias the Theban call his
name. But in reality the call came from a foreigner who
had been shoved aside roughly by one of the slaves.
"There is something peculiar about courage," Socrates
reflected, striding on again. "Each of my friends would
assuredly prove his valor in the field, and many of them
in fact have done so, and all would think it utterly disgraceful to disobey a general's command because of the
risk it implied—and yet none of these same men will
come to me now and walk with me down to the court,
though the only risk he'd run would be some abuse."

But by now, whatever words were called out as Socrates was passing were all but deadened by the great clamor
rising from down below in the court.

Across the plane trees lining its longer eastern end,
Socrates saw the agitation that had seized the crowd of
lookers-on behind the barrier. Veniremen not picked by
the lot always formed that throng's solid forefront; and
their traditional chant of protest was mingled, today, with
the general angry reaction to the unusual press of new
arrivals. For, overflowing with men though the little
square seemed, still others issued from the Royal Portico's
end and elbowed their way forward.

They might have left the covered walk earlier, crossed
the corner of the marketplace, and posted themselves behind the low brick wall—whose top, to be sure, was already occupied by an unbroken row of men who sat, dangling their legs or clasping their hunched-up knees. But
the very violence of the bustle in the rear of the court

appeared to attract the citizens come to see Socrates being tried. Their hubbub grew so vociferous now, and engaged so much of even the jurors' attention, that the appearance of the accused in the court went almost unno-
ticed.

Escorted along the side wall of the Royal Hall, Socrates
had found himself blocked by a team of slaves about to
lug the great water clock out of the back door and into
the narrow lane that separated the dais from the building.
From this lane, two steps led up to the oaken boards
of the three-foot-high structure; but Socrates climbed onto
the platform from the side, slowly. And since at the same
time a platoon of police was rushing forward to drive
back a swarm of spectators who had clambered over the
railing and trickled into the aisle bisecting the rows of
the jurors' benches, all of the jurymen, bent on watching
the clash, had their backs to the dais.

But Socrates, walking across its empty expanse, past
the empty seat of the king archon, felt as though these
five hundred and one pairs of eyes were turning away
from him deliberately to make him aware that he was of
no greater importance than any citizen summoned before
his peers. As soon as he reached the three-legged low
stool that stood near the shorter end of the platform, he
spun round.

Afterward some people said it had been obvious that
Socrates must have lost weight during the "worried days
when he was trying to prepare his defense," and that one
could barely see his belly protrude as he was facing the
court. The truth was that his erect posture came as a
surprise to those who at last looked at him.

Meanwhile the unwieldy brass clock had been placed,
down below, close to the farther end of the dais. A large
vessel filled with water had been brought out, and three

officers had stepped up to the timepiece and begun filling its upper globe; and as always, the number of pitchers to be poured into it—which regulated the speaking-time of the parties—was creating a good deal of discussion. Two other magistrates were supervising a couple of slaves who had hauled the two ballot-urns out of the Royal Hall and carried them to the passageway without crossing the dais. There, in front of it, they put the two vessels in their places—they were of uneven height and shape, one of them of shining brass, the other earthen—and then the two officers convinced themselves that the ballot urns stood firmly on the ground, and knocked a crooked finger against them before sitting down on the edge of the elevation.

Although the police had not yet succeeded in clearing the aisle, the pushing and shouting there had ceased to attract the jurymen's undivided attention. They were slumping in their seats, or sticking their heads together, or calling to someone farther off across the never-still arms and heads of others, or standing up to spread soft mattings over their part of the bench. Only from time to time did one or another of the five hundred and one cast a glance up at the platform.

Socrates was standing motionless. He remembered another day when, silent and alone, he had listened to a babel of voices, trying to find words likely to keep his fellow Athenians from doing injustice—and that memory brought a smile to his face, and he raised his shoulders, gradually and without any trace of defiance or scorn . . . and this is why it was said later that the wild shriek which at this moment went up from among the spectators must have come from the same intoxicated man who, apparently having drifted into the throng straight from some revel, then cried out:

"At last! At last he stands where he belongs, the corrupter!"

But there was hardly any response to the raucous shout
of the drunkard. For of a sudden a group of men had scaled
the low wall at its rear end, and those sitting on top of
it gave room without demurring, and all the men on the
benches stared at the new arrivals; for, conforming with
usage, the friends of the accused should have approached
the place allotted to them—to the left of the dais—from
somewhere near the Royal Hall.

Socrates saw them jump down into the lane between
the low wall and the outer ends of the benches, some
being helped by others, and start to walk forward. Adimantus was among them, the son of Ariston; and Nicostratus, Theosdotides' firstborn; and Chærophon's, the
impetuous Chærophon's, brother; and Paralus; and Antisthenes and the excitable Apollodorus; and Adimantus'
young brother, Plato; and the two Thebans, Simmias
and Cebes; and the aged father of Epigenes; and the
handsome Phædo, whom Crito had bought out of slavery
for his great gifts; and the bright-eyed Glaucon; and the
brothers Æantodorus and Apollodotus; and Crito, the
noble Crito, setting his staff before him serenely, by
the side of his son. . . .

There were well over two score of Socrates' friends—
young men who only a month before, on some of the
wrestling-grounds, would ask him to talk to them while
they scraped the oil and the dust off their bodies; and men
who had fought the Spartans in many a battle; and white-
beards who had been exposed many a time to Persian arrows, and behind whose veined temples and heavy eyelids long-bygone glorious days must still be alive, and
days and nights resonant with man's greatest glory, his
search for truth. . . . They had come! And Socrates,

watching their progress through the veil which joy cast over his sight, knew that he had, in his core, never doubted that they would come to lend him support. Here they were, yesterday's companions and interlocutors, and the companions of twenty years earlier, and the fathers and brothers of companions dead now—fallen in battle, drowned in the sea, killed by the plague, slain by the Tyrant—and the sons of men long with the Shades who once had sat with him on the bank of the Ilissus while they all cooled their feet in the brook, with the summer-time's scents and whispers about them. . . . Was it not there that he had said to the charming Phædrus: "For you see, Fate has ordained that there shall be no friend-ship among evil men, and there shall be everlasting friendship among those who are acting justly"?

Overmastered by this onrush of memories, Socrates had not noticed the renewed flow of spectators into the pas-sageway. With the Scythians withdrawing, more and more men had seeped out from behind the barrier, and inching forward surreptitiously, soon were clogging the whole breadth of the aisle. There was, to be sure, some immediate protest from the jurors. But the sight of four magistrates stepping out of the Royal Hall one after an-other—marching ahead, as everyone knew, of the king archon—hushed all voices and made all men in the pas-sageway halt their steps. As a wind-swept wave subsides on a pebble-strewn beach, so the great clamor died away in a rustle of murmurs.

"The accusers—" said the king archon as soon as he had stepped onto the boards of the dais, "the accusers, by tak-ing the oath in my presence, have promised to speak with fairness."

Meletus and Anytus and Lyco had followed the king archon out of the door, and Meletus, spurning the wooden steps, leaped onto the platform with a clatter. His two associates remained down below; and Socrates, looking past the poet and the triumph written all over his face, saw Anytus walk by the clock with studied slowness and then halt.

Socrates took a step toward the king archon, who had seated himself.

His robe of bleached linen, falling in a profusion of folds down over the tips of his sandals, made him appear taller than he was and broader of shoulder. His face, however, seemed small. His hands, which held a rolled parchment, reposed in his lap. He did not move. The hieratic pose custom demanded of him at a trial must have been intended—so Socrates was thinking at this moment—to conjure up, behind the raiment of the priest-kings of old, the image of their infallible judgment.

The king archon unrolled his parchment. "Socrates, son of Sophroniscus—" he began reading.

V I I

Not a few of those who sneaked through the spectators'
railing had edged to the side, in the rear of the benches,
and then slunk forward along the plane trees. When the
king archon's first words stayed their movement, many
of them already had reached the space to the right of the
dais; and Anytus, who stood at two or three paces' distance from it, found himself hemmed in by a tight cluster of men.

But no sooner had they recognized the tanner than they
opened a lane in their crowd, and he stepped up to the
platform and with marked determination propped his
clenched fists against its boards. No one dared come close
to his side; and when the king archon had finished reading the indictment, rolled up the parchment, and pronounced the name of Meletus, Anytus felt that the emptiness about him had widened. He was looking with intense
eyes at the poet's sallow face. But his gaze kept straying
down to the thin hairy legs of Meletus and his knees'
oddly cavernous hollows.

At last Meletus thrust out his right arm, and cleared
his throat. "O Athenians—" he began, but his naturally
high-pitched voice miscarried, and he coughed and had to
clear his throat again. He presented a pitiful sight. To
dissemble the narrowness of his chest, he had drawn his

tunic somewhat up through his girdle, thereby shortening it more than was seemly. Adopting the custom of
orators, he had enlarged the slit of the garment by lowering the uppermost of the silver pins that held it together; and his stiffly outstretched arm seemed to test
that newly won freedom. Earlier in the morning he had
worn his mantle wrapped gracefully round his torso; now
he had taken it off, and the cloth was dangling from
his left hand, a shapeless bundle. He lifted his chin and
took a step forward. "O my fellow Athenians," he started
again, "this is a grave day for you. For many people think
it hard—"

"State your case, Meletus, son of Meletus," an uncouth
voice made itself heard, trailing a wave of sniggers.

Disconcerted for no longer than a moment, Meletus
continued: "Many people think it hard to accuse a citizen of impiety, for the law against it is appealed to seldom,
and men are prone to wonder whether a law appealed to
rarely may not be infringed with impunity. . . ."

Anytus barely suppressed a loud gasp. Had Meletus
gone out of his mind? He was using the selfsame words
he had fought against in Lyco's draft of the complaint!
True, he, Anytus, had advised him to refer, in the opening of his speech, to the harm done to piety and the worship of the gods in the city; but never would he have
dreamed of having Meletus address the gods themselves
in the priestly manner that now was tinging his diction.
Was this the "valuable last-hour counsel" Meletus had
boasted of having received from Lyco on his return from
the harbor? Anytus raised himself on his toes to locate
Lyco in the crowd behind him and to read in his face
an explanation of the poet's conduct. But Lyco seemed
to be nowhere.

The tanner never had speculated about the gods. He

participated in festive observances, made sacrifices at the proper altars, and occasionally called upon one of the soothsaying women, convinced that what he was doing was the thing to do. Piety was part of the Athenian way of life. It "pleased the gods," as the saying had it. The gods' own mode of existence, however, and the motives they acted upon were none of man's business. Now, the phrase "irate gods"—this was the notion Meletus proceeded to dwell on—was by no means his coinage; it was a commonplace among men partial to unctuous speech. But such was the stress Meletus put on these words, such the display of his compassion for the insulted immortals, such indeed the display of his own human emotion, that it made the gods appear more and more human themselves, pettily vengeful.

There were impatient murmurs and a shuffling of feet along the benches, and the spectators resumed their pushing and nudging and jostling; and to aggravate Anytus' misgivings, it was Socrates who seemed to encourage the restlessness.

When Meletus had commenced his oration, Socrates had leaned forward a little, swaying on the balls of his feet, and had inclined his head to one side and clasped his hands low on his back. This stance of his, well known to many, denoted the frame of mind of a man sure to make a laughingstock of his interlocutor. Still, Meletus' audience had been fairly attentive up to this point and, at any rate, little concerned with what the accused was doing. But now Socrates sat down on the low stool. He did not make a show of his sitting down, as accused men often did, feigning exhaustion. He seated himself with almost gingerly caution, crossed his legs, and, taking his eyes off Meletus—whose voice was droning on while his arm was beating time to the monotonous rhythm—

arched his brows and looked, lips drawn, down at his unshod feet.

Anytus inched toward the clock, to tap against its brass and thereby urge Meletus at last to start talking about matters more material. But just as he lifted his hand, the name of Hermes fell on his ear, and he grasped at once the turn the evocations of the irate gods had taken. And so did every last man present.

To recount the sordid story of the mutilation of the sacred statues, as Meletus set out to do, was a double-edged undertaking. For one thing, the sixteen-year-old story had only by implication any bearing on the trial, and the Great Amnesty robbed that implication of its effect. Further, Alcibiades had been found guilty then— in his absence—and when he returned some years later, hailed as Athens' savior in spite of his treacheries, no one of course had thought of enforcing the old sentence. Was not that sorry record likely to set today's jurors wondering about the effectiveness of the sentence *they* would pronounce? Moreover, Anytus was fearful lest a tale told a hundred times should weary the men.

Meletus was talking with great force. He appeared to have gathered the most lurid details about the old crime. Some of those busts of Hermes had a picture of the erected male parts carved in bas-relief on the dado; and the salacious accuracy Meletus used in describing the offense to those phalli spellbound his listeners. "To desecrate what is most ancient in our worship," he said, "only enhanced the impudent lust of Alcibiades, a concupiscence the wildest orgies could no longer sate. He rubbed himself against the god as a dog does against a tree in pursuit of satisfaction. And was Alcibiades afraid in the least of the god's ire? He was not! Why should he be? Had not his loving teacher taught him there were no gods?"

"The amnesty, Meletus!" a stentorian voice cried out. "Respect for the amnesty, poet!"

Anytus held his breath. From the corners of his eyes he saw many faces turning in his direction. He forced himself to keep looking straight at the speaker, who, his head lowered in a pretense of yielding to the reprimand, waited for the noise in its wake to abate.

When he lifted his head again, his eyes were wide open, as though in a trance, and in a tone overcast with abhorrence he alluded to "that other sacrilege Alcibiades committed," that "outrage surmounting even the foul disfigurement of the holy statues—"

The king archon was seen raising both hands.

"The blundering fool should know better," said Lyco, standing at Anytus' elbow—and the tanner, overcoming his surprise at the orator's sudden reappearance, snarled agreement. Of course no one must tell in public the story of how Alcibiades and some of his cronies one day had parodied the Eleusinian Mysteries at a drunken party! When the informers then had laid their evidence before the Assembly, its president had ordered the place cleared of all men not initiated into the secret cult; and the king archon no doubt would have to do likewise now should anyone in the court, for whatever purpose, start talking about those rites. The tactlessness of Meletus was all the greater in that the king archon, by dint of his office, superintended the Mysteries of Eleusia himself . . . and suddenly it came to Anytus that Socrates once had been rumored to be an initiate, too! Struck by the new light this old rumor seemed to throw on the "trickery" of the king archon, Anytus started to watch him closely, so as not to miss any signal he might give the accused—one of those secret signs that Eleusinian initiates were said to exchange in delicate situations.

But the king archon merely dropped his arms, thus ending the general suspense; and Meletus, his inflection a shade less steady, resumed his harangue.

Anytus, leaning against the dais sidewise, was scrutinizing the jurymen's faces. He was not unprepared to read foreshadowed defeat in them. To fortify himself, he called to mind the many storms he had weathered. But even while he groped for that premature consolation, he noted with keen surprise that Meletus' speech was not displeasing his audience. The blending of obscene anecdotes from Alcibiades' life with sardonic references to the "superhuman knowledge pursued by Socrates and his hangers-on" had called forth a favorable response. And as the poet, his voice strained, declared that Athens' gods most assuredly had no room in their midst for that very own special deity of Socrates—"that thing!"—a mood of fulfilled expectation swept the court, very much like the delight sweeping the Theater's throngs when the protagonist stepped onto the stage.

Emboldened, Meletus went on: "It is true that Alcibiades at the time of his worst crimes was no longer consorting with Socrates. But let us assume a man trained a horse from its earliest youth, for three years, let us say, as good horsemen do—"

"What would you know about horses?" a juror threw in, amused in advance by the hilarity that, in fact, did not fail to spring up on all sides.

"You are right, my excellent friend," Meletus replied, "the simile came to my lips rashly. I know nothing about equestrian pastimes. I grew up under the clouds of war and of the famine and of the plague—"

"Did you ever go to war yourself, Meletus? The man you accuse did, and he distinguished himself in battle!"

"Since when have distinguished veterans been free to

engage in crime?" Meletus rejoined, his head turned to the heckler. "Did not the infamous Critias win distinction in the field, too, at one time?" And with that retort, he began to hurl vituperations at the late Tyrant, calling him the "very best of Socrates' students." "Be on your guard, Athenians, lest Socrates deceive you through the fiendish power of his eloquence. He will try to persuade you that Critias came to him when he was young and of no consequence to the city, as many hundreds of young men did. And did they not all, so he will ask you, also flock to any number of other teachers, Athenian and foreign? He will tell you that only rank ill will would call him *the* teacher of Critias—"

"Why do you insist on ignoring the amnesty, Meletus, son of Meletus?" a ragged venireman, getting up in his seat, called out severely.

"My memory does, my friend," the poet answered with a presence of mind which amazed Anytus, "for there are crimes no amnesty can erase from my thoughts. Who indeed could lay greater claim than Critias to having translated Socrates' contempt for our institutions, his hatred of our laws, into action?"

Lyco was pulling at the tanner's cloak. "I did not brief him in vain last night, after all," he said in an undertone, while Meletus proceeded to talk with great fervor about the youth of the city—the "mainstay of tomorrow's lawful rule."

Anytus shook Lyco's hand off his shoulder. He could not detach his stare from the speaker. Cheeks puffed up, he blew out air. He had maneuvered Meletus into his role to keep the trial free from the suspicion of political motives; no one must be tempted to wonder whether the men of popular rule might not be bent on destroying dissenters and critics!

Meletus, his rigid index finger drawing circles in mid-air, had embarked on listing pedantically the "disastrous effects of Socrates' teachings upon the young." He employed fancy words such as "otiosity" and "incivism." And did not everybody know of Socrates' disinclination to put his wisdom to use for the commonweal in the Assembly? "To that," Meletus said with mock regret, "this wise citizen has preferred speculating on things under the earth and in heaven and passing his findings, so called, on to the young." He stopped to give way to shouts of approval.

Hands were clapped, and quite a few jurymen jumped to their feet and with outstretched arms pointed toward Socrates as though they had caught him red-handed.

He too had stood up. Determined, so it seemed at first, to silence the vociferators with his poise, he almost at once turned toward Crito, whose commanding shape had come to the foreground down below, and who raised his staff to draw Socrates' attention to those many jurors who had remained seated calmly.

"A sober-minded gentleman, our lord Crito," Lyco whispered to Anytus behind a crooked hand. "He's not fooled by the noise—these shouters don't form a majority."

The tanner refrained from telling his associate that those shouters seemed to constitute more than a fifth of the jury and thus would at least protect him from paying the fines. He only mumbled: "Wait and see," hopeful that Meletus would go on to exploit the theme that had won him the first applause.

But, instead, Meletus started to reiterate and to rephrase the indictment's charge that Socrates was corrupting the young.

Anytus was looking fixedly at Socrates and his mien of utter blankness. If anything, boredom was written on it.

All of a sudden Meletus cried out: "Athenians, O Athenians! The city is in danger once again. Socrates turns the young into supporters of a tyranny he schemes to bring about by deriding our institutions!"

"Evidence!"

"If evidence is needed to the effect that Socrates is deriding our popular rule—"

"Evidence to the effect that he is scheming to bring about a tyranny!" an aged juror called out in a tremulous tone.

Meletus, shifting his weight from one foot to the other, let a moment pass before making a gesture meant to express the immaterial nature of that question. Apparent though his failure to meet the challenge was, it seemed to impress the men as little as had his awkwardly solemn warning of tyranny.

A mere fraction of the jurymen's number were former exiles—men who themselves had fought against tyranny. Most had stayed on in the city, like most Athenians, through Critias' terror. They had survived it each in his own way—by making themselves scarce in public, or by turning their eyes from injustice done others, or even by saying: "Why, yes . . . yes, my Critias," where stouter hearts might have said: "No." For four and a half years now those ordinary Athenians had been cursing the late Tyrant and drowning the not-so-proud recollections of their own conduct in a flood of abuse. The far-fetched notion of a possible new tyranny, held up to them unawares, embarrassed rather than chilled them. Also, the cry for "liberty's protection against tyranny" had stood many a politician in good stead in the four and a half years past and no longer fired the citizenry's imagination. So great was the apathy of spectators and jurors alike at this moment that not even the sound of Socrates' words stirred them.

"Come here, Meletus, son of Meletus," he said in a casual tone. "Let me ask you a question. You have thought a great deal about tyranny, have you not?"

"I have indeed."

"Now, which of the two do you think a tyrant can subdue more easily: the man who speculates about his life and about the city, or the one who thinks as told?"

"The one who thinks . . ."

"Well?"

"The one who thinks as told," Meletus said with a fretful shrug.

"Do tyrants, then, prefer to rule over his kind?"

"They probably do . . ."

"Do they?"

"They do."

"Do they, therefore, dislike men who are speculating about their lives?"

"Everybody dislikes such men!"

"Tyrants, too?"

"I said 'everybody'!"

"Tyrants, too, then. . . . So in urging young men, as I am, to think with their own heads—"

"I will not be dragged into one of your word-juggling arguments, Socrates!" Meletus interrupted at the top of his lungs and whirled around to turn his back to his questioner, who neither by sign nor sound commented on the evasion.

Anytus stood with bated breath. He had looked forward to Socrates' first words in the court with the fierce hope of finding his language stripped of its fabled ease. To be sure, a shadow had fallen on his ironical lending-the-ear countenance as Meletus cried out that the city was imperiled; but in the exchange that followed, Anytus had detected neither lessened self-assurance in Socrates' voice, nor one false note.

Meletus was facing the jury again. He extricated two small scrolls from beneath his cloak, which had lain at his feet for some time. Holding these parchments aloft, he asked, nearly squealing with rancor: "Did not Socrates ask sons to disobey their fathers? Did he not teach the young to regard their elders' beliefs as old-wives' tales, or as the concoction of poets? He did . . . he did do all of that!" He caught his breath, coughing. "But how can Socrates help disdaining the laws, contemptuous as all of us know him to be of the lawgivers in the Assembly? How indeed . . ."

The reference to the decline of parental authority had cut Anytus to the quick. He felt as though every single man were staring at him. While he tried to give the appearance of profound unconcern, he heard Meletus, rather abruptly, aver that he had never had any quarrel with the accused and stood where he did as a lover, a true lover of the city.

"As none other than Pericles said, we differ from men in other cities in that we consider him who keeps aloof from public life not a modest citizen but a useless one," the poet continued, and presently set out on what sounded like a veritable disquisition on civic duties. But, spluttering, he was caught in his own words. "A man different from all others is not a righteous man," he proceeded after a pause, "for if he were, all others—all of you, Athenians!—would be unrighteous, evil men. Do not allow Socrates to blandish you with the dexterity of his words. Remember what is said of his ilk: they make the worse appear the better cause. . . ." By now, Meletus' evident

desire to say all the things that were in his mind and his
natural inability to give tongue to all of them at one and
the same time had thrown him into utter confusion. Repeatedly he darted, half over his shoulder, a glance at the
clock, the sound of whose dripping water was growing
less and less distinct as more and more of the liquid collected in the lower globe. And then, in the midst of a
sentence, he stopped.

"It is over," Anytus breathed out between set teeth,
glad to have the air cleared of the petulant, croaking voice.
He did not comprehend why the men still were talking
only in murmurs, and why none of the jurors stood up
to stretch his legs; no longer looking at Meletus, he had
not noticed what kept them attentive.

The poet had unrolled one of the scrolls. He had re-
gained his composure. He said: "Socrates will tell you
that there is courage in challenging ancient beliefs. Should
you reply: 'A warped, an ill-placed courage it is,' he will
rejoin: 'Courage still.' But I say: courageous men attack
singlehanded, and that is not what Socrates did. He
looked for support in his assaults on the gods and the laws
and custom. He looked for authority to vindicate these
attacks—for voices stronger than his, for men superior to
him, men whose words, unlike his, were not given birth
amid the vulgar jokes of street-corner argumentations or
at drunken parties. Homer! Hesiod! Pindar! Those illustrious poets, long with the Shades now, Socrates forced
into being his helpmates. He fell upon their works to
falsify the meaning of certain passages and pervert their
pious spirit, so that those noble lines seemed, to unwary
minds such as the young have, to uphold his ungodly
teachings." And deaf to the half-humorous howls of protest which went up, Meletus began to read from the
Pindaric odes on his scroll, interrupting their flow now

and then to explain in which way Socrates had been imputing impious thought to his own long-departed august confrere.

At one point a wit broke in to inquire when precisely "Meletus the younger" had consulted with Pindar in Hades. But though many men must have understood the allusion to the Aristophanean comedy in which Meletus the elder had been shown taking counsel with the great playwrights of old in the nether mansions, there was no more than a ripple of laughter. The men were bored.

When one of the officers came up onto the dais from the clock and touched Meletus on the hip, no one waited for a proper conclusion of his oration. Whatever he may have been trying to say was swallowed up by an outpouring of chatter; and he at last lowered his scroll and retreated.

Only now that Meletus was walking away to lean down to his two associates, talking in rapid whispers—only now did Socrates feel the weight of his indignation. The poet's barefaced distortion of facts had not upset him: he always had taken deceit for granted in men rushing toward a preconceived goal. Nor had the salacious comments on Alcibiades' misdeeds upset him; he was inured to hearing the once-beloved abused, and his own grief was too great to feel such abuse as a blow. What stung Socrates was Meletus' protestation of his great love of the city.

Socrates was not deceiving himself: Meletus' love of Athens was closer akin than his own to the feelings he could assume in the jurors. Could he possibly say to them: "What you love is the security that Athens is offering you once again, what you love are the conveniences of liberty, not liberty itself"? Could he say to the five hundred and one: "Do you know what the commonweal is, in truth? Pericles held that what distinguished Athens from other cities was her denying instruction to no one—instruction, mind you, which is the search for truth"? Could he tell them that he for one loved the city with an affection making demands on the lover as well as the beloved? He could say all of that to his judges; yet they would only hear rebuke in his words and never appreciate his own unerring love of Athens—

Anytus had ascended the dais from its rear, Lyco behind him. The orator's gaunt figure towered over Meletus, who, his hand rid of the scrolls, kept stroking his beardlet.

The king archon leaned forward. "Anytus, son of Anthimion," he said, his voice as expressionless as his face.

"You at the clock there," the tanner called out even before the king archon leaned back again in his seat, "stop pouring water. You need not measure my speaking-time. I shall talk very briefly."

"Take all the time in the world, Anytus!" a front-row juror cried up to the platform. "Take all the time you need to cut this Socrates down to size, my Anytus! Do you remember me from Phyle?"

Though the veteran had leaped to his feet, Anytus gave him no sign of recognition. He stood bolt upright, straddling his legs. His arms, akimbo, spread the mantle he wore in spite of the heat. "Men of Athens," he began with his firm, metallic voice, "I shall add little to the speech of Meletus. That is as it should be: the main accuser must present the facts, and the facts must speak for themselves. Do not blame Meletus for their great number or their bewildering diversity. His speech would have been easier to follow if Socrates, let us say, had stolen a horse.

"Socrates will tell you that three men of small consequence have complained against him—against him, a man priding himself on being the wisest of all, and who indeed has been talked about a lot in our city for a long time. Three citizens of small consequence, then—to wit, a poet, one out of the two or three hundred orators plying their trade among us, and a tanner and maker of leather goods.

"That I am first and foremost. True, the gods gave me the strength to carry out what all good men wanted done, to wit, dispose of the infamous Critias. True again, I have been listened to in the Assembly on certain occasions, and if I may say so, I was not always wrong there. But neither of these things gives me a special claim to wisdom. To be right in the council of one's equals means only to lend breath to their common thoughts. Therefore I say: what I did by complaining against Socrates was to make my fellow citizens' wish and purpose come true. Once again the gods gave me—gave us three Athenians of small consequence—the strength to fulfill a desire common to all good Athenians.

"And the magistrates? Were they not free to turn down the complaint and collect the fine imposed on anyone who presents an absurd accusation, or an obviously selfish one, or one dictated by personal enmity? Why, instead, was the indictment written out as drafted by us? Why was not one single objection raised when the parchment was posted in public? As you know, shouts of dissent and even riots in front of the Royal Hall are by no means uncommon when people disfavor an indictment or regard it as the result of the shoddy work of informers. Ours being a free city, every citizen may to his heart's desire object to what he thinks wrong or unrighteous. Nothing of that kind happened in the present instance. I submit: it is not three men who complained against Socrates—it is the people of Athens; it is not the magistrates alone who thought the complaint worth looking into—it is the people of Athens.

"I shall not talk about Socrates' crimes. One thing alone I will mention. Socrates is likely to say: 'You accuse me of introducing new practices. What kind of accusation is that? Innovations—what about them? Does not whatever we cherish stem from some innovation?' I say: so it does; but to lay down the laws which you see graven on this wall, to give the city rules to act on, as those ancient law-givers did in moves which I admit had the character of innovations—that is one thing; to start a continuous flux of innovations, to make innovation as such the rule of men's conduct, that is an altogether different matter. It makes lawlessness the law. It replaces common belief with individual doubt.

"Socrates, affecting naïveté, will say: 'I did not introduce new gods. You confound me with some of those foreigners who brought their idols to the city.' But the practices of Socrates—through their very vagueness—deify doubt, men of Athens, and are a thousand times more pernicious than is some outlandish Ashtoreth a handful of foreigners may worship in our midst!

"Socrates must be found guilty. He must be got rid of—destroyed. If the men of Athens had not wanted him to be found guilty, they never should have permitted this trial to take place. Not to try Socrates would have been immeasurably better than to find him not guilty and let him return to his ways unscathed. To declare him not guilty would be tantamount to writing out a charter making it legal for him—or anyone, for that matter—to poison your sons with continuous doubt and a hankering for innovation for innovation's sake. If it should be your opinion that the most valiant of the men who went to

Thebes gave their lives for anarchy—if that should be your opinion, acquit Socrates.

"That is all I will say," Anytus added and stepped back. He had all the time scowled into nothingness.

Lyco did not linger. Strutting forward, he nearly bumped into the withdrawing Anytus.

The orator's name came in a mere mumble from the king archon's mouth. It must have been heard nevertheless in every last corner of the court, for a profound stillness had descended on the men everywhere while Anytus had spoken.

"Not as one well versed in our laws," Lyco commenced, "not as the rhetor known to some of you, as I venture to hope I am, do I appear before you, O Athenians . . ."

The expertly built periods did not reach Socrates' ears. He had been watching the jury closely throughout the speech of Anytus. The tanner's hammering sentences had made a deep impression on the men, totally different from the transient interest evoked by some of the utterances of Meletus. Anytus' warning of the lawlessness that "continuous innovation" must spawn had filled the men with alarm. Benighted though Socrates thought them, he pitied them for it; and as Anytus had ended his speech, Socrates had averted his eyes from the men's faces narrowed and paled by the shadows of fear.

Now he was gazing past the tall shape of Lyco. . . . Afterward some men recalled the old story about his "thinking bout" in the camp before Potidæa, and suggested that the stupor appearing to lay hold of Socrates "while Lyco was putting in his two obols' worth" had reminded them of that well-known earlier incident. But Socrates was not attempting to solve a problem this time —as he had been on that long day before Potidæa. It was not the strain of his intellectual faculties which petrified his features; it was the image of common fear.

After a time Lyco's speech seemed to lift from his listeners the clouds that had hung over them; his workmanlike cadence set them at ease. When he fell silent, some jurors cheered. He spread his arms wide, and this traditional gesture did not displace one of the folds of his immaculate cloak. He stood thus, statue-like, for a moment or two, and then turned measuredly to make obeisance to the king archon—an outdated civility both his associates had omitted; and again there was a certain amount of cheering, though many of the jurymen by now had started munching the onions or figs or garlic they had brought with them.

Socrates heard the friends down below call out his name in tones of reassurance.

VIII

He walked unhurriedly to the center of the dais, from which Lyco had withdrawn. "Well, men of Athens," he began, clasping his hands behind his back, "I cannot of course tell what effect the speeches have had on you. As for me, they nearly made me forget who I was, so persuasively did my accusers talk. And what a pack of lies!" he said, very slowly.

"But none of their lies amazed me more than their warning you against my eloquence. Really, that Meletus did not blush as he came out with that falsehood, knowing quite well it must stand unmasked once I opened my mouth—that I can only call impudence. Everybody knows I am anything but a great speaker, though I admit I've been a great talker all my life. But as I was saying, my accusers spoke hardly one word of truth—so why single out that one lie?

"Why? Because I must say a few words about the manner in which alone I can, and in which I will, speak to you. You see, men, I am a stranger to the parlance of law courts, standing in one for the first time in all of my seventy years. So I'm asking you this favor. As you would allow a stranger to use his own tongue in a court, so allow me to use such words as come to my mind, and don't be surprised—and do not interrupt me—when you hear me talk as I would in the marketplace. That isn't too much to ask of you, is it? And anyway, men, what counts in an accused is truthfulness—even as the sense of justice does in a judge—and whether my speech will be better or worse than those of my accusers, never mind that. Truth has an eloquence of its own and can do without a prepared ornamented oration."

He paused, unclasped his hands, drew himself up, and said: "The point, men of Athens, is that I am convinced of the righteousness of my cause. Yet, in obedience to the law, I will make a speech of defense.

"But let me, before turning to my present accusers, talk to you about my accusers of old. There have been many of them, and I still fear them more than Anytus and his two associates. For those earlier men set their slander afloat when most of you, who today are my judges, were children and your minds were more malleable and less wary of falsehood. So I have to fight ingrained opinions. . . .

"Now who were those calumniators of mine? Except in the case of a certain comedy writer, I've never succeeded in putting my finger on any of them. Therefore I now have to challenge shadows, as it were, and argue when there is no one present to argue against. And how short is the time given me to dispose of defamations heaped on me for so long!

"Now what have those shadowy scandalmongers been saying for so long? This, for one thing: 'There is a certain Socrates among you who speculates about things in heaven and beneath the earth.' Of course you all know that Aristophanes introduced such a savant into one of his comedies and put a lot of nonsense into his mouth and chose to call that stage figure Socrates—and only the gods know how much that whim of Aristophanes has contributed to the baleful gossip about my pursuits. But it so happens that I am not engaged in that sort of research—though I do not disparage those who are, and do not subscribe to the view that investigations of nature must needs cause a man to deny the gods. I simply am not a student of the cosmos—that is what I wanted to say.

"However, if any of you believes he did hear me talk about the universe and related matters at some time or another, he should say so now. . . .

"Why do you remain silent, all of you? . . .

"Because you know I'm talking the truth. Well, you may conclude from that how much truth there is in the rest of those old accusations against me.

"Still, I shall go on. What else have those calumniators of mine been saying? This: that I taught my doctrines—doctrines about the cosmos, I presume!—to others, and that I made the worse appear the better cause, as the phrase has it. Falsehood, again falsehood! Not only did I not pass any doctrines on to others; I also was never a teacher. The mere thought strikes me as ludicrous. I—a teacher? And for money, perhaps? What absurd fabrication! What did you say?" he asked, reflecting on some mutters along the front-row benches. "That taking money for money's worth is no disgrace? Of course it is not. If a man is in a position to pass actual knowledge on to others, a payment only does him honor. I don't know whether any man is in such a position; I only know that I am not. I do not have that knowledge which alone is worth paying for—the knowledge which might raise men to excellence the way a horse-trainer's knowledge enables *him* to raise his steeds to their perfection. If I had such knowledge, I would be proud to charge a very high fee for imparting it to others. But, as I was saying just now, I do not have that knowledge, men. So you see again I have been accused falsely—"

"That's what you say!" an oafish voice broke in, coming from somewhere among the men perching on the low brick wall.

"I am aware," Socrates said, "that some of you feel like asking me: 'But what is the origin of those persistent accusations that you declare to be false? What did you do to give rise to them? For you must have done *some-thing*—something that made you conspicuous—or else you would not have acquired that sort of reputation. So tell us what the cause for your bad reputation is, unless you want us to jump to the wrong conclusion.' Now that is a sensible question, and I was just about to take it up. I shall try to answer it. Please bear with me. Please do, even though you might come to think I am joking. I am not. I shall speak the truth. Listen to me. . . .'"

The racket along the wall had spread to the men behind the barrier, and now a good many jurors too were whistling and booing to show their impatience.

"Did you not ask me a question?" Socrates exclaimed, a flicker of annoyance crossing his face, "and will you not listen to my answer? Well, then—what attached that harmful reputation to my name must have been the kind of wisdom I do possess. Please don't interrupt me again. I'm not speaking from presumption. It all goes back to a word not mine. It all goes back to a witness worth listening to, to say the least—"

"Speak up!"

Socrates passed his hand over his bald head. "It all goes back to the god of Delphi," he said. "His word might tell you, as it told me, what kind of wisdom I possess—if such it is."

"Do you mean to say," Meletus asked in the baffled silence, "that the god of Delphi does not know whether your kind of wisdom *is* wisdom?"

"*He* does, Meletus. But unlike those teachers who take

money, I do not pretend that I share the gods' knowledge."

"A shrewd man he is, not a wise one!" Lyco threw in, opening his arms and bringing them up in a quick spiral motion.

"I am inclined to believe that I am wise—wise, my good Lyco, to the extent of such wisdom as mortals can attain to." He hesitated for another moment before he began: "I take it most of you knew my friend Chærophon, who is dead now. Those of you who did will recall his impetuous nature and his habit of carrying through his every plan. So one day he took it into his head to go to Delphi and inquire of the oracle—I beg you not to interrupt me again, for remember I am only giving an account of what Chærophon did—inquire of the oracle, then, whether there was any man alive who was wiser than Socrates. Whereupon the priestess told him that none was wiser. If you men doubt the truthfulness of that story, why don't you ask Chærophon's brother, who stands over there?"

No one in the court so much as shifted his eyes toward the group of the friends. The jurymen's faces had turned stony.

"When Chærophon came back from Delphi with his report, I was at least as puzzled as you seem to be now, men. I asked myself: 'What does the god mean? What is the solution of his priestess's riddle? The god does not lie. Truth is of the essence of the divine. He cannot possibly lie.' After much deliberation I made up my mind to examine my fellow citizens, especially those whom others deemed wise, so I might go to Delphi myself and tell the priestess: 'I detected this or that man to be wiser than I am. So there must be some hidden meaning in the god's word that you related to Chærophon. What is it?'

"So I resolved. First, I went to see a politician who enjoyed great fame in those days as a man of resource and wisdom. The more I talked with him—discussing basic and really quite simple matters, mind you—the more convinced did I become of his lack of insight. And since he himself thought highly of his cleverness and his knowledge, and appeared to take their sum for wisdom, I tried to explain to him why he was not in truth a wise man. I failed in that attempt, and he did not love me more for it, though I assured him I had not set out to show him his lack of wisdom, let alone to prove that he was wanting in the kind of wisdom it then dawned upon me I possessed. Dawned upon me, I am saying—because only a long time after I left that man did it become clear to me that I *was* wiser than he: neither of us knew the final answers, but he was convinced he did, while I was not.

"I could talk for hours about my wanderings among men and what I might call my Herculean labors in examining them. I could, for instance, tell you about my conversations with poets and how I found out they thought themselves superior to everyone else in wisdom simply because they had written some poetry. Or I could —and in fact, will—tell you how I investigated a great many artisans and tradesmen. Now in approaching *them*, I was thoroughly conscious of all the things that they knew and I was ignorant of. Nor did I forget my ignorance as I proceeded to talk to them. At the same time, however, I discovered that each of those men permitted such knowledge as was his in his own field to persuade him that he also knew the answers to the essential questions human life poses; and that delusion befogged what wisdom he might have culled from his special knowledge.

"You will ask: 'That, Socrates, is how you came to feel

that you were wiser than other men, is it not?' No, men. What I came to do first was to ask myself: 'Would I trade my kind of wisdom for any man's special knowledge plus his blindness to the nature of actual wisdom?' My answer was: 'No. I am better off as I am.' And then I realized at last the meaning of the Delphic word. What it had said was that only the deity has true wisdom, that man's knowledge is worth little or nothing, and that the mortal who knows this is so, is indeed the wisest of men. In other words, I realized that the oracle had spoken of me by way of illustration, for I for one acknowledged the limitations of human knowledge.

"So you see the god did not single me out as a man more knowledgeable than others. Certainly not. I myself never felt I was more knowledgeable than others. Yet my investigations caused many of my fellow citizens to turn against me. No matter how often I may have assured them that I did not consider myself wise, they only perceived that I failed to acknowledge *their* wisdom. That, Athenians, is the source of the widespread hostility I have encountered, the origin of those accusations of old.

"I might have stopped going about in that fashion, and ceased to examine men—and myself, too, if I may say so. But how could I? How can I? I still may come across a man whose wisdom would cause me to doubt the result of my investigations. In actual fact, no investigation which deserves that name is ever concluded.

"That one quite absorbed me. It took up so much of my time, hardly any was left for public affairs, and none for my own. And *their* neglect, men, has kept me in poverty all my life. . . ."

Socrates added: "And all that happened because of my devotion to the god," but these words came out in a mere murmur. What was stifling them on his lips? Fervently as he wished it were a sign from the god, he knew with assurance that the divine voice had not spoken. Had he, then, been afraid of provoking his judges, afraid that they might say: "Look here, Socrates, no other man ever proved his devotion to Apollo by examining his fellow men, and therefore what you call devotion to the god must be different from everybody else's piety"? Had he been afraid that, if asked: "Do you, then, think you are different from everyone else?" he might answer: "I do"? And *if* that had been the apprehension smothering his words, had it been born from ordinary fear? He was firm in his belief that he had never ruled out a sentence of death as a possible outcome of his trial. But had he ever contemplated his death as such? Had he ever divorced the vision of the supreme penalty he might have to pay from the envisioned injustice that might bring it about? He had noted the absence of the word "death" from Meletus' oration. Nor, though hinting at it, had Anytus pronounced it. During Lyco's speech it had occurred to Socrates that he might use the word "death" in his own, admonishing his countrymen not to "go too far" ("for you see, men, the malice of my accusers and your own naughtiness actually might push the hemlock cup up to my lips, and you'll regret it afterward")—and now he wondered whether the playfully testing tone of that imagined admonition had not issued from a biased incredulity barring the image of his own non-existence.

The hard voice of Anytus called Socrates back from those unanswered queries. "Granted," the tanner said, "granted for argument's sake that you believed the god sent you out to examine men. Did he also urge you to seduce the young to do likewise?"

"Seduce?" Socrates replied with a new animation. "Those young men came to me of their own accord. Most of them belonged to well-to-do families and hadn't much to do—"

"Of course not—"

"They liked listening to my investigations and began to imitate them. Should I have told them: 'You mustn't do that, for I alone know how to ask questions'? Why, that would have been the height of arrogance! Now, those young men went about questioning men and frequently made them conscious of their shortcomings—hazily conscious, but conscious still. And such men, instead of getting angry with themselves and their shortcomings, cry out now: 'That accursed Socrates! He teaches those lads how to pester their elders with unending queries. He is a misleader of youth, a wrongdoer.' And if someone asks them: 'What wrong did he actually do?' those men cannot tell, and to justify their anger they take recourse in those accusations that have always been raised against men, citizens or foreigners, who dedicate their lives to thinking about what underlies human existence.

"Those ancient ready-made charges have come in handy to those who over the years have grown to hate me for the plainness of my speech and the directness of my questions—in other words, for my speaking the truth. And now Meletus and Anytus and this orator have made their own those time-worn charges—'disseminating doctrines about the cosmos' and 'denying the gods' and 'making the worse appear the better cause,' and so on. They hate the truth that I voiced at times about their own pursuits.

"So I'm coming to my present accusers, men. Take Meletus. He says: 'Socrates corrupts our youth.' Much does he care about it! He should, though, for he plumes himself on his great love of the commonweal. Let me say bluntly that he doesn't even know what this noble word stands for, or what it means to be a genuine lover of the city. In short, this poet pretends to be concerned with a matter he doesn't care a straw for. To come forth with such a piece of make-believe—is that not, I'm asking you, a nasty trick to play on a law court?"

"How do you propose," asked Lyco, "to prove it is pretense on his part?"

"I shall try to prove it. Meletus, son of Meletus! You implied, did you not, that you have given a good deal of thought to the improvement of our youth?"

"A great deal."

"A great deal," Socrates repeated, shaking his head and pursing his lips in mock appreciation. "Will you, then, tell the court who in your opinion improves our youth?"

"*You* corrupt it, Socrates!"

"You misunderstood my question, Meletus."

"Still, you corrupt our youth—"

"Come, come, Meletus, think. Let me ask you this: can anyone who cannot be influenced possibly be corrupted?"

"Of course not, for being corrupted is proof of one's being influenced."

"Good! Now, can anyone be influenced and yet not be susceptible to improvement, as well as corruption?"

Meletus gave no reply.

"You do not seem to have made up your mind as to who is improving the young. That doesn't mean that no one is, to be sure. It merely bears out my contention that you spoke untruth saying you gave a great deal of thought to the improvement of our youth, and that you in actual fact are not interested at all in that problem."

"I am! . . . The laws!"

"The laws—what?"

"The laws are improving our youth."

"Yes, the laws hold up the good to our youth. I agree. But what person, or persons, in your opinion, so instruct the young that they grasp the honest good with their own minds and strive to attain it?"

Meletus started. "The judges in this court do!" he exclaimed.

"All of them, or only some?"

"All of them."

"And what about the other citizens present here?"

"They too are improving our young men."

"A great many improvers, I must say! And what do you say about the men in the Assembly?"

"They too are improving our young men."

"Does not every citizen serve on a jury at some time or other? Do not most citizens at some time or other sit in the Assembly?"

"They do."

"Then every Athenian is improving our young men while I alone am corrupting them. Would you say so, Meletus?"

"I would. I do!"

"You do not have much faith in this overwhelming majority of your fellow citizens, Meletus," Socrates said, nodding contentedly. It was smooth sailing from here on. Soon he elicited some giggles from the jury by engaging Meletus in a discussion about the training of young horses, for the men recalled the poet's own ill-starred attempt to introduce that comparison earlier.

Then Socrates went on to inquire of Meletus whether he thought that anyone in his right mind would aim at turning those he had to live with into bad men; so why should he, Socrates, ever have aimed at so foolish a thing? Or did Meletus mean to say that he was corrupting those lads unintentionally? If that was the case, Meletus should have warned him betimes; any man, shown his error, ceased erring, for no man erred willingly. . . . And as

Meletus opposed nothing but a sullen silence to those arguments, Socrates said: "Well, men, is it not clear as daylight that this poet is not in the least concerned with the improvement of our youth?"

A rustle of approval could be heard, and not a few judges got half up and nodded with dignified contentment. But there was no gratification in Socrates. He did not feel, as he so often had in asking a man questions, that he had asked them, in verity, of himself.

Still he proceeded. Did Meletus, by charging him in one breath with corrupting youth and not revering the city's gods, perhaps wish to say that he was instilling the young with disrespect for the gods whom the city worshipped? Did Meletus suggest that he, Socrates, urged those lads to worship other gods? As Anytus had foreseen, he, Socrates, did not understand the expression "introducing novel practices." Meletus wouldn't, by any chance, accuse him of atheism, would he?

"That is precisely what I accuse you of!" the poet cried out, sapped by now of his self-control by the semblance of sincere curiosity in Socrates' tone; and in the next moment he allowed the relentless questioner to trick him into bringing up once again, and more specifically this time, the atheistic doctrines about the cosmos to which, so he maintained, the accused was adhering.

"Are you sure you are talking about me, Meletus?" Socrates countered. "You appear to take the judges here for illiterates, my good man. They know—as who wouldn't?—that it was Anaxagoras who taught those theories about the sun and the universe. They can be found in the pamphlets he wrote before leaving our city, and which sell everywhere for one drachma—"

"Athenians!" Meletus, bounding forward, interrupted at the top of his voice. "Do you see now why I warned

you of his deftness with words? Let him not deceive you!
I swear he does not believe in the gods. I swear he does
not!"

"But did you not say yourself, Meletus, that I believed
in divine agencies?"

"Divine agencies!" Anytus cried out—he had grabbed
the poet's tunic and with a severe scowl admonished him
to calm down—"we are talking about the gods!"

"So we are," said Socrates and forthwith began to prove
that no one could possibly believe in divine agencies—in
something that is of the gods—without at the same time
believing in the gods themselves. He used the most common similes to lead his hearers to conceive of the "apparent inconsistency" of Meletus' accusation. He extracted
from him the very answers his own deductions stood in
need of, and having won his point, spared him none of his
scorn.

He felt a new boldness surge up in him—and it was
not fed by the inability of Meletus to hold his own in
their dispute. Watching the poet shift his weight from one
leg to the other, Socrates knew of a sudden that this new
imperious courage must be designed for a higher purpose
than bearding the little wretch. Even convincing the unjust among the jurors of their injustice seemed a petty
purpose, considering the magnitude of the courage that
Socrates felt, and its fire. It had freed him of the fetters
of fear.

He turned away from Meletus and said that he had
talked enough about him and also about those enmities
of old—"though they," he added, "and not Meletus or
the tanner would be responsible should I be condemned
to death." Then he remarked, with a shrug: "But obloquy
and envy have destroyed many a just man, and I am not

the last one they will destroy." ("Why," he was reflecting, "why, upon saying: '*should* I be condemned to death,' did I go on to say: 'I am not the last man they *will* destroy'?" Had the jurymen noticed that slip of his tongue? And *had* his tongue slipped?)

The men's faces were bent upon him with an unwholesome expectation.

"Now someone might ask me: 'Are you not ashamed, Socrates, of a way of life which has brought you to this pass and threatens to destroy you? To him, I would reply: 'Should I be ashamed of having not dreaded destruction?' In my opinion, no man worth his salt must permit that menace to influence his conduct. Does not every Athenian face destruction in war? Yet few are known to have deserted their posts out of fear. Several times in my life— before Potidæa, at Amphipolis, and at Delium—my superiors enjoined me to stay in a certain place irrespective of mortal danger. So I did, of course, and all those who were with me did, too. Yet the superiors who issued those orders were only men—men the Assembly happened to have put over me. Would it not be strange if I disobeyed the *god,* then, who—of this I am convinced—enjoined me to stay at my post and gave me to understand that this was the right place for me? Would it not be strange indeed if, for fear of death, I had disregarded his command to search into my fellow men and into myself?

"It would have been more than strange! If I had slighted the order of the Delphic pronouncement, I would stand before you indicted justly. For would not turning a deaf ear to a divine command be like saying: 'I merely fancied it was such, but it isn't and can't be, since gods do not exist'? If, on the other hand, I allowed common fear to overrule what I knew was the god's command, you might accuse me rightly of claiming superhuman wisdom. For being afraid of death, men, is tantamount to pretending to wisdom beyond human attainment."

And while Socrates, with a determined nod, went on to say that there *was* a point in which he seemed to differ from most men—his incertitude about Hades—it struck him that he no longer appeared to dread, as most men did, the unknowable for its very unknowableness. "I know nothing about death," he declared. "I know not whether death, of which men are afraid as of the greatest of evils, might not turn out to be the greatest good. But I know that disobedience to one's better, be he a mortal or the god, is dishonorable and therefore evil. How, then, could I possibly engage in what I know to be evil only to avoid something that might turn out to be a boon?

"Even if you refused to believe Anytus—who told you I must be destroyed unless you wanted your sons to be utterly ruined—and even if you said: 'Socrates, we will acquit you on the condition that you stop your inquiries and keep in mind that you will be put to death if caught at them again,' even then I only could make this reply: 'Athenians, I love and respect you. But I shall obey the god's command rather than yours. As long as I am alive and in good health, I shall not cease telling anyone who comes my way: "You are an Athenian, a citizen of the most famous and most civilized city of the world. Are you not ashamed of spending your life amassing money, or thinking how you might do so, and running after honors and public notice, while all the while you care very little about wisdom and truth and your inner being?" And if the man I am arguing with rejoins: "But I do, Socrates, I do," I yet shall not let him go. I shall interrogate him about what he maintains he cares about, and if I find out that he is not really concerned with his inner being and

with truth, I shall tell him so. I shall tell him that he un-
derrates what is of the greatest value and has a ludicrously
exaggerated notion about what is of far lesser worth. And
I shall repeat these words to everyone I happen to talk to
after my fashion.' That, men, would be my reply to a
conditioned offer of acquittal.

"But, honestly," he asked, "what do you think I am
doing in going from one man to another after that fashion
of mine? What, if not trying to persuade them that an
Athenian should be as little concerned with comfort and
riches in civilian life as he is in the field? What, if not
trying to make each of those men realize that, unless he
strives to think with his own head and perfect his own
inner being and seek after truth by his own judgment,
neither he nor Athens will ever profit from whatever
he does? That is what I'm doing in going about among
men. And if anyone says that is not what I talked about
to the young, I must call him a liar, or at least say he's
talking rubbish. . . . But do as you like, believe Anytus
or don't, condemn or acquit me—I will never alter my
ways. I will not, men—even if you threaten to put me to
death a hundred times over!"

Not one sound save Socrates' voice had been heard.
Even when his plea to reason had turned into a declaration
ringing loud with defiance, the jurors had sat unstirring
with set features. But now a few stood up, and some
folded their arms over their breasts to pit a mute disapproval against the temerity of the accused.

"Do not interrupt me again!" he exclaimed, riding high
over the first shouts which broke the silence pregnant
with fury. "We agreed you would listen to me to the
end! I have something more to say that might cause
you to cry out. I must tell you that I am not talking about
my death in a manner of speaking. I am well aware of

the seriousness of the danger. But I am equally well aware, men, that being killed is a far lesser evil than taking away a fellow man's life unjustly." Although he had to shout out these words to drown the incipient uproar, Socrates was in reality calm. He had committed himself.

He had stepped forward and stood over the brazen urn, and as soon as the clamor began to subside, he said: "I am not going to argue for my life any further. Let me talk, instead, about you, my fellow Athenians. Once you have killed me, men, you will not easily find such a one as me—someone who's acting as a kind of gadfly to the city. Don't laugh. A city, perhaps by its very size, *is* very much like a heavy horse—though it may be a well-bred one—and tends to grow sluggish, and therefore must be prodded into action. And as nature attaches gadflies to horses, so the god has attached me to the city. I have been fastening myself onto your necks and I roused you from your twilit slumber, one after another, and now it may well be that you will strike out at this gadfly, as men aroused from a doze often do—or, to drop that comical figure of speech, kill me with no further ado. But if you do so, you will drowse on for the rest of your lives, as will your sons for the rest of theirs, unless the god takes pity on you and on them and orders some other man to act as I have."

"The god!" Meletus called out. "I tell you, Athenians, this Socrates is hiding behind a god he does not believe in!"

"Oh, Meletus . . ." said Socrates with a weary tone. He had lowered his head as if to peep into the darkness of the urn's hollow. A sense of futility encroached on his thoughts. A memory had risen to them, as may a dream that reality seems to re-enact many years after. "Would not a physician," so he had asked one of the Sophists many a long year previously, "were he arraigned before a jury of children, be found guilty forthwith? Imagine his accuser saying: 'This man, children, did evil to you. He coaxed you into swallowing bitter potions. He made you vomit and then fast again. He applied leeches to you and made you bleed.' What would it avail that physician if he answered: 'All that, children, I did to improve your health or cure you from ills you failed to recognize as such'? Would not that man be condemned just the same?" The Sophist had been amused by the parable; and recalling it now, Socrates himself could not help smiling, and the smile was still on his face when, raising his eyes in feigned despair, he asked, over his shoulder: "Meletus is grumbling again, is he not? What did you say, my Meletus?"

"You heard me! I asked you how you intended to prove that it was the god who sent you on that mission of yours."

"A good question. The judges are entitled to get an answer to it. Well, then. Is it perchance within human nature to neglect one's own affairs as completely as I have, and, for as many years as I have, watch the miserable circumstances of one's household without lifting a finger to better them? Assuredly it is not. You must admit yourselves that it is not within human nature to cast all personal concerns out of one's mind and take on those of others unasked. Measured by the standards of ordinary conduct, to act in that manner might make sense, to be sure, if money were to be gained. But I never took money —I told you before why I didn't—and even Lyco, who should know something about taking money for words, did not have the insolence to say that I ever asked for, or got, any pay from those men, young or old, I held discourse with. Now what, men—what, if not the god's bidding, could ever have made me act contrary to human nature?

"I must go on, so that you won't get restless again. . . . I am told it seems inconsistent to some of my fellow citizens that I should have gone about, trying to make each of them see what is wrong in his way of life, while I hardly ever spoke in the Assembly—the proper place, so I am told, to advise one's fellow citizens and talk to them about concerns common to all. Now, friends," he said with an ease that surprised and gratified him, "I assume most of you heard me talk, on one occasion or another, about those signs which come to me, that voice. . . . And, come to think of it, my paying attention to that voice may constitute those 'new practices' Meletus says I'm introducing. That voice, then—you don't need a name for it as long as you hear it—never urges me to do this, or that, but always prevents me from doing something I am about to do. It doesn't say to me: 'Do this, Socrates,' or: 'You must do that.' It says: 'Be on your guard, you must not do what you are about to do.' That is the way in which long ago I was deterred from going into politics. I am glad I was, for, had I entered public life, I would have perished long ago—which would have done no good to you, or to me, for that matter. 'Why would you have perished?' you are likely to ask. Do not take offense at my reply, men. It is a truthful reply, and you mustn't shy away from truth. The short and the long of it is that no man who wants to prevent injustice and opposes a multitude can possibly stay alive very long—"

"Is every multitude, then, unjust, in your opinion?"

"Determined as I have been never to yield to injustice, Anytus—"

"In what capacity? In what capacity—since you shied away from public life, as you just admitted yourself, and never once appeared in the Assembly?"

"I appeared there on at least one occasion, and my present accusers, who keep interrupting me, should recall that occasion and also the fact that I happened to be in the president's chair on that day. . . ."

Curiously, Meletus and Anytus and Lyco had not stepped forward during that exchange, and Socrates had refused to look behind him. He had drawn away from the top of the ballot-urn, and after squinting up at the sun and running the back of his hand over his brow, he began to relate the story of "that day seven years ago" on which the Assembly had been so eager to have tried— "summarily and in a body, against justice and law"— the generals returned from the Arginusæan bay. "I for one," he said, "I as the only one opposed the motion. I enforced adjournment in the teeth of dire threats hurled at me. But I then and there determined to run any risk rather than side with the breakers of the law, rather than side with injustice. As you recall, the multitude that I opposed—vainly, in the end—soon regretted their injustice; and that, I think, is why I survived the fury of the populace. But would I have survived it if, holding various offices or merely joining the Assembly with regularity, I had found myself compelled to oppose the multitude on a succession of occasions? Incidentally, Anytus, those six generals were tried in the days of popular rule, and it was in the days of popular rule that I was in mortal danger upon opposing unlawful procedure. Do not interrupt me, Anytus! You may take comfort. The greatest danger I was exposed to in public life came to me when the Thirty were in power—"

Shouts of "Critias, the infamous Critias!" stopped him

short. One man had climbed one of the plane trees, and, precariously straddling a bough, formed his hands into a horn to yell from on high: "Your disciple Critias, your good student, your pupil Critias!"

"When the Thirty were in power," Socrates proceeded to say, "they summoned me one day and ordered me to voyage to Salamis and, with the help of some henchmen Critias had on that island, fetch a certain Leon and bring him to Athens. Leon of Salamis was guilty of no crime —in fact, was accused of none—yet the Thirty wished to put him to death. They also wished to implicate me in their misprision, for, as you know, they were eager to implicate as many citizens as they could. But their great power and ruthlessness did not browbeat me into becoming an accessory to that crime. I did not say to myself: 'What is there to do but obey? How can I oppose the despot? No one possibly can within the city.' None of those things did I say to myself. I simply disregarded the odious order and went home. And had it not been for the end of the Tyrant's rule, which took place soon afterward, I most probably would have lost my life at his hands."

"At the hands of your pupil Critias!"

Socrates shook his head vehemently. "I had no truck with the usurper, and well you know it! Who can say that I ever submitted to those whom malice now chooses to call my pupils? The truth is I've never had pupils. Anyone, rich or poor, young or old, can come to me and hear me talk and talk back to me and watch me follow my occupation. . . ."

He looked into space. He had been speaking haltingly in the end, and with an oddly abortive motion, raised his shoulders. He may have seemed tired to his listeners, and some must have thought he was losing the thread of

his speech. But to Socrates himself, it was as though he
were once again looking for the great illusion which
had gone out of his life many long years before, and
which yet seemed to have lived on as an unfulfilled
promise and been with him all the time like a tone too
high for human ears. . . . No man in the Great Court
knew why he stamped his foot as he was saying: "I wish
to make this clear. If one of those who came to me turned
out later to be a bad man, for that I can be blamed as little
as any credit should be given me for another one's turning
out to be good. I never passed any theories on to others
and never taught any doctrines. And no secrets either.
If anyone says he ever heard me talk to one man about
things I didn't also discuss with others—let me assure you
that fellow is a liar.

"I am an old man and I have been going about among
you for a very long time. Uncounted are those who,
grown up by now or past middle age, held discourse with
me when they were young. They all have had ample
time to find out whether I then corrupted their judgment
or trained them in evil skills. If they have arrived at that
conclusion, now is the time for them to say so. Now they
ought to speak up, and so ought the fathers and brothers
and sons of those who are dead, or of those who do not
wish to step forth themselves for some reason—in case
those relatives think that I did harm to their families
and can also say what harm I did. . . . There is Crito,
who is of my own age, and with him is his oldest son,
Critobolus . . . and over there stands Nicostratus, the
son of Theosdotides . . . and there I see the face of
Theages' brother, Paralus. . . ."

It was a long roll call. Of course Socrates knew that
it was not customary for a citizen accused of impiety to
introduce character witnesses, and he did not deliberately

challenge established practice. The names of the friends came to his mind as a matter of course at this juncture, and he lent them breath as a matter of course. Was it not a farewell he sang out as he pronounced one name after another?

His friends and companions might have rushed forward now to crowd about the dais on all sides, or even, flouting usage, leap onto its boards and cry out: "He did us nothing but good, men of Athens, and nothing but good to our departed! He never foisted any doctrines upon us after the manner of the Sophists. He gave us an inkling of what wisdom is and showed us that excellence can issue only from knowledge. He imbued us with a yearning for knowledge and kindled in us the desire to know ourselves. He put us on the road to wisdom, and sometimes we wondered whether that road was not part of the goal." Thus they might have spoken. But they merely raised their hands, standing on tiptoe, and chanted: "Socrates, Socrates . . ."

The massive aversion that had frozen the jurors' faces when Socrates mentioned the generals sent to Hades was melting away. Some compassion seemed to be mingling with the curiosity that kept the jurymen's heads cocked toward Socrates' friends even after their chorus had ended; a goodly number of the men on the benches seemed reluctant to direct their eyes back to Socrates' unmoving shape, and their glances wandered across his head to the slope and its boulders and the spectators standing atop them.

The two officers who had been sitting near the urns on the edge of the dais had got up, and Socrates saw them thread their way to the door of the Royal Hall.

"Well, men of Athens," he said, "that is about all the defense I have to proffer. Except for one more thing—"

"Hurry up, will you?"

Socrates recognized the heckler—it was the veteran of Phyle. "There may be some in your midst," he went on, and tardily shook a finger at the loudmouthed man, "who have had to stand trial themselves at some time or other. Such men are bound to recall how they entreated the judges with supplications and tears on this very platform and produced their families clad in mourning and made them wail and sob—and yet the charges brought against those men were less grave than those brought against me. Such men might grow incensed because I, an accused for whom a sentence of death has been suggested, so serious is his case, fail to do any of those things, and are likely to cast their votes against me in anger. I do not know how many such men are among you. Still I do not dismiss the danger—"

"So why—" Anytus set out to ask, his head tilted in a pretense of attentiveness, but the veteran of Phyle broke in:

"Do not ask him, my brave Anytus, ask us. He just doesn't want to act as all Athenians do."

"My friend," Socrates said—to his dismay he noticed a trembling in his voice—"my friend, I am a human being, a creature of flesh and blood. I have a family, three sons. One of them is almost a man, the two others are still small children. All the more, I admit, you have the right to ask: 'Why do you not bring your sons here, together with your wife, and have them petition us for an acquittal?' I shall give you my answer. It is out of respect for the good name of all of you, out of respect for Athens, that I refuse to stage any such spectacle. It would be disgraceful to this court, as to the city, if a citizen of my age, a man who rightly or wrongly has acquired a reputation as a man of some insight, and whom many

think a man outside the run— Let me talk, men. . . .
It would be disgraceful, I'm saying, if such a one would
stoop to having his family ask for clemency and weep
and lament. I refuse to debase myself in that fashion and
make a laughingstock of myself and the city."

A torrent of angry voices deadened these last words.

The fracas had started with a wrangle between some
men on the brick wall and some others who had collected
behind them. A group of those latecomers had tried to
clamber across the wall and had been held back. Now,
venting their long-suppressed resentment, they turned it
against the defiance of the accused. One of them, a fellow
tall as a giant, who had managed to scale the wall, cried
into the court: "Outside the run! Did you hear it, judges?
Outside the run of all good Athenians! Superior to all,
superior!" And along the brick wall and under the plane
trees and in the passageway and behind the barrier, hundreds of voices took up the new charge.

At the same time, the name "Alcibiades" was heard
reverberating in the lanes of the benches. Some gray-
beards had got involved in a discussion about the merits
of a law, dropped nearly a generation before, that used
to rid the city—by a simple majority vote in the Assembly
(provided six thousand men were present)—of any
citizen considered dangerous to popular rule, of any man
suspected of deeming himself superior to his fellow Athenians. As it happened, Alcibiades had been responsible for
the repeal of that law, which used to send such men
straight into exile; in one of his sardonic moods he had
one day hectored the Assembly into ostracizing a little
schemer of no consequence whatsoever and, thus making
a mockery of the ancient institution, had discredited it.

That discussion now spread from the benches to all
sides. Becoming more heated among the spectators and

less to the point, it incidentally made them aware that
Socrates had by no more than an innuendo answered
the many impassioned words with which Meletus had
blamed him for Alcibiades' crimes. Hardly anyone
stopped to recall Anytus' reticence on that score, or Lyco's,
and the obvious consideration for the Great Amnesty
behind their omission. Socrates simply seemed to have
evaded the issue—and deprived his audience of hearing
the man said to have loved Alcibiades most discuss his
abominations in public!

In no position to reproach Socrates with having availed
himself of the amnesty's benefits by keeping silent on that
point, the crowds seized upon whatever they now remembered had aroused their indignation in his speech—
above all, his avowed unconcern with public affairs. He
had, in a way, apologized for his aloofness from the Assembly. But he had done so with a sting! Everybody knew
that participation in the Assembly's proceedings was on
the downgrade, and that the magistrates sometimes had
a hard time insuring a quorum. And this Socrates talking
of "the multitude" in the Assembly! Now even the most
simple-minded of the citizens present believed they
grasped what Socrates' critics meant by calling his talk
"ambiguous"; and the passionate shouts of disfavor,
drowning the jurors' cries for order, grew shriller with
every heartbeat.

Called into action by the officers at the door of the
Royal Hall, police rushed into the court, fanning out to
quell the tumult; and as the two magistrates charged with
handing the jurors their ballots had come forth to the
urns again and were standing ready, each holding a large
brass bowl—into which the voting-disks had been sorted
—the Scythians redoubled their efforts to clear the aisle.
Egged on by the impatient jurymen, they pushed and

pressed the obstreperous men all the way back behind the barrier.

The desperate energy of the police seemed to amuse some of the lookers-on—in particular, those along the plane trees, who for some reason had not joined in the hubbub; and it was their derisive laughter and the twits they hurled at both the rioters and the Scythians, rather than the latter's own exertions, which put an end to the turmoil.

Throughout it, Socrates had been gazing across the heads of the throng, his face showing not the least emotion. Now, his hands low on his back again, his overlong tunic somewhat disarranged, he focused his glance on the front-bench jurors and said in a loud even voice: "You have sworn to judge according to the laws each case for which the lot might pick you. You have sworn to do no favor to anyone and not to make a present of justice according to your own good pleasure. If I now urged you," he proceeded, thrusting out both arms to silence the last lingering noises in the rear of the court—his eyes did not release the jury—"if I now urged you to think of my family and have mercy on them, would I not try to make you forget your oath? Would I not appear to be saying to you . . . wouldn't I be saying to you in actual fact: 'You have sworn by the gods to uphold the laws—what of it?—there are no gods'? Would I not thus convict myself of the very crime I stand accused of—that is, of not believing that gods exist? But I am far from believing that there are no gods, men of Athens. And since I believe in their existence—believe in it in a sense far higher than do my accusers—I commit my cause to the god, as well as to you."

I X

Even while Socrates was concluding his defense, the two magistrates, each carrying his bowl, had advanced along the front row of the benches. Upon reaching its end, they turned into the next row and, progressing from row to row, wound their way past the jurymen; and the intermittent clank of the brazen ballots the two magistrates handed the men—one out of each bowl to each of the five hundred and one jurors—skimmed the subdued gabble.

A stranger chancing into the Great Court at this moment might have asked: "What difference is there between those two voting-disks every juror receives?" In fact, they were of identical shape and color, and through the center of either ran a short axle. However, the axle of one disk was hollow—an open pipe—while the other's was solid; and any Athenian could have told such an ignoramus that the hollow-axled ballot condemned whereas the solid-axled acquitted. "Look, later, as closely as you can at any juryman as he approaches the narrow-mouthed brass urn," so such a stranger, pressing for further information, would have been told. "He will hold the axle's ends between index finger and thumb, so that no one can possibly tell which of his two disks he's about to drop into this vessel. Its opening, mark, is so narrow that, no matter how nimble a man's fingers, he cannot insert both disks at one and the same time (as some might be tempted to do from indecision); and dropping them in one after the other would give away his deceit. So, in addition, would his appearing empty-handed at the wide-mouthed earthen urn—into which each juror must throw his waste check. You'll agree this mode of procedure is ingenious."

It may have been that. But speedy it was not, for no juror was permitted to leave his seat till all of them had been given their ballots. Also, custom bade the juror remain silent once he held the two disks in his hand.

With one of them after another thus halting their whispers, the spectators too were keeping their peace. It was very warm now, and an odor of garlic hovered above the crowds.

The three accusers had left the dais, but remained close to it, by its right side.

Socrates had sat down. He seemed to be contemplating the jury. After a while Crito extended an arm from down below to lay his hand on Socrates' shoulder, but Socrates did not move, and no words were exchanged between the two old friends. Critobolus brought a bowl of water, and Crito took a sip without glancing at his son, and so, without looking back at either of them, did Socrates.

Two slaves had begun to hoist onto the elevation the table for counting the ballots.

Then the king archon left his seat.

At last the two magistrates had filed past the five hundred and one, and holding their emptied bowls upside down, walked back to the urns.

No signal was given by anyone to get the jurymen to their feet. They rose, one after another, and shuffled up to the passageway. Although the men seeped into the aisle from both sides at one and the same time, they formed their file there without pushing or trying to get ahead of one another. When the line began inching forward, each man was careful to keep at some distance from the one in front. Not one word was spoken, nor were any signs or glances exchanged. From time to time some juror seemed to hesitate before discharging his duty at the narrow-mouthed urn, and then the whole file came to a brief standstill.

Having voted, each juryman returned to his seat by walking along the outer ends of the benches, and the spectators in these two lanes stepped aside as best they could to make room for the one-day judges.

However, for all this orderliness, the intervals between the clankings of the ballots increased as the voting progressed—and it sounded as though the latecoming votes, which were to decide the verdict, hesitated before taking the irrevocable plunge. At the same time, each new ballot inserted, colliding with a larger mound of disks at the bottom of the urn, produced a clank less metallic and duller.

The table had been put up in front of the king archon's seat.

No slave must touch the urns once the votes were in. As it happened, the two magistrates who had to lift the urns onto the dais were elderly men . . . and sprinkles of laughter and some half-suppressed taunts accompanied their panting efforts.

When the voting had drawn to its end, Socrates—sitting on his stool, knees wide apart, his spread fingers upon them—had taken his gaze away from the shortening line of men in the aisle, and looked before him with a blank face. Now, with the two officers turning the brazen urn out on the table, he slowly moved his head toward them.

Some of the disks rolled along the top of the table, and the two officers, leaning forward quickly, shot out their arms to prevent the disks from dropping.

As soon as they had patted the five hundred and one ballots into a pile, Socrates stood up.

"Socrates, son of Sophroniscus," said one of the magistrates mechanically.

Socrates shook his head.

"Meletus, son of Meletus."

Meletus raised a fluttering hand; abiding by usage, he too was rejecting the invitation to watch the count.

The two magistrates bent low over the table. There was hardly any clanking to be heard as they began to sort the hollow-axled checks from the solid, so gingerly did they lift one ballot after another and put it on the mound of its like.

High overhead, a phalanx of wild geese crossed the sky, flying seaward. There was not one man in the court who did not crane his neck to observe the course the boisterous birds were taking, and the two magistrates too followed them with their eyes, interrupting the count. Only Socrates did not look up to the sky.

The magistrates kept counting.

The two piles of ballots seemed fairly even.

When the count was complete, they started counting all over again. Not once did either of them so much as part his lips. Meanwhile the other officers left their places to come up onto the dais, step by step, and approach the table.

Someone must have gone to inform the king archon that the count was over, for no sooner had one of the two tallying magistrates written its result on a tablet than the king archon returned to the platform.

Even before sitting down, he accepted the tablet. While

again assuming his stately posture, he held the tablet before him at some distance.

A profound stillness reigned over the whole expanse of the court.

The king archon said: "Socrates. Socrates, of your judges, two hundred and eighty found you guilty—" He went on to say that two hundred and twenty-one had found Socrates not guilty . . . but a swelling rush of mutters and murmurs swamped what he said.

His first words had released jurymen and spectators alike from the bondage of their suspense. Yet no one shouted out his emotion or leaped to his feet, as men would in some of the lower courts upon the pronouncement of the verdict. However shadowy the judicial power the Athenians had left to their one-year "king" may have been, this one moment seemed still to bring back some of the ancient awe. Thus the place resounded with the restrained mumblings of a thousand Athenians or more, and their turning to one another with abortive shrugs and questioning miens stressed the eerie force of their low-pitched chorus.

But all of a sudden Anytus, leaning forward over the edge of the dais, brought his fist down on its boards and exclaimed, his voice shaken with bitterness: "It cannot be true! Two hundred and one and twenty!"

"I too am astonished at the number of votes that are *for* me, Anytus," said Socrates, his face still uplifted to the king archon and the spark of expectation that seemed to have come to his unstirring countenance. "To think of it: had a mere thirty votes gone over to the other side, I now would stand acquitted! Frankly speaking, I expected a far greater majority to go against me. That is one of the reasons why I am not incensed or grieved. Be not so proud, Meletus," he continued, swinging his eyes to the poet. "Believe me, you'd be in dire straits now except for the assistance you received from the tanner and from Lyco. Without it, I dare say not even a fifth of the judges would have found me guilty, and you'd have incurred a fine of a thousand drachmæ. So I am not upset, really. No, men, I am not grieved." Was he really as untouched by the vote of condemnation as he told them he was? It had pushed him still closer to death—to that state of his non-existence which he still could not picture. "About my penalty, then," he said. "As you know, Meletus proposes death. What, then, shall I propose? What I deserve, of course. But what does a man deserve who, though never idle, has never tended his own business and never cared *this* much about any of the things most men are running after—"

"You've said all that before, Socrates!"

"Perhaps I have—"

"The question at hand now, Socrates—"

"The question, my friend, is this," Socrates said, casting a stern glance at the interrupter, and the casual inflection was gone from his voice. "What should be done to a man for having said to every man he met: 'Before worrying about what you may get, worry about what you are and what you might be; and before worrying about what your city owns, worry about what she is'? What shall be done to such a one? In case a man's deserts are supposed to fit his actions, something good should be done to him, I'd say. How would you pay off a benefactor of yours who happened to be poor? I suppose you would reward him with the privilege of a lifetime seat at the public table in our City Hall—and he'd deserve it far more than the Olympic victors you confer this honor upon as a matter of course, for the victories of those athletes afford you only a fleeting pleasure—a semblance of happiness—

while what I have been doing is likely to give you genuine, lasting happiness, men. Moreover, those athletes are not as a rule in want, while I am. In short," he declared, "inasmuch as it is my duty to say what I think I deserve, I suggest maintenance at the City Hall."

It was as though a cloud had descended upon the whole court, a thick bank of clouds, so impenetrable was the solid silence. No one could have singled out from the jury, at this moment, the two hundred and twenty-one men who had judged the accused not guilty.

Socrates said: "I was not spiting you or making fun of this court. Nor did I talk out of impertinence. I advanced this proposition simply because I am convinced that I never did any wrong intentionally. However, I seem to have been unable to convince *you*. The time was so short. . . . If it were not for the law which decrees that a capital cause must be decided in one day, a law unknown in other cities—"

"Why don't you go to live in one of those cities?"

"I shall answer your question," Socrates said, but he had to wait for the enthusiastic endorsement the heckler's proposal received to die down. From the moment the vote had been in, he had not doubted that most of the judges were expecting him to suggest banishment as his penalty. But could he possibly behave as a booed-down actor would and run off the stage? Could he possibly say, though not in so many words: "Forget I ever opened my mouth, let me go, do no longer think of this Socrates, do no longer discuss his doings, imagine he never was talking to you"? He felt certain that the divine voice would stay his first step should he thus try to abscond and turn his back on the whole meaning that his existence had gained. And though he realized that he was courting death by not complying with his fellow citizens' wish—

and that braving death was one thing, but courting it another—he yet heard himself say: "I told you that I don't know whether death is good or bad. Should I, then, to escape something of which I don't know whether it is good or bad, propose to have inflicted on me something I do know must be bad? Shall I, in other words, ask for my own banishment—"

"Yes, Socrates!" an outburst of howls broke in. "Exile! Exile!"

"Exile? I would be blinded indeed by the love of being alive should I propose to have banishment inflicted on me, and fail to consider that I cannot expect people abroad to endure me when even my own countrymen don't. Why, I would be driven from one foreign city to another! For the young would flock to me in whatever city I stayed, of that I am sure, and no sooner would I have started holding discourse with them than their elders would expel me from their township. A nice kind of life that would be for a man of my age! 'But can you not hold your tongue, Socrates?' some of you may ask and explain to me that no one would object to my presence in such a foreign city provided I kept my mouth shut. Now if I say to that that I cannot keep silent because keeping silent would be a disobedience to the god—if I say that, you will not believe me. Nor will you think me sincere if I tell you that the urge to examine one's fellow men's lives—and one's own—is man's greatest boon, and that an unexamined life is not worth living. No, you'd not believe me.

"Remains a fine. Well, any man who's got the means to pay a fine should not be reluctant to offer such a payment, for parting with money is not too bad. But I don't have any money, men. . . . Maybe I could raise one mina. . . . Be it, then. I propose this sum as my fine."

"Clown—" said one of the front-row jurymen. But on the whole the stupefaction was much too great to find words. Then Anytus began laughing. It was a labored guffaw, fitting ill his glowering face, and, probably to make his amusement appear more natural, he started to pound the boards of the dais with both fists. And then a fat man, appearing by Anytus' side, began to laugh equally loud, and then Lyco did, and then a third man, and then a fourth, and then the entire crowd about the tanner burst out, and at length the court was ringing with this envenomed pretense of mirth.

It was primarily to evade the sight of the laughers—who carried their affected good humor to the point of making their mouths gape up to the sky and holding their bellies—that Socrates veered half round. But he had also seen the beckoning hands in the direction he turned to—Critobolus' hands and Plato's and Apollodorus'.

Crito laid his staff aside, and, fingers splayed, lifted both hands high and brought them down again and then up again twice. And Apollodorus did likewise, and Plato kept pointing to them both, his alert eyes wandering from Crito to Socrates and back again, and finally Critobolus, who was standing so close to the elevation he had to lean far back to expose his face to Socrates' view, formed with his lips a soundless word with the exaggerated care used in communicating with deaf-mutes.

Socrates nodded to signal that he had understood the recommendation. He was deeply moved. Yet there was something almost like repugnance in his inflection when he said to his judges: "Thirty. Crito and his oldest son and Apollodorus ask me to offer thirty minæ. They will stand surety for me. Let a thirty-minæ fine be my penalty, then."

To himself he was saying: "Men threatened by death

act strangely. They seem to fancy that they will live on forever if only this one threat is removed." He wondered why the divine voice had not spoken to prevent him from acting as strangely as men in general acted when threatened by death.

X

The Royal Hall's deep shadow had slipped over the platform. The king archon was holding his gray-bearded chin cupped in one hand, with the other supporting the elbow. He seemed to be contemplating from under his brows the thickened knot of well-wishers about Anytus.

The waste-check urn had been emptied on the table even while Socrates spoke. And no sooner had he pronounced his final offer than the two magistrates started separating the hollow-axled disks from those with solid axles, and sorting them into the bowls. Like a whimsically irregular echo of the ballots' clanks, the sounds of the dripping water of the clock, purposeless now, fell into the quiet that had followed Socrates' proposition.

Although the bystanders resumed their conversations after a while, there was scant animation in them. The proposal of a fine had dispirited the men. Had Socrates suggested banishment, they would have looked forward now to the exultant procession that guided a banished person out of the court as a rule (much as an ostracized man used to be chanted and cursed out of the Assembly in the days of the *óstrakon* law). The payment of a fine— and by rich guarantors, at that—was a drab affair, to be settled the morning after at the Exchequer. Moreover, the onlookers were tired. Few had been able to sit down for even a short rest since the trial had opened. Only up on the slope of the hill, where more and more men had assembled on both sides of the Royal Hall, some could be seen squatting on their haunches atop the boulders.

A formidable silence was hanging over the jury. Usage kept their lips sealed once the man they had found guilty had come forth with his alternative offer; and that enforced calm appeared to turn the jurors' fatigue into torpor. Most of them were slouching in their seats, legs stretched out or feet propped up against the bench in front, and, their hands clasped behind their necks, were staring upward, as if brooding over their judgment. Some were dozing beneath the makeshift hoods of their pulled-up cloaks.

Socrates had drawn the stool closer to himself with his foot. But he did not sit down. What weariness had been in him was gone. A curious question preyed on his mind (and the most curious thing about it was its sounding as though it had come from the person least likely to interfere with his meditations, Xanthippe). He had known perfectly well what the multitudes in a law court were expecting, and never had doubted the impact of their reactions upon the jury. Why, then, had he avoided talking at length about what these men wanted him to enlarge on with gusto—Aristophanes and his old comedy, party politics and postwar popular rule, or Alcibiades' crimes? What indeed had made him withstand the temptation of giving his audience its due, as it were? Could it have been his old disinclination to cater to his listeners' tastes, his habit of broaching subjects they were not eager to have discussed before them?

The two officers had finished sorting the ballots. Each with bowl in hand, they turned, waiting for the king archon's nod. Meantime the urns had been carried back to their former places.

As through a mist Socrates saw Meletus draw himself up, down below, on tiptoe, an unabashed sneer on his face; and he heard Crito say in an undertone: "A fool to the end, this poet. Victory is not his yet. Be of good cheer, my Socrates."

"What victory?" Socrates murmured. Yet, as the two magistrates now descended from the dais, he became aware with dismay that his heart was beating faster. "Am I still that eager to have those thirty votes come over to my side," he was asking himself, "so that I can go home and have a long night's sleep with no dreams in it, and can talk tomorrow to the men in the square again? . . . Would I say to them: 'I was not afraid of death'? What does a man back from war prove by saying: 'I showed courage'? Are not such veterans laughed at if they talk once too often about the courage they showed? Once the danger is past, their courage does not seem real. Only those who have died with fortitude give reality to this thing 'courage.'" Was it the seduction of that thought which had lured him into antagonizing his judges? Or had he perchance enjoyed antagonizing the five hundred and one? Joy had come to him, that was true. But it had been the joy of his growing assurance that the god approved of a man's being true to himself and of his provoking the judgment of mortals.

The two officers were passing through one juror's lane after another, handing two disks to each man.

"I more than provoked this multitude," Socrates went on in his mind. "I gave them to understand that all of them had been wrong all their lives and that their lives had been worthless. . . . But did the image of so many lives wasted sadden me? To be sure, I am only mine, and my love of the truth, and my striving for a way of life that would have some meaning, have come to me in my aloneness. Yet, am I not theirs also? If I reject their claim, does not my love of the truth float in a void?"

Once again the king archon had retired to his chambers.

Once again then the silent judges rose from their benches.

A little more hastily this time and with a shade less of punctilio, their file was moving along the passageway —through the golden light of the afternoon up into the adumbration about the two urns.

Socrates did not succeed in taking his stare off their inch-by-inch progress; and finding himself bent on reading their faces, he told himself sternly that it was merely his penalty (death or the fine) they were voting on this time—while, before, these peers of his had decided whether or not he offended against the law. He admonished himself not to overrate what was of less value, and to think of what was of genuine worth. But his glance could not be deflected.

At last the brazen urn was once again hoisted onto the platform, to be turned out on the table.

The two tallying magistrates proceeded speedily with the second count of the ballots. The intermittent metallic noise was in Socrates' ears, but he did not once look toward the table.

Then the king archon came back again. He was stooping a little as he mounted the steps, and when he was handed the wax-covered tablet his fingers at first failed to meet the magistrate's hand.

His seating himself and lifting the tablet evoked no sign of suspense in the court this time. Anyone who had caught, as all could, a glimpse of the two mounds on the table had noted their disparate heights; and since everyone knew on which side the votes in favor of accepting the fine must be piled up, and on which those turning down the proposal, its rejection had been apparent to all long before the king archon's return.

He said that three hundred and sixty of the jurors had voted the death penalty.

According to practice, he should have taken himself away now; and the pose of indecision—unbecoming his office—in which he remained in his seat puzzled the men and seemed to make them uneasy. Only when Meletus was seen to throw up his arms rigid in unbridled triumph did the buzz of voices grow louder.

Socrates took an abrupt step to the center of the dais. "Let me tell you this," he said in a tone so hard it pierced the air like an arrow, "you judges who sentenced me to death. You did not gain much by it, for if you had waited only a little while, your desire to see me die would have been fulfilled anyway, for I am quite old. And you needn't have laid open the city to the accusation of having killed a wise man, which her detractors *will* level at her, for, eager to find fault with Athens as they are, they will be only too delighted to call me a wise man—which I am not—and, making it appear as though my judges had voted unanimously for my death, those critics will say: 'This is how proud, enlightened Athens deals with her wise men.'

"You then might retort: 'Wise? Socrates—wise? Where was his wisdom when he defended himself?' For you may think I was convicted because I lacked the wit to present my case properly. Let me tell you that it was no such lack that prevented me from talking to you in the manner in which you are accustomed to hearing accused men defend themselves, and in which you'd have liked me to talk to you. It was my disinclination to toady to my judges—or, to express it more correctly, I lacked the impudence to curry favor with an Athenian jury. Or, more correctly still: I was determined rather to die having spoken after my fashion than to speak as you wanted me to and save my skin. As in the field, where a man often may save his life by throwing away his arms and going down on his knees before his pursuers, just so an accused, be he guilty or innocent, has a fair chance of escaping death by saying and doing everything likely to please his judges. That's easy enough. In fact, avoiding death in that situation is not difficult; avoiding unrighteousness is. It runs faster than death and pursues a man more fiercely. Death, though the slower pursuer, has caught up with me, for I am old and moving slowly myself—while my accusers, though nimble-footed and quick, yet have been overtaken by the fast-moving pursuer, wickedness. . . ."

No one had interrupted Socrates. His right to speak once more might have been questioned if anyone had given thought to the matter earlier. As a rule, a man sentenced to die—and who knew he'd have to drink the lethal potion before the next day's sun set—lacked the composure to address his judges; he would burst out in laments or protest his innocence with screams as savage as they were futile. Few men in this court had been unaware that Socrates, if condemned to death, would still have twenty-odd days to live; and for that reason, rather than any trust in his imperturbability, no one had expected him to behave as did men literally at death's door. And though his self-possession might have angered the crowds, they did not jeer, and in fact seemed intent on not showing their anger.

The king archon finally rose to his feet and walked away with marked unceremoniousness—he almost slipped away into the dusk—and thereupon the judges got up and began to gather their cloaks and mattings. Yet none seemed ready to leave. Although they were ostentatiously turning their backs to the dais, they had still been attentive to Socrates' words; and as he mentioned the "faster-moving pursuer" and with accentuated clarity formed the word "wickedness," a new unrest rippled their rows, and some of them raised their clenched fists, yelling: "You! You—"

"I—" Socrates broke in strongly, "I now shall go to suffer the penalty of death, while you who have doomed me will leave this place condemned to bearing the mark of unrighteousness for the rest of your lives. And as I abide by the sentence passed on me, so you have to abide by the judgment that truth will pass upon you. And if you think that by killing a man you will have protected yourselves from being censured for what is wrong in your way of life, you are mistaken. After my death, others, younger men, are going to censure you, and since I won't be here any longer to keep them in check, they will talk to you less softly than I did and will hurt you far more. There is but one way of escaping that punishment," he added with a suddenly mellowed and almost compassionate inflection, "and that is to mend your ways and to improve yourselves. That is a way open to all, and an honorable road it would be for you."

The spell that the novelty of a convicted man's exhorting his judges seemed to have cast on the court had worn off rapidly. Impatient feet were scraping the ground, benches being knocked against by men who were scrambling over them or pushing them aside in a concerted effort, trying to get out of their seats as best they could. At the same time, the spectators—who, no longer held back by the Scythians, had flooded the aisle and whatever space there was at the bench-ends—began to pour from all sides into the jurors' lanes. As in the Theater, where many in the audience would make haste to get back to their homes as soon as the chorus had sung its last verse and danced its last step, while many others would rush down to the stage as though to test their emotions by themselves treading the boards on which the actors had enacted the play—so now in this law court did swarms of men push forward to get near the dais, forcing their way through the stream of those eager to leave the place behind them, their job done.

Socrates was standing in the purple dusk that now enveloped the whole elevation. "Friends . . ." he said. He had not expected the outvoted judges to come up to him and thereby lift the secrecy of their ballots; but here they were, thirty and fifty and a hundred of them, and still more, flocking toward him. "Friends," he began again, "you who have found me not guilty and wanted me to be acquitted . . . I would like to talk to you. And to you, too . . . to all of you. Stay with me, all of you, for the short while the magistrates over there are still busy—"

He had not seen the Eleven approach. They had trudged down the hill to the right of the Royal Hall, and their garb of unbleached material had kept their shapes fairly indistinct in the gathering gloom. Now they were ascending the platform, one by one—men of uneven height, some rather ungainly, some very old—and were beginning to assemble between the marble seat and the table, while the magistrates yielded their places.

In a flush of happiness Socrates noticed that the lugubrious presence of the Eleven did not come to him as a shock. He drew his overlong tunic somewhat awkwardly up through the girdle a span, and after bending down sidewise to prop his hand against the boards, sat down and let his legs dangle over the edge of the dais. "Stay with me," he repeated.

The surge of the men was emptying the court's right-hand section. Already the space under the plane trees' foliage was as good as deserted. Yet there still was a sizable group about Socrates' three accusers, who, fore-heads creased and lips drawn, were watching the ardor with which those willing to stay with Socrates for another short while were forming a semicircle.

This arc of men finally stretched from the lower part of the rock-strewn slope, along a good thirty feet of the brick wall, down to the front rows of the vacated benches; and a fair number of men had got up on them and, to steady themselves, put their arms around their neighbors' shoulders.

The chatter of the men leaving the court lost itself more and more in the distance. And at last Anytus could be seen striding away with his two associates and the troop of their hangers-on.

Socrates had tilted his head and seemed to be sniffing the air of the oncoming evening, wrinkling his nose. "As I was saying," he repeated, "I'd like to talk to you and explain what, in reality, happened to me. You see . . . throughout my life, that voice I know so well, that divine voice, opposed me, even on the most trifling occasions, whenever I was about to commit an error, or turn into the wrong path, or risk disaster and evil. But today, when there has come to me what might be, and generally is, thought to be the worst of all visitations—the last and greatest evil that can befall a man—today that voice did not speak to me once. Not once did those familiar signs stop me, as they so often did, in the midst of my talking, as indeed in mid-sentence, or when I just opened my mouth. Not once . . ." he said again, under his breath. His glance, wandering slowly over the frieze of the men's uplifted faces, had come to a halt on the face of Crito—and to his amazement, Socrates noticed the total absence from it of the embarrassment that used to tighten the old friend's lips and deflect his eyes at the merest allusion to the voice that came from the god.

"How can one account for the voice's persistent silence?" he continued. "How, if not by assuming that what has happened to me is a good thing, or, in other words, that those who hold that death is an evil thing must be mistaken. For surely the divine signs would have warned me in the manner familiar to me for so long, if what I was doing had been likely to result in something bad. Honestly, men, if we now reflect on this outcome of the whole affair ourselves, is it not safe to say that it is all to the good? For death, if you think of it, can only be one of two things: either it is a state of nothingness—of complete unconsciousness—or else, as tradition has it, a change occurs. . . .

"Well, then. If there is no consciousness in death, and it is something like a sleep without dreams, is not death a good thing? Ask any man to think of one night, out of all the nights of his life, in which nothing disturbed his rest, not even a dream; and then ask him to compare that one night with all the others in his life, and also with all his life's days—any man, and be he the King of Persia himself in all his affluence, will tell you that few were the nights or days he spent in anything like the comfort that he felt in the dreamless long sleep of that one night. Now if death should turn out to be like that, and all the time after one's dying not different from a single night of undisturbed solid sleep—would not to die be a gain?"

He stopped, closed his eyes, passed his hand over the

whole length of his face, and, looking up again, continued
with animation: "Let's consider the alternative now. Let
us consider what has been surmised so often—that to die
is to travel elsewhere from here. I'm asking you, my
friends," he said, his tone edged by a shade of irony, "if
that ancient assumption *should* prove to be valid, what
greater boon could come to a man than finding himself on
that journey? Perhaps it *is* as it is said, and all the dead
are present where that journey leads to. Imagine one's
arrival in that place. Imagine, friends, one's being rid of
those fellow citizens who take it upon themselves to administer justice, and one's coming upon the true judges
of good and evil at last—upon Minos and Rhadamanthus
who, as our tradition has it, sit in judgment in Hades.
Imagine further one's meeting a Homer or a Hesiod, as
one well may; would not many a man give a great deal
for that chance alone? In short, if I were sure that our
tradition is right in that respect, I for one would willingly
die many times over. Of course I for one would also be
eager to meet those heroes of old who were put to death
unjustly, for it would afford me no small satisfaction
to compare my fate with theirs."

At first the men had stared at Socrates with ill-hidden
perplexity. Gradually they all averted their eyes to look
down at their hands or up at the deep-blue sky.

Socrates had not adopted the ancient images frivolously.
The train of his thoughts had issued from a notion of
justice cleansed from human error and untainted by human passion . . . and the imagery of tradition had joined
that notion unawares, much as pictorial memories may
accrue to a scent. But with those pictures and their growing solidity, an overmastering trust had come and fortified
his belief in the existence of infallible justice. The testing,
half-teasing, self-teasing inflection that at first seemed to

tinge his descriptions of Hades had faded completely from his voice. He was not defying his baffled listeners alone when he went on to remark: "Perhaps I will also be able in Hades to proceed with the search for truth after my fashion. What delight it would be to ask questions of those men and women who have done away with the selfishness of the living!"

One of the Eleven, who were still standing behind the table, had lifted a handful of voting disks from its top in a thoughtless motion, and let them drop down one by one.

"And think of this," Socrates said, "there they don't put a man to death for asking questions, or, better, they can't—if what is said is true, and those in that place lead a deathless existence, as well as a happy one.

"So let me tell you, men," he proceeded with great serenity, "you too must not fear death, and must be confident that evil cannot touch the true being of a just man either in life or death. . . . And that, I suppose, is why the divine agencies refrained from warning me. You do not really think, do you, that it was mere chance which made things go the way they did in my case? Most certainly not! I clearly see—I do now—that it is better for me to die and be freed of life's tribulations than to live on and be at their mercy." He got to his feet, not without some effort, and after catching his breath, said: "Thus I am also no longer angry at my accusers and at those judges who found me guilty—well though I know they did not intend to do me any good, to say the least. And for that they must still take the blame. Yet I wish they would take an additional revenge for my having annoyed them so often. In fact, I wish all of you would repay me the annoyance I caused you so often. Seriously, I beg you to annoy my sons, once they are grown to manhood, exactly the way I annoyed you—in case, that is, they should turn out to care more

about money and all the rest than about their inner perfection. And if they think the world of themselves while
they are in truth worthless, tell them so—as I told you. If
you will do that, men of Athens, my sons and I myself
will have been treated justly by the city, after all." Having
spoken these words, Socrates turned and took the first
step in the direction of the Eleven.

The breeze of the evening was running languidly
through the plane trees. The shadows had fallen over the
entire court, and of a sudden its expanse seemed enormous,
and the dark benches seemed to stare at the deliberate
slowness of Socrates' progress across the dais, as though
at a strange intrusion of the obscurity's peace asserting
itself. Not until he had reached the end of the platform
did the Eleven, who had stood still, start following him.

Someone near the low brick wall was sobbing; and Socrates, at the point of climbing down from the elevation,
turned half round. It could be seen that he wished to open
his arms wide, but somehow this gesture miscarried. "It
is time we leave," he said into the immense calm, "night
is falling. Now, then, men . . . It is time for all of us to
depart from this place—I to die, and you to go on living.
Which is better, none but the god knows."

PART III

X I

"He is kept in chains day and night."

"And Crito?" Cinesias said in a challenging voice. "And Simmias the Theban? And Apollodorus? Are they chained, too? Each of them is wealthy enough to bribe a dozen jailers, my Anytus, let alone one."

"You do not trust that one, I take it."

Cinesias arched his eyebrows, saying nothing, and his very silence impressed Anytus as impudence.

He disliked the fat man, who had unexpectedly ambled into the tannery yard awhile earlier. Anytus recalled the way the obsequious fellow had sidled up to him toward the end of the trial and lent support to whatever the accusers had been saying at that late stage of the proceedings. The advice that Cinesias now had come to offer prejudiced Anytus against him even more. He said: "The answer, my friend, is still no," and then remarked lightly that the Eleven might be interested in the suggestion.

Cinesias wrinkled his nose to show his poor opinion of that body, but checked the grimace quickly—aware, perhaps, that the tanner might think it a reflection on the stench hanging over the place—and in the tone of one whose patience is not easily taxed began, as he put it, to "review the situation." He declared that it was only natural for the moneyed among Socrates' cronies to try to get him out of the prison and out of the city. Even if their devotion to him were less strong than they pretended, they would be careful of their good name among like-minded men and do everything in their power to bribe the jailer—this one, or any other the Eleven might put in his place if they were urged to give some more thought to the notoriously easygoing disposition of that freedman. But Socrates was a human being with a human body and could not possibly walk out of the prison compound without being seen—being seen, that was, if a couple of vigilant men were present, with their eyes accustomed to keeping watch at night as well as by day. Now those two islanders whom the excellent Anytus himself had met in the Royal Portico on the day before the trial—

Why didn't Cinesias recommend their services to the Eleven?

"Because the Eleven, like other magistrates, hardly appreciate trained informers these days," Cinesias answered sententiously, wetting his lips. "Their commendable zeal for the purity of public life sometimes seems to dull their sense of reality. The most they would do, come to think of it, is to send two or three of their Scythians to the prison —dolts a man like Crito would know how to cope with. No, my Anytus, I would not think of making recommendations to any of the magistrates. What chance, to put it bluntly, does a simple citizen have nowadays of being listened to by magistrates? Now and then I feel, Anytus, that our present-day popular rule tends to breed a deal of self-righteousness in them."

"Are you not being rash in your judgment?" Anytus asked, casually. He stood with his back to the large wooden trough in the center of the yard; and though Cinesias, by a fidgety step or two, had made several attempts to lure him away from this spot, the tanner did not budge. "Self-righteousness—nonsense!" he mumbled while he plunged a hand into the opaque liquid of the trough to stir it a little.

"I warned you I was going to talk bluntly," said Cinesias. "Nor are you responsible for the magistracy." He paused, breathing thickly. "Believe me, Anytus, I do not intend to upset you again. Who would know better than I," he added familiarly, "that the verdict upset you greatly, and that in the nineteen days since—"

"Why should a verdict of guilty upset an accuser, you know-it-all?"

"The margin might."

"Oh, the margin! It took me by surprise, I admit. I did not realize right away that Socrates' eloquence was to blame for it, together with the blundering of Meletus."

"But who were those two hundred and twenty-one men so easily swayed by Socrates' eloquence?"

"Eighty of them," Anytus said gruffly, "thought better of it at the second ballot."

"Who, then, were the remaining one hundred and forty-one? Lovers of tyranny, men in favor of the rule of the few, hangers-on of the noblemen? That's unlikely. Very unlikely indeed, what with the veniremen's lists purged of all such characters four years ago—"

"Untrue! The lists were purged only of men known to have served the Tyrant. I marvel at the frivolity with which you are repeating slander."

"My excellent Anytus," Cinesias said, after yawning on purpose, "you know I've never criticized you, and never once opposed you in the Assembly. I am your friend. Why, then, not face the truth together? Why not face the lamentable fact that the vote for Socrates was swelled by loyal supporters of popular rule—"

"Who, as I was just saying, were not proof against Socrates' dexterity with words!"

"Or, as I have been trying to say, were influenced by their own feelings, by a certain discontent noticeable even among the most devoted adherents of our popular rule—a discontent with certain high-handed methods that have been used in the Assembly, especially when the attendance is small."

These words, pronounced in a curious singsong, were entirely baseless, to Anytus' mind. Yet their very baselessness, together with the sneer that appeared on Cinesias' fleshy face, made the tanner wonder about his caller's ulterior purpose. At the same time he remembered that Cinesias had done business as a money-changer in the old days—an occupation injured not a little by the collapse of the city's imperial trade—and when the obnoxious man started to refer again to a "certain discontent," Anytus broke in rudely: "Is there such? Where? Among money-changers?"

"I did not know—" Cinesias said, his features twisted by a flash of hostility, "I really did not know that our new Athens looked askance at a law-abiding citizen's efforts to do well in his trade." And suddenly his gaze went past the tanner out to a pile of oxhides stacked against the rear wall of the yard, and he began to mutter, as though to himself, such phrases as "the victims' garlanded heads strewn with barley" and "barley mixed with salt" and "barley grown in the Rhenean plain"—which would all have been gibberish to anyone not conversant with the Athenian ritual of sacrifices, but was of course perfectly clear in its intent to the tanner and maker of leather goods.

In the days immediately after Socrates' trial, full-bodied columns of smoke had been seen rising from the sanctuaries, and the greasy odor hovering over the temple compound had proved that no mere fowl or skinny lambs were being offered the gods. In actual fact, not only oxen and heifers had been laid down on the altars by men careful again of their duty; young bulls too had been immolated in sizable numbers. Anytus himself, in the company of some veterans of the civil war, had taken a bull uphill to one of the shrines of the maiden goddess, and had watched, his face furrowed by pride, the crimson-clad priest stab the bellowing animal in the neck. Anytus had also, some days later, availed himself, as a matter of course, of the increased supply of hides at several temples—

Cinesias stopped his meaningful muttering. Smiling genially at Anytus and putting both hands against his chest, he averred inconsequentially that he had not come to talk politics.

Anytus sat down on the broad rim of the trough. While bent on returning Cinesias' protracted smile, he tried to recall whether the ludicrous joke about the shortage of oxhides *had* come to his mind when he bargained with the acolytes at the temples. But his memory, gripped by a more urgent concern, failed to serve him. Had not certain barbed quips, deftly spread and repeated once too often, though just as ludicrous and just as baseless, done great damage to the men they had been aimed at? Nor, so Anytus realized with a pang, was it a matter of mere repetition in his case, for scandalmongers might actually not scruple to point at those smoke plumes—

Cinesias had gone on to say that Anytus need not talk to those two islanders himself. He, Cinesias, knew best how to handle their like. But he was not a rich man, alas. If he were, he would not importune his friend Anytus. He simply would post the two informers near the prison at his own expense, and perhaps hire another pair, too, so as to be kept informed of what was really going on there, and be able to warn Anytus of any danger.

By now it was apparent to the tanner that Cinesias had come to extort money from him. Far from being enraged, he determined to humor the man. Raising his hands as if to calm a troubled friend, he said: "I am well informed on what is going on there." Cinesias knew—or did he not?—that Socrates had been visited regularly by a varying number of his intimates since the first day of his confinement. These friends of his sometimes stayed with him for hours. There was no regulation against it; a man sentenced to die could have visits from as many of his friends and relatives as he wanted. In view of the short time left such an individual as a rule, any restriction in that respect would no doubt be barbarous. Furthermore, the magistrates had never been averse to having loud wails and laments issue from the prison house, counting on their effect as a dire warning against offending the law. "I am calling all this to your mind, Cinesias," the tanner continued, "to stress the fact that there is no way of preventing Socrates' band from keeping company with him. There are no special regulations concerning a man sentenced to death while the Sacred Ship is absent. Not that no thought was given to the peculiar situation. Plenty of it was, as I happen to know. I also happen to know that Crito, right after the trial, offered thirty minæ of silver as a bond to have Socrates released and left at liberty until the return of the ship. The offer of course was turned down."

The more Anytus by mien and tone pretended to take Cinesias into his confidence, the more an expression of coldness and even scorn replaced the feigned attentiveness of the latter. "I do not censure the magistrates," he said when Anytus had finished. "I appreciate the peculiar situation and the limits it sets to security measures. But you'll agree, Anytus, that all that only vindicates my suggestion. Those limits make it imperative for you to have the prison

guarded by competent, incorruptible men. Do not forget,"
he proceeded, in his eyes a twinkle which ill suited the
evenly threatening inflection of his voice, "that people will
blame you as much as the magistrates, should Socrates
manage to get away."

"The accusers have no say once sentence had been pronounced."

"Is that so?"

"Such is Athenian custom."

"Custom, custom . . ." Cinesias echoed while he began
to inch away from Anytus along the longer end of the
trough. "Didn't you say in court that Socrates must be
destroyed? Now it almost seems as though his being tried
and found guilty had been more important to you than
is his destruction."

"Did I not succeed in having his proposal of a one-mina
fine laughed out of court? And didn't that laughter bias
the judges against the acceptance of *any* fine?"

"These are subtleties not likely to stick in the minds of
ordinary men, my Anytus. What they are likely to say is
this: 'Anytus was eager to have Socrates called to account
for impiety. He was eager to have a well-known man
called to account for not giving the gods their due. He
must have had motives besides his concern with the gods
and the law, or else he would be less satisfied now with the
verdict as such and less indifferent toward the execution of
the sentence.'" During these words, Cinesias, speaking
over his shoulder, had advanced toward the rear of the
yard, and no sooner had he come close to the stack of
hides than he put a hand on top of it and started to beat
a slow tattoo with his fingers.

"Go away!" Anytus, having whirled round, shouted at
a slave who had come out into the yard, and after the
frightened half-naked man had withdrawn, his master

glowered into space for some time before directing his eyes back to Cinesias.

The extortioner had stopped his drumming. He was leaning against the pile of hides, his legs crossed, looking at the ground. A rhythmically pounding noise that had started somewhere behind the rear wall emphasized the silence of the two men.

Anytus got to his feet. He could no longer deny that he was beaten, for the time being. He had to meet the menace forthwith—and he had learned in the field that, to meet a menace, a man must take one step back first! Walking over to Cinesias, he made at the same time a half-humorous sign toward the trough, as if apologizing for the foul smell, and in a voice so amiable it wiped the smirk from the blackmailer's face, inquired how much those two "island friends" of Cinesias would charge for their services.

The suddenness of his victory took Cinesias by surprise. He actually stuttered as he started to say: "Well, if you'll leave all arrangements to me, Anytus . . ."

The tanner, his stare glued to the adversary's tense face, reflected that no businessman would resort to this kind of money-making unless his fortunes were broken; and he decided to strike a hard bargain—as any Athenian worth his salt must in dealing with a man in dire straits. This resolution steadied his self-assurance immensely.

The haggling that followed became more and more whining on Cinesias' part, more and more spirited on Anytus'.

The sum they agreed on in the end was far from being a strain on his coffers. Although he knew of course that extortioners always returned for more money, giving a new, sinister twist to their threats, Anytus' initial alarm was as good as gone when Cinesias at last took his leave amid protestations of his "supreme passion for justice."

He would have to be placated only for a comparatively short time! His weapon was fated to dull. Two months hence the funny story he had threatened to peddle would be dated and most unlikely to give pause to any Athenian. As for Socrates himself and the memory of him, Anytus had already made up his mind. Socrates had not put any of his teachings down in writing. There had been no splendor about his life, and in his transgressions no wild daring such as kept brilliant the colors of, say, Alcibiades' image. Whether he was to die now or to live out his old age in some foreign city, the remembrance of him would become shadowy soon.

To be sure, Athenians, though no longer discussing *him,* would yet be discussing his case for some time to come. For any trial was greater than the citizen tried, and cast a shadow longer than his. As long as no new lawsuits engaged the emotions of men, they would continue to argue about the speeches delivered at Socrates' trial and, perhaps, also about the verdict. But new litigations were bound to come up for trial! And even before they did, those who had disapproved of the complaint against Socrates and the sentence passed upon him could be relied on to put less and less passion into their disapproval. Athenians never held fast to minority views with any deep passion once the die was cast—of that Anytus, for one, was sure. Where, for instance, had the frenzied passion of the Tyrant's supporters been once he was slain?

Public opinion, then, did not trouble Anytus. He was troubled nevertheless. His thoughts could not get away from the deal with Cinesias. He wished he had had the courage to tell him: "Look here, my good man. You want money, and as it has turned out, you have persuaded me that I should give you some. All right. You'll get some money. But forget the pretext you thought up to get it. Forget those informers. You wouldn't give them more than a tenth of what I'll give you, anyway. So drop this pretext. Leave security measures at the prison to the Eleven." For, to put it as clearly as Anytus' desire presented itself to him at long last in this hour—he wanted Socrates to escape.

He did not doubt that plans were afoot for the prisoner's rescue. He had talked with Simmias the Theban twice since the trial, pursuing him, in one instance, across the whole length of the plaza; and the hectic and then again mawkish prattle of the young man—his extolling of Socrates' "superhuman composure" and the "all but unearthly wisdom at death's door"—only served to confirm Anytus' suspicions. He assumed that the jailer had already been plied with silver, and that some way had been designed for spiriting Socrates out of the city.

Although Anytus did not care a straw for Socrates' life, he wanted these plans to succeed. He wanted to know—know for certain—that Socrates' attitude toward the thought of his death had been no more than another forensic trick. Once he stood unmasked as a common trickster and liar on that point, the rest of his oration in court could be dismissed as falsehood also.

In Anytus' opinion, the most dishonest part of the speech, next to Socrates' pretended joy in anticipating the arrival in Hades, was the protestation of his utter contempt for money. True, Anytus had heard similar protestations before: many unsuccessful men cloaked their envy of the success of others in that feigned disdain. But Socrates had gone beyond it. He had gone beyond declaring that he himself was not concerned with riches. He had implied boldly that a man's striving for them jeopardized his love of the commonweal and prevented him from being a just man.

Anytus could have sworn a sacred oath that the sight of the smoke plumes ascending from the temples uphill had gratified him solely as a man intent on seeing Athens return to her wholesome old ways. Moreover, compared with what Anytus owned, the profit to be expected from the increased supply of hides was utterly negligible!

But suppose that profit were great enough to make him as wealthy a man as Crito, and suppose he'd known in advance that it must make him that rich; would this foreknowledge have interfered with his thoughts as he pondered Socrates' guilt? And *if* he had been mindful of some such fabulous profit, would he have arrived nevertheless at the right conclusion—to wit, that a revival of traditional piety must be beneficial to Athens, whatever the way it happened to affect her tanners' fortunes?

These were curious questions, even if considered apart from their fantastic premise. They did not stagger Anytus. His wish to see Socrates run for his life seemed to have inured him to thoughts of a kind hitherto alien to him.

Not by any stretch of the imagination could the prisoner's escaping profit the spirit of the Athens for which Anytus had fought. Surely the criminal's self-exile, no matter how pathetically pictured, could not warn men more effectively against lawless innovations than would his lawful execution. His flight could afford Anytus himself neither profit nor honor. On the contrary. Even after casting aside Cinesias' trumped-up warnings, the tanner had to ask himself whether the escape of a convicted felon he himself had brought to trial might not destroy his reputation as a man who meant what he said and carried through what he meant.

Thus, his wish was downright paradoxical. But so, measured by the standards Anytus had lived by and prospered through, was the root of that wish—his burning desire to know more about himself than his eyes and ears had taught him to take for granted.

X I I

At about the time Anytus, burdened with a problem he would have deemed completely unreal less than a month before, went back to his tannery work, Meletus the poet entered the Piræus.

This was his first visit to the harbor town since the day of the trial. Most of the time since that day he had stayed in his dingy house near the street of the potters, devoting himself to his *Marsyas*—the unfinished tragedy that he had abandoned shortly after Anytus drew his attention to Socrates' "monstrous transgressions." Alas, since buckling down to his work again, he had made little headway, constantly though he had reminded himself that he was not, after all, cut out for a public career, and that a stage success was still the goal he must strive for.

He had also kept in mind how important it was that he finish his drama, and finish it soon. Within the coming month the magistrates would decide which of the plays submitted to them were to be produced in Dionysus' honor this year, with some rich man, in each case, "giving the author his chorus." Meletus had mentioned his *Marsyas* repeatedly to Anytus during the months of their association, hopeful that the tanner might influence the magistrates in favor of the drama once it was ready, or even volunteer to pay for the chorus himself; and Anytus had listened to him benignly. Therefore, the snail's pace at which his work was progressing disheartened Meletus doubly. For Anytus' cordiality toward him was on the wane—to put it mildly!

Directly after the trial, Anytus, walking away, had wished his two associates a good-night; and not once in the nineteen days since had he asked Meletus to his house—Meletus, the spokesman of their common complaint, the man who, when all was said, had borne the brunt of Socrates' fiendish skill in the court!

Meletus was not unaware of the errors that had crept into his oration, and he suspected Anytus of blaming him for the appalling margin on the first ballot. Given the opportunity, he would have refuted that view, or at least told the tanner that only the vulgarity of the rabble had unsettled his speech at some of its turns. But no such opportunity had arisen.

When one day after another had passed without his receiving word from Anytus, Meletus had begun to look forward with waxing impatience to Socrates' execution. His death, putting the seal of reality upon the sentence, was bound to obliterate its antecedents in court, efface the memory of his main accuser's forensic errors, and restore him, Meletus, to Anytus' good graces.

Such selfish considerations yet left ample room in the poet's heart for an honest desire to see the insulted gods avenged with all the power of vengeance that was the law's. The fickleness of the jury, and the spectators' changing humors, had strengthened immeasurably his confidence in the immutable gods, and his resolution to remain their uncompromising defender seemed to draw him still closer to the solace this faith afforded.

This, then, was the state of mind in which he had set out for the Piræus. He was not fool enough to consider standing on the pier to look out for the Sacred Vessel, as children were doing in a game throughout her absence. Even the most favorable of the winds could not possibly bring the craft home for another five or six days; besides, her arrival was announced regularly a day or two in advance by runners dispatched from Sunium to report that she was about to double the cape. What drew Meletus onto the highway was his feeling that the smells of the harbor town and the sea might enhance his joyous anticipation of the vessel's return, add assurance to his impatience, and benefit his work's progress.

But later, on the road, he had also grown conscious, and most pleasantly so, of his wish to lie with Glycera. He realized that the outcome of the trial was not likely to please her. Even if her sympathy for Socrates, voiced on that other day, stemmed only from her mischievous nature, she, an accuser's victim herself, hardly could be supposed to rejoice in the victory of an accuser. On the other hand, women of her calling were known to side with success; and Meletus, counting on their notorious indifference toward the hazards of a man's road to success, had persuaded himself that Glycera must consider the trial's outcome his personal triumph. He meant to extract not a little pleasure from her new respect for a successful Meletus. He would more than get even with the hetæra! To be sure, her galling oxhides-and-leather tale had long since ceased to discomfit him. He had, in the court, been quite fearful lest that slander should be hurled at Anytus; but when none of the hecklers so much as alluded to it, he had told himself, for the last time, that the "whorehouse rumor" simply must be unknown in Athens. In short, he bore Glycera no grudge on that score. It was different with the humiliation she had inflicted upon his dignity, on his very manhood! The memory of her sending him to the couch of her slave—

the recollection of his obedience—had kept his self-esteem smarting amid all the harder blows dealt it since that hour. Thus, the new docility he assumed in the hetæra lent her image a keenly novel attraction.

The afternoon was warm. The ocean breeze that had met him halfway along the road had failed to cool his forehead. He decided to stop for a short rest at the Great Temple of Artemis, whose steps were a favorite place of the town's gossips waiting for the latest news from the city.

As it turned out when Meletus came closer, the wide steps were empty of men. But not a few had gathered on the upper landing and perron in the shade of the protruding roof of the building. Oddly, none of these men seemed to be looking in the direction of the highway. They had all turned their heads the other way. Ascending the steps, Meletus noticed what was engaging their attention. A troupe of Cretan acrobats was performing at the farther corner of the structure, whose thick roseate-painted columns earlier had cut off the spectacle from his vision.

Having joined the men on the perron, he looked about him. An acquaintance of his, an Athenian, a teacher of music, was standing near by, and Meletus tapped him on the hip, saying: "Waterfront entertainment, eh, friend?"

"Not bad, though," the tall man remarked, barely glancing at Meletus, and shifted his eyes back to the artists and the tight ranks of their spectators.

Arms stretched out sidewise, three of the acrobats had just jumped onto the shoulders of three others, and two boys, naked except for their brilliantly patterned loincloths, now leaped high into the air to grasp the hands of the men above and gain a toe hold upon their shoulders. At the same time other members of the troupe began to turn somersaults, circling the precarious tower of human bodies.

Loud gasps of acclaim rippled through the crowd, and the onlookers on the temple perron threw in their more measured applause. The acrobats jumped down, and after bowing to all sides, were getting ready for some new stunt. But an elderly man who had mounted one of the curbstones was drawing one pair of eyes after another away from the Cretans. In a mountebank's tone at variance with his dignified pose, he announced that he was "not only one" though being one mortal only. He inclined his head to one side in a pretense of straining his ears, and was rolling his eyes below studiedly quivering eyelids—and in the same instant a hollow-sounding voice started sermonizing somewhere about, or within, him, admonishing "all good men" to hearken to the dæmon he asserted was talking out of his own innards.

It was the openmouthed bafflement of some Spartan soldiers in the assemblage, rather than the ventriloquist's tricks—or indeed the balderdash of his "dæmon"—that fascinated the audience, swollen now by those who had drifted away from the Cretans. Still, when the ventriloquist paused, pretending a possessed man's exhaustion, a good many coins were dropped at his feet.

"There's another superhuman voice for you," the music teacher said to Meletus. "Do you plan to complain against the old fellow, too?"

"Your joke is in poor taste," Meletus said, drawing himself up with a jerk.

"Did you say it wasn't to your taste?"

"I said your silly remark was out of place," Meletus declared in a tone loud enough to cap a burst of laughter evoked by something the ventriloquist had said to the Spartans.

"What silly remark?" a husky man wearing a sailor's hat inquired, turning half round, and another, evidently a merchant, pointed a waggling finger at the poet and asked:

"Who, by the dog, is this pompous pygmy?"

"Jokes that trifle with Athenian justice—" Meletus began at the top of his lungs, only to be outshouted at once.

"Why, this pygmy is Meletus, the son of Meletus!" the teacher of music called out—and no sooner had the poet heard his name pronounced than he felt a thwack on the nape of his neck and a blow against his buttocks and a kick against his calves, and before he could open his mouth again, or look to see who his assailants were, he was hustled off the perron, down the whole flight of stairs, and catapulted into the crowd, which a moment before had been thrown into a new fit of laughter by the capering Cretans and the wild yells they let out to deaden the ventriloquist's double-voiced mouthings.

The first thing Meletus became conscious of, besides the pain in his calves, was the total indifference of everybody within his sight to what had happened to him. His hands trembling, he rearranged his tunic and mantle as well as he could in the throng. Gradually craning his head then, he noted that the men up on the perron appeared to be no longer concerned in the least with what he was doing or might have attempted to say.

Say—to whom? The anonymity of the assault, checking any thought of redress, added to its inexplicableness. For inexplicable Meletus insisted on calling the incident to himself. He was about to extricate himself from the mob when he saw a familiar dark-skinned face with eyes staring at him in unbridled glee. The man—Glycera's doorkeeper—stood opposite the temple, a basket bulging with provisions at his feet, and by his side a conspicuously foreign-looking fellow with another pannier and some garlands of roses and violets in his arms. Meletus felt tempted to beckon the doorkeeper over and urge him to hasten home and announce to his mistress that Meletus the poet would be calling on her. But his legs were aching and he bent down to nurse them. When he straightened up, the two men had gone.

Without wasting another glance on anyone about or behind him, he threaded his way through the crowd, which, though still in high spirits, had begun to disperse. His calves seemed to hurt less now. He progressed with prudence, keeping close to the buildings on the left side of the road. After a time—whether short or long he would have been at a loss to tell in his daze—a string of chariots overtook him, and to escape the dust in their wake he nimbly sought refuge in a side-street.

Only after advancing a hundred steps or so into its growing stillness did it come to Meletus that some passersby in the thoroughfare's reckless traffic had shouted at him. He had not grasped their foulmouthed lingo, and now concluded that his dignified, measured gait amid all the bustle must have angered those men.

He wished Glycera were living in Athens again. He also reflected that, instead of wearing himself out on a five-mile march and then being pushed about by uncouth harbor-town idlers, he might have made an attempt to find Anytus in the plaza. Whatever the reason for the tanner's recent aloofness, he would not dare turn his back on him in public! Honestly, it was not fitting that the three men who had in concert prevailed over criminal impiety should that abruptly break the tie of their common purpose. And Lyco had gone—gone out of town, to Platæa.

Meletus did not censure the orator for going on that

journey. A man in Platæa, indicted for wounding a boy
with the intent to kill, had engaged Lyco to coach him for
his defense, and the promised fee would have tempted a
speech-writer of far greater repute than Lyco's. Nor had
Meletus minded the blatant conceit with which Lyco,
coming to say farewell, had boasted of his great new
fame. However, the poet had expected Lyco to drop a
few words about their long conversation on the eve of
Socrates' trial and say that he, Meletus, had put the advice
received to very good use indeed. As it was, the trial
scarcely entered their talk. Not until Lyco was about to
leave Meletus' house did Socrates' name come up, with
the orator mentioning a "certain hearsay." What hearsay? "Oh, about some plan to get Socrates out of the
prison house," Lyco replied; "and, come to think of it,
Meletus, you ought to be on your guard lest a mockery
be made of the sentence." Had the excellent Lyco talked
to Anytus about the danger? "I did not see him in the
square, and knowing the surly manners of tradesmen
when they are busy, I felt no desire to go to his workshop.
You'd better be on your guard yourself, then, that justice
be done to the last," the orator repeated, and all of a
sudden, as though in an afterthought, he lifted his jointly
cupped hands—an imaginary bowl—up to his mouth and,
in a mimicked death struggle, issued a rattling sound and
dilated and contracted his nostrils and finally let his jaw
drop, his tongue dangling. And in the following moment
Lyco had gone—gone on his business trip to Platæa.

Pondering the matter afterward, Meletus had satisfied
himself that the hearsay must have reached Anytus
also, and that, being the man he was, he most assuredly
had alerted the Eleven by now. To apprise him of the
rumor as if it were news would serve no purpose. It also
would be unwise to offer Anytus a chance to say that

such hearsay might arouse public opinion far more than it apparently was doing, if the speech of Socrates' main accuser had made a lasting impression on the men of Athens! In brief, the poet had decided not to force superfluous warnings upon the man who still might be willing, once the *Marsyas* was finished, to pay for the chorus.

Proceeding along the quiet street now, Meletus congratulated himself once again on the cleverness of that decision, and gave himself up to musings about his drama and what it would be like. After a while, a new verse for it fell into his thinking. It was a beautiful line, and he recited it over and over again—under his breath first, then with sonorous loudness—each time moved more by its euphonious perfection, until at length he could not help picturing the audience at the Theater swept by the edifying emotion that line must call forth. So profound was the poet's surrender to this daydream that he failed to notice the circular temple somewhat set back from the street until he found himself in front of the stelæ that stood, in two rows, at the approach to the small building.

He mounted the three steps to enter. But the oaken door was locked, and Meletus sat down on the stone floor of the narrow circular porch, gingerly because of his aching limbs. He slipped off his sandals, put his back against the wall, and stretched out his legs. The sun hurt his eyes. "These foreign acrobats!" he said to himself indignantly, "and that foolish ventriloquist! Was not public merrymaking while the Sacred Ship was away, though not strictly unlawful, frowned upon in the old days?"

He thought of Lyco again, and then of Lyco's speech in the court, and then, once again, of his own, and then it occurred to him that he had not once in the nineteen days past stopped to consider the wounded pride of those one hundred and forty-one among Socrates' judges willing to spare his life, and he told himself, moved anew, that enjoying the hurt feelings of men who'd opposed him did not seem to be in his nature. Probably it was not in poets to resent their fellow men's mistakes and their indecision! And with that observation, the new verse for his *Marsyas* floated back to his mind, this time trailing a second beautiful line and a third and a fourth—which at last made him perceive that these were all verses written by Sophocles, his departed great confrere. "What pranks a poetry-lover's memory plays on a poet," he said to himself dreamily, and clasped his hands behind his neck and cushioned his head in the bend of his right arm. Though fatigued, he did not feel bad, and even smiled as he half closed his eyes. He would get to Glycera's in time for the meal. He wouldn't allow her this time to indulge her fancy by spinning a yarn, and would brook none of her second-hand Sophistry either —so he resolved with firmness. He felt like changing his posture, but a sharp pain in the small of his back stayed the movement, and he remained as he was. . . .

When he looked up again, the sun stood low in the sky. A flock of children were playing in the street. Their shrill voices must have wakened him. For, by Hercules, he had dropped off! "All to the good," he mumbled while at the same time he started rubbing his neck. Then, leaning forward to put on his sandals, he noticed a rakish-looking man with a cock under his arm who was lolling against one of the stelæ, staring at him.

"Lost your way, stranger?" the fellow called over to him.

"By no means," Meletus, after clearing his throat, called back, and scrambled to his feet. Before stepping down from the porch, he blew his nose. "I know precisely where

I am, my good man," he said with marked animation and, looking straight ahead, strode by the man with the rooster.

He did not feel tired the least bit. The air was pleasant. The Piræus was not such a bad place, after all, he was saying to himself, enjoyably mindful of his destination. Why, nothing really had happened to him in front of the Artemis temple! He had not been set upon, really. Some men put in good humor by a bunch of enter-tainers had jostled him about a little, no doubt provoked by his conspicuous contempt for the cheap performance. Good gods, who didn't know of the practical jokes of Piræic roughnecks! Poor Glycera!

His impatience to get into her presence seemed to sharpen his sense of orientation. He swung into an alley, guessing that it would lead him toward the neighborhood of her home. And in actual fact it was not long before he had reached the street on which her house stood. He walked on at a brisk pace, whistling through his teeth.

He had been strutting along for a short time, nose in air, when a succession of oddly ornamented footprints caught his eye on the ground. But the tiny sparks kindled by the sun on the sand blurred the peculiar pattern each time he focused his glance on one of the imprints. His curiosity aroused, he finally made a halt to bend over one of those marks—and almost at once emitted a faint cry of surprise, having spelled out the words "FOLLOW ME" left on the soft ground by the sole of a woman's sandal.

He chuckled and even snapped his fingers, so much did the newfangled streetwalkers' trick amuse him. Yet, con-tinuing on his way, he was not concerned with what that lowly sister-in-calling of Glycera's, who evidently was plying her trade near by, might look like. In fact, he at first failed to connect the telltale signs on the sand with the female shape that he saw, after advancing some more, emerge from the recess of one of the buildings.

The woman was walking with mincing steps, obviously hampered by the outlandish gown she wore, whose garishly patterned wide skirt fell from her astoundingly narrow waist down to her unseen feet. A saffron-colored veil fluttered about her shoulders.

Still chuckling, if rather studiedly, Meletus could not tear his eyes off the woman. She was about fifty feet ahead of him now, but the distance decreased. It occurred to him that she might belong to the Cretan troupe—and some very special stories about the harlots of Crete started hammering at his imagination.

Suddenly she was walking faster, as if eager to hurry past the bay trees to her left and the building behind them; and Meletus, at its door directly the woman had passed it, recognized Glycera's house.

He was on the point of calling the doorkeeper, when the woman made a motion as though to look back over her shoulder, and then, as if on the spur of the moment, lifted her arm in a curious manner and, with a swish of her skirt, disappeared into a lane on the right side of the street.

He went after her, entering the dim passage, which was no wider than the span of a man's arms. She had stopped and spun round to face the pursuer . . . and Meletus beheld, to his profound amazement, her breasts, which protruded from her tight bodice, totally bare in their roundness.

She contemplated his speechlessness, smiling.

It was Glycera's slave.

"The goddess is good to me," she said with a faint voice.

He had to swallow hard before saying: "Why, you little cheat—"

"I cannot linger here," she breathed.

He did not know what to say next. Had Glycera fallen on such evil days that she would send a slave girl out on the street, as aging hetæræ sometimes did? It could not be—

"I cannot stay here, Meletus," the girl repeated and went on to explain, as though she had read his mind, that her mistress was ignorant of this escapade.

"I won't betray you," he said with unsteady lips. He had meant to put standoffish reproval into his voice, but mechanically adopted her whispering tone.

She drew closer.

The scent of her skin threatened to bemuse him, and he retreated a step and asked severely where she'd come by this outrageous attire of hers.

She shrugged.

"You sly little strumpet . . ." he kept muttering with a forced scowl.

"Did I not please you the other day, my sweet Meletus?"

He did not have the strength to disclaim the memory. It already had seized upon him with a power stronger than the mere pictures of recollection.

She started slinking toward the farther end of the passage, and keeping close at her heels, he said: "I strongly advise you to return to the house. Remember that the police never fail to apprehend a runaway slave. Your mistress is likely to have you thrashed soundly. I'd hate to see these shapely buttocks of yours flogged—"

She interrupted him with a giggle. Having reached the corner of the lane, she extended an arm to point out a high sepulchral monument that rose, at some distance, over a matted hedge of laurel.

He let out an exclamation of indignant refusal. In the fading light, the place she was pointing to offered a hidden spot such as the lowest of prostitutes were known to take their customers to, foreign sailors, waterfront laborers, scum—

A shaft of the sinking sun fell aslant her naked bosom. His name dropped from her lips in a coaxing sigh.

"What of it?" rushed through his head. "I would not be hers—she would be mine."

She made an almost imperceptible motion that brought her hands close to his thighs.

"No!" he said to himself, shaking off her hand. "A Meletus does not play around with her sort in dark nooks. Certainly not a Meletus who carried the day in the Great Court and who is destined to win greater and grimmer fame still once the Sacred Vessel makes port." But the thought of that day at once played havoc with his resolve to rebuff the woman. The submissive expectancy on her face made him relive the feeling of limitless power that had been his on that other day as he had lorded it over her body; and the lure of this sensation seemed to hold out the assurance that no one and nothing could cheat him of his final and lasting triumph. Like the image of a nightmare past, the gossip about Socrates' planned escape flashed through the poet's confusion, and following the slave girl out of the lane, he saw himself, with his mind's suddenly unclouded eye, watching the prison house day and night—the truest guardian of the gods' honor.

X I I I

Glycera's doorkeeper had rushed home immediately after watching the humiliation of Meletus in front of the temple of Artemis.

The doorkeeper had been sent to the market with a servant of the hetæra's present houseguest—a Thessalian gentleman by the name of Phocion—and certainly should not have lingered in the street to gape at entertainers. He thought it politic, under the circumstances, to confess his fault to Glycera. For he supposed Meletus to be on his way to the festive meal in preparation at the house and feared that the garrulous poet, in describing the incident, might refer to him as a witness. Moreover, the dark-skinned slave had overheard his mistress ridiculing Meletus with gusto on a recent occasion, and surmised that an account of his rough handling by apparently like-minded folk would please her.

As soon, then, as the man encountered Glycera, he started with his report. But she, far from being amused, flew into a rage and slapped his face.

The news that Meletus was on his way to her house alarmed her. She realized that having him come upon her three guests would be nothing short of disastrous, and at once made up her mind to try to keep him away. Instead of rejoining the gentlemen engaged in weighty talk in the courtyard, she withdrew to her chamber; and it was not long before a scheme meant to thwart the unwelcome visit had matured in her mind.

As it happened, she had only the day before purchased a curious garment from some Cretan buffoons who'd come a-begging to her with a tearful tale about their one woman performer's death on the voyage. Glycera, then, had her young slave girl brought to her and set to work dressing her in that garment, apparently an archaic costume. The attire—which, as the hetæra put it in relating the exploit to her guests some hours later, "must attract even a blind man's attention"—proved to fit the young thing very well. While informing the girl of what was expected of her, Glycera also recalled a pair of "talking sandals" she owned—a keepsake of her late mother's—and she fetched the old Corinthian footgear and had the slave put them on.

She would recognize Meletus the poet, would she not? Well, he was likely to think himself a man of great consequence now—never mind why—and therefore reluctant to trade a Glycera's company for that of a woman walking the streets, however alluring. To waylay the puffed-up fellow might not be easy. The girl must apply every artifice taught her. If need be, she might go so far as to promise Meletus her favors for nothing. Nor must she release him any too soon once he was lying with her. She must submit to his every whim. None could possibly hurt her more than would the merciless whipping at home—her punishment should she fail! Finally Glycera led the girl out into the back yard and to its door, and sent her off to "play the Sirens' part to this half-size Ulysses."

Indubitably the intrigue, though born of apprehension, had amused Glycera more and more while she proceeded with those preparations. Delight in mischief,

rather than any pride in her ingenuity, tinged the tale as
she told it—with success assured, that was true. For
neither had Meletus appeared at the door nor the slave
girl returned, and the evening's shadows were already
shrouding the head of the little statue that Glycera could
see outside the hall's half-curtained door.

The meal was over. One of the slaves of the Thessalian
was mixing and spicing the wine and kept pouring it
for his master and for Critobolus and Glycera.

Crito, lying on the couch facing hers, was not drinking.
Although he was looking at the hetæra across the flower-
strewn low table, he had stopped listening to her story;
and from time to time his glance strayed to the manly face
of Phocion. It had always inspired him with affection.

Phocion was the son of a propertied man who, for many
years prior to his decease, had been connected with Crito
by the bond of mutual hospitality. Phocion, an athlete of
distinction, had himself been Crito's guest on some occasions, and also his host in Thessaly on some others.

Upon receiving Crito's urgent invitation, he had
without delay set forth on the journey to Athens. It had
been slowed by the springtime slush on the mountain
tracks and, later, by a gang of robbers (who did not live
to rue their foolhardiness); and Critobolus had been kept
waiting for the Thessalian's arrival for two solid days,
cooling his heels on the highway beyond the Acharnian
Gate.

The thought of welcoming Phocion outside the city was
his own. "Is it true, my father," he had asked Crito,
"that your entire property might be seized as a penalty
for your having done what you intend to do?" That
might be the punishment, Crito replied, should he be
accused and judged guilty; however, anyone making
such a complaint would have to prove it. "Would he not

prove it by saying: 'Socrates is known to be staying in Thessaly, living in the house of a certain Phocion, and this Phocion, an athlete familiar to not a few Athenians, was Crito's houseguest on the eve of the prisoner's flight'?" This might be admitted as proof in court. "Why, then, bring the Thessalian to your house, my father," Critobolus suggested, "or to mine, for that matter? He would be far less conspicuous at the Piræus, and least so in the home of some foreign woman. I happen to know one of them fairly well—that Corinthian banished from the city for the alleged theft of a necklace. She is a shrewd person and can be confided in, too." And Crito, the noble Crito, had agreed to the plan.

It had worked out well. Phocion appeared to have taken a fancy to the woman, and as he was a generous man, as well as handsome and virile, her affection for him was not hard to explain. It did not, however, explain her enthusiasm for Socrates' projected rescue. Being a party to it was risky for her. To be sure, only a citizen could be indicted for persuading a man in the city's employ to connive in an illegal act that involved his duties. Still, the men of popular rule, if such was their wish, would know how to wreak their vengeance upon a woman with a criminal record. They might get some wretch of an informer to denounce her for some vaguely defined transgression—perhaps for procuring—and ruin her completely.

All this was rushing through Crito's head while the woman's lively voice fell on his ears. He could not help comparing her indifference to the peril she must have discerned with his own swift acquiescence in the cautious scheme of his son. No matter how firmly he told himself that this caution, since it helped keep their plan a secret, also heightened the chances for its success, he continued to feel uneasy. The beautiful smile that had brightened his face when the hetæra commenced her account had, as she concluded it with a peal of laughter, given way to a tense and tormented expression. Only with the merest nod of approval did he support his son's praise for Glycera's inventiveness and her wit.

Phocion leaped to his feet as soon as she fell silent, stepped behind her couch, and leaned down to embrace her and kiss her on the mouth.

"Now, my lord Crito," she said after disentangling herself from Phocion's caresses, "I beg you to proceed with your instructions."

"There is nothing left to instruct our Phocion about," Crito said. "He knows where to wait for Socrates before daybreak—"

"On what day, though?"

Crito, who had been lying on his back, turned sidewise and propped up his elbow to support his raised head. "You will be told in time," he said dryly.

"I heard a sea captain say," Glycera remarked, "that the new sail of the Sacred Vessel should bring her in far sooner this year than expected."

"The runners from Cape Sunium—" Critobolus tried to throw in, but his father stopped him short:

"As I was saying, Glycera, someone will come to your house in good time to notify our Phocion," and to stress the finality of his words, he nodded several times. But the apparently uncontrollable motion of his head seemed to change into a sign of wonderment and even regret, and at the same time Crito's eyes went out to his son, who had risen from his couch and gone to the little altar as if to contemplate there the charred remains of the offering laid down before the dinner.

"I shall defer to your judgment, my Crito," Phocion

was saying. "Yet permit me to ask a question. You told us the jailer was as good as yours. I admit I fail to appreciate fully the activities of those informers—"

"In free Athens, eh?" Glycera intervened. "Athenians, my sweet Phocion, have no master over them save their informers!"

Crito signaled Phocion to go on.

"As for those informers, then. Did you not say yourself, Crito, that the best thing to do was to give them their bribe on the spot? Didn't you say that it could not be foreseen which of them would be there? At any rate you don't seem to doubt that they too are yours for the asking. Why, then, do you hesitate to decide on the day of my departure with Socrates? Why do you hesitate to say: 'Tomorrow'?"

"We friends of Socrates have grown used to leaving decisions to him, Phocion."

"Why, then, does *he* hesitate to say: 'Tomorrow'?"

Critobolus spun round. "He doesn't know of our plan yet!" he burst out, heedless of his father's gestured protest.

"What makes you reluctant to inform him?"

"Socrates—" Crito said after another pause, "Socrates might be afraid of harming others by his escape. He has, for one thing, grown fond of the turnkey, a whimsical man—"

"Were you not assuring us yourself that this turnkey will be taken into hiding somewhere and kept there until the excitement dies down and he can be guided safely out of the city?"

"Such is our intention. The Theban I mentioned—or did I not? Simmias, his name is—has already arranged for such a hide-out. But there are others Socrates might fear he'd get into trouble. Critobolus. And me, too."

"Would he?" Glycera asked.

"Not if my father will do as I have suggested," Crito-bolus said. "Not if he'll do as Simmias the Theban and his friend Cebes have been suggesting all along. Being foreigners, they could not be indicted for bribing the jailer. They have offered to pay him out of their own funds."

"Well, in that case no harm whatever can come to anyone!" Phocion exclaimed. "Is that not so? Can you not, my Crito, convince Socrates—"

"It has always been hard to convince him of something of which a man may strive to persuade him," Crito broke in, and as the Thessalian shook his head in bewilderment and looked toward Critobolus and back again at his father, Crito averted his face and picked his tall staff up from the floor and stood up and returned the smile of the hetæra, who had asked:

"Do you feel tired, my lord?"

He said that he apparently was no longer used to rich meals, and when Phocion mentioned one of his slaves who, being a physician, carried a draught for an upset stomach in his bag, Crito waved the offer aside and, still smiling, said that he merely wished to get a breath of fresh air—"my habit at this hour, as my son will affirm." And glancing at Critobolus with a twinkle, he walked to the door, stepped out into the dusk, and advanced to enter the eastern colonnade of the yard, setting his staff before him at every step.

But as he began to walk back and forth, the end of the staff sometimes trailed behind him over the flagstones of the portico—and then he would grasp it more firmly again and angrily square his shoulders.

In the hall, the conversation had been resumed. The evening breeze ran through the foliage of the trees outside the wall, and Crito sniffed the air, which seemed to carry over to him the smell of the sea, through whose waves, placid or choppy, the Sacred Vessel was voyaging home.

Critobolus' indiscretion had been justified! The loyalty of the Thessalian was deserving of frankness. And as the two younger men appeared to trust the hetæra, her presence should not have interfered with the resolve to tell Phocion the whole truth.

The whole truth? Was not Critobolus ignorant of some of it himself? Socrates' friends had agreed not to take Xanthippe into their confidence at this stage. Yet Crito had gone to see her—though he had gone to Socrates' house merely to tell Xanthippe that neither she nor her sons would want for anything after the death of her husband.

But she had said: "Crito, I know you are determined to save his life. I know you have been making preparations for his escape. No one has told me you have. I myself have not for a moment assumed that you would stand by and watch his destruction. Why have you not come to apprise me of your plans? Did you think me indifferent to them?" He said that he hadn't wished to raise premature hopes. "What did you think I live by but hopes?" she exclaimed. "There is more to consider than our own peace of mind, Xanthippe," he countered with a severity summoned up to hide his emotion. She said: "You haven't informed him either, Crito! I know you have not. You are afraid he will reject your plans. You have kept me in the dark because you fear that Socrates would be even less willing to follow you wherever you mean to take him, if *I* begged him to do, for his family's sake, as you say. I am not angry with you. He has a way of confusing those closest to him and making them doubt the self-evident—and well you know it, Crito!"

They stood in the small back yard, and the two little

ones played noisily inside the house . . . and Crito suddenly recalled that long-ago night when Xanthippe, "little Xanthippe," had stood before him on this very spot and had given rein to her tears while her husband, to elicit a smile from Alcibiades, made game of her and her "goslings" within. How strong she had grown since that night!

"Crito," she was saying, "not one man in Athens would be surprised, and Socrates knows it." Surprised—at what? "And what is more," she proceeded, disposing of his needless query by a frown, "there are few who would not condone his escape into exile." Few though they might be, he said, they were dangerous men. "You do not fear *them,* Crito. It is Socrates whom you fear. You are afraid that he too may have learned no one would be surprised should he get out of his chains and away from the city. For you know as well as I do that my husband detests doing things apt to surprise no one."

Again Crito had no reply ready. Several of Socrates' friends had maintained from the first that his escape would not come as a shock to Athens; and Crito felt relieved hearing Xanthippe confirm that assumption, for a great many women must have talked to Socrates' wife since his trial (and younger men nowadays were not altogether averse to discussing public affairs with their wives). But Xanthippe's assurance about public opinion was rendered worthless by her assertion that Socrates would not consent to let himself be rescued.

Crito could not bring himself to ask Xanthippe: "How can you know Socrates' thoughts so well, since you have not once gone to see him?"

Every morning Socrates' intimates gathered in front of the Royal Hall at sunrise, waiting for word that the gate of the prison compound had been opened. And standing there in the chill of the early hour, wrapped in their cloaks, they would stop their talk whenever a woman came into sight with her slave or with some other woman, wondering whether it was Xanthippe. Never to this day had it been she. But Socrates himself had not once asked his friends to bring her to him; and thus some of them should have rebuked Apollodorus when he cried out one morning: "First the jury condemned Socrates in defiance of justice, now his wife does so in defiance of conjugal devotion!" But not one of the men, and not Crito either, had contradicted the rash Apollodorus.

Perhaps it was that smarting memory which caused Crito to remain equally silent when Xanthippe accused her husband of pride. For that, she went on to say, would be at the root of his refusal to do what nearly everybody expected. "And where," she asked with a bitterness so great it threatened to break her loud nasal voice, "and where will this thing 'pride' be once he is dead? With his Shade, perchance? And will it help his Shade reach up from Hades to feed the children?" Crito said that there was not one ounce of pride in Socrates—not one ounce! But at the same time, following an impulse, he dropped his hands on her shoulders—as he had on that other, long-ago night—and he felt, almost at once, a shudder run through her ample body, while a weird sound rose from her throat, a choked outcry or sob, and she herself, her shoulders sagging, seemed on the point of letting her head sink on his breast.

But her head had been high again in the very next moment, and her tight-lipped countenance set in irrevocable disapproval.

Who was it that once had called her, in jest, "the implacable goddess of common sense"? . . . Crito, still pacing the covered walk of Glycera's courtyard, which now lay in deep shadow, tried to recall the originator of that ambiguous quip—as though the search for that trivial detail could keep away the suspicion that, so he had felt when leaving Xanthippe, must have been growing in him for days.

From the first day on, Socrates had astounded him and all his friends by the way in which he was spending his time in the prison. When alone, he wrote verse—the last thing he would have done before, ever. When his companions were with him, he asked them questions, as was his wont, and listened to their answers only to ask more questions again. But were these questions ever concerned with what had been done to him in the court? They were not! Not one single time, in all those days, had he touched on the verdict against him, or on the penalty it had decreed he must suffer.

Was he loath to add one single word to the many that he had spoken to the men of Athens in court? Had he made up his mind to impress upon them by more than mere words the injustice done him and the wrong done to justice? Did he want the men to perceive with their own eyes, at his bier, what they had done or allowed to happen? Was he, then . . . was he willing to pay with his life for the hope that his death might move Athens' men to mend their ways really?

This was the question, this the suspicion, still too dim for words while Crito had talked with Xanthippe, which, after he left her, had struck terror into his heart. And now, having stopped walking to and fro in the portico and standing near its farther end, his unblinking gaze on the quivering shaft of light from the hall, where the lamps had been lit—now he found himself wishing that Xanthippe were right, so that he could say to Socrates: "Everything is ready for your escape. Overcome your pride." For how could he say to him: "Overcome your concern with the ways of your fellow Athenians" without being told: "That, Crito, I never shall do"?

Crito passed his hand over the wreath of his white hair and over his forehead and temples, and closed his eyes for a long weary moment. When he opened them again, he saw his son standing in the illuminated doorway.

Glycera's sudden laughter broke the stillness, and then Phocion's voice could be heard, thick with annoyance, and then another burst of Glycera's laughter.

The old man stepped out of the colonnade, waving a hand toward his son.

"You are angry with me," Critobolus said, coming nearer. "You were worried lest the Thessalian should inquire the reason for your reluctance to inform Socrates of our plans. Phocion asked no such question, though, and I do not think that he would have asked any even if you had stayed inside. I believe he feels that, whatever the answer, he would not grasp it. And how indeed could he, who knows so little about Socrates and his ways, understand your hesitancy?"

"Do you understand it, Critobolus?"

"I do," Critobolus replied; and as Crito, his head low, and clutching his silvery beard, kept his silence, Critobolus said with a rapid voice which could not fully conceal his awareness that it was not a son's business to force advice on his father: "What you must tell Socrates is this: 'When you were saying in court: "I shall suffer the penalty of death, abiding by the sentence passed upon me"—when you were pronouncing these words, Socrates, you were talking to unjust men and you were justly indignant. Surely what a man says to unjust men does not bind him.' That, my father, will disprove Socrates' view that he must live up to those words."

"If we agree on the premise—" Crito began, but his perplexity deadened the rest of his sentence. Was his own, and Xanthippe's, surmise that Socrates would say no to the proposition of rescue shared by all those who knew and loved him? And had each of them hidden his dread all these days from all the others? And how many theories about the motive of the dreaded refusal had ripened among them? The irony of the situation nearly seduced Crito to chime in with Glycera's laughter, which had grown louder, even though the Thessalian seemed to be remonstrating against her gaiety now.

"They have been drinking hard," Critobolus said, following his father, who had started walking toward the doorway.

Phocion stood in front of the hetæra's couch, his arms folded across his breast, and his somber expression contrasted not a little with the wreath of roses which Glycera must have put on his head and which had slid down and was tilted over his eyes.

"May I make a third at your jesting?" Crito asked.

"Jesting!" Phocion cried out. He did not object when Critobolus, coming to him straight from the door, took the flowers off his head. "You did not hear, my excellent Crito, what this woman proposes to do!"

Glycera stood up from her couch. "Will you lie down, my lord?" she asked. "And will you permit me to sit by your side? I need your help, your protection."

"If Crito should say there's any sense in your scheme—"

"Let her talk, Phocion," Crito said as he accepted the cup of wine the hetæra had brought him. "Let her expound her project herself. Perhaps she too will give me good counsel. Eh, Critobolus?"

"What is that project of yours?" Critobolus, turning crimson, asked Glycera. "What is it about?"

Crito sat down on the edge of the couch.

"Meletus," the woman said.

"What about him?"

"He must be lured away from Athens before you take Socrates out of the prison and guide him through the Acharnian Gate."

"Why Meletus?" Phocion threw in heatedly. "Why not this tanner, surely the far more powerful of the two?"

"Will you, my lord Crito, tell this wild Thessalian that I couldn't possibly send Anytus the letter I plan to dispatch to Meletus?"

"What letter?"

The hetæra lifted a hand to toss back some ringlets of her golden hair which had loosened. "Oh, something like this," she said. "'In vain, O Meletus, did I try to banish the thought of you from my mind. I treated you shabbily some days ago in the hope that my meanness would make me so deeply ashamed of myself I would not dare face you again. That hope has deceived me. I am longing for your company and willing to hear you berate me as cruelly as I deserve it. But do not punish me by keeping aloof, my Meletus. Come and lie with me.' Could I possibly send such a missive to Anytus? I have never even met the tanner."

Critobolus had grasped Phocion's arms to calm his temper. "What would we gain, Glycera," he asked, "by having Meletus out of the way as long as Anytus is free to have us watched—if that really is the intention of Socrates' accusers?"

"There is no common intention of theirs," Crito said. "Lyco, as we know, left for Platæa, and no one has seen Anytus and Meletus together since the trial. Of that my own informers have assured me. In actual fact, the tanner is said to be busier than ever—"

"Making his profit on the oxhides Socrates' judges provided him with!" Glycera interjected. She had remained standing.

"What oxhides?"

"That is not a lovely story, my sweet Phocion, and our two Athenian friends here might not want it repeated. Although Anytus has brought to grief the man they love most, they yet are prone to doubt the dismal baseness of Anytus' motives. For Anytus too, my Phocion, is an Athenian."

Crito took a sip of his wine before he remarked in a tone subdued but distinct: "I understand you have lived a long time among us, Glycera. Still, I wonder whether you know us."

"Why do you sneer at my father's words, Glycera?"

"Have I done so, Critobolus? The point is I heard them so often. I seem to remember Meletus using them when I saw him last."

"What makes you side with Socrates, Glycera?" Crito asked suddenly.

"Do not a great many people side with him?"

"Athenians, my naïve Phocion," said Glycera, "a great many Athenians! As for myself, Crito, I hate Athenian law courts, and this may be reason enough for me to side with their most recent victim. I hate your law courts and their purveyors," she repeated, draining her cup and at the same time lifting the pitcher to pour another drink for the Thessalian, who echoed in a murmur:

"Purveyors—?"

"Complainants, then, plaintiffs, accusers, informers . . . You see, Phocion, Athenian law courts must be fed regularly, and so must the Athenians' hankering for news and excitement and scandal. In the old days, so I was told, it was mainly Athens' allies who were feeding her courts. Their generals and their magistrates and their rich men would be haled into Athens' law courts on the strength of treaties we who are not Athenians may still fail to appreciate. Now, with no allies left to Athens, other special fare must be offered her justice—"

"You should stop drinking!"

"She is not drunk," said Crito to his son in a very low voice. "Nor do I believe that her hatred of law courts alone has turned her into a party to our undertaking."

"Whatever it was," the hetæra called out, a smile breaking out from her eyes and around her mouth, "it cast me into the strong arms of this Thessalian. Look at his glowering face, my lord Crito. We will have to shackle his hands unless we want him to kill Meletus."

"You seem to be convinced that Meletus—"

"Oh, my Critobolus," she said over her shoulder, having thrown her arms about Phocion's neck, "how little you know about weaklings!"

"Is there any sense in what she proposes, then?" the Thessalian inquired across the head of Glycera, who was trying to gag him with her caresses.

With an abrupt motion, Crito stood up. Throughout the general bantering, as well as the woman's outburst, the most contradictory reflections had crowded his brain. Phocion's final query restored clarity to his thoughts. It made him realize that, whatever Xanthippe's suspicion or Critobolus' or his own, he had not in truth despaired of Socrates' willingness to let himself be rescued. A score of arguments seemed to be rushing to his mind, each persuasive and sound and valid enough to be heeded by the beloved man in the prison! "There is a great deal of sense in Glycera's suggestion," he declared with authority as soon as she had let go of the Thessalian. "I have been troubled myself by the thought of Meletus. One never can guess what his sort will do next."

"Very true," Critobolus said. "One has only to think of his silly attempt to read a Pindaric ode to the jury."

"Did he do that, the dirty little cribber? Pindar, of all the poets!"

"Do you dislike his work, my clever Glycera?" Crito asked. "Pindar was not an Athenian, you know. Yet it was he who wrote: 'O Athens shining white, and violet-crowned and celebrated in song—' "

" 'Fortress of Greece and her glory, the god's own city . . .' " the hetæra joined in, arching her brows high and opening her arms, fingers spread, in a gesture whose obvious scorn, however, vanished midway. With a defiant toss of her head, she took her eyes off the unstirring face of Crito, and then clapped her hands twice. "Let the slaves bring us some of the Chian wine. And some more lamps, too. And if it pleases you, my lord, let us listen to music. Surely," she said into the first twangs of the cithara which penetrated the hall, "surely it would not displease Socrates to know that those who want him to go on living cherish life's beauty themselves."

XIV

Socrates had spoken, he himself had spoken! He had, if not in so many words, let his friends know that he would not choose death. "For that is, that must be, the meaning of what he said to Phædo of Elis this morning!" Simmias exclaimed, still out of breath from his hurried ascent of the hill and his search for Crito in the porticoes of the Gate House. He had found him seated on the parapet that enclosed the small precinct of the temple of the Victory-bearing Athena, the gracefully modern edifice perched on the angle of rock jutting out from the plateau, to the southwest, like a bastion.

"What did he say to Phædo?" Crito asked, and, startled though he was, brought a finger up to his lips. No one, to be sure, seemed to be within hearing. But voices rang sharp in the limpid air of the hill, and while the hours for sacrifices and supplications were over, a number of men were still lingering about the Gate House, a mere sixty feet to the north, higher up. Moreover, some of the temple sweepers were known to double as informers; in fact, one of them had earlier followed Crito on his stroll through the maze of votive shrines and statues and outdoor altars and storage buildings.

"It happened this way," Simmias said, stammering with excitement—Crito had motioned him to his side. "Phædo was sitting on the low stool by Socrates' bed, and Socrates, who had just won us over to his view on a certain point, started to stroke Phædo's head, and, in his usual manner, clasped his hair and let it run through his fingers. And then, quite suddenly, he murmured: 'These fair locks must not be cut off, my beautiful Phædo,' and he was no longer looking down at Phædo's bent head, as he had been before, but was gazing up at the aperture in the wall. And then, Crito, then he repeated distinctly what he had first said in a murmur."

"And you assume—"

"Do you not? If he died, Phædo *would* have his hair cut off, would he not, as all of us in common decency would. The implication is clear! Oh, you should have been present!"

"Who was?"

"Apollodorus and Hermogenes and Cebes and I myself," the young Theban replied; and as Crito only repeated these names, looking fixedly out on the sea visible across the roofs of the city and the orchards and pastures and vineyards beyond the walls, Simmias gripped his arm and urged him to say whether he *didn't* share his own conviction and Hermogenes' and Cebes' and Apollodorus'.

"And Phædo?"

"Phædo was clumsy. He said: 'I do wish, Socrates, I could keep my hair unshorn.' Whereupon Socrates said with a laugh: 'My dear boy, you seem to forget our last night's discourse and the proof that you advanced shortly before leaving, which you seemed pretty keen on. We are going to resume our argument now, are we not? Well, I know that this proof of yours will die, and so you'll have to mourn it and *will* have to have your hair shorn.' Now did *you* ever hear him use the phrase 'a proof dies'?" Simmias went on, the lowered voice blurred strongly by his Bœotian accent. "None of us had ever heard that figure of speech, and, frankly, we did not think it happy. But we realized that Socrates had coined it in haste and only to turn his earlier words into a joke. Perhaps he had expected us to call out: 'Phædo's hair will remain untouched, Socrates, for you will not die in this prison,' and was embarrassed at our lack of response. Actually, Apollodorus, for one, *would* have burst out, if we others had not restrained him, keeping in mind the promise that we gave you."

Crito had begun drawing small squares and circles on the gravelly ground with his staff.

"Why do you remain silent?" Simmias asked and irritably put his hand on Crito's staff.

"You say that he announced his decision not to choose death," Crito said slowly without glancing at the Theban. "I believe he did not. He may have meant to say that, being human, he was saddened by the thought of his approaching end."

"Must he not therefore choose life if offered the choice?"

" 'Therefore,' Simmias, 'therefore'? A man may hate to depart from a place and nonetheless leave it."

"Some of us *were* convinced that he longed to be rid of the tribulations of life, to quote his own words in court. To live among men so closed to reason as his fellow Athenians may indeed become unbearable to a man. That disgust, so some of us felt, had made Socrates tired of life—so some of us *had* felt until this morning. But now— You are not listening to me, Crito," Simmias interrupted the rapid flow of his words. For all their intensity, he had spoken with no great assurance. "What are you thinking about?"

"The Sacred Ship."

"So am I, Crito! So are we all, day and night. Time presses. The ship sailed twenty-seven days ago. Not in the

memory of men, I have been told, has she been away for
so long, and though there are those rumors about contrary
winds off the eastern islands, and though no one can tell
how good that new sail of hers really is—"

"The memory of men! How long, I wonder, was she
away when Theseus sailed her to Crete?"

"Did you say Theseus?" Simmias asked on a note of
surprise.

"So I said. You see, my Simmias, this is the very spot
on which Theseus' father stood to look out for the craft
and her sail." And ignoring the young man's exclamation
of undisguised impatience, Crito began to retell the ancient
story about the tribute that the city had had to deliver to
Crete every ninth year in those faraway times—seven
youths and seven maidens—and about noble Theseus and
his resolve to die rather than watch these victims being
thrown to the Cretan monster, that creature part bull and
part human. "But I am certain you know all that and also
know that Theseus slew the horrible creature with the
help of the Princess Ariadne and thus put an end to the
abomination. What you may not know, however," he said,
raising his hand, "what you may not know is the story
of Theseus' father. Theseus had promised that he would
hoist a white sail on the homeward voyage should he succeed in killing the monster—whereas, should he perish in
the bold venture, his shipmates would leave untouched the
dark sail the ship had set out with. But after the loss of the
charming Ariadne (this is another story again), Theseus
in his grief forgot his promise. And when his father, from
up here, saw the vessel drift into the bay with her dark
sail, he thought that Theseus was dead, and he threw himself down from this cliff." Crito pointed his staff at the
edge of the tawny limestone platform and the fearsome
precipice yawning below. Then he said: "When you came,

Simmias, it just had occurred to me that now this self-same vessel—"

"The selfsame?"

"Never mind, Simmias. To us who are getting on in years, the mist that envelops those times and their men seems to grow thinner and thinner. You may say that older men are prone to slip into those ancient tales much as an artist does into an ancient pattern. But perhaps it is the tales that slip into them. . . . Older men seem to breathe more easily in the knowledge of the vast spaces of time's endless circle. . . ."

"You do not wish to answer my question," Simmias said with a subdued growl, snapping out of the bewilderment into which Crito's digression had cast him.

It was true that Crito, unable to explain Socrates' words, had embarked on retelling the age-old myth to evade Simmias' prodding. Also, he did not quite like the thought that Socrates should have opened his heart to Phædo alone.

A native of Elis, Greek land siding with Sparta in the latter stage of the war, this Phædo had been taken prisoner in one of its last battles, and then had been a slave of his captor in Athens. A change in that man's fortunes had brought Phædo up for sale after a couple of years or so; and Socrates, strolling past the slave market with Crito one day, had asked him to buy the young Elian and manumit him, so deeply had his handsomeness and his poised demeanor struck Socrates on the spot. Crito had done as bidden. And within a few months the extraordinary gifts topping Phædo's beauty had made Crito admire the great perspicacity of his old friend. Phædo had little schooling; yet by now he seemed to follow Socrates' discourse with profound understanding.

Crito had always been conscious of the quicker and surer grasp others had, when compared with his, of the hidden meaning of Socrates' talk and its more subtle aspects; and only the down-to-earth parlance Socrates was partial to had alleviated those misgivings. But ever since the trial Socrates' language had more and more risen above that plainness. Images of tradition would crowd into his speech and seem to assume a new meaning, and sometimes he seemed eager to push beyond the very limits of words. The wider Socrates' talk had ranged, however, soaring higher and higher, the more firmly had Crito kept his own thoughts down to earth and warned himself to apply them solely to the task of Socrates' rescue.

Now, growing aware of how far his own thoughts threatened to roam, Crito could not but wonder whether that single-mindedness he'd admonished himself to hold fast to had not begun to falter under the strain of these days. So he said, somewhat gruffly, that he could see no gain in guessing the true meaning of Socrates' words to Phædo, and added curtly: "We will know his mind soon now."

"When, Crito—when?"

"Do not make common cause with my son, who reproaches me for not yet having forced Socrates to speak his mind. Or do you suspect me of wavering? Surely I could not say to Socrates: 'Such and such are our preparations, I beg you to leave this place,' before knowing where we want him to go."

"Did I not suggest he might go to my own city?"

"Did I not tell you that Socrates might not be welcome in Thebes? The men of your city came to respect Anytus when he lived among them—so you have told me yourself —and might not think any too highly of a man Anytus calls a felon. Anyway, we decided on Thessaly then, did we not? And need I remind you that my Thessalian friend did not arrive until recently—"

"Eight days ago!"

"I didn't see him until the day after—"

"Seven days have passed since, Crito!"

"So you do blame me! Do you not see . . . don't you all see that Socrates must be overborne, must be rushed into choosing life just as the jaws of death are about to close over him? I had to postpone my talk to the last possible moment, Simmias. This is the course I made up my mind to hold fast to, as I returned from the Piræus."

"Why did you not breathe a word to any of us about that decision? Why, in fact, did you make all of us promise you once again we would not broach the subject in Socrates' presence?"

"You are all superior to me in reasoning, Simmias," Crito said. "But reasoning alone will not prevail over his hesitation, whatever its motives may turn out to be. Was it perhaps reason that made him defy death in court?"

"To defy death is one thing," Simmias rejoined, "to choose it when life beckons is an altogether different matter. For a soldier to say: 'I shall not surrender and ask for mercy though my doom is certain'—such conduct is not without reason. It still may turn the tide of the battle, and at any rate will keep unsoiled the name of a warrior surviving defeat. But who ever heard of a defeated soldier telling himself: 'The fight is lost, the battle over, yet I must ask the victor to put me to death'?"

"*Is* the battle over?" Crito asked under his breath.

"Do you, then, dismiss what Socrates said this morning?"

"No. Nor do I belittle what you and the others present read into his words."

"Your son, Critobolus, came in later with Antisthenes," Simmias said, "and Hermogenes and I took them aside and told them what had happened, and they agreed that our interpretation was sound. And so did three or four others of our friends I ran into as I stepped out of the prison house."

"Was Adimantus' young brother among them?"

"Plato? No. He's ill."

Crito stood up. He several times passed his hand over his forehead before, with slow steps, he traversed the short space between the parapet and the outermost edge of the cliff. The wide sweep of the gulf lay resplendent in the unchangeableness of its waters—blue and cobalt-colored, and silvery farther off, as if skimmed by scrolls of mother-of-pearl. Fishermen's boats, moving lightly to the eastward, dotted the surface; a low-sterned outlandish craft lay becalmed in the offing.

"Forgive me for pressing you so hard," said Simmias, who had followed, and now closed his fingers about Crito's elbow.

Crito said that he understood the urgency of Simmias' concern, and then he turned his head toward the rock of Munychia, which obstructed the view of the harbor. The blazing light of the western sky ridged with purple the contours of the rock and the fortress atop it. There were men, so it came to Crito, who apparently did not mind the Spartan garrison on the hill of Munychia when they climbed it to stand up there in the shade of the citadel's ramparts, as men used to do by the hundreds on summery mornings in the old days. They would stand there, those foolish men of today, and, glimpsing Salamis, the Holy Island, would talk about the Persian armada sunk on the bottom of the straits, and about the battle that had saved Athens eighty long years before—

"Do not take offense if I repeat myself," the Theban was saying, "and beg you once again, Crito, to yield to our entreaties. Cebes and I have the money ready for the jailer. Parting with it will be easy for us. You know that my father is a well-to-do man, and as for Cebes—"

"I know of his affluence, as who wouldn't?" Crito interjected with an acerbity born not merely of a rich and generous man's pique at finding others equally open-handed. There was more than that to Crito's vexation. At the trial, shortly before the second ballot, Cebes had tried to sidle up to some of the more poorly clad jurors and slip them some money. The Scythians had shooed him away. His design had been utterly naïve, to begin with; and so Crito had told him when, afterward, Cebes showed the friends the Æginetan gold coins hidden among the figs in the basket that he had carried throughout the proceedings. Recalling that incident now, Crito also recalled his melancholy annoyance at Cebes' assumption that votes were for sale in an Athenian law court.

"Let us two Thebans, then, give the fellow his bribe," Simmias concluded. "Whatever Socrates' reasons for hesitating may turn out to be, should he indeed still be hesitating, this one consideration of his, his fear of getting *you* into trouble—"

Turning his head sharply, Crito raised a warning finger again. A group of rustics had come within earshot. They had stopped near the small temple, and some of them had mounted the parapet, and all of them were arguing, in loud tones, which parts of the famed frieze depicted Greeks fighting with Persians, and which, Greeks fighting with Greeks. Keeping an eye on these men, Creto finally said in a whisper: "Do not worry, my Simmias. He will be informed of your offer."

"When—when?" Simmias asked in an equally muffled voice.

Crito's gaze had traveled past the chattering men. The glare of the afternoon sun lay on the helmeted head of the colossal bronze statue of Pallas Athene which towered over the shining-white marble roof of the Gate House. The tip of the mighty lance upon which the armored goddess was leaning had been bereft of its gilt many a year before; yet a gleam as though of pure gold dazzled the vision of the old nobleman and moistened his eyes. He realized with a pang how intense was his revived awareness of the city's grandeur. It seemed to have stolen into his heart at Glycera's house—

Simmias stood expectant with parted lips.

"Did you see Meletus this morning? Was he slinking about the prison again?"

"No. None of us saw him this morning."

"You see, my boy?" Crito said with sudden animation. "Things work out according to plan. I sent someone down to Glycera yesterday to let her know the time had come—"

"Crito, my Crito!"

"She must have dispatched that amorous missive of hers to Meletus last night, and he no doubt hastened to throw himself into her wide-open arms."

"And Phocion? Did you alert Phocion too?"

"Not yet. He must have moved out of Glycera's house, though, by now."

"You said he wasn't alerted yet."

Crito chuckled. Had not he or Critobolus told Simmias that Glycera called in another woman later that night, a fellow Corinthian of hers living near by? Simmias hadn't heard of that part of the intrigue? Well, then. Egged on by Glycera, this other hetæra, a pretty young person, assured Phocion in no uncertain words that he would be welcome at *her* house should he get tired of the company of a brainy woman. For Glycera had foreseen that she would have to rid herself of the Thessalian before Meletus' arrival. She *was* a brainy woman, Crito declared. There

also was no question about her ability to keep Meletus
from leaving her for the next two or three days or four.
She'd know how to keep him in thralldom—on her couch,
at her table with the cups filled all the time and the hall
resounding with beautiful verses and with music, and then
on her bed again, perchance with a well-trained slave girl
as a third—

"So the time has come at last!" Simmias cut Crito short.
He had attempted several times to interfere with the ver-
bose levity that so ill suited a graybeard.

"Tonight, Simmias," said Crito. The labored smile had
left his face. He had not adopted his frivolous manner for
its own sake, or to humor the persistent young man. He
had taken refuge in it—as though such talk about the
hetæra's professional wiles could blot out his memory of
her jibes at Athenian institutions, together with the memory of his own curious reaction. It had been curious indeed,
hearing himself rebuff her sarcastic hints and extol Athens
with mounting passion—an Athens that had brought to
the brink of destruction the man he loved most! All
through the rest of that night these contradictory feelings
had raged within him, though the resinous wine the hetæra kept pouring for him and the wanton twangs of the
cithara permeating the hall without respite had made his
head heavy and his thoughts slow.

Again and again in the days that had passed since then
Crito had weighed that conflict and wondered how greatly
it would weaken his eloquence should Socrates really say
"No!" And it was the desire to resolve his antagonism of
feelings, this grating discord, that seemed to have drawn
him up the hill, into the hoped-for afternoon solitude of
the acropolis of the city. . . . No solution had come to
him amid its Periclean splendor. But as he said "Tonight"

at long last, he knew as a certainty that his love for Socrates would override all inner conflicts that might plague him.

He looked at Simmias with eyes cleared of the veil which the glitter of Athena's lance had cast over them, and which had kept dimming his sight even while he talked of Glycera's tricks. Although the chattering rustics had retreated from the temple of the Victory-bearing Athena and were on their way back to the Gate House, Crito reproved Simmias by a little frown for the joyous shout and the upflung arms with which he reacted to the one word "Tonight!" Then he said: "You must go down to the prison house now and ask the others to leave at sundown, as you will yourself. And tell the turnkey I shall come before the moon is up. He owes me some gratitude, you know."

"So you have given him the money!"

"Some only. A gratuity meant to strengthen his confidence. Oh, I wouldn't give him his bribe now. We in Athens have learned that bribes mustn't be paid too far ahead of performance. We have learned many things since Pericles' days," he remarked with a bitterness that yet did not cloud the composure of a man about to carry out at long last a great decision. "Come now. I shall go with you up to the Gate House, and there you will leave me behind."

Simmias did not stir. His eyes narrowed, he stared across Crito's head toward the east.

"Come now. Don't start asking questions again."

But Simmias nudged Crito and pointed surreptitiously at the flagstoned road whose winding course led down from the Great Temple of the Virgin, which, from the awesome height of its substructure, dominated the whole expanse of the temple compound. The brilliant colors of the frieze of the enormous building were shimmering in the golden glow of the hour.

Not for a good while could the old nobleman take his eyes off this marvel of the world, which stood out serenely against the azure; and only when Simmias stretched out his arm with a rigid finger did Crito see the man who was hurrying, with a jerky gait, down the road all but emptied of traffic. Two heavily laden donkeys and their driver were trudging far behind him. "Anytus . . ." he breathed.

"And on business too . . ."

"Do you think the asses are his?" Crito said, watching the tanner's progress.

"It does not matter," Simmias muttered absently.

"His son got involved in a waterfront brawl the night I was at Glycera's house, and nearly lost his life in the drunken scuffle. So Glycera's pretty friend told us."

"Anytus doesn't care. He's been heard saying that as far as he is concerned, his son is dead."

"Still . . . Who knows," Crito said, barely moving his lips, "who knows what really lures a man up this hill?"

"Do you wish to avoid him?"

For a moment Crito's shoulders had sagged. But now he drew himself up again, grasped his staff firmly, and started walking.

Simmias, by his side, kept his eyes focused on the advancing tanner, and in low tones vented his detestation of him.

But his mumblings floated past Crito's ears. "If you do not want to think of yourself, my Socrates," so he would say to the beloved man, "think of us who are your friends. Think of what would be said about us should you perish in this prison. We would be accused of callousness. Men would even say we lacked courage." Thus he went on to call to mind all the reasons likely to impress as valid a man concerned, as all good men were, with the good name of his friends. But at this moment Simmias, who happened to have stepped ahead a little, halted abruptly—and Crito saw Anytus standing on the uppermost of the three steps that, hewn out of the rock, connected the flagstoned road with the pathway to the Gate House.

The statuary clustered at the end of the road had concealed Anytus on the last leg of his approach. Apparently he had halted some moments before. He stood still, his arms akimbo, looking down at the two men without in the least bending his head. His face showed no surprise; perhaps he had espied Crito's tall figure and silvery beard from high up and was prepared for the encounter.

"*Chaire,* Anytus," said Crito.

Anytus responded in an expressionless voice. As he shifted his glance to Simmias, Crito believed that he noted in it a flicker of troubled compassion.

Except for the unceasing murmur of the breeze, hardly any sound interfered with the silence of the three men. The donkeys were no longer to be seen; their driver must have led them off the road onto a short cut.

"I take it," the tanner began with marked slowness, "you are planning to return to your native town soon, Simmias—"

"A town well known to you, Anytus!"

Anytus came down a step. "You are going to tell a long tale to your father, I take it."

"The news will travel ahead of Simmias," Crito threw in, astonished at his own calm.

"Still Simmias is likely to give his own version—"

"I shall tell my father the truth. The truth, Anytus!"

"Yes, Simmias. . . . Your father might say then: 'I can see why you came to dislike Anytus so strongly. But he, my son—did he dislike you with similar strength?' To that you ought to say no, Simmias, if you wish to be truthful."

"My father is most unlikely to inquire after your feelings, Anytus, great though his concern with your feelings was when you lived as his guest in Thebes."

"This is what I am driving at, Simmias. Suppose your father asks you: 'Did not Anytus appreciate the extent of your love for your teacher? Did he not realize that great harm to *him* would also hurt you greatly? Could it be that he did not think of the good done him in my house five years ago?' "

" 'Little do you know his kind, my father'—this would be my answer to any such question."

Anytus shook his head, while his glance for the barest moment strayed toward Crito. "If you meant what you said about telling truth, Simmias, you must say this to your father: 'Anytus will never forget the good that you did him. He swore to that within sight of Athena's Great Temple. Then he said to me: "When your father dissuaded his countrymen from delivering me and my fellow exiles to Sparta, he virtually saved Athens. Surely we exiles never could have joined battle with the infamous Thirty had we fallen into the hands of the Spartans. Others, it is true, might have mustered up the courage some day and overthrown the Tyrant. Still, that thought does not detract from the good that your father did us. He was our benefactor. He turned out to be the benefactor of Athens. But he also was his own city's benefactor. He taught his fellow Thebans to refuse the unjust and lawless requests of the Spartan king. Your father strengthened his fellow citizens' love of their city and its sense of justice. He knows that no man can possibly love his city and yet take its laws lightly. He will understand the love that I feel for Athens' laws and her order." This, my father, is

what Anytus said to me up on the acropolis of his city.'
And this, Simmias, is what you must tell your father unless you do not actually wish to speak truth." The voice
of the tanner, slightly tremulous in the beginning, had in
the end reassumed all of its natural metallic firmness.
His face, caught by a reddish beam of light, seemed to be
struggling against any display of emotion.

" 'This is what Anytus the tanner said to me in order
to mock my despair'— that's what I will tell my father,"
Simmias retorted after a pause, his jaws taut with hatred.

The tanner looked toward Crito again. It could be seen
he was tempted to say something to him. He opened his
mouth twice, wetting his lips with the tip of his tongue.
But then he spun round and stalked away along the upper
road.

"Leaving, Anytus? Leaving to look for your donkeys
and the wares on their backs?" Simmias shouted after him,
and in his anger withdrew from the hand that Crito had
laid on his shoulder.

The altercation had affected Crito in a most equivocal
manner. He could not perceive any purpose in Anytus'
pretense of opening his heart to Simmias. Protesting
gratitude toward his father was senseless under the circumstances. Yet there had been a ring of honesty in
Anytus' appeal to "truth"—if only the honesty of his desire to make his appeal.

"Why is it that men so readily cloak their selfishness
with love of their city?" Simmias asked as soon as they
were walking again. "Why is it that this love, used as a
cloak, seems to convince them at once that they are just
men?"

"Is not any lover likely to think of himself as being beloved? And is not the commonweal supposed to love only
just men?" Crito ventured to reply.

They reached the Gate House in mutual silence.

The sun sat lightly upon its Pentelic marble. The six huge snow-white columns, forming five gateways, were thrown into profile by the shadowy expanse of the great hall behind them; the colonnade at its farther end lay in deep shadow. The projecting wings of the building kept the breeze away from the area in front of the central gateway, where the two men had halted.

"I shall go down now," Simmias said, trying to catch Crito's eye.

But Crito was looking skyward. Inside the hall, the sweepers had suddenly started their work, and the swishing of their brooms had roused a cloud of birds from their perches on the cornices and the architraves of the columns; and Crito, leaning more heavily on his staff, was craning his neck to observe the birds flying seaward.

"Will you stay in this loneliness until sundown?"

Crito put his hand on the arm of the young friend and with the other hand, which held the staff, made a wide gesture. "Do you call this hill lonely?" he asked. He expected no answer. A beautiful smile brightened his countenance as he nodded with deep assurance. He was still nodding after Simmias, having taken his leave without words, had entered the hall.

The fierceness had gone out of the sun, and Crito wrapped his mantle more tightly about him. But he remained standing at the central gateway, whose width bisected the four high steps of the structure.

He was about to sit down on the bottom step when he heard his name called and thrown back by a succession of echoes.

"Crito, hey, Crito," the voice repeated, lower this time though no less pressing.

"Anytus! Where are you?"

"Here . . . here I am," Anytus said as he emerged from behind the easternmost column.

"How have you gotten here so fast by the detour you took?" Crito asked while the tanner darted down the steps toward him.

"Fast, eh? Don't you know I'm supposed to outrun the stench that sticks to my clothes?"

"I am in no mood to exchange jokes," Crito said, eying Anytus. "Nor, let me warn you, in any mood to listen to mockery."

"In what mood are you exactly, Crito?"

"I told you—"

"Or, to put my question more correctly, what are you occupied with? And what, to get to my point, is your great friend occupied with on this balmy day—which, to me, signals the end of those gales rumored to have delayed the return of a certain seagoing craft? Is he basking in contentment, your friend? Does he enjoy spiting the city once more, spiting her for the last time? Is he? Is he, Crito?"

The hoarsened voice, the constantly twitching nose, and above it the perpendicular crease cleaving the lower part of the forehead and suggesting an open gash, so deeply had its edges reddened—to say nothing of Anytus' black scowl and his violent gestures—all this left Crito speechless even after he had stopped gaping at the change that had overcome the tanner since his talk with Simmias. He sensed where Anytus' words were aiming. But he could not account to himself for the reckless desperation ringing through their coarseness. "Spite?" he finally managed to say. "Socrates spiting you—or anyone, for that matter?"

"The city, the city! He's keeping the whole city on tenterhooks!"

"On tenterhooks?" Crito repeated tonelessly.

Anytus laughed. The laughter seemed to come out of him against his will—and of a sudden it dawned on Crito that this crackling guffaw might be reflecting a man's helpless wonder at his own nature.

"He is kept in chains day and night," he muttered.

"Chains or no chains, he'll run for his life, take my word for it. He pretends indecision, right? Right? Perhaps he hopes to extract a promise from . . . from whom I wouldn't know . . . a promise that he'll be recalled from exile, as his darling Alcibiades was, and his sentence forgotten as Alcibiades' sentence was. Any other reason you'd know for the indecision of the old Alcibiades-lover, my lord Crito? Eh? Indecision, my eye!" he cried out, and in the next moment, inclining his head with a wild thrust and clasping his hands low on his back to mimic Socrates' favorite stance, he said in an affectedly pensive inflection: "Now tell me, my Phædo, tell me which is more beautiful —the blissful abandon on the face of a handsome youth giving in to his lover's yearning, or the forbidding visage of Charon the ferryman waiting for the Shades on the bank of the Stygian river?"

Crito averted his head to hide his true emotion. The gods were just! Anytus was fearing retribution! Had not the populace, seven years before, sent to their death the unjust men responsible for the death of the generals back from the Arginusæan islands? Now Anytus the tanner was afraid of the retribution that might come upon him after Socrates' death! Crito did not rejoice in the terror he assumed in Anytus. What he thought of were the words he'd speak to Socrates. "None other than Anytus told me that the whole city wants you to go on living," so he would say, "and who knows public opinion better than he?" So great was Crito's happiness at this moment that he paid no attention at all to the nasty performance which Anytus, after catching his breath, had resumed.

He seemed to have embarked on a parody of the way Socrates censured men for their striving for honors and power and riches.

X V

An owl was calling through the stillness. Now that Athens' men, the just and the unjust, had gone to sleep, Athena's bird was on the wing.

A cloud was journeying across the full moon; and Socrates, lying on his cot, was waiting for the shadows to pass from Crito's face. He could not bring himself to say: "So that is why the jailer let you in at this late hour. Because you were 'kind to him,' as you put it! Why don't you speak plainly, Crito, and say: 'Because I bribed him'? Not that I haven't known it for many days. I have been watching the change in the good fellow—his mutterings about stingy magistrates, and, above all, the way his eyes wander sidewise whenever I try to meet them. I have known all along, Crito, that you were bribing the man—and not merely to have him open the door for you at some unusual hour. I have known all along that you want him to open the door for me." Socrates could not bring himself to say: "Did you—did all of you—really think I would not guess your plan and follow its progress by your faces? Nor were your expressions the only telltale signs. Would it surprise you to learn that I knew something was threatening to go wrong with your project when your son did not come here for three days? And your going down to the Piraeus 'on business' with Critobolus the day after! As if a Crito had ever gone there to collect debts, or engage in waterfront trading! Incidentally, did you persuade one of the foreign captains at the Piræus to take me to Crete or perhaps as far as Sicily? I wonder, though, how you'd get me through the Piræic Gate. Do you intend to have me sewn into the skin of a billy goat and loaded onto a wagon like a carcass? Or would you disguise me as a sick old crone, with my head swaddled lest informers or the guards at the gate should see my bald head and my beard and cry out: 'Why, this old hag is none other than Socrates'? But that is beside the point. Just tell me, Crito, do you, or do any of your men, seriously think that your absent-mindedness escaped me while we were holding discourse these past days? I wish you could be more attentive than you have been of late, all of you, because there is much I still want to discuss with you. We might get closer to the solution of the problem that a man about to die needs must be occupied with —and which, come to think of it, is the one problem every man is occupied with all his life, for the one certainty he has about the unknowable future is that he is going to die, and perhaps the thought of his death is indeed the best vantage point to consider what he should live for. However, I may be prejudiced. Having been told that I should not have meddled with things that were none of my business, I may indeed be biased in favor of occupying myself with something that definitely is." All this, Socrates could not bring himself to say to Crito. When the old friend had appeared in the doorway a short while earlier, his tall figure thrown into profile by the torch the jailer outside had held aloft, the stooping shoulders and bent head had filled Socrates with tender pity; and when, with the door shut again, Crito had advanced and lifted the stool by the bed and carried it to the opposite wall, his face, in the dim light, had looked weary and drawn.

The intensity of his hopes, his fears, and the unsolved

questions preying upon his mind had nearly worn out the old man. On his descent from the hill, he had decided to start this talk by reminding Socrates of how often he had pleaded with him, before the trial, to get away from the city. Though Crito was aware that escaping from a sentence imposed was a thing different from evading a trial, he had planned to refer once again to the many men charged with crimes who, wary of the city's justice and not thinking it worth suffering for, had fled Athens, at one time or another. Then Crito had meant to proceed to talk about Anytus—the repentant Anytus. . . . When the tanner had left him at the Gate House and rushed off like a madman, Crito had still been foretasting the effect that the story of their encounter would have on the beloved man in the prison. But as he walked down the hill in the gathering dusk, a new suspicion had risen in him—the fear that he might have misinterpreted Anytus' outburst. Could anyone be really afraid of retribution without at the same time admitting his wrong to himself? And could anyone aware of having wronged a man still hate him with the kind of ferocious rancor that Anytus' wild parody of Socratic discourse had revealed? What if the tanner's oblique contention that "the whole city" expected Socrates to escape had only been designed to encourage his flight so that he could be caught red-handed and his friends be utterly ruined? The men of popular rule must hate Socrates' intimates more than Socrates himself now, and Anytus must be appalled by the prospect of leaving untouched their wealth and their influence on public opinion. Seen in this light, Anytus' outburst gained a new, sinister aspect—and Crito, in fact, had reached the prison compound with his self-assurance at low ebb.

He had found no words after Socrates, having been told of the jailer's friendship for Crito, had muttered: "So, so," and had lapsed into silence. Now Crito, leaning his head against the rough masonry of the wall, was looking steadily at the prisoner's inert shape. The night was fairly warm, and Socrates had not drawn his cloak over him. A timid sheen gleamed on the chain that shackled his ankles.

"I know why you have come, my Crito," he said at last, "and inasmuch as we have hardly ever been alone these past days—"

"Everything is ready for your escape!" Crito exclaimed, "and I feel that we have made the right preparations. Do not say no, I beseech you do not say no!"

"You sound as though you took it for granted that I will. . . ."

"Oh, my Socrates, there are so many things I was sure I'd tell you as soon as we were alone. But now I seem to be unable to say any of them, except—Socrates, need I really tell you in so many words that an irreplaceable friend would go out of my life should you die?"

"Would he?"

"Do, therefore, think of me," Crito said, insensitive to the irony of the interjection, "think of my loss and my sorrow and grief. But think also of my good name," he went on with a determination so abrupt it tinged his tone with reproach. "Think of the many men who do not know you. Should you die now, they would not say that you chose death. They would say you might have been saved if only Crito had been willing to spend some money, but that he did not care what happened to you."

"But why should we care about what those many people will say? What the many say is never of importance."

"Is not what happened to you proof of the great evil that the many can inflict on a man once they have formed the wrong opinion about him?"

Quite suddenly, stars, enormous and brilliant, stood in

the frame of the wall aperture; and both men turned their heads, as if in a concerted motion, toward the pale light floating in.

"*What* is it, Socrates, that makes you reluctant to listen to me?"

"Am I not listening to you most carefully, Crito?"

"Do not jest, my Socrates. Do not make sport of my clumsiness with words. Please, answer me. What is it that makes you so reluctant even to inquire what the plans for your rescue are? Be honest now," he said, feigning a stern reproof, "be honest and tell me whether you're hesitating to consent to our plan simply because you are afraid that you might get me and your other friends into trouble."

"That is *one* thing I fear—"

"Dismiss it from your thoughts! We are more than willing to run this risk. Nor is it a great risk, by any means."

"Is it not?"

"Perhaps you worry about the expenses we would be put to. If you do, believe me, you overestimate the sums needed. You never were good at figuring money. Our friend out there, who owes me some gratitude, is far from exorbitant in his demands, and actually eager to close the deal on our terms. As for the informers, they are cheap nowadays, with so many men taking up this wretched profession. Rest assured those informers will be satisfied with little. And if you think of my means, Socrates, which certainly are ample— And if you have any scruples about letting me defray the costs alone, I can tell you truthfully that Simmias of Thebes is prepared to disburse whatever sums should be needed, as is Cebes, who has a tidy pile of gold coins in his possession."

"Is it only their wealth that makes you consider having the foreigners pay the bribes?"

"Frankly," Crito said listlessly, or pretending to be listless, "I would not approve wholeheartedly of their paying the ransom. I who am your oldest friend and companion—"

"Did you say ransom, Crito?"

"This may not be the correct word. But it is a good word to apply to money spent to lead a good man back to freedom."

"Freedom?"

"Do not say, Socrates, as you did in the court, that you would not know where to go once you are free, and cannot picture yourself being welcome abroad. I happen to have a faithful friend in Thessaly—"

"So it is Thessaly!"

"Not a bad part of the world, I assure you, though I know it is still fashionable to talk disparagingly about its mores. I recall clearly a certain morning, Socrates, when you were talking with Meno the Thessalian, who is dead now, and you were saying yourself—"

"What did I say to Meno, exactly?" Socrates broke in, the irony gone from his inflection.

"Why, you said that his countrymen, known only for their riches and their fine horses in the past, had since acquired the reputation of being knowledgeable and even wise men—"

"Meno! Meno of Larissa! Was not Larissa the town he came from?"

"I cannot remember what town he came from," Crito replied, emphasizing his patience in the face of what he could not but think willful discursiveness. "But he came from Thessaly, and that is where this loyal friend of mine, a man still young, Phocion by name—"

"He once asked me a bold question, Meno did," Socrates interrupted again. "Come to think of it, it was the boldest question anyone ever put to me. He asked whether

excellence can be taught. Did you say he was dead? I wonder . . . I wonder, Crito, whether he has received an ir-
refutable answer to his question by now."

For a moment Crito was speechless. A lesser man, he
said to himself, might take in bad part this constant
evasion, and ask that attention be paid to his love and its
pain. He changed his posture so vehemently that his staff,
which he had lain across his knees, fell on the earthen floor,
and said in a forceful voice: "Phocion is the name of my
friend. You will be treated with the utmost courtesy in his
house. He and his relatives and his acquaintances will
love you, and no one in Thessaly will cause you the
slightest trouble. In fact, Phocion is sure that his countrymen will consider themselves honored whenever you talk
to them after your fashion, for men in all Greek cities have
heard about your wisdom, though you have never left
Athens and traveled about." Crito picked up his staff. "But
speaking of your wisdom, Socrates—you cannot in earnest
think it wise to let your enemies, who are unjust men, have
their way to the end, and let them destroy you when you
can get out of their reach with no great exertion. And,
think, further, of this. If, for reasons we still do not fathom,
you should choose to die, you would also be choosing to
desert your children. Instead of bringing them up and edu-
cating them, you would be exposing them to the hazards of
a life without the guiding hand of a father and his protection. It is true you could count on their being spared the
misery that is the usual lot of orphans, for we who are your
friends would never forget them. But would you not be
deserting them just the same? Wouldn't you, in short, be
shirking your duty?"

"Imagine a soldier," Socrates began, "imagine a soldier
in battle. Imagine him coming face to face with an adversary stronger than he and far better armed. Imagine

him taking up that adversary's challenge with no thought of danger while aware that his very courage is likely to orphan his children. Would you say, Crito—"

"A soldier fights a battle," Crito cut in—at last the eloquence he had so fervently hoped for seemed to have accrued to his speech—"and, fighting, he chooses the hard and the manly road. You, so it seems to us, are about to decide on the easier way. And should not a man who has been concerned with men's excellence all his life decide on the manlier road under any circumstances? In short, Socrates, I would be ashamed of you, if I were not far more ashamed of myself and of all of us. We will no doubt be blamed for this whole business. And it is true that the trial need never have taken place, for we who are your friends should have prevailed upon you to leave the city betimes, and I for one should have told you then all the things I am trying to tell you now. And after you refused to take yourself away from the city and decided to stand trial, I should not have given in to you, and should have insisted on having a man versed in legal matters write out your defense. And while I did not beforehand know that you would provoke the jury by not bringing your family, clad in mourning, with you, I should have mended the situation directly I saw what your intention was, and should have hastened to your house and brought Xanthippe and her two little ones into the Great Court myself. And truly, Socrates, we who are your friends should also have spoken up in your behalf there without mincing words, and should have compelled the judges to listen to us even though our speaking would have been against custom. We have ample reason indeed to be ashamed of ourselves. But what you appear to be planning now—this crowning folly of the whole affair—this, if you carry it through, will be laid on our doorstep unjustly. We will be blamed for it as long as we live. For no one will ever believe that it was not our cowardice, or our negligence, that allowed this horrible thing to happen."

"Whichever way I act, then, I am bound to get you into trouble," Socrates said with a short laugh. How much there was to refute in Crito's impassioned words, how much in them did not tally with reason! The ardor of the noble friend, however, had affected Socrates deeply. He wished Crito would go on talking nonsense out of devotion. It was curious: another voice seemed to have joined Crito's—the memory of another, a charmingly lisping voice that in another, a far-away night had implored Socrates, in the face of reason, to comply with its entreaties. . . . "My dear Crito," he said, sitting up on the edge of the cot, awkwardly because he was trying to muffle the clanking of his fetters, "your zeal is beyond praise. Let us now, as coolly as is our wont, reflect on its aim. For only zeal that goes in the right direction furthers a venturesome undertaking, whereas the other kind only adds to its risks."

"I urge you not to talk about risks again," Crito exclaimed. The evenness of Socrates' words had stung him into a courage that made him feel nothing but contempt for any wicked scheme Anytus might harbor. "Suppose there is a certain amount of danger attached to our undertaking. Does not a soldier carry his wounded comrade-in-arms out of the rain of the enemy's arrows, with no regard for his own safety? Did you perchance think of your safety when you carried young Alcibiades out of the midst of battle at Potidæa?"

Socrates, throwing back his head, looked up at Crito, who had come over to him. His face was in shadow. Not for many years had any of Socrates' friends pronounced in his presence Alcibiades' name. Was Crito inserting it into this talk to tempt him with the image of the once-beloved—with the never ending promise of life?

"I beg you to listen to reason," Crito was saying, over and over again.

Socrates did not move. A murmur had risen somewhere in the night, a murmur insistent and startling—

"You must not leave your friends alone amid all the confusing changes that seem to have come over the city! We need you, Socrates, all of us, and though you would be staying in Thessaly, we still could communicate with you whenever we needed your wisdom. . . ."

Might not his death, Socrates reflected, reveal to this loyal dear man what in truth he had striven for all his life? Might not his death show Crito the higher truth of the many words he had spoken to him? And had he, Socrates, not striven, above all, to help men harvest the fruit of the seed of true knowledge implanted in them?

Crito, exhausted, had ceased to talk. He put his trembling hand upon Socrates' shoulder, and as he bent down toward him, moving his head out of the shadows, a feeble ray of light caught the silvery glimmer of tears in his eyes.

"Were you mentioning reason, Crito?" Socrates asked. "Do you not think I have always been one of those who cannot help letting themselves be guided by reason?"

"You have, you have," said Crito, his voice choked. "So do not discard reasonable advice!"

No reply came. The owl had stopped calling its mate.

Socrates had averted his glance from Crito. He was staring up at the aperture. A bat was flitting past it, outside.

"Really, Socrates, I have not been talking in haste. . ." Crito tried to say, but did not continue. The old story of the "thinking bout" in the camp before Potidæa crossed his mind, so perfectly immobile was Socrates now, so faint was his breathing, so impervious did he seem to the reality about him.

After a long time he asked: "Will you come back tomorrow, Crito?"

"I will, I will. I will, Frog Face," Crito said. A pitiful abortive laugh broke from him, begging for an echo; and then he turned slowly to pick up his mantle, which he had left lying on the floor by the stool.

But Socrates, though he had not heard that nickname since his schooldays, remained silent and motionless.

Crito was trying to put on his mantle—all the while mumbling Socrates' name, in pleading accents and in reproving ones, and then again in accents of wonder and of despair—but he finally left the cloak hanging down shapelessly from his shoulder.

The jailer must have been eavesdropping, for no sooner did Crito make for the door than it was opened and the glare of the turnkey's torch fell for a moment into the bluish near-darkness.

Socrates listened to the retreating footfalls. Even when they had died away in the distance, he kept his head cocked toward the door. The air was cooler now. The smell of ripe barley and of flowers seemed to be wafted into the room—

Did violets grow on the banks of Thessaly's brooks in springtime? Could one sit there and hold discourse with friends in the sunshine dappled by swaying foliage? Spring came late to Thessaly. . . . Socrates closed his eyes, overmastered by the sense of life's seduction.

It had penetrated his heart innumerable times since the trial. It had gripped him through the mere awareness of his revived senses when he woke up from sleep. It had come to him in smells and sounds, imagined and real. It had approached him through pictures entering his

mind's eye unsummoned—some of them still and soundless, as if arrested in mid-movement beneath an unmoving
sun, some others advancing toward him, out of the
shadow, with spirited motion. And above all, life had
been beckoning to him through the remembered faces of
men and their words echoing out of the no-man's-land
between recollection and dream. And sometimes, in a
dream, there had been a face shining with the great light
of comprehension. . . . Was there in the whole universe
—was there anywhere—a felicity greater than watching
the first spark of true knowledge appear on a living face?

"Tell me . . ."

Socrates opened his eyes, with a start.

The stream of murmurs gliding through the night was
shaping itself into words soft and distinct: "Tell me, Socrates, what are you about?"

Who had spoken? Had it been the voice familiar to
him since childhood? Were the signs, which had failed
to manifest themselves for so long, coming to him at long
last?

"Are you not in the habit of asking questions?" the
gentle murmur proceeded. "Do you object to being questioned yourself?"

Socrates changed his position slightly. But he did not
turn his head. Not only the lack of command assured him
that he was not being spoken to by the familiar voice.
At his right side the air seemed to have grown more solid,
seemed to be pressing against him—

"How say you, Socrates?"

A human shape seemed to be sitting on the edge of the
bed by Socrates' side, so he noted without wonder when
with an effort he cast a guarded glance sidewise. A man
of his own height appeared to be seated there, his face
veiled by an opaque penumbra.

"Tell me, Socrates . . ."

"What is it you urge me to tell you?" the prisoner asked, using the very phrase he had employed thousands of times in the marketplace. He did not marvel at the naturalness with which he entered upon this converse.

"Tell me, Socrates, are you not about to overturn the laws and the very life of the city? Or do you suppose the commonweal can continue to exist once decisions arrived at lawfully no longer have any power—or, in plain words, when each citizen decides for himself whether or not to submit to such a decision, and sets aside the laws, if he so decides, and tramples them under foot?"

"Might not a law court have set aside the laws?" Socrates objected, almost instinctively. "Might not the commonweal—the men it consists of at this particular moment —have trampled the laws under foot?"

"O you lover of wisdom," came the answer, "do you hold that the commonweal consists only of the men alive at a particular moment?"

The draft from the aperture in the wall was growing stronger. Outside, the night was resonant now with a downy rustle. A cloud had begun to eclipse the moon again, and the shape by his side all but vanished from Socrates' vision.

"Imagine that you are reaching the Acharnian Gate, Socrates—or is it to be the Piræic one?"

"Never mind," Socrates muttered.

"Imagine the laws waiting for you there."

"At the gate?"

"Precisely. Imagine them standing there, arrayed in all their ancient glory. Imagine them saying to you: 'Was this our agreement with you? Were you not to abide by any sentence imposed upon you by the city?' What would your answer be, Socrates?"

For the first time since this curious discourse had started, Socrates felt something like a tremor. "I would say," he answered, "that the city has injured me by an unjust sentence."

"To that, the laws would reply: 'Do you, the accused, set yourself up as the judge of the city's judges? But suppose they did injure you—and suppose, further, it was we, the laws, who gave them the tools to do so—do you propose to set things aright by denouncing your agreement with us? What complaint do you have against us, Socrates—what complaint grave enough to justify your attempt to destroy us and the life of the city? Do not answer rashly again'—so this chorus of Athens' laws would warn you."

"The chorus of Athens' laws!" Socrates exclaimed under his breath, heartened rather than intimidated by the solid blackness now about him and his eerie interlocutor. "I know the trick! Putting words into the mouth of some unassailable body! It is true that I have been concerned with justice all my life. But laws that permit—"

"Were you not warned against answering rashly? Are you not about to propose that justice should exist without laws, or laws without law courts, or law courts without judges?"

"Continue."

"Will you follow me and imagine the laws standing at the Acharnian Gate when you reach it?"

"Continue."

" 'Remember,' the laws would say, 'that your father married your mother through our good services. Remember that you would not be Socrates of Athens without those among us who regulate marriage, for this man *we* brought into existence. Do you have any objection to those among us who regulate marriage?' "

"I have none," said Socrates to the man whom he seemed to be seeing again, though, so to speak, in a fluid manner only, very much as one sees the outlines of a person or a thing mirrored in rippled water.

"Good. Then the laws would inquire: 'And what about those among us who regulate the upbringing of children? Do you have any objection to them? You have none? Well, then. Since we brought you into existence as an Athenian and watched over your upbringing—are you not our child, are you not our own, are you not ours, Socrates? And being ours, do you not realize that you have no right to do to us as we do to you? Did you ever think you had the right to strike your father because he struck you? Do you think now that you have the right to destroy us because we think it right to let you be destroyed? Have you, O wise man, failed to discover that the city must either be convinced of her wrong or, if not convinced, must be obeyed?' "

"Obeyed!"

" 'You did not question her right to send you to war, did you? That command exposed you to the danger of being mutilated or even killed. Still you abided by it and, in later years, frequently sounded quite proud of your obedience. Must you not, by the same token, also abide by the decision of one of the city's law courts? You have been at liberty, ever since coming of age, to try to change the city's view on what is just, and as free to persuade her of our unfairness as you were to persuade your father of his. But violence an Athenian must not do either to his father or to the city.' Would you say, Socrates, the laws speak truth?"

"Truth, I would say," Socrates heard himself saying.

"Whereupon the laws would proceed: 'Consider now that, if you failed to convince the city of our unfairness, and still did not like us, you were free to betake yourself to some other city. Such was your right ever since coming of age. But you remained within the walls of Athens. Did you not by so doing enter into a tacit agreement with us to do our bidding unless you convinced the city that we were unjust? Now think of this, Socrates. Not even at your trial did you complain against us, except for finding fault with the regulation that restricts a trial in Athens to one single day. And speaking of your trial, Socrates, you did not propose banishment there. We, who refuse to let you go now, would still have let you go then—and well you knew it. But you declared that you preferred death to exile. Where, O our Socrates, are those gallant words now?' "

The interlocutor seemed to pause. The calm was so absolute now, one could have thought that this room, this building, that Athens herself had been lifted into the void.

" 'Where, O you lover of wisdom, are those fine words now that you run away like a miserable slave and turn your back on the covenant you made with us? Answer, Socrates of Athens. Are we right in saying that you agreed to do our bidding in your actions, as well as in words?' Do you think, Socrates, you would find yourself assenting if you were spoken to in this manner at the Acharnian Gate?"

Socrates said: "I think I would find myself assenting."

" 'Now consider further that you are breaking this agreement not under any compulsion, or without perceiving the issue, or under the stress of haste. You had seventy years to make up your mind about us, the laws, and your compact with us. You seem to have judged it equitable, for you scarcely ever left the city, though you had the choice and could have gone and traveled about as the Sophists do, or taken up residence in some town abroad.

And now, after seventy years, you—you, of all men—break your covenant with us and run away. O our Socrates, let us warn you. Do not besmirch your cause and make a fool of yourself into the bargain.' "

"A fool?"

"Yes, Socrates of Athens. Or do you propose to prove the injustice of your judges by acting unjustly yourself? Would not your escape only confirm their conviction that they acted justly? Would they not say: 'Surely he who corrupts the laws is more than likely to have also corrupted the young?' And you, Socrates, meantime would go about in some foreign city, talking about goodness and excellence and justice! Perhaps men would listen to you for a time. But most of the time they would amuse themselves by telling one another funny stories about your flight from the prison of Athens and how you got yourself smuggled out through the Acharnian Gate. They might not say to your face: 'Were you not ashamed, old man, of doing violence to the laws of your city just so that you might live a little longer?' Or, rather, they might not talk to you in that fashion so long as you flattered them by declaring how perfect *their* laws were and how just their commonweal and how infallible their law courts. Still they would keep in mind that, when all is said and done, you broke a sacred pact so that you might continue to eat and drink, and thus, in a manner of speaking, traded your birthright as an Athenian, and that of your sons, for a dish of porridge."

All of a sudden the mellow light of high moon was flowing freely into the prison room, and a broad band of brightness fell aslant the prisoner's bed. He turned his head sharply to make out the man, or the phantom, that was speaking to him. But there was no one at his side—

nothing save the deep shadow cast by his own form on the cloak spread over his bed.

"Listen, Socrates. If you abide by your agreement with the laws, you will depart an innocent man—a sufferer, not a doer, of evil; a victim not of the laws, but of man. But if you go now and repay evil with evil, returning blow for blow, wronging those you should least wrong —the laws, the commonweal, your friends, your sons, and yourself—then you will be deemed an utterly unjust man as long as you live, and after. And after . . ." And then, upon a long silence, came the words: "You must not follow Crito's advice."

And these words—words that no longer argued or counseled, but forbade—had been pronounced by a voice different from that which had spoken before. No longer did Socrates wonder, as he intermittently had while being interrogated, whether what was happening to him in this hour was outside the natural order of things and beyond the ken of reason. The reasonableness of the injunction, penetrating his consciousness, seemed to make what had happened part of his own being.

X V I

"What is the time?"

"Dawn is breaking, Socrates."

"Have you been here long, Crito, or did you just come?"

"I've been here for some time."

Only now did Socrates turn his head away from the wall to look at Crito, who was sitting close by the trestle bed. "Why did you not wake me?"

"You were sleeping soundly. Should I have robbed you of your slumber, this last refuge from your great troubles? As I was watching you," Crito continued, "I could not help marveling at the peacefulness of your sleep. It is true that the evenness of your disposition has always amazed me. But never would I have thought that any man could bear with such calm the misfortune that has come to you now."

"Would it not be foolish—" Socrates said in a voice still somewhat dreamy, "would it not be foolish for a man who has reached my age to fret over the approach of his death?"

"Men older than you have been known to fret over it."

"That may be so," Socrates remarked. He hunched up his knees and began nursing his fettered ankles. "But tell me, Crito. You left very late last night Yet you've returned at this early hour. . . ."

A yellowish tinge was trickling into the paling grayness of the prison room. "I have come to bring news," Crito said with an earnestness free from the tearful despair of the past night. "Bad news, my Socrates."

"Has the ship arrived?"

"She has not made port yet," Crito answered, his tired, kind eyes meeting Socrates' lifted glance. "But the runners have come from Cape Sunium. I saw them myself, on my way home last night, near the Royal Hall. Socrates, at this very hour the ship may be setting sail to double the cape. She may well put in tomorrow! Let me therefore ask you once more, let me beg you to heed my advice. Everything is ready. Phocion, my Thessalian friend, will be waiting for you this coming night, shortly before daybreak, on the highway beyond the Acharnian Gate."

"Beyond the Acharnian Gate . . ."

"Make up your mind then, Socrates—or rather, have your mind already made up, for the time for deliberations is over. If you do not let yourself be taken away from here this coming night, we will no longer be able to rescue you."

Socrates had stopped rubbing his feet and legs.

"Listen to me, Socrates. You were saying last night—"

"What *was* I saying last night?" Socrates interrupted his old friend's anguished voice, and without waiting for a reply, swung his legs over the edge of the bed and got to his feet. The chain made a sharp clank.

"You were saying that you had always followed the course reason told you was the best. Did not reason now, in your long deliberations, tell you that the best, that the only course to take was to choose freedom, to get away from this place and leave the city?"

"Strictly speaking," Socrates said, "that was not the subject of my deliberations, Crito. Strictly speaking."

Crito shook his head. He watched Socrates stretch out

his arms sidewise and drop them again, and again stretch them out, fists closed, in the fashion of athletes.

Then Socrates slipped on his tunic, but left it ungirded. "You see, my dear Crito," he said while stepping away from the cot, the chain on his feet trailing, "I went further back in those deliberations of mine, in my pursuit of the best course, to use your happy expression."

The speed with which Socrates had shed the aftereffects of sleep might have startled Crito. But his undismayed single-mindedness left no room for such observations. Having slowly turned round on his stool, he saw Socrates halt beneath the aperture in the wall.

"I have been thinking a great deal about those rules of conduct, those principles which my earlier reflections led me to regard as the best, Crito. And I've been asking myself whether I can repudiate them now because this calamity has befallen me."

"What rules of conduct?"

"We will come to them presently. The first problem is this. Can I say: 'Those principles were the best as long as I happened to be in one situation, but are worthless now that I am in another'? That I clearly cannot say. But I can and will examine whether I wasn't mistaken in my earlier reflections, and whether those principles are, in truth, the best. And since you, Crito, are not to die upon the return of the ship from Delos, your judgment will not be influenced by the change of circumstances that may cloud mine. Let us therefore deliberate in common—"

"The time for deliberations is over!"

"No, my Crito, it never is," Socrates said with mellow reproof, and clasping his hands on his back, he said: "Now, where shall we start? Perhaps by recalling what you were saying last night about the multitude and the opinions of the many: Now tell me, Crito . . . tell me, to whose advice do you think a man should listen on the wrestling-ground—to the various opinions of the many bystanders watching his performance, or to the judgment of his trainer and physician?"

"To the latter, of course."

"To one man, then?"

"To one."

"To the one whose praise he has come to value and whose censure he fears. Right?"

"Right."

"And he ought to proceed with his training, and regulate his eating and drinking, in the manner this one man thinks best. True, Crito? For would not following the opinions of the many do harm to his body?"

"It would."

"It might, in actual fact, ruin his body completely, might it not?"

Crito nodded. A wan smile traveled over his features. It was as it had been thousands of times, and as thousands of times before, there was no way of resisting the inexorable lure of Socrates' questions.

Socrates went on: "Now, we agreed long ago that there is something within us which thrives on justice and deteriorates if we act unjustly. Would you say that this result of our reflections still holds true?"

"Certainly, Socrates."

"Let us assume now that there is one who to this—to the soul—is what the physician and trainer is to the body. If that assumption is justified (as I believe it is), should we not, in matters of fair and foul, good and evil, just and unjust—should we not in these matters follow the advice of the one and dismiss the opinions of the many? For would we not, in following *them,* corrupt the soul exactly as a man corrupts his body when he does as the bystanders on the wrestling-ground say?"

"But those bystanders, few or many, do not kill a man for not doing as they say!" Crito cried out. "Those many, on the other hand—the multitude you're actually talking about—can kill us for rejecting their opinions!"

"Granted. But does that invalidate our finding, Crito? And then, is life worth having if a man's body is utterly diseased? It assuredly is not. And should life be worth having with one's soul corrupted? Did we not, my Crito, on several occasions agree that not life as such, but only the right kind of life is of value?"

"Yes, on that we agreed."

"And did we not always maintain that only the man who is acting justly leads the right kind of life? Is this finding of ours still true and valid?"

"I suppose it must be."

"Let us go on from these premises, then. The problem you urge me to resolve is whether I should, or should not, leave this place without the consent of the city—"

Crito made a start, twisting his shoulders. He was on the point of saying that nearly everybody in Athens would condone the escape. But in the same breath, he foresaw Socrates censuring him for failing to distinguish between "consenting" and "condoning."

The orange-colored and pearl-blue tints of the quadrangle of sky visible through the wall-opening had kindled to a reddish luminescence. Cloud strips, as translucent as Egyptian veils, were journeying seaward.

Socrates' head and shoulders were untouched as yet by the oncoming brightness. Once or twice while talking he had glanced backward. Now his gaze went out into the shadows that, thinning, still lingered in the shallow recess

of the door. . . . Not until this moment had the interlocutor of the past night come to his mind—though the
night's experience seemed to have been with him, in a
provokingly disembodied manner, ever since he had
awakened. The tardiness of his memory did not astound
him. Had not the divine agencies often given him leave,
in like fashion, to test their injunctions in the channels
of reason?

Crito had risen; and as he advanced, the dawn illumined his face, which looked more seamed than ever.
Above the untrimmed beard, the pallor of his cheeks
failed to reflect the vivid hues of the nascent morning.
"The injustice of our fellow citizens—" he started to say
with a new firmness which, however, faltered almost at
once under Socrates' stare.

"We must stick to our problem, my Crito. Time is running out."

"It is, it is, Socrates! If you don't follow me—"

"If—" Socrates broke in, "if we should find that I would
be acting justly in leaving this place, then I will follow
you; if not, I will make no such attempts. And, mind you,
inasmuch as we now must determine what is just and
what unjust, Crito, neither death nor any other contin-
gency must enter the argument. Now, then," he began,
inclining his head, "are we to say that we must never
do wrong intentionally—or that we may do so in certain
instances though not in certain others? Or is doing wrong
always evil? Remember, Crito, that we long ago decided
it always was."

"I remember."

"Thus doing injustice is evil regardless of circumstances?"

"Yes."

"Is not, therefore, doing injustice to those who did injustice to us evil, too?"

"It is," Crito answered after some hesitation, with a sigh short and faint.

"Are you certain of your conclusion? This view, let me remind you, has never been accepted by any sizable number of men, and never will be. And those who hold this view have no common ground with those who do not, and the gulf between them can never be bridged. I, as you know, made up my mind long ago that repaying injustice with injustice cannot be right ever, and I still think this view sound. However, I cannot proceed to the next step of our argument unless you too say, as you have done on earlier occasions, that this principle is valid."

"Proceed. I have not changed my mind on that point."

"Let me now ask you this question. Should one act in accordance with what one has admitted to be right, or may one act contrary to it?"

Crito remained silent. A glowing thread of the new light fell on his lowered head.

"Or more specifically—or rather, in other words: if someone promises a man something he found to be this man's due, must he also give it to him?"

"I would say he must."

"If all that is so, let us go on to consider how it bears on the question of my escape. Did I not admit—as we all do—that it is the right of the commonweal to summon me before a court of law and to pass sentence on me? Would I not, therefore, by trying to undo that sentence, refuse to give the city what I myself admitted to be her due? Would I not wrong her? And by so doing—by acting unjustly—would I not also be wronging myself? We have just agreed that a man's soul is utterly corrupted by his acting unjustly. And we also found that a man acts

unjustly if he discards the rules of conduct that his reason
has led him to regard as the best. What do you say, Crito?"

"I cannot tell, Socrates, for I do not know. . . ."

"Oh, my Crito!" Socrates exclaimed under his breath.
Should he tell the dear man that he himself had been asked
those questions in the past night—and that, for all his
initial objections, he had found himself soon concurring
with the answers suggested? But how could he tell Crito
of the past night's experience without having to meet the
incredulity that nearly always had shown in Crito's mien
when he was told of the voice that came from the gods?

The birds were wide awake now all over the hill.

"Then look at the matter this way," Socrates said, un-
clasping his hands and assuming the impish expression,
nose wrinkled, which he had always favored in starting
out on an invented tale. "Imagine that I am trying to
abscond—or shall I say, play truant?—and that you and
your son have taken me, in some clever disguise, through
the whole length of this part of the city and led me to
the Acharnian Gate—"

"Beyond it, beyond the gate!" Crito called out in exas-
peration. "Beyond the Acharnian Gate, where the faithful
Phocion is waiting! Do you assume that we have failed to
make the right preparations for getting you through the
gate?"

But Socrates paid no attention. He proceeded to repeat,
as though in an invented allegory, what the shadowy
interlocutor had told him during the night. It came back
to him far more clearly than dreams ever had; and while
he talked on, he knew for a certainty that what had preceded the god's injunction last night had not been a
dream. It all returned to him now word by word; and his
words painted the image of the laws waiting for him at
the Acharnian Gate, as this awesome image had been

painted to him. And the objections that Crito, in feigned self-control, from time to time raised seemed to mirror his own.

But the further Socrates went on with his tale the less Crito interfered with the mounting intensity of its flow.

The sun was rising over the hill as Socrates was concluding his story. His eyes had not let go of his loyal old friend. Had Crito understood at last that the laws belonged to an order different from man's will and his will to survive? "That, Crito," he said, "that is the way we must imagine the laws would speak to me. . . ." And of a sudden he felt determined to undo the pretense of a made-up parable, sustained throughout his account, and he said in a voice lowered and slow and yet distinct: "Thus I *was* spoken to, Crito. And in the end I was told that I must not do as you suggest. And all the words spoken to me are lodged in my ear, and I seem to hear them all the time now, as the Corybants who follow the great mother of the gods along the mountainous path in springtime hear the sounds of the flutes even after they've ceased playing. Indeed, those words, ringing and ringing on in my ears, keep me from hearing any others. Yet, Crito," he added in his habitual matter-of-fact tone, "if there is still something you wish to oppose to those words, speak up and say what it is."

"I have nothing to say," Crito breathed.

"Let me, then, act as I must," the shackled man said with a serenity born of a sense of fulfillment—a sense of supreme freedom—"and let me follow the god and go where he leads."

The great stillness received the irrevocable resolve without echo. Crito barely managed to prevent his head from nodding—whether in helpless grief or in agreement, he would not have known. Unable to dissimulate the shimmer of understanding that he felt must show in his face, he turned away and walked back to the stool, and sat down with an aged man's awkward slowness.

Day had come.

After a time the voice of the jailer broke the calm. He was talking to some of the friends outside.

Then the door opened with hardly a sound—the turnkey seemed to have failed to put up the bolts and chains after letting in Crito (or had he neglected to bolt the door last night after Crito left?)—and Apollodorus came in and Critobolus and Hermogenes and Antisthenes and the two Thebans. While they filed in without a single word, the jailer chattered away behind the door in what sounded like encouraging accents.

Socrates had not moved from the spot. From the corner of his eye he noticed the men's timid attempts to salute him. They were all looking at him from under their brows. As they finally stopped to huddle about Crito, bending down to the seated old man, whose head had sunk low on his chest into the wretchedly crumpled folds of his mantle, their whispers did not reach Socrates' ears with a force greater than the hum of the jailer's bees.

Then the door was opened again, a crack only this time, and Phædo of Elis stepped in. But though he too seemed reluctant to come close to Socrates, he did not join the others. He halted midway between the door and the group, one foot thrust forward with lifted heel, one hand on his hip, his head lowered. On his beardless face expectation mingled with deep anguish.

Was it the onrush of unanswered questions behind his shining-white forehead and delicate temples which tautened Phædo's features? Or was it the anticipation of questions he seemed to know he himself would be called upon to answer? "What questions will I be asking him

and the others in the two days left our friendship?"
Socrates asked himself. "Or, rather, how will I shape into
questions the many things I must tell them—and the one
thing? Along what road must I guide their thoughts so
that my departure will not leave them totally orphaned?
For I must, like the bee, leave my sting in them before
dying."

A host of images crowded into his mind—memories,
buried for years, of those foolish days of his youth in
which he had hoped that investigating nature might
actually divulge the ultimate cause of all things; and
remembrances that seemed to have been in him before
he came into existence; and the imagery of tradition;
and notions wrenching themselves from the Mysteries'
matrix. . . .

But out of this welter and its longing for order rose
to Socrates' mind an image of the realm where the god
was to lead him, and of the judgment there of man's
soul. . . . The murmur of that realm's unchanging waters seemed to mingle with the harmony of the spheres
. . . and while Socrates realized that this had been the
music, this the poetry, for which he had been preparing
himself throughout his life, the only changeless reality—
truth and justice—stood, in all its realness, before his
mind's eye.

What would he answer should one of the friends say
to him: "You are talking about man's soul, Socrates, as
if man were not like a stringed instrument, and the harmony could survive once the lyre is broken"? Would he
convince them that the decay of the body was not the end,
and that the harmony was imperishable and real? He
would say to them: "I cannot guarantee that the descrip-
tion I'm giving you of the soul's arrival in her eternal
mansion is accurate. But you may safely assume something

of the kind to be true." He might fail to make them behold in all its realness what he was beholding himself. Still, they would grasp—of this he was convinced at this moment—that, wherever a man's soul was to be once his body was in the grave, the promise of her immortality, as long as he was alive, must be the beacon charting the course of man's life and guiding his ship, with life's glittering cargo gone, into port.

The men had stopped talking. They seemed to have turned to look at him, and one of them, perhaps Apollodorus, kept pronouncing his name in stifled outcries.

But Socrates had not taken his glance away from Phædo. A solid beam of the sun was caressing the youth's uplifted face and the smile of reassurance with which he was trying to cloak his sorrow and his confusion. The draft from the aperture was stirring the honey-colored hair ever so lightly. . . .

Was not another beautiful youth standing over there, one hand on hip, smiling at his older companion, eager to listen to his words, and as though in truth craving true knowledge? "Have you come once more, Alcibiades, risen out of the Tartarus' lightless abyss? Have you come, for the last time, to tease me and mock my hope for human excellence? Do not smile at me, traitor—"

"My Socrates," Phædo of Elis said and took a step forward, "oh my Socrates, I do not know how to greet you on this morning. With the fall of the wind, the Sacred Ship may by now have rounded Cape Sunium—"

EPILOGUE

The return of the Sacred Vessel had never been celebrated with elaborate rites; and since the city's defeat, even the common curiosity her homecoming used to arouse had been on the wane. Certain people would forget themselves to the point of saying that the arrival of any grain ship these days was likely to draw more men to the Piræus than was the return from Delos of the bireme "which Theseus himself once had sailed." As for news from the temple island, nothing spectacular could be expected. The festival there had grown to be a rather stale affair; and not many Athenians were interested, these days, in the outcome of the choral competition. It was taken for granted that the men from the foreign cities would pay none of the former respect to the delegation from Athens, no matter how well it acquitted itself—and no one was eager to hear *such* stories again!

For all that, a sizable crowd had assembled this year on the wharf. Suspense was written on every face long before the vessel dropped anchor, and excitement was ringing out of the continuous chatter.

Yet when the ship's commander, Cleomedes, stepped ashore, no wild cheers went up—though the fortitude he had shown in the storms that had beset the homeward voyage was common knowledge by now. As he advanced up the pier, his head bandaged over an injury suffered in the tempest, few men rushed forward to watch him handing the priests the traditional gift from Delos, a sprig from the olive grove of the god. Instead, nearly everybody elbowed his way out on the jetty, trying to get hold of one or another of the sailors who were busy making fast the hawsers. Or else the men shouted questions up to the mariners who were leaning over the bulwarks. Not even the homecoming chant of the choristers arrayed on deck could drown out the passionate inquiries hurled aboard.

Thus, even a blind man could have told that there was something special about the return of the vessel this year. There was. An all but incredible piece of news, abroad since the runners' arrival from Cape Sunium, had stirred the souls of all men.

It had all begun when the runners, reaching the city late that night, had gone straight to the Royal Hall. The next morning it was bruited about that they had roused the king archon himself from his sleep and stayed with him "until daybreak." It also was said that he had enjoined them to keep their mouths shut until the ship cast anchor. But long before that, every schoolboy knew what had happened—and the crowds had come down to the harbor less to have the outrageous story confirmed than to get its details firsthand.

The helmsman, Xenias, had deserted in Delos and left the island with the pilgrims from Chios! This was a thing unheard-of indeed, nothing short of a crime. It was the breach of an agreement so self-evident that its hallowed nature was beyond any contract expressed in words. Many a man who long before had ceased to believe in the actual sacredness of things sacred felt a shudder chill his bones at the news.

A brooding, a grumpy, an entirely humorless man—as

such Xenias was known to a good many Athenians; and the ship's crew and the choristers, unable to furnish the curious with the story behind his defection, enlarged, after coming ashore, upon the steersman's notoriously surly disposition. At the same time, however, some declared that his conduct on the island itself had given no indication of disloyal or treasonous thought. He had watched with pious attention the Crane Dance of the various choirs preceding their sacrifices at Apollo's altar and, in fact, had been in good spirits. He had talked a good deal when the Athenians were alone at their meals, preferably telling stories about the old days when Delos had been "more than a shrine for a once-a-year visit." It may have been hindsight that caused some of the sailors to mention also the spiteful censure they supposed they had heard as an undertone to those tales of the glorious past of the island—the days when Delos was headquarters of the pan-Greek alliance sternly presided over by Athens, and the place where the League's fabulous treasure was kept. So, for instance, one of the mariners reported that Xenias had spoken of "the Athenians who all of them wrecked Athens' glory themselves. . . ."

Not one out of a hundred of the hearers of those reports —or, for that matter, not one out of a hundred Athenians who heard them later—recalled the discussion, current almost five years before, about the propriety of letting Xenias stay in his well-paid job in spite of his having sailed to Delos a year earlier with the brother of the infamous Tyrant. Too many similar discussions had taken place after the Tyrant was slain! Even those men who remembered the dated issue failed to connect the pilot's desertion with the bitter feelings that debate might have left in his heart.

The one man who could have informed his countrymen about that connection, Cleomedes, kept his silence.
He had disembarked with his mind made up to say
nothing about Xenias' great fear of his fellow Athenians.
When the runners who came aboard as the ship anchored
to the eastward of Cape Sunium had reported that
Socrates had been sentenced to death, Cleomedes had
realized at once that this was no time to repeat, even with
the utmost disapproval, any of Xenias' bitter remarks
about the justice of present-day Athens and her "blatant
unfairness." He therefore invented a spicy fib about a perfectly enchanting Chian youngster the pilot had fallen
in love with at the Crane Dance, whom he had later followed aboard the vessel from Chios.

To be sure, the commander planned to tell the truth
to Anytus, his admired old friend and comrade-in-arms.
But when he inquired why Anytus hadn't come to the
harbor, he was informed that the tanner was bedridden
with fever; and Cleomedes could not, at least for another
three or four days, think of going to Athens. It was,
under the circumstances, incumbent on him to see the
vessel into her roofed slip and to supervise the removal
of her rudder and oars, her sail, pulleys, cordage, and
the rest of her tackle. Moreover, she had sprung a leak
aft on the last day of the voyage, and he was by no means
certain he might not himself have to negotiate the repair
with the shipwrights. He had grown to be quite a salt,
Cleomedes had, since bravely leaving Delos on the ap-
pointed morning without the pilot.

He could have postponed that departure and looked
for a substitute among the natives of the island. A reliable
navigator, however, would not have been easy to come by,
for Delos' able-bodied men were known to have emigrated

in droves after the collapse of the League. Also, Cleomedes had felt more than doubtful about the lawfulness of having a foreigner steer the Sacred Ship home.

Another consideration, more weighty still, had counseled him against delay on that fateful morning. The memory of the two men who, at the Piræus, had warned him against "racing" the ship on the homeward voyage had kept haunting Cleomedes on the outbound trip every day and during many a night. After Xenias' desertion he therefore could not but wonder whether those two men— or some others bent on having Socrates' period of grace extended, should he be sentenced to die—hadn't bribed the helmsman into running away and leaving his shipmates all but helpless. He dismissed this suspicion, telling himself that a man as deeply concerned as was Xenias with the good name of his sons was not the sort to be corrupted. At the same time, Cleomedes perceived that a delayed departure would play into the hands of the pro-Socrates clique back in Athens—whose existence he had come to regard as a fact. Confronted thus by the choice of involuntarily playing *their* game, or proving to Anytus that he was siding with him, the commander had arrived at his resolve with no great struggle.

Now, ashore, he could not help asking himself how much thought he had given to old Socrates on the voyage from Delos. The simple truth was that Cleomedes' initial concern with Socrates' trial had been displaced entirely by the wearing and hazardous nautical tasks he had so nobly shouldered. Surely a man so little experienced at sea as he, finding himself on the pilot's bench in those horrendous gales—surely such a man could not be expected to ponder the subtleties of a lawsuit or, for that matter, the subtleties of human conflicts!

Most probably a trained pilot would have brought in

the ship faster in spite of those gales; and it might have been argued that the stouthearted decision of the commander to leave the temple island without such a man had extended Socrates' period of grace, after all. But to the best of Cleomedes' knowledge, no one said so upon his return.

He was, of course, asked a great many questions. In answering them, he went out of his way to give credit to the courage, the loyalty, and the efficiency of his crew. A succession of sailors and even some choristers, so he declared, had been of vast help to him at the tiller, and had offered valuable advice as to how to handle the sail —"as fine a piece of cloth, by the way, as ever breasted the winds."

In actual fact, the number of those helpers had been small, and nearly all of them had lost heart once the westerly storm had sprung up. . . . But Cleomedes was not, out of mere generosity, praising his crew beyond their deserts. He was doing so in order to leave unmentioned the name of the one man aboard who had stood by him virtually alone throughout the days and the nights (the nights!) of the savage ordeal. For this one man— hardly more than a beardless boy—was not the kind of person to be talked about with admiration under present conditions.

His name was Diocles, and he was the same chorister who, on the first day of the outbound voyage, had annoyed Cleomedes with that old playful question about the identity of their ship with the craft that Prince Theseus had once sailed to Crete. Nor was this the only bodiless question the handsome youth had thrown up while a benign breeze had borne the vessel along over placid seas. It soon had turned out that he loved that sort of discussion and had a way of inveigling others into such talks.

Once Cleomedes had also overheard Diocles debate with some of the boys the charges against Socrates and vent his doubts as to their justice!

Cleomedes talked to the youth after disembarking. He again thanked him for what he had done in the great storm, and lauded him for his pluck and sang-froid. But he also warned Diocles against indulging his fancy for worthless speculations. "You have an alert mind, my son. Apply it to things constructive. And as for your extraordinary courage, mind you, there are situations in an Athenian's life in which courage alone may be of little worth. . . ."

Although the choir dispersed even before the ship was unrigged, Diocles stayed on at the Piræus. His parents were dead, and he was not any too eager to see his guardian, an ex-magistrate, a man of means, but also a coarse man, to Diocles' mind.

Thus the youth sauntered through the streets of the harbor town, still slightly dazed by the toils and perils behind him. When asked about them by strangers, to whom he was pointed out, he was chary of words. He had no contribution to offer toward the scandal about the pilot's desertion. Now and then he stopped at some street corner and listened to men as they talked about the day's news—the "riddle of Xenias," or the brawls some of the ship's crew had engaged in after entering Athens, or the plays that the magistrates were said to be contemplating for this summer's production; or why old Socrates had been fool enough not to escape; or the complaint against a foreign adulterer lodged with the magistrates by an irate husband. For many long hours, however, Diocles merely loafed about the harbor, looking out on the sea.

It was there, on the jetty, that Phædo of Elis came upon him on the fifth day after the vessel's return.

Phædo had met Diocles some months before on one of
the wrestling-grounds. Only three or four years older than
the chorister, he yet had been struck by the skillful queries
Diocles put to him, though the youth knew next to nothing
about higher learning and also confessed that his guardian
was hostile to it. Phædo, urged by the youth to tell him
what Socrates was really talking about all the time to
those lucky enough to be talked to by him, had finally
promised Diocles to take him into Socrates' presence. But
the final training of the choir had then kept Diocles away
from the wrestling-ground, and thus that promise had
come to naught.

At the sound of his name, Diocles looked up, but he
did not at once recognize Phædo with his hair cut off.
Only when Phædo said that he was glad to see Diocles
back from the terrible voyage—only then did a spark of
recognition appear in the eyes of the youth. "Did you not
wish we would never return?" he asked.

"The Sacred Ship of the Athenians always returns,"
said Phædo.

It was midday. In the offing, the waters mingled with
the cloudless azure. The orange-colored or vermilion sails
of the becalmed fishing-boats spotted the luminous space.
The thinnest of mists rested on the rock of Munychia.

Diocles asked: "Were you at the prison house yourself
when Socrates took the poison?"

Phædo nodded.

"How did he die?" Diocles inquired in a low tone. He
now had his eyes on the low-sterned foreign craft in one of
the roadsteads. "Were his friends with him? Or did the
Eleven not allow anyone to be there?"

"Several of us were with him when he died."

"I wish you'd tell me about his death. That is, Phædo,
if you have nothing else to do."

"No, I have nothing to do," Phædo said. He had come to the Piræus with the vague plan of finding out whether some ship would be sailing soon to foreign parts. Simmias and Cebes were already on their way back to Thebes; Antisthenes was said to be visiting relatives in some obscure hamlet; and there were rumors afoot about some great journey the wealthy Plato was to embark on. Phædo too was determined to get away from Athens. He could no longer bear the sight of the city. Only the day before he had seen Meletus strutting about the square, carrying his ugly head higher than ever; and then the poet had entered the Royal Portico to join a group of men who, while visibly little pleased, had yet forced their faces into obliging smiles as they listened to him. Early this morning Phædo had gone to his favorite wrestling-ground with Critobolus, and they had both turned round at the gate, overmastered by the memory of Socrates' love for the place. . . . But, for all that, Phædo felt no desire to return to his native Elis. He might be reproached there for having allowed himself to be taken prisoner in the war. "No, I have nothing whatever to do, my Diocles," he now repeated and sat down by Diocles' side, "and I wish I could tell you everything about that day, that last day. . . . But to begin at the beginning, I do not know how to describe my own feelings in those hours. I should have pitied Socrates, and did not, for again and again I found myself disbelieving that I was in the company of one about to die, so utterly fearless was he, and so calm. I suppose those ambiguous feelings were shared by all the others who were there."

"When did you enter the prison that day?"

"The sun was barely up. You see, we had, on the previous days, formed the habit of assembling in front of the Royal Hall at dawn to wait there for word that the gate

of the prison compound had been opened. Then we would
go up—"

"All of you at one and the same time?"

"All who came on a particular morning. Not all of us
came every morning. Some had business to attend to on
one or another of those days. Critobolus, for instance, did
not come for three days at one time. And Crito too. But
that is another story."

"And so you—those of you who came—would go
up . . ."

"Yes. And we would spend the whole day with him."

"In discourse?"

"Yes."

"The gods were good to you," Diocles said, and Phædo
continued:

"On that last morning we had assembled even earlier
than usual, for we had heard that your ship was about to
put in. And as soon as we got word that the gate was
open, we walked up. But the jailer did not let us in,
telling us that the Eleven were with Socrates to take off
his chains. We were alarmed. We knew he was to die at
sundown, such being the custom, and asked the jailer why
the Eleven had come at this early hour. The man explained
to us that the hemlock potion affects a man's body much
faster if he has moved his limbs freely for some time before drinking the poison. That is why the Eleven had
come to remove the fetters—"

"Did you see the Eleven yourself?"

"No, they left through the rear gate."

"And after that all of you went in—"

"Yes. Crito and his son and Apollodorus and Hermogenes and Antisthenes and Epigenes and the two Thebans.
I entered last."

"And Plato, of whom you spoke to me once?"

"He was sick. How, by the way," Phædo asked and for the first time turned his head toward Diocles, "how did you learn of the outcome of the trial?"

"As we anchored that night before doubling the cape, the runners came aboard. They brought the sad news. And with them was one of the priests of the temple of Poseidon, which, as you certainly know, is near by, and he boasted of having journeyed up to the city early in the month of Thargelion and having been in the court himself. Moreover, I have listened here at the Piræus to several men talking about the trial."

"Did they say the verdict was unjust?"

"Some did, some didn't. Those who think it unjust blame it on that orator Lyco, and say he must have known why he left town in a hurry after the trial. But do proceed, Phædo. So you went in. . . ."

"Yes. And there was Socrates' wife, Xanthippe. You have heard about her, have you not?"

"I have heard about her since I was a child. A nagging woman—"

"Yes, that is her reputation. But some of us have been wondering about it these past days. After we had buried Socrates, we returned to the prison to fetch his cloak, and we were unable to stop the jabbering of the jailer; and one of the things he told us then was that he hadn't slept a wink the night before the execution, and had sneaked up to Socrates' door to hear what Xanthippe would say to the doomed man, for, like most people, the jailer knew of her unpleasant disposition—"

"Do you mean to say that she spent the night with Socrates?"

"She did. There seems to be no law against it. So the jailer—who, as I was saying, admitted to eavesdropping—told us that Xanthippe never once raised her voice and never once asked Socrates a question. You see, this—those persistent questions of hers—is what more than anything else seems to have given her her bad name. 'As it was,' the jailer said to us, 'the two were sitting side by side on the bed when I took the Eleven in, and to me they looked like two people who have been sitting together in silence for a very long time.'" Phædo made a pause. He had propped his flattened hands up on the slippery edge of the stone wall, and let his feet dangle over the sluggish water beating against it below. Now he leaned forward a little as if to look at his image faintly reflected in the wavelets. "However, when *we* came in," he continued, "she jumped to her feet and broke out in laments, after the manner of women, and covered her head, and finally said amid sobs: 'Oh my husband, this is the last time your friends will be talking to you, and you to them!' Then Socrates, who had been gazing at her with compassion, took his eyes off her and said: 'Yes, I must talk to them. Crito, let someone take her home now.' You must know that Crito had some servants with him that morning. They were waiting outside, and so he led Xanthippe out of the room, trying to comfort her and calling her 'little Xanthippe,' and then we heard him order one of the slaves to accompany her to Socrates' house. We were all of us quite moved. For we knew that Crito had promised Xanthippe to take care of her and her children after Socrates' death, and so we realized that she was not pitying herself. And this also was when Apollodorus burst out in a loud wail, and we others had to restrain him—though, to ourselves, we too were weeping at times as the day progressed. Or, rather, we were weeping and laughing by turns."

"Laughing?"

"Yes, as always . . . for we laughed at times whenever Socrates held discourse with us."

"Was he, then, holding discourse with you on that last day also?" Diocles asked.

"Until sundown. . . ."

"There is some talk out here about certain plans—" Diocles said after a brief silence, "plans supposed to have been made for his escape, which miscarried."

"Miscarried! Do people say they miscarried? Oh, Diocles, let me not talk about those plans. For again I would not know whether to weep or to rejoice. . . . Was I saying he was fearless and utterly composed in his last hours? He was both, Diocles, because, in actual fact, the god led him."

"I do not understand you," the other said, his forehead furrowed, and uncrossed his legs.

On the pier, farther off, some slaves laden with heavy tackle were trudging toward the arsenal in a file. They were singing at the top of their voices, and their ditty rang out sharp in the limpid ocean air.

"What did Socrates do, what did he say, Phædo, after Xanthippe had gone?"

"He sat up on his cot and began to rub his legs—"

"What did he say, though, and what was he talking about till sundown?"

Phædo put his arm around Diocles' shoulders. He made no reply. How could he hope to give this boy even an inkling of the knowledge that Socrates had imparted to his interlocutors in those last hours?

Ever since those hours Phædo had felt like a man who, having tried hard to look at the sun—into its very brightness—has closed his eyes, and opening them again, finds his vision assailed by spectral forms—multicolored stars and fiery circles and ellipses that follow trajectories determined by inscrutable laws; and as these forms, these images, vanish and retreat into the universe, his sight seems purer, as though the sun, which he has tried to behold in its life-giving realness, were giving a new life and reality now to his own vision. . . . This, in a manner of speaking, was the way those hours' discourse was living on in Phædo; and it dawned upon him that Socrates' farewell gift to those he had loved was more than knowledge. In truth, he had urged them to try ever and ever again to look, with eyes feasting and smarting at once, into the great light—

The portal of the arsenal was thrown open with a protracted clatter, and the laborers, entering it, fell silent one after another.

There was a new sadness in Diocles' voice as he said into the stillness: "Tell me at least . . . at least tell me how he died."

"Yes, my brave and modest Diocles, I will tell you about it. The sun was low in the sky when our discourse was over and Socrates had done speaking. Then Crito asked him how he wished to be buried. 'Any way you like,' he replied, 'but be careful lest I escape you. Indeed,' he said to the rest of us, 'I do not think I have succeeded in convincing Crito that I am the same Socrates who has been talking all day long about those things you must keep thinking about as long as you live unless you do not love me; instead, our dear Crito fancies that I am the Socrates he will see soon, a dead body. Hence his concern over what should be done with me. That I spoke to you at such great length, telling you I will leave you after drinking the poison—go to the good and the wise god—that Crito believes I said merely to comfort you and take heart myself. Therefore, men, I beg all of you to stand surety for me with Crito, just as he—at the trial, and again after it—offered to stand surety for me with the king archon and the Eleven. But whereas he did so as a guarantee for my remaining in the city, do you now guarantee *him* that

I will not remain, but will depart. For I do not want this dear man to be beside himself when he watches my body being buried or cremated and cry out: "Here you are, O Socrates, to be turned into ashes!" Be of good cheer, then, my Crito, and do with my body as you see fit, and say: "Now I am lowering Socrates' body into its grave," or, as the case may be, "Now I am giving to the flames Socrates' body." ' And after he had said that with the most gracious of smiles, he rose and left the room.

"The jailer was waiting outside to take him to a chamber where a bath had been prepared. For Socrates had told us earlier he wished to bathe so that the women would be spared the trouble of having to wash his dead body. Crito went with him.

"We others started talking again, and we tried to discuss the many things he had told us, and especially how the two Thebans had questioned him when he'd spoken of what is immortal in man—so that he had said he seemed to be obliged to deliver another speech of defense. All that we tried to discuss as best we could, but we soon turned to talking about the magnitude of our bereavement. For had he not been as a father to us?

"Then he came back again. And then Xanthippe returned. She carried one of her little sons in her arms, and a woman relative who was with her led the other by her hand, and Lamprocles, Socrates' firstborn, who is almost a man, followed the little group. You must know that he had been sent to stay on the farm of Xanthippe's family some days before the trial. When they had all walked in now, we left the room, and then we stood in front of the building and argued about Xanthippe, and whether or not she had ever sensed what manner of man her husband was, and as Crito had known her longer than any of us, we asked *him*, but he said he would never be able to answer that question.

"After Xanthippe had gone, all of us went back to Socrates. Crito, come to think of it, went in earlier, for Socrates wished to give certain instructions to his family, and being uncertain that they would listen carefully, he wanted Crito to be present.

"Now sunset was near. The jailer came in, and with him the messenger of the Eleven. 'Socrates,' the jailer said, 'I know for certain that you will not, as other men do, rage now and be angry with me and curse me—or this man either—for I have come to know you well, and, by the gods, you are the most gentle of all the men who ever came here, and thus you will not blame me, or this man either, for what has to be done. You know who in reality must be blamed,' he added in a hushed tone, and then, speaking loudly again, he said: 'You know yourself what this man has brought. Try to bear the unavoidable as lightly as you can, Socrates.' And at that, the man's voice broke, and we saw tears rolling down his lumpy face as he murmured: 'Fare you well. . . .'

" 'Fare you well yourself, my friend,' Socrates said; and the jailer, after a last glance at his prisoner, walked out. 'He is a good man,' Socrates said to us. 'He often came to me early in the day or late in the evening, and he would talk to me, and never would he talk about this hour. And even the nonsense in which you men tried to involve him did not corrupt his goodness. He has been all along as good to me as he could be. And now it really looks as if he were honestly grieved.' "

"What nonsense was Socrates alluding to?" Diocles asked.

"Never mind. It *was* nonsense. . . . As none of us said

a word, Socrates stood up and said: 'Well, then. Let me do the bidding of the good man.'

"The messenger of the Eleven had not left the room with the turnkey. He was standing in the shadows which by that time had gathered in the recess of the door. 'Is the poison ground,' Socrates asked, 'and has he over there brought the cup? If not, he should go out now and grind the poison.'

" 'But the sun is still over the top of the hill!' Crito cried out. He was standing near the wall aperture. 'No one can say that the sun has set yet! I know of several instances in which men took the poison long after the messenger of the Eleven came to announce that the hour had come. In fact, I know of more than one man who had himself brought a good meal and plenty of wine, and ate and drank, and all that even though the sun was as good as down. Do not hasten, my Socrates, I beg you do not. There is still time, there still is!'

" 'I suppose those men acted rightly in their own way, Crito,' Socrates said with the greatest composure, 'for they were sure of gaining something by the delay. I, on the other hand, am right in not following their example, for I am sure that I would gain nothing at all if I swallowed the potion a short while later. I'd only make a fool of myself—I would in my own eyes. So, my dear Crito, do as I say.'

"Then Crito gave a sign to the messenger of the Eleven, and the man went outside, and all of us held our breath, as though we expected to hear him grind the dried leaves of the hemlock herb in the hallway. Of course we heard nothing.

"Then the door opened again, and we thought the man was returning, and Apollodorus broke out in a horrible lament—he is that kind of man. Actually, it was not the messenger of the Eleven who entered, but a very young boy who carried a torch. For dusk comes soon to that prison room.

"But it was not long before the messenger came in again with the earthen vessel into whose water he had put the poison. He was holding the cup rather gingerly, so that none of the liquid would be spilled. Socrates motioned him closer and said: 'Now then, my good fellow, you are experienced in these matters. Tell me what I ought to do.'

" 'It's simple enough,' said the man. 'Once you've drunk it, you walk about until your legs feel heavy. Then you lie down.'

"With that he offered Socrates the cup, and Socrates took it with both hands, and his hands did not tremble. Nor, I think, did the color of his cheeks change. He looked straight at the messenger of the Eleven, inclining his head a little, and asked: 'What would you say, my friend, if I made a little libation out of this cup? May I?'

" 'No,' said the man. 'You see, I put just as much of the stuff into it as will be enough, no more. That's what I always do.'

"Socrates said he understood that. 'But surely,' he added, 'I may ask the gods to watch over my journey. I really must.' And after another moment he lifted the cup to his lips and drained it.

"Until that moment, all of us, except for Apollodorus, had managed to control our emotions fairly well. But now we could no longer restrain our tears—

"But Socrates, who had begun to walk about, as he had been told to do, said to us: 'Why do you behave so strangely? I sent the women away to have nothing of this, for I was told that a man should die in peace. Be quiet, then.'

"Thereupon we felt ashamed and stopped weeping. But we remained in the corner we had withdrawn to in our previous attempts to conceal our grief—some of us pulling our cloaks over our heads—and thus we stood with bated breath while Socrates kept pacing the room. The boy with the torch had advanced a little, and as he raised the torch, Socrates' shadow, rising and falling on the walls, seemed to be all over the place.

"After a while he said that he was feeling a heaviness in his legs, and lay down on his back.

"The messenger of the Eleven, who hadn't moved away from the bed, now touched Socrates' feet and legs, and this he did again after a time—gently, so it seemed to us. But finally he pressed one of the feet hard and asked Socrates whether he was feeling the pressure. Socrates said he was not, and thereupon the man pressed his calves, and so upward and upward, and then, casting a glance at us over his shoulder, he said that the legs were getting cold and stiff, and that this was as it should be. And after that, he again leaned down to Socrates to touch his thighs and also his groin, and said in an undertone: 'When the poison reaches the heart, that will be the end.'

"At that, Socrates pushed the cloak he had covered himself with away from his face, and his eyes beckoned Crito, and the messenger of the Eleven stepped aside so that Crito might get close to the cot. At the same time the young boy, perhaps overcome with fright, lowered his torch—"

As Phædo, his voice choked, stopped and took his arm off Diocles' shoulders and raised his fingers to his brow, his younger companion, who all the time had refrained from looking at him, asked wether Socrates had said anything to Crito.

"Yes. He said: 'Do not forget we owe a cock to Asclepius—'"

"To Asclepius the Healer?"

"That is what Crito understood him to say."

"Do not men bring offerings to Asclepius' altar after recovering from illness, Phædo?"

"We too, all of us, have been wondering about this request. Socrates' voice was very feeble, you must know, and no one but Crito really could hear what he was saying. And Crito was in tears. Perhaps Socrates was in reality asking him to sacrifice that cock to Hermes. For the cock, as you may remember, is also sacred to *him*. Does not he, Hermes, guide men's Shades to the Stygian river? And does not the cock herald the reborn light? These, mind you, are speculations."

"And did Crito reply to Socrates still?"

"He said: 'The debt shall be paid. Is there anything else you wish to say?' But no answer came. Socrates, though his hands no longer were steady, had drawn the mantle over his face again. Meanwhile Critobolus had taken the torch from the boy and, holding it high, stepped behind his father, and we, who too had stepped close, saw a quiver run through Socrates' body. . . ."

"And then?"

"The messenger of the Eleven, after another moment or two, uncovered Socrates' face. His eyes were set. And then Crito closed them, and he also closed Socrates' mouth. . . . This, my Diocles, was the manner in which he died—the best and the wisest and the most just of all men we ever can hope to see."

For a very long while the two youths remained seated side by side without stirring. Below, the eternal sea was lapping against the jetty.

Even as Phædo concluded his account, the shipwrights' hammering had begun to be heard in the distance. Diocles cocked his head, and then he got to his feet. Protecting his eyes from the glare of the sun with his palm, he gazed intently to the eastward, as though from where he was standing he could in reality see his ship beached over there under the gabled roof, unrigged, her brazen prow dented, the wickerwork shields of her sides in tatters, and the hole aft gaping wide between splintered planks—yet still his ship, and Theseus'.

A NOTE ON THE TYPE

This book is set on the Linotype in GRANJON, *a type named in compliment to Robert Granjon, who in 1523 began his career as type-cutter and printer, working in Antwerp, in Lyon, at the Vatican and Medici presses in Rome, and in Paris, where he died in 1590. Granjon, the boldest and most original designer of his time, was one of the first to practice the trade of type-founder apart from that of printer.*

Linotype GRANJON *was designed by George W. Jones, who based his drawings upon a face used by Claude Garamond (1510–1561) in his beautiful French books.* GRANJON *more closely resembles Garamond's own type than do any of the various modern faces that bear his name.*

The book was composed, printed, and bound by The Plimpton Press, Norwood, Massachusetts. The typography and binding designs are by W. A. Dwiggins.

WAD